COPPER BEECHES
was originally published by Trident Press.

Also by Arthur H. Lewis

THE AARONSBURG STORY
THE WORLDS OF CHIPPY PATTERSON
THE DAY THEY SHOOK THE PLUM TREE
LAMENT FOR THE MOLLY MAGUIRES*
LA BELLE OTERO*
HEX*
CARNIVAL*

*Published by POCKET BOOKS

 *Are there paperbound books you want
but cannot find in your retail stores?*

COPPER BEECHES

Arthur H. Lewis

PUBLISHED BY POCKET BOOKS NEW YORK

COPPER BEECHES

Trident Press edition published September, 1971

POCKET BOOK edition published August, 1972

This POCKET BOOK edition includes every word
contained in the original, higher-priced edition. It is printed
from brand-new plates made from completely reset, clear, easy-to-read
type. POCKET BOOK editions are published by POCKET BOOKS, a division
of Simon & Schuster, Inc., 630 Fifth Avenue, New York, N.Y. 10020.
Trademarks registered in the United States and other countries.

This book is for Ken Souser, my Copper Beech sponsor, and for Charlie Howland, Jim Montgomery (who claimed kinship with Irene Adler), A. Carson Simpson, Joseph W. Spelman, M.D., and all my other fellow Sons who have withdrawn from active membership on our rolls to join Mr. Sherlock Holmes, John Watson, M.D., and Mrs. Hudson, wherever they are.

I ASK forgiveness for certain liberties I took with Philadelphia's geography and Pennsylvania's history as well as "amending" a few articles in Copper Beech bylaws. For example, those looking for a carriage house at Nineteenth and Spruce streets won't find one there. "The Bean Soup" is not celebrated when I said it was and Bill Scranton didn't open his gubernatorial campaign at McClure. Meetings of the Copper Beeches are held in October and April and no—repeat "no" —woman ever has been admitted to one and, despite Women's Lib, chances are no woman ever will be. But I swear by the old Shikari hunter that, to the best of my knowledge and belief, I took no liberties with the Canon.

For their editorial skills, I am particularly grateful to Marvin E. Aronson, M.D., Donald A. McDonough, and H. W. Starr, the last named being one of the great Sherlockian scholars.

For their willingness to assist me in this effort, I acknowledge my gratitude to Herman Beerman, M.D., Francis I. Gowen, David H. Roberts, and Ben Wolf.

For their technical advice I owe a debt of thanks to "Miss Jean" Puciato of the Philadelphia Bureau of Missing Persons, and to Chief Police Inspector Harry Fox.

For the idea behind this book I am extremely grateful to Herbert M. Alexander (no Son, alas!), who believes it is a simple matter for people to disappear, and finally, to Paul Gitlin, Esq., who wishes most of them would.

My task of recording recent Copper Beech activities at an end, I stretch out in a chair high up in the Sierras beneath a hot Mexican sun and, perhaps for the hundredth time, pick up my dog-eared copy of the Sacred Writings. In an instant there is no sun; the pure, clear air has become London peasoup fog, and the mountains are no loftier than the second floor of 221B.

"... it was a wild tempestuous night ... Holmes and I sat in silence all evening, he engaged with a powerful lens deciphering the remains of an original inscription upon a palimpsest. ... Outside the wind howled down on Baker Street, while the rain beat fiercely against the windows."

San Miguel de Allende
Guanajuato, Mexico
August, 1970

COPPER
BEECHES

CHAPTER

1

WHEN THE bet was placed it was my ill fortune to be far from home. However, lest you think my information has been obtained second hand, let me assure you that I was an active participant in the Chase almost at its inception and I most certainly was present at the payoff. Besides, I am the duly elected Historian of the Sons of the Copper Beeches and could thereby, without seeming to pander to my insatiable curiosity, collect information from all parties concerned. Ergo, I know more about this tragi-comic affair than anyone else including the Federal Bureau of Investigation, the Philadelphia Police Department, and the Sheriff of Snyder County, Pennsylvania.

As Sherlock Holmes himself might have said, "There are points about the case which promise to make it an absolutely unique one." But before I begin this strange tale I should tell you who and what the Sons of the Copper Beeches are. As a matter of fact, my start ought to be with a brief history of our better known parent body, the Baker Street Irregulars.

However, since the very thought of offending a fellow Sherlockian pains me, I hereby state categorically that such a history is totally superfluous for those scattered millions of Canonical devotees, who, through force of bitter circumstance, remain unaffiliated. Because of the widespread distribution of our members' well researched and frequently inspired monographs, they (enviously, no doubt) are aware of our existence. Furthermore, they share with us the belief that Conan Doyle was an impostor, an unscrupulous literary agent who cunningly grasped credit for writing Dr. John Watson's factual accounts of the Master's deeds.

And, except for a few pig-headed agnostics, we are all convinced that Holmes is alive and well and living in England where he has become one of Great Britain's leading, albeit

1

unpublicized, apiarists. There may be a legitimate question as to his present whereabouts. I, for one, because of certain information I am not as yet at liberty to reveal, am inclined to believe his minuscule farm, originally on the outskirts of Swinton, is presently in the vicinity of Crow Trees, Barrowfield, near Nelson, Lancashire, to which rural area he moved within the past decade.

One need look no further than into "The Adventure of the Lion's Mane" for evidence not only of Holmes' current activities, but also of Mrs. Hudson's state of health.

"My villa," said the Master, long after his involuntary retirement, "is situated upon the southern slope of the downs commanding a great view of the Channel. My house is lonely. I, my old housekeeper and my bees have the estate all to ourselves."

What could be more specific? Furthermore, a medical acquaintance of mine, a British physician who had done considerable research in the field of geriatrics, told me recently that Mrs. Hudson, despite arthritis and other creeping infirmities of old age is still the Master's housekeeper, performing her duties with as much enthusiasm if not vigor as she did when Holmes and Dr. Watson occupied rooms at 221B Baker Street.

We are grateful to the London *Times* for news of Mycroft, Sherlock's only close relative. That paper, on April 16, 1941, announced Mycroft's death must be presumed because a buzz bomb demolished his club, the Diogenes. I might add parenthetically that the body of Holmes' obese brother never was recovered although I am not one to aver that he, too, is still among the living.

Scoffers who decry our confidence in Sherlock's tenacity, offer "proof" of the Master's death by commenting on his absence from the columns of the London press these past three or four decades. To this, we faithful say, "So what!" Holmes never sought fame. As he reiterated to Dr. Watson time and time again, sufficient for Holmes was the joy of the hunt. "I play the game for the game's sake," he said. I know he meant it. I'm sure that were it not for the connivance of Doyle, the Master would have been known only to grateful clients and to his pedestrian colleagues—Inspectors Gregson and Lestrade and Detective Stanley Hopkins—and not have become a household word.

An admission must be made here that the Master's last *known* assignment was undertaken shortly before World War I. It was only because of Mycroft's appeal to his younger brother's patriotism that Sherlock came out of retirement to frustrate plans of the evil German spy, Baron von Bork, thus paving the way for an Allied victory. His client was none other than the British government. It detracts not a whit from the Master's *amor patriae* to note, as Holmes himself did, that "occasionally, he [Mycroft] *was* the British Government."

Although this exploit occurred more than half a century ago, I among many, do not doubt that if a matter of sufficient interest were presented, Sherlock Holmes could be persuaded to return to active duty.

Believe me, I wish we Sons had called upon him for help instead of relying upon our own meager powers of deduction, meager despite years of concentration upon Canonical methods. Well, what's past is past and instead of brooding we should thank our stars we emerged from our escapade with not much more damage than to our pride.

And now, this unavoidable digression at an end, I resume the task of providing sufficient information about the Baker Street Irregulars and the Sons of the Copper Beeches for non-Sherlockians to understand, if they can, just how six mature, conventional residents of the Quaker City could become involved in a preposterous man hunt.

In the spring of 1934 (or so the story goes, although I will not vouch for its complete accuracy) the late Christopher Morley and several other devotees of the Master were lunching at Manhattan's Murray Hill Hotel. Included in the coterie, which met with more or less regularity in this elegant relic of a bygone era, were Morley's Pulitzer Prize-winning older brother Felix; Alexander Woollcott, raconteur and radio's Town Crier; Gene Tunney, Shakespearean scholar and a pugilist of some note in sporting circles; actor William Gillette, most famous of all Thespian portrayers of Sherlock Holmes; Elmer Davis, newspaper columnist, and Rex Stout, teller of a hundred Nero Wolfe tales and President of the Mystery Writers of America.

Exactly how it came about none of the survivors of that noteworthy luncheon is able to recall, but shortly afterward Mr. Davis agreed to write bylaws for a newly created society to be known as the Baker Street Irregulars. This was not the first congeries of Holmes' devotees to bear a like name.

Historically speaking, the original Baker Street "irregulars" (spelled with a lower case "i") were street gamins Holmes recruited for special assignments that required both anonymity and familiarity with London's slums. Mention of the "irregulars" comes in Dr. Watson's spellbinding monograph he called *A Study in Scarlet*.

" 'What on earth is this?' I [Dr. Watson] cried, for at that moment there came the pattering of many steps . . . accompanied by audible expressions of disgust upon the part of our landlady.

" 'It's the Baker Street division of the police force,' said my companion [Holmes] gravely: and as he spoke there rushed into the room half-a-dozen of the dirtiest and most ragged street Arabs that ever I clapped eyes on.

" 'There's more work to be got out of these little beggars than out of a dozen of the force . . . The mere sight of an official-looking person seals men's lips. These youngsters . . . go everywhere and hear everything. They are sharp as needles, too.' "

There is no need to quote more than a small portion of Mr. Davis' efforts (which elevated the "i" in "irregulars" from lower to upper case) to show both character and aims of the newly created organization.

"The purpose of the Baker Street Irregulars," states Article II of the Constitution, "shall be the study of the Sacred Writings." Article I, of course, simply notes the name.

"The officers," states Article IV, "shall be: a Gasogene, a Tantalus, and a Commissionaire."

Section 1 of the bylaws declares that "an annual meeting be held on January 6th, or thereabouts, at which the Canonical Toasts shall be drunk after which the members shall drink at will."

For the record it might be stated that these toasts honor Irene Adler (always "The Woman" to Holmes), Mrs. Hudson, Mycroft, Dr. Watson's second wife and conclude with one to "The second most dangerous man in London."

Section 2 states that "all other business shall be left for the monthly meeting."

The final section, 5, declares "There shall be no monthly meetings."

I am proud to say that one of the first of many score branches grown from the parent tree is our own Copper Beeches founded in 1947. With certain minor exceptions, e.g., our chief officer is the Headmastiff and the fourth Canonical Toast is drunk not to the second Mrs. Watson but to Miss Violet Hunter. Our constitution and bylaws are quite different from those drawn up by the late Elmer Davis.

Our name itself, Copper Beeches, chosen after considerable study, is a fitting one for the Quaker City sodality. The heroine of this Sherlockian experience, "The Adventure of the Copper Beeches," is Miss Hunter, "a governess, forced by her unscrupulous employer to wear a particular shade of electric blue . . . belonging to my dear daughter, Alice, now in Philadelphia."

Divisions of the Baker Street Irregulars currently exist nearly everywhere in the world including one at the base of Mount Kilimanjaro. That African outpost was established in 1948 by the missionary father, Francis Philben, C.S.S., who tells me all meetings of his kraal are conducted in Swahili. Despite the fact that the only Kiswahili I know is a dirty limerick which Father Philben did *not* teach me, I'm sure I'd find great enjoyment auditing a regular meeting of the Kenya branch of our society. Unfortunately the only African city I've ever visited is Marrakech, Morocco, where no branch exists. While in the course of my travels I have attended BSI sessions in Copenhagen, Rome, Calcutta, and Mahoopany, Pennsylvania, I have yet to thrill at hearing, if not comprehending, a group of Kikuyans discuss the Master in their native tongue.

I digress again; all this has nothing whatsoever to do with the case and its unfortunate and near fatal involvement of several Sons of the Copper Beeches. I'm sure had it not been for Colonel Eberhardt's insuperable egotism, plus his greed for acquisition of the Carl Anderson manuscripts, he'd have gotten away with it. Admittedly, this superb collection of Doyle's original writings (copied, of course, from Dr. Watson's notes) is something every Sherlockian in the world covets.

Nevertheless, only after the *alleged* (and I emphasize the word) suicide of the cherished collection's Pittsburgh owner was this great prize offered for sale. Even though the famous Ben Wolf Gallery, which handled the estate, set a purchase price of $47,500 I still marvel at the fact that these unique documents were not gobbled up at once. That, however, is beside the point. The fact is they *were* available and so became the bait the Colonel used to hook six unwitting Sons to his line.

We Sons hold two meetings a year, on the last Friday in September and the last Friday in March. Since we do not have our own clubhouse, we gather at the spacious quarters of the Diogenes, which by a most peculiar concidence bears the same name as that of Mycroft Holmes' sodality. But there the resemblance ends. Membership in the former consists of some fifty garrulous old men, not one of whom ever shuts up long enough to listen to anybody else, while in the latter, according to the Canon, "no talking save in the Stranger's Room is, under any circumstance, allowed, and three offenses, if brought to the notice of the committee, render the talker liable to expulsion." Were I possessed of a waspish tongue, I could point out even more striking dissimilarities.

Ever since I can remember, and I became a member of the Copper Beeches twenty-three years ago, it has been customary for some six or seven Sons to continue study of the Sacred Writings for several hours after regular meetings adjourn. These late evening gatherings invariably take place in the townhouses of members who live within walking distance of the Diogenes' Camac Street shelter. Long ago many of us swapped suburban living and the Chestnut Hill or Paoli locals for the dubious pleasure of dwelling on the fringe of a jungle convenient to City Hall. Hence it is no problem to find a place for an extension of Sons' erudition and conviviality.

Although several of these sessions have been held in my home and sometimes in that of my neighbor, Arthur Redstone, it occurs to me that ever since Colonel Eberhardt became a Copper Beech neophyte five years ago, we began gathering more frequently than elsewhere in his converted brick carriage house on Locust Street near Nineteenth.

The place is huge. I don't know how many rooms there are, but house and garden occupy approximately a half-acre of ground which, for a center city residence, is positively overpowering. My townhouse, for example, is on a lot eighteen feet wide and forty feet deep. If my mathematics are correct this would be roughly one-thirtieth the size of the Eberhardts'.

A quaint, and frequently pretentious, custom of rich and very rich suburban Philadelphians has been to give their homes a name, just as did their English ancestors. E. T. Stotesbury called his palatial mansion "Whitemarsh" and the social-climbing Wideners whose fortune was founded on profits from the sales of tainted meat to the Union Armies, called their monstrously ugly residence "Lynnwood Hall."

Several Sons, including Eberhardt, have taken up the fashion but, I hasten to add, with tongue in cheek and the Sacred Writings in mind. As many Copper Beeches as could crowd into our tiny Jessup Street home for dedication ceremonies six years ago, heard me christen it "Pondicherry Lodge." My neighbor, and fellow Son, Arthur Redstone, the distinguished brain surgeon, calls his home "Shoscome Old Place." H. W. Starr, the Headmastiff, labeled his Rittenhouse Square apartment "Wisteria Lodge." Sherlockians need no source guide to these appellations; non-Sherlockians are welcome to search for them in the Sacred Writings or remain in ignorance. The choice is theirs.

Even before Eberhardt's admission to the rolls of the Copper Beeches, which certainly is one point in his favor, he called his home "Baskerville Hall." I would not demean myself to point out, even to the most ill-informed, from what source *that* historic name is derived.

Eberhardt added a touch of the macabre to a building that already had seen more than its share of violence since it was constructed by Daniel S. Knight, the Quaker Abolitionist, more than a century and a half ago. It was in the vast, gloomy, and unfortunately soundproof basement of Patterson's carriage house, a station of the underground railway, that a score of slaves on their way to Boston starved to death when their patron, a bachelor who lived alone, succumbed to an apoplectic stroke in the main house. No one heard the piteous cries of the hungry Negroes whose skeletons, some dangling from rafters and others prone on the earthen floor, were discovered two years later. An account (brief, presumably because of more important war news) is to be found in the *Public Ledger,* March 5, 1861.

Shortly before the turn of the century, death once more found its way into the basement of the carriage house, then in the possession of Dr. Gerald Mott Foster, member of an old Quaker family.

"Late yesterday (April 21, 1899)," stated the *North American,* "Gerald Foster, Jr., four-year-old son of the distinguished physician, was trampled to death by his Shetland pony, in the basement of the Fosters' stables.

"The strange accident occurred when the animal, which young Gerald had just mounted, for some unknown reason plunged with the child astride into a cellar door a workman had carelessly left open. The terrified beast kicked his charge to death before the hostler could effect a rescue."

Eberhardt made his *outré* contribution to the scene shortly after he and his bride moved into Baskerville Hall by planting a double row of yew trees along the forty-foot path which lies between the iron entrance gate facing Locust Street and the rear exit, which leads into Sassafras Alley. In the years between the Colonel's rise from Apprentice to Journeyman to Master, these conifers had grown so tall and their piney foliage so dense that they cast a permanent shadow all along the narrow passageway they enclosed.

Not in the least do I mind admitting I never have been able to walk that path, even in broad daylight, without thinking of the dreadful fate which lay in store for poor Sir Charles at the south end of the yew-lined passageway, nor of the agonies his nephew, Sir Henry, endured, before Holmes laid low the legend of the Baskervilles' unearthly hound.

I do believe it would have been the Colonel's pleasure to have added no artificial illumination to the scattered shards of light which filtered through the dense, green needles, leaving the pathway in total darkness other hours. However, Ellen, his wife, insisted that lamps be installed at both ends and in the center, so Eberhardt, with reluctance, I don't doubt, acquiesced.

But on some of those postprandial sessions in Baskerville Hall, when I happened to drive rather than walk to the carriage house, he invariably managed to switch off the lights ("an accident," he would claim later and offer profuse apologies) a few moments after I parked my car in Sassafras Alley. He knew that I would then scurry along the yew-lined path, my heart palpitating wildly, and arrive at the front door, barely able to control either breath or emotion. I am not the only Son upon whom Eberhardt played this sadistic trick.

My good friend and fellow Sherlockian, Henry Shalet, told me that upon one occasion the moment the Yew Alley lights went out he heard a deep growl close at hand and only by exerting the strongest willpower, managed to walk instead of running wildly along the path. When Henry, his face blanched with fear and his body shivering uncontrollably, asked the Colonel whose dog it could have been—the Eberhardts owned only a small, gentle spaniel, Ellen's pet—his host shrugged shoulders saying it must have belonged to Judge Ulmebaum, his neighbor to the rear. This explanation, given with a grin, never satisfied Henry nor me. Henry says the Judge's family are cat lovers and wouldn't dream of owning a dog.

It was in front of the Colonel's great open fireplace that the wager was made just a few hours after the conclusion of the regular March Copper Beech session. Under normal circumstances I would have been among those present. Simply because I had to catch an early morning flight I begged off and went home to get a good night's sleep. Considering what happened that evening during my absence, I wish I hadn't been so damned anile. In the long run I'm certain this would not have made any difference. However, for the rest of my life I shall always regret not hearing Charlie Starr, the Headmastiff's nephew, utter that classic Sherlockian phrase at 1:40 A.M., March 28, 1969, after he and four other Sons bade goodnight to the Colonel and his Lady, then stepped into snow-covered Locust Street.

"Come, Watson, come!" said Charlie, turning to his colleagues. "The game is afoot!" As subsequent events proved, how right he was!

CHAPTER

2

To TELL this story properly I must return to that spring meeting of the Copper Beeches. Beginning about 6 P.M., we'd had our usual assortment of *apéritifs*, drunk the specified Canonical toasts of the SOCB and thus were in a proper mood to enjoy the excellent dinner which followed. The first paper, an excellent one, "The Smoking Holmes," was delivered by Dr.

Herbert P. Middleton, of Princeton University. In it our distinguished ecologist, by the use of various artifacts, verified the Master's complete familiarity with tobacco in all its forms.

After this, Monsignor Lallou, at 91, our oldest member, led a brief but erudite discussion on the specifications of watercraft mentioned in the Sacred Writings. This brought chuckles to several attending Sons who have named their own boats, seagoing and otherwise, in honor of vessels which played roles in a number of Sherlockian adventures. Ames Johnston, for example, christened his sixty-foot Chriscraft *Sophie Anderson II*. You will remember that *Sophie Anderson I* was a British bark, "lost at sea in '87."

John B. Koelle, who used to row single scull for the University in Jack Kelly's day, has a catamaran he named in honor of the steam launch *Aurora,* which played an important role in the *Sign of the Four. Tonga* is what he calls his wife who frequently sails with him, and I hope Betty never discovers that the original Tonga was the "little hell hound" poison-dart-shooting Andaman Islander. I could go on with other examples—Bert Olisandro's *Gloria Scott,* for instance—but I think I've made my point.

At this March 1969 meeting one apprentice, Dr. Orville Horlach, was raised to Journeyman, and joined the rest of us singing the "Apprentices' Emancipation Anthem" to the accompaniment of Bill Smith, assistant conductor of the Philadelphia Orchestra.

The tune is not unlike "Here We Go 'Round the Mulberry Bush," and the words follow:

> Pour, oh, pour the Highland Whisky
> Slop some Bourbon in a glass;
> And, to make us mildly frisky,
> Let the brimming bumper pass!

> For our Copper-Beech apprentice
> Rises from indenture freed:
> Strong his elbow, keen his scent is:
> He's a journeyman indeed!

> From his bondage now he's rising
> And alone he's fit to fly
> Which we're bent on signalizing
> With unusual revelry!

Justice of the Pennsylvania State Supreme Court, Frank J. Eustace, Jr. (our Recorder of Pedigrees), then read a precis of the second volume of *Huxtable's Sidelights on Horace,* as told to this distinguished member of the judiciary by Thorneycroft Huxtable, M.A., Ph.D., etc., of the Priory School, near Mackleton. In retrospect, Sons who soon were to become involved in the disappearance of a fellow Sherlockian were forced to arrive at the grim conclusion that Frank's choice for his master's thesis was a rather strange coincidence. But the Justice's paper was well-received and Frank, this same evening having completed his many years as a Journeyman, was elevated to the lofty rank of Master Copper Beech. This achievement gives him the right to wear the famed Sherlockian cap, to smoke the famous curved meerschaum, and attend sessions of the BSI anywhere in the world with or without invitation.

There was another intermission, essential since the Sons' mean age hovers slightly above the midcentury mark. Ten minutes later the meeting was resumed with the usual quiz. I should state that an amendment to the bylaws changed the original form of interrogation, wherein members hurled questions at each other with little regard to parliamentary procedure, to a more formal and less rowdy method of judging each other's erudition. Under the old system these examinations occasionally became chaotic, perhaps because two or three normally polite Sherlockians by this hour were, as the expression goes, "in their cups."

On the evening of which I speak, "The Adventure of The Solitary Cyclist" was the Adventure selected to rate our Sherlockian scholarship. I have an extremely retentive memory and I'd studied my lesson well. Thus, I was able to answer every question correctly even recalling the exact times (9:13 and 9:50) morning trains left Waterloo for Farnham Station. A few Sons complained to the Headmastiff that this last question was unfair but I backed him completely and would have even had I not known the answer. I've always said that if it appears in the Sacred Writings, it becomes a legitimate inquiry.

The first prize which I won hands down was an autographed copy of *Lament for the Molly Maguires.* I must say, and I did say it openly though its author is a Son and was present, that this tale of nineteenth century hard coal region

violence was far better told by John Watson, M.D., in his re-
cital of *The Valley of Fear.*

The final toast was drunk to Miss Violet Hunter. Then our
Headmastiff adjourned the meeting and with my early morning flight to Lisbon in mind I regretfully bade goodnight to
members of our tight little postprandial group and informed
the Colonel I would not be able to accept his and his Lady's
hospitality.

So Arthur Redstone, my neighbor and a "regular" at these
late evening extensions of Sherlockiana, and I walked home
together. Redstone, who heads the Department of Neurologi-
cal Surgery, had an operation scheduled for 7 A.M. and he,
too, had denied himself the pleasure of added conviviality.
For the sake of his patient, whoever that might have been, I
was glad of the doctor's decision. He seemed quite unsteady
on his feet and had to cling to my arm as we strolled through
Rittenhouse Square and down Spruce Street to Jessup. His
hands were shaking so violently that after three or four futile
attempts to insert his key into the lock he turned to me with a
sickly smile and asked me to do it for him. Although I'd im-
bibed as much if not more than the good doctor, I had no difficulty performing that task.

Since I always try to be completely fair and aboveboard
about everything I do, and I am even more meticulous when
it comes to putting facts on paper, I must point out once more
that I was *not* present when the bet was placed. But my research has, as usual, been thorough and my knowledge of
character and background of those involved is complete so
that I properly assume the author's prerogative of omni-
science and relate the opening phase of the chase just as
though I had been at Baskerville Hall when the Colonel en-
trapped his unwary guests into an action they lived to regret.

In truth, very little time elapsed—less than a fortnight—
between the hour the bet was placed and the hour I became a
full-fledged member of the "hunt." This was the first one to
which I belonged since I dropped out of the Radnor Hunt
some dozen years ago when my mount stumbled over a stile
which had no right to be there.

Before I relate what I know about the Colonel (and I know
a *great* deal now) let me first talk about those five innocents
who were led into a trap devised by that unscrupulous retired

member of our Armed Forces. With the exception of Eberhardt, whom I have saved for last, I shall now call the roll.

First comes Marv Abrams, aged forty-five. Marv is not only an M.D. (he led his class at Temple which, while not the University, has certainly deserved, albeit limited, recognition) but also an LL.B., earned not honorary. He is short, fat, and bald. As coroner's chief pathologist his take-home pay cannot exceed $19,000 per annum, hardly adequate to support a wife and four sons, the oldest of whom entered Swarthmore last semester and the other three all at Friends Select. There is no doubt that Marv could earn at least five times as much in private practice but his great love, excluding the Sacred Writings, is forensic medicine. I dare say he ranks among the top ten U.S. scientists in that field.

Marv's particular discipline is dissection and in this area he is most accomplished. You would be amazed, as were quite a few individual murderers and several members of organized crime's hierarchy, at the amount of knowledge Marv was able to glean after a prolonged session with a minuscule section of a previously unidentified corpse.

I've known Marv ever since he became engaged to my wife's second cousin, a Biddle no less, and subsequently married Helene, much to the dismay of the bride's family, which has never quite gotten over the shock. I say if a man has the instincts of a gentleman, even if not born one, it should matter little what his ethnic origins are although at a certain point I do draw the line. I readily admit that at first I did not think the marriage would last, so disparate is the upbringing of Helene Biddle Patterson of "Grey Oaks," Chestnut Hill, and Marvin Abrams of South Philadelphia.

I am happy to say the marriage has been a complete success and not for one moment do I regret having been present with my wife (the only representative of the Family) when Magistrate Estes Bigelow tied the nuptial knot nineteen years ago. Furthermore, I am godfather to Frank, Marv's youngest son, and attended his circumcision. Prior to that ceremony I admit that in my ignorance of Hebraic customs I thought the "bris" for which Marv had asked me to be on hand would be some kind of wild pagan rite.

Marv developed his Sherlockian interest because of me and quite properly I was one of his three Copper Beech sponsors. He proved to be a noble Son, indeed, and his dissertation on the poison used by the fourteen-year-old Jack Ferguson in the lad's attempt to murder his baby stepbrother (see "The Adventure of the Sussex Vampire") has become a classic in the annals of BSI literature. I realize, of course, Marv was able to draw upon his knowledge of chemistry for this superb monograph.

Next on my roster is Charlie Starr, an architect. Charlie graduated from Harvard, then went on to further his studies in Paris under Le Corbusier and now heads one of the Quaker City's leading firms, as did his father before him. Charlie is about my height, which is slightly under six feet, has red hair, freckles and is a rather quiet, almost shy man. At fifty he is still a bachelor and lives with his mother in a penthouse in Society Hill Towers, which he himself designed.

Although Starr is a Philadelphian by birth, his first formal affiliation with fellow Sherlockians was in Paris where he joined *Les Dévots du Maître*. It was only after the death of his father that Charlie came home and transferred his membership to the Copper Beeches. While there is nothing in the constitution or bylaws which denotes what action we must take, we have always accepted, without question, every transferee. At this moment, I'm not sure what would happen should one of Father Philben's protégés move to the City of Brotherly Love and decide to affiliate with us.

One more item of interest about Charlie Starr. He has a French mistress whom I'm sure he sees at least three times a year. His purported reasons for these frequent returns to Paris are to attend the sessions of *Les Dévots*. However, two years ago, by chance I was in Paris the very evening *Les Dévots* were holding their regular midwinter session. I saw the notice on the events list of the George V where I always stay.

Naturally, I attended and was asked by the Commissionaire, their equivalent to BSI's Gasogene, or second in command, to give a brief report on Copper Beech activities. I accepted and in my rather fluent French brought my hosts up to date on our progress. All the while, during dinner and afterward, I kept looking around for Charlie. When we'd drunk our final toast and I still hadn't seen him, I asked the Commissionaire what could have happened to Starr. I told him I'd been led to believe Charlie was a regular at meetings of *Les Dévots*.

The Commissionaire glanced down at me from his lofty

heights—he must have had at least two inches on de Gaulle—
and gave me a puzzled *coup d'oeil*. Then he lifted his left eye-
brow, shrugged his shoulders, raised his hands, palms out,
fingers apart, turned his lower lip down and glanced heavenward with the kind of look only a Frenchman can give, thus
telling me in the flash of a second more than he could have
said in a hundred words.

The following morning, quite by accident I assure you, I
happened to drop into the coffee shop of the Lancaster Hotel,
a popular hostelry although not quite up to the standards of
the George V. I'd almost forgotten Charlie stayed at the Lancaster when he came to Paris. I'd been sipping my *café au lait*
and nibbling at a *croissant* for no more than an hour when I
saw him walk down the center stairs, a magnificent brunette on
his arm. It's entirely possible that Charlie observed me out of
the corner of his eye but he gave no sign of recognition. I certainly said nothing to him then nor have I ever mentioned this
encounter although I've given Starr countless opportunities to
discuss it with me.

Next comes Donald Donaldson, a tall, husky "boy" of
thirty-nine, one of the youngest and among the least affluent
of all Sons. Don is a reporter on the Philadelphia *Inquirer* and
the only Pulitzer Prize winner I know. He got his coveted
award by exposing the thievery of Philadelphia's corrupt mag-
istracy. Sadly, however, Don's well-merited honor was almost the only thing of value to emerge from a grand jury
probe which followed his series of byline articles. Despite the
fact that a half-dozen high ranking politicos were indicted by
a blue ribbon grand jury on numerous counts of mal and mis-
feasance in office, not one member of this lower judiciary was
sent to jail or paid a fine for his crimes. Such discouraging results are typical of Philadelphia which, as Lincoln Steffens
once said, is a city "corrupt and contented." Ofttimes I think
some of us should roll up our sleeves, get into the arena and
clean up the mess just as we did a few decades ago. Don and
his paper do their best but obviously it isn't enough.

Don is not a Philadelphian by birth. As I recall he was born
in Chester and attended Franklin and Marshall, Dickinson, or
one of those colleges. But Melvin L. Sutley, who heads the
Department of English at the University, told me Don has
been taking courses there and even though he has a wife and
three children to support eventually will get his Master's. Mel

was one of his sponsors at the Copper Beeches. While I'm genuinely fond of Don, until we both became involved in the Chase, I saw him only at regular or postprandial sessions of the Sons. He has the kind of curiosity I myself possess and which, had I wanted to enter the field of journalism, might have won an award such as my youthful friend attained.

Ed Johnson, aged sixty-one or thereabouts, is fourth on my list. I've known him for any number of years and, if I'm not mistaken, Dorothy, his wife, came out the same season Juliet did. We entertain the Johnsons once or twice a year, usually at large dinner parties and they entertain us about the same number of times. But we see them in between at the homes of closer mutual friends.

Often I try to figure out just what makes this distinguished member of the Philadelphia and New York Bars dress as though he came straight out of Dickens. He wears heavy, four-button, three-piece square-cut woolen suits obviously fashioned by a tailor who hasn't changed patterns for the last three-quarters of a century. Across his vest he sports a thick gold watch chain, the kind my grandfather had. He's hatless at all seasons and the only man I know who still wears spats. I wouldn't be at all surprised if they cover high button shoes. I'm also convinced he must be his own barber; no professional could make such a botch of Ed's thick, short cropped, iron-gray hair, which always looks like a field of clover lacerated by a lawnmower with dull, badly nicked blades.

Ed may not have kept up with contemporary masculine attire or tonsorial styles, but he most certainly has kept abreast of contemporary federal, state, and municipal tax laws. Johnson, MacMitchell and Harrison, of which Ed is the most senior partner, represents the pick of the Quaker City's blue chip corporations. Ed is Quondam Fellow at the University where he holds a yearly seminar to acquaint several hundred members of the Bar with new legislation in his particular discipline.

I almost forgot that Ed, in addition to his dedication to Sherlockiana, has another extracurricular activity—he is a railroad buff. On his Downingtown farm is a Reading Company caboose, the inside of which he remodeled to hold his great collection of the Sacred Writings. He is also President of the Doylestown, Perkasie, and North Wales Short Line. And short it is, from depot to terminus the total dis-

tance covered is slightly over two miles. But the three ancient
Erie coaches and the 1900, 4-6-2 steam engine that pulls them
pass all ICC regulations. We Sons hold our annual picnic
aboard the D.P. and N.W.

Fifth, and but for the Colonel, last on my list is Jack Wharton, aged seventy-four, a tall, elegant, slender, white-haired
gentleman from an old Philadelphia family. Jack is chairman
of the board of Hyer and Company, which, I have been told,
is the second largest advertising agency in the world. Hyer
and Company is based in Philadelphia and not Manhattan for
purely personal reasons. Jack's fifteenth floor office has a
wood-burning fireplace and a superb view of Washington
Square and the Delaware River. The Whartons' red brick an-
cestral colonial home is a mere three-minute walk from his
office and Jack lunches there every day with his wife. That the
agency will move to New York City next year when Jack re-
tires is beyond question. The Whartons' only heir, a son whom
I knew well, was killed driving a Red Cross ambulance during the Battle of the Bulge.

Jack has a razor sharp analytical mind and, for a man his
age, remarkable physical strength. He played cricket with the
great George Patterson and boxed for the University. Only
two months ago Jack was threatened by a young knife-wield-
ing thug. He knocked the fellow to the ground and then stood
over him until a passerby summoned police.

The Whartons no longer entertain except at small family
gatherings, but both Jack and Veda (an odd Christian name
indeed for one from a conventional family as the Cadwal-
laders) are active in civic affairs. Jack was chairman of the
United Fund Campaign in 1968 and Veda still heads the Epis-
copal Hospital Women's Auxiliary and is a Friend of the
Free Library on Logan Square.

I've never heard either of the Whartons utter a disparaging
remark about anyone, even about those who have told me
they consider Veda and Jack complete snobs. When I attempted to report these unkind and certainly untruthful remarks, as I felt it my duty to do, Jack turned a deaf ear and
brushed them aside with a smile. While I admire him for such
a display of Christian forbearance, which I myself practice, I
do believe it just as important to know who your enemies are.
Wasn't it Thomas Mann who said, ". . . the actual enemy is
the unknown"?

CHAPTER

3

Now we come to the Colonel. I do not intend to stress the striking similarities in character, if not in physique, possessed by Colonel H. Wesley Eberhardt and Colonel Sebastian Moran, "the first link in his [Professor Moriarity's] chain and, consequently, 'the second most dangerous man in London.'"

I've said it before and I say it again, I never liked Colonel Eberhardt and I felt this antipathy almost from the moment of our meeting at the fall 1964 session of the Sons. I think I should explain the significance of an invitation to attend one of these meetings. While nothing in our bylaws restricts the number of guests, the Diogenes cannot handle more than eighty persons comfortably at a sit-down dinner. Since we average seventy-eight Sons per session, it's obvious that a maximum of two outsiders may attend and these invariably are men who previously have shown more than a casual interest in the Sacred Writings. Should a visiting BSI appear at the last minute, it is the duty of the neophyte lowest in seniority to surrender his seat and eat (or drink) his dinner in the downstairs lounge.

It may sound like a gross exaggeration to state that such a high percentage of Sons are present every time, particularly when you consider our average age. Nothing except death or a confining and possibly near fatal illness stops a Son from being on hand those two important evenings. We've even had to roll invalid members up the club steps in wheelchairs.

All of us belong to other organizations which meet with some regularity, but whenever there is a conflict you can be certain to which sodality Sons extend "regrets." On one occasion, and I hope I'm not telling tales out of school, Thomas Hart, then the Majority Whip of the United States Senate, pleaded serious illness and sneaked off to Philadelphia instead

18

of staying in Washington to attend a dinner at the White House. Even more startling was Monsignor Lallou's appearance at the fall 1966 session, when the Philadelphia *Evening Bulletin* that very afternoon carried a story about his departure for the Ecumenical Conference in Rome.

But for me the greatest surprise of all came when I saw Marv Abrams walk into the Diogenes in September of 1961. I happened to know this was the Eve of Yom Kippur, a very High Holiday indeed for one of Marv's faith. In the hope of slight mitigation I'm glad to report to Anyone Whose task it is to record mortal sins that to the best of my knowledge neither food nor beverage passed Marv's lips that evening.

Bearing these facts in mind you should see why we Sons consider it a signal honor to be a guest. And if guests live long enough they eventually do become members. Attrition accounts for approximately three vacancies a year.

We had two invitees that evening. Who the other one was I've long since forgotten but Ken Souser's was the Colonel. I recall exactly my first impressions of that gentleman. Charlie Starr, Bill Smith, Marv and I were standing around the bar waiting for refills. My predinner drink is a martini. I happen to like the taste of vermouth so when a bartender serves me an eleven-to-one concoction, I invariably send it back after the first sip. If he gives me an argument and asks why I didn't say so in the first place, all I do is tell him to look it up in the Guide where he'll find the correct formula is three to one. Certain people I know would rather drink something they do not like rather than complain, or as they say, "make a fuss about trifles." They think I'm too finicky. But I always say what's right is right and if you're paying for something you should have it.

Well, to get back to the Colonel. Ken was making the rounds with his guest, a tall, handsome, dark-haired man who carried himself like a ramrod. I took him to be in his early forties but later, to my surprise since I'm usually accurate about ages, I discovered he was a full decade older. Moving from left to right Ken introduced the Colonel to Charlie, Bill, me, and then Marv. As he heard the name "Abrams," I distinctly noted a slight elevation of Eberhardt's eyebrows and what appeared to be more than a momentary hesitation in extending his right hand.

I'm well aware of the fact that there are plenty of clubs in our City of Brotherly Love that will accept none of Marv's faith even as "tokens." I even belong to a few of these and have seriously considered doing something about it and probably would if I were more of a crusader. You can be sure of one thing, though, and that is when I am introduced to a Jewish luncheon or dinner guest at the League or Racquet I never, by word or deed, indicate disapproval and am as cordial to him as I am to members.

Later, Marv told me that his evening was almost spoiled by the Colonel's involuntary reactions, which he noted as quickly as I had. I can explain my own perceptiveness since I *was* his sponsor and *am* his friend and demand Marv's complete acceptance, which he has *always* received in the Copper Beeches. As for Marv, I suppose those who belong to minority groups have highly sensitive antennae which alert their owners to potential discrimination.

Actually, before the meeting ended, I'd almost convinced myself that I'd made a mistake about the Colonel's latent prejudices, or if they existed he was, like a good fellow, trying to lay them aside. I'm aware now that this was arrant nonsense on my part. The Colonel, who had strong personal reasons for wanting to become a Son, must have considered the possibility of a potential blackball.

Not that any sponsored guest has ever been rejected. As Tom Hart, who is chairman of our Membership Committee, said many times when neophytes are being proposed, "Unlike the United States Senate, Sons never rise on a 'point of personal privilege.'" All of us feel that if a man is properly sponsored by two Sons he should be admitted. To act in a contrary fashion would be casting aspersions on the judgment and good taste of other Sons. Of course the Colonel could have had no way of being aware of this.

Something else, far less important than dislike for ideological reasons, was my reaction to a pair of spectacles the Colonel wore. These were rimmed with thin gold and hung from a black cord attached to a buttonhole in his left lapel. I realize it is a sign of immaturity to form opinions about a person for such a silly reason. Human nature being what it is, however, I am not the only one who judges a fellowman for equally inane reasons and lives to regret these instantaneous and frequently erroneous conclusions. A girl I once knew told me she'd broken her engagement because she grew to despise the way her fiancé crooked his finger each time he held a glass, a cup, or a spoon. She learned, only after it was too late, that the digit had been bent permanently as a result of an automobile accident.

I think it quite possible that had I not been with Marv when we met Eberhardt I might have formed less strong opinions about him and even enjoyed his company. Then, too, the Colonel always did seem to go out of his way to treat Marv with extra if sometimes what I concluded was exaggerated courtesy, even after Eberhardt became a Son. As for those gold rimmed glasses, I never saw him wear them again. Once, quite jocosely, he told us that just moments before Ken called for him the night he was a Copper Beech guest, he was so nervous about being accepted by the Sherlockians that he dropped the horn rimmed spectacles he normally wore; they smashed to bits and he had to dig out a pair he'd worn only once and that was in Kuala Lumpur where he attended a state function in the full dress of the military.

All this sounded most convincing and quite jolly. We know now that the Colonel never had been to Kuala Lumpur and as for the lenses, rimmed with gold or tortoiseshell, they were made of plain, unrefracted glass. "Twenty-twenty vision was what the man had," Martin J. Moynihan, a Son and our only ophthalmologist member, reported when he was in a position to make a diagnosis. "The bastard didn't even have astigmatism."

In fairness, I must admit the Colonel knew the Sacred Writings better than almost anyone else I've ever met including Sir Julian Wolff, a Cantabrian and *the* recognized authority. I'll give you an example when Sir Julian himself was present as Tantalus (presiding officer at special occasions) and principal speaker.

Sherlockians by the scores from all over the world gather at the annual meeting of the New York City Baker Street Irregulars held on the second Friday of January in a famous West Twenty-third Street restaurant. As part of the regularly scheduled program, the Gasogene calls for a volunteer to perform any act he chooses with, of course, Sherlockian substance. One year a member of the BSI from Topeka, Kansas, played two bars of music ("Tra-la-la-lira-lira-lay") on his piccolo and asked that it be identified. I'm proud to say that without a moment's hesitation our own Bill Smith called the tune—a

Chopin etude—and its source—*A Study in Scarlet*. Then Bill, at the Gasogene's request, which in a sense made it a command performance, completed the etude on his violin and I'm sure he did as well as Norman Noruda "whose attack and bowing are splendid." (Perhaps I should explain that Bill teaches at Juilliard, which was why he had his violin with him.)

Although I think it would have been more seemly for the Colonel to have waited until he had reached Master status (he was still only a Journeyman), he did the Copper Beeches just as proud as did Bill. To the amazement of everyone present Eberhardt quoted the complete story of the "Musgrave Ritual" verbatim. When the tumultuous applause died down, Sir Julian, who'd followed the text in the 1930 Morley Edition of the Sacred Writings, shook the Colonel's hand and declared the reading had been letter perfect.

"However," said Sir Julian, "I must add one mild criticism. The gentleman from Philadelphia placed an accent on the first syllable of the word 'laboratory.' I prefer it placed on the second."

I have a pretty fair accumulation of Sherlockiana myself but I was overcome with envy every time I saw the Colonel's. His occupies seven floor-to-ceiling library shelves. He has a copy of practically every book, treatise, monograph, and thesis ever published on the subject as well as eighty-four pages of original manuscript. The only missing item of real value was the Carl Anderson collection, and it was Eberhardt's avowed intention to fill that gap no matter what the cost.

With rain falling heavily and a high March wind blowing through the leafless trees on Rittenhouse Square, deserted at this late hour, indeed "it was a wild, tempestuous night," when Ellen welcomed her husband and his guests into their home. I always found something sweet and feminine about Ellen although, even when she was far younger and her hair was a warm, rich brown, I never heard anyone refer to her as a beauty. My parents would have labeled her an "old-fashioned girl," meaning she neither smoked, drank, nor used profanity and saw to it that the needs of her husband were satisfied before considering her own.

Ellen comes from solid Philadelphia stock, the Dawsons. While her Colonial ancestors did not, as did mine, disembark from William Penn's good ship *Welcome,* nevertheless they arrived in the Quaker City a decade or so before the Revolution. Ellen went to the correct schools—Agnes Irwin and Bryn Mawr—attended the Assemblies and had a proper coming out at Horticultural Hall, almost the last one held in this relic of the Centennial.

Shortly after, Ellen was reported to have an "understanding" with a dashing member of the First City Troop but nothing came of it. The young gentleman married somebody else and the "bud" remained unplucked. Personal tragedies filled Ellen's life. Her grandparents, maternal and paternal, went down on the S.S. *Empress of Ireland*. Her parents were killed while touring a Nevada copper mine they owned; a sudden power failure plunged the elevator in which they were riding into a pit several hundred feet below. The Dawsons' only other child was a Mongoloid son. When her parents died, Ellen took care of the boy in the family's Wyndmoor home and when he died at the age of twenty-seven, Ellen moved into the Rittenhouse Plaza, one of the few remaining center-city apartment houses which does not cater to the *nouveau riche*.

With the death of her brother, Ellen became the last in the family line. I believe there were a couple of cousins, several times removed, who lived in some dreary midwestern town, Indianapolis, if I'm not mistaken, but I doubt if Ellen had seen or heard from them more than a few times since early childhood.

Money, of course, never was a problem for Ellen. In addition to a sizable fortune bequeathed to her by her parents, she was one of only two or three legatees of her four grandparents. There is no question in my mind that it was solely money which attracted Colonel Eberhardt to Ellen Dawson, who was in her forties when they met. During the ten years following her brother's death she had been a volunteer social worker and, as everyone says, a truly dedicated one. Unlike so many other women in her social and economic position, Ellen took her duties seriously and put in a full eight-hour day, five days a week at the Friends Settlement House on Poplar Street.

Ellen and the Colonel met at one of those charity lunches which usually wind up raising so little money that the host and hostess must either confess failure or write out a personal check sufficiently large to prove the affair was a financial success. This was different, it was run by a Hicksite Friend, to which sect the Dawsons gave better than lip service, and no money was wasted on hired help, liquor, or food. At these efficiently managed affairs you serve yourself, you drink no cocktails, and you go away hungry. But you can be certain that every cent of your contribution is delivered to its beneficiary.

Holding a platter of dainty sandwiches (watercress sliced thin, no doubt) balanced in one hand and a cup of coffee in the other, the Colonel maneuvered himself into a chair next to Ellen. I'm sure he'd done his research thoroughly, knew exactly who she was, and went to the Hopkins' for the purpose of meeting the Dawson heiress.

Perhaps, subconsciously, I've forgotten to tell you that the Colonel's full name, at least the one we knew him by, was H. Wesley Eberhardt. Call it a silly prejudice if you will, but I always had an aversion to men who part their names in the middle.

The Hopkins' luncheon was quite casual, a buffet, and since everyone present was supposed to be a friend of the hosts and thus automatically a lady or gentleman, it was quite proper for the Colonel to introduce himself to Ellen even though he had not been formally presented. I hate to admit it but Eberhardt is a handsome man and he can be charming as well. He must have charmed the hell out of Ellen from the moment of their first encounter because that night she wound up in the Colonel's bed. My facts are correct. I have them from an unimpeachable source, an ancient page "boy" at the League where the Colonel was then living. When you consider that Ellen was a properly raised, diffident if not shy woman past forty, whose one fleeting romance with the First City Trooper was in the distant past, this was an incredible feat.

Three weeks later they were married at the Friends Meeting House on South Twelfth Street, in the shadow of the towering PSFS Building. Juliet, my wife, who'd known Ellen for many years and served with her on committees frequently, and I were among those present.

If the only weddings you've ever attended are traditional church ceremonies you would have a hard time believing the simplicity of a Quaker marriage. They are not all exactly alike but do follow a similar pattern. I've been to many but never ceased to wonder at their uncluttered approach to holy wedlock. There is no preacher, best man, maid of honor, bridesmaid, nor music. The bride, sometimes dressed in traditional white but just as often not, enters the bare Meeting Room and sits on a straight-back chair directly opposite and at arm's length from the groom.

For perhaps as long as a half-hour, they stare at each other in a silence broken either by a Friend who rises to say whatever he feels like saying, or by the snore of a dozing Quaker, nudged into startled wakefulness by his wife. Finally the couple stands up to face each other, the groom makes his formal pledge to love, honor, cherish, and possibly adds "obey"; the bride does likewise; the groom places a wedding band on his bride's finger; they sign the marriage register; and the ceremony is over.

There's usually a sweet table with cakes and unspiked punch at a reception in an adjacent room, and I have been to formal dinners, which some Quaker parents give for their daughter, the groom, and guests, at the Barclay, the Warwick, or the good old Bellevue-Stratford.

At most church weddings, the bride's relatives and friends are seated on one side of the aisle, the groom's on the other, thus affording each team a chance to measure and comment upon the strength of the opposition. There's one thing to be said in favor of a Quaker ceremony. You can't tell who belongs to whom—everybody sits together. So at the Dawson-Eberhardt nuptials, neither my wife nor I could hazard more than a guess about the quantity and quality of those who came to see the Colonel join his Lady in holy matrimony. My estimate as to his relatives was a big fat zero and as to friends, perhaps a half dozen, and these appeared to be business acquaintances or colleagues from Valley Forge Military Academy where the Colonel, since his retirement, was a teacher.

While the Meeting House was packed with Ellen's friends I know that the only kin at her wedding were those two or three dismal Indianapolis (or was it Peoria?) cousins several times removed who, after their introductions, faded away. I recall one of them, a large bespectacled, scrawny, middle-aged woman who had to be either a history teacher in a midwestern cow college or a small-town librarian, asking me whether it was much of a walk to the Liberty Bell.

The honeymoon was brief. This was between semesters at

Valley Forge and Ellen was in the midst of setting up a new program at the Settlement House. The couple was back from Palm Springs in ten days.

CHAPTER

4

I NEVER could call myself a close friend of Ellen, although my wife knew her well; and until he became a Son, I was hardly aware of the Colonel's existence. It occurred to me later that I'd actually seen Eberhardt at the League of which I am a very lukewarm member. But I used to lunch there from time to time because the food was the best in the city until the Diogenes lured their chef away. I know why, but that's another story and like that of the Giant Rat of Sumatra, one "for which the world [in my case only Philadelphia] is not yet prepared."

The Colonel became a member of the League as soon as he established the required residency and proved his unswerving devotion to the principles laid down by the late William McKinley. His sponsors, as we discovered during the "Chase," were far to the Right; both of these gentlemen were, like Eberhardt, retired members of the military.

However, despite my own political liberalism (I firmly believe there are many decent Democrats) I'm sure had I known of Eberhardt's deep Sherlockian interest I would have gone out of my way to meet him and might very well (God forbid!) have become one of his Copper Beech sponsors. I certainly must have met him at the wedding when Juliet and I passed through the reception line. But, as I recall, we had another engagement immediately following the ceremonies and did not stay for the sweet table. I'm sure our absence was unnoted and I doubt if I gave any thought to either Eberhardt for some time to come. Juliet continued to work with Ellen who still continued to spend considerable time on Poplar

Street and unquestionably remained a substantial contributor to the Cause.

It was quite a while later, and certainly following the Colonel's admission to the Copper Beeches, that Juliet and I were entertained at Baskerville Hall. It was then that I learned something about the Colonel's background—or at least what he led us to believe about it. The dinner party was small, four or five couples and the inevitable "extra man," frequently a homosexual. After we'd dined, the gentlemen retired to the library for brandy and cigars, a quaint and rather pleasant custom to which we Philadelphians still adhere.

The Colonel claimed Chicago as his "home town" (the exact phrase he used), and there was as little reason for us to doubt this as there was for him to tell us what turned out to be a fact if not the truth. It was the kind of distortion that permits a school to advertise that it is an "international" institution because one of its seven hundred students comes from Toronto. Eberhardt also told us his father was a doctor and this, too, fell into the same category.

I used to wonder if this equivocation was a result of the Colonel's training (he was in military intelligence for years), congenital instincts or, as I am now convinced, the result of deeply laid Machiavellian plans. The Colonel rarely did anything spontaneously. With just a tinge of regret in his rich, baritone voice he admitted that his alma mater was not the "Point" but The Fortress, a violently reactionary military institution in the Deep South. This time he told the unvarnished truth.

"I make no claim to a liberal education," Eberhardt once said with a deprecating half-smile, and you had to give him credit for admitting that much. "I guess until I met Ellen I thought there were only two kinds of people in the world, military and civilian. And then to marry a practicing Quaker!"

He laughed a bit. "I dare say Ellen's had serious misgivings about getting tied up with a husband whose training and philosophy has been the complete antithesis of hers. She has a lot more tolerance than I."

These were the rare moments when I felt that Ellen's gentle qualities were effecting a change in her husband's mold even if only slightly. Then he'd say something so outrageous that I'd tell myself this would be the last time I'd ever visit the

Eberhardts despite the man's collection of Sherlockiana and
my wife's growing fondness for Ellen.

I recall one of those bigoted remarks which made me
furious. I would have asked for my coat then and there had I
not been loathe to embarrass either Ellen, my wife, or other
Eberhardt guests. It was the day following President Kennedy's assassination. Believe me, I am *not* a Kennedy fan. I have
never voted the Democratic ticket in my entire life, although
from time to time, when I felt our candidate was personally
obnoxious, I have been tempted to cast my ballot for his op-
ponent in the other party. That I have not done so I attribute
to strength of character.

There were only four or five guests that evening. I'd gotten
up, as I often did, to peruse Eberhardt's fantastic collection. I
may have drunk a bit too much and certainly I ate too much
and consequently had not been following the conversation. I
climbed up the library ladder to re-examine a unique Brazil-
ian edition of the Sacred Writings, hand-printed and designed
in Rio in 1930, the year of Sir Arthur Conan Doyle's death,
and illustrated by an unknown artist who depicted Holmes as
a gigantic Negro.

I was wide awake then—I had to be or I could have fallen
twelve feet to the floor below—when I heard the Colonel
calmly say, without raising his voice a single decibel, "It was a
legitimate assassination. That man deserved to die, he was
disrupting an entire world. I disapprove only of the method.
Very, very amateurish and sloppy. The executioner might easily have failed and never gotten another opportunity.

"You'll find the killer, whoever he was [Oswald had not yet
been identified] was no professional."

Almost in shock I heard Tom Gilford ask the Colonel
whether he'd reward or punish the murderer. The Colonel
looked puzzled. His answer which came a moment or two
later utterly baffled me.

"Reward the culprit? Tom, you must be kidding! He shot
our Commander-in-Chief. When they get him they ought to
string him up from the nearest tree. That's how *I'd* handle the
bastard!"

I made no attempt to join the conversation. Pleading a sudden, severe headache I asked to be excused, collected my wife
and my coat and went home. We didn't see the Eberhardts
again for a good many months. But Juliet had been to an af-

ternoon meeting with Ellen and afterward the pair of them dropped into Schrafft's for tea.

"It wasn't so much what Ellen said," my wife told me later, "because she said very little. It was her attitude. Remember you once commented on the fact that you never saw a woman who appeared more at peace with the world than she did?"

I nodded.

"Well," my wife went on, "whatever it was she had, she has it no longer. I don't think she's happy. We're not the only ones, you know, who've been refusing invitations to the Carriage House [Juliet never could get used to calling the place Baskerville Hall]. Ellen's beginning to feel isolated, and I gather the type of people who *do* see them are definitely *not* her type. She's always been far more liberal than you or I. Let's face it. She's often entertained Negroes; we've talked about it but never did anything."

I shrugged my shoulders. I'm as tolerant as the next man but there *are* limits. Juliet went on.

"I'm sure I know what's distressing Ellen most at the moment. Remember how you'd make a wry face when you saw her name in the newspapers listed on a committee you disapproved of? Like the time she supported that Youth Movement for Peace in Vietnam which you said was a Commie outfit. And that other time she was active with a group trying to elect that nice Jewish man for Governor. Coleman, or something, and we sat at the same table with him and his pretty wife at the Orchestra and you told him about your friendship with Marv and that witty rabbi we met at the Pattersons'."

I remembered these incidents quite well and I tell you honestly I was more than pleased to find other members of my friend Marv's race so completely acceptable. Naturally I didn't vote for Coleman, but it wasn't my vote which decided the issue since he was defeated quite badly. Coleman had gotten the Democratic nomination for Senate this time and I had the feeling I knew what Juliet would tell me next. I was right.

"Apparently, without asking the Colonel's permission, Ellen made a contribution to Mr. Coleman's committee, and it must have upset her husband quite a bit when he saw it listed in the *Inquirer*."

I smiled, thinking it must have upset Eberhardt's John Birch friends even more.

"That wasn't all," Juliet continued. "It seems Ellen invited the Colemans and some of their friends to dinner at the Carriage House. She had a wry smile when I asked her point-blank what the Colonel's reaction was. 'He was quite reserved,' she answered. Then I asked Ellen [you can see my wife is a very forthright woman] whether they'd ever dined at the Colemans' home. 'Mrs. Coleman asked us,' Ellen said, 'but we declined.' "

From what Juliet went on to say I gathered that Ellen had become completely estranged from the circle of friends she'd always enjoyed associating with. I'm sure others besides ourselves had pleaded "previous engagements" when Ellen's invitations came 'round. The point my wife was trying to make in her indirect fashion was to ask me if I'd mind including the Eberhardts at a small dinner party we were giving for a visiting columnist scheduled to speak at the Art Alliance in a couple of weeks. He would be our overnight guest. I agreed in spite of recalling how unpleasant Eberhardt had been the last time we'd been to the Hall.

Our guest of honor was Ed Gifford, whose family was our nearest neighbor when we had a farm outside Paoli. Ed was at the University then. We'd invited only four other couples and Eberhardt, to my surprise, stayed far away from politics and all other controversial subjects and exuded every bit of his old charm. He discovered at once that he and Ed, who'd been a UPI war correspondent for the *Bulletin* before his column was syndicated, had met and spent a few days together in Korea.

Ed is a superb raconteur and did much of the talking. But the Colonel, without using offensive, four-letter words, told several funny stories about the peculiar mating habits of the Koreans. The evening, to my complete surprise, turned out to be delightful. I know our guests enjoyed themselves; they certainly stayed late enough. As for myself, that dinner became an almost memorable occasion. Just as he was leaving, the Colonel took a small, carefully wrapped package from his overcoat pocket and handed it to me.

"I think you'll enjoy adding this to your collection, Frank," he said and smiled slightly. "I know you don't have it."

I couldn't wait until I unwrapped his gift. It turned out to be an original edition of *The Case Book of Sherlock Holmes*, published in England by McWilliams, Ltd., and hand-bound in limp leather. While this was not a true collector's item, I'd never gotten around to buying a copy. I showed the thin volume to Ed (poor, benighted fellow, he collects *Lepidoptera*) who admitted he'd not read the Sacred Writings since high school days. Nevertheless I think he sensed my delight at the unexpected acquisition and probably related it to the pleasure he himself might have had had he suddenly been presented with some desiccated butterfly stuck on a pin.

Then over our last few brandies, after Juliet retired, we let the logs burn down to ashes while I told Ed about Ellen, the Eberhardts' marriage, and how the Colonel kept throwing me off balance. Ed is a good listener and did not miss a word. He'd been seated next to Ellen at dinner and I know he enjoyed her quiet humor. She'd even looked pretty. Of course Ed sensed nothing amiss in the Eberhardts' relationship because that evening nothing was amiss. They treated each other as any husband and wife do—a slight diminution of interest when the latter relates an oft-told tale and a look of frustration when the former tries to tell a joke certain the punch line will be muffed. Usually the husband is right.

Ed was smiling. "Tell me, what is it about the man that seems to fascinate you?"

I grinned, admitting he was the only person who baffled me completely. I gave as an example what the Colonel said about the Kennedy assassination although by this time still another Kennedy had been slaughtered.

"Then, all of a sudden," I went on, "the Colonel comes along and does something completely out of character. He *knew* that book was sure to please me enormously and he could have had no other reason for giving it to me than for my pleasure. And yet, in so many other ways his actions are repugnant. I sometimes believe he's a throwback to the Roman republic's bullies and a potential menace to society."

Ed shook his head.

"You don't understand the military mind, Frank. I think I do. Let me try to explain. The Colonel and I were hardly what you'd call bosom friends. Actually, the only time I spent with him until this evening was back in '52 when I was covering the last gasps of the Korean 'police action.' I'd been assigned to do a series on the basic attitudes of the average Gook; to dig behind the gung-ho crap the Army was putting out. You know the stuff, that the Koreans loved America, the

Mummers Parade, the Rose Bowl game and simply detested the ideologies of their brothers to the North.

"I didn't want the usual guided tour. I pulled strings at the Pentagon and was promised freedom within certain mutually agreed-upon limits. I was to 'tell it like it is.' My escort out of Seoul [they were still calling it Keijo] was Lieutenant Colonel Eberhardt. He hadn't gotten his chicken wings yet.

"He was G2, he looked it and at our first meeting was quite formal. It was obvious he mistrusted the press and besides, he was a member of the military and I, a mere civilian. I've been around enough to know that despite orders that I assumed would have filtered down from above—although you never know, some stupid one-star might have decided to countermand a four-star—I was to see only what the Colonel wanted me to see. And I was going to talk only to those the Colonel wanted me to talk to. In other words, more of the same junk, which I had no intention of taking. I had enough handouts in World War Two."

Ed said he'd asked for and finally gotten an order that the Colonel would escort him only as far as a village ninety miles southwest of Seoul.

"GIs called the place Chickamauga, which was to be my starting point. There a staff car and driver would pick up my interpreter and me, and the Colonel would return to his base. Naturally I insisted on my own interpreter; I wasn't having any the Army suggested. My guy's name was Mr. Kim. He was a bald, ageless, little yellow man, sharp-eyed, completely honest and dependable. He'd worked for UPI and AP, too, and had top clearance.

"Whether or not he was a gentleman by birth I wouldn't know and couldn't have cared less. But he sure didn't belong to the servant class. He was clean, neat, his table manners were excellent—Western style—and, within the limits of his salary which wasn't much, he dressed well. I'd used him twice before, once when the Korean action began and again six months later. Naturally, I treated him as my social equal, which he certainly was, and probably a wealthy landowner before the Japs took over. I addressed him as 'Mister' Kim; he was as formal with me.

"Important from my point of view was that Mr. Kim translated exactly what I said and gave in quite precise English the exact answer. There were no shadings, no raised eyebrows, and no ad libs to impart his own philosophies. And he never belittled you to the natives, a quality damned few interpreters have. Most of them feel that by denigrating us they upgrade themselves. My knowledge of the language is limited, but at least I can tell when I'm being conned."

Ed paused while I stirred the ashes and poured another brandy.

"It took a few days for Mr. Kim to arrive at Seoul and I spent those with the Colonel as a guest in his home. I must say he was a most considerate host and did his best to make me comfortable. He was witty, a good listener, and knew the score from the military point of view. Those two or three days passed pleasantly enough.

"I didn't want any other newspaperman's opinions so I deliberately stayed away from our office, AP, and the Overseas Correspondents' Club. Consequently I was in the Colonel's company most of the time. He lived well, like our officers over the rank of Major do on foreign soil. He had a house and a Korean family to serve him hand, foot, and bed besides. If he had one fault it was his egotism and that did anger me at times. He was so goddamned sure he was right and those who disagreed with him, wrong.

"He *knew* Rhee was finished, he *knew* what diplomatic mistakes we were sure to make at the peace talks [we made 'em!], he *knew* there'd be a power vacuum in Indochina and that the U.S. would step in to fill it. You got to remember the Colonel was saying this a long while before Dien Bien Phu. He even predicted Russia's involvement in the Arabs' behalf in the Mideast."

Ed shook his head in reluctant admiration.

"He was right about damned near everything. However, I don't want to sound as if all I did during those few days was listen to the Colonel expounding his philosophies or making political predictions. On the contrary. We played tennis and swam at the Bachelor Officers' Quarters and after dinner we were at the chess board. I was no match for the Colonel, he was superb."

I interrupted to tell Ed what the Master had said about chess players.

"Amberly [in *The Adventure of the Retired Colourman*] excelled at chess—one mark, Watson, of a scheming mind."

My guest smiled and went on.

"He was very gracious, a good winner and I almost liked him. In fact, come to think of it, I did most of the time. He was considerate to his family and servants and the woman, a pretty native, who I'm sure was his mistress. But never did he openly show signs of intimacy with any of them. They kept their distance and so did he and yet, as I learned quite inadvertently, he was paying, out of his own pocket, for the education of two or possibly three of the kids who were living in the servants' compound. And I'll tell you something else; not once did he mention his personal life or his past.

"After those few days together I developed one overriding feeling about my host—that he never did anything spontaneously, that he had to be right *all* the time, that he had to win *every* game. A great man for our side in time of war but a potentially dangerous one otherwise.

"He was the correct age and the right temperament for his rank and I was sure he would have been a two-star by now. So I was shocked to learn he'd retired as a mere colonel. I wonder why."

I wondered myself. Ed went on.

"In the evening of the third day my office informed me Mr. Kim was ready to start our venture the following morning. At seven o'clock a staff sergeant who was our driver pulled up in front of the Colonel's residence. My interpreter was with him.

"I was delighted to see Mr. Kim and he was as pleased to see me. We shook hands, I asked him about his nephew, or grand-nephew, I don't know which, but who I believe was Mr. Kim's only relative. We chatted for a few minutes about past shared experiences and mutual friends, then the Colonel stepped out of the door, and I introduced him to my interpreter. Eberhardt nodded curtly and did not extend his hand. Fortunately neither did Mr. Kim so no face was lost.

"There wasn't any question about where Mr. Kim would ride. He climbed up with the sergeant, a very faint smile on his face. He knew I'd have wanted him in the back of the staff car which had plenty of room for three. It took us nearly eight hours to travel those ninety-odd miles. We stopped twice to eat and stretch our legs before climbing back in the jeep. The sergeant opened a hamper, passed out sandwiches and poured coffee from a thermos.

"I sat with the Colonel; the sergeant ate by himself a dozen yards away. On the other side of the jeep Mr. Kim munched

his sandwiches and drank his coffee alone. I've often thought
about that scene. Here were four men brought together by the
fortunes of war to this remote spot in the Korean hills. Yet,
because of the Colonel, we were not a group, only four individuals. Eberhardt simply could not yield under circumstances where the General or Admiral would have eased up."

I poured our last brandy.

"The second and final stop for that day before Mr. Kim
and I would be delivered to Chickamauga was at a small military outpost which had an officers' mess. Eberhardt and I
joined the local commander, a captain, his first louie and two
seconds. I looked around for Mr. Kim. The Colonel noticed
my glance, there was no trace of a smile on his face.

" 'Don't worry. Your man's being fed.' "

"I raised my eyebrows. 'Where?'

" 'Out with the other niggers.'

"Then the goddamnedest thing happened. As we were
about to eat the Captain turned to Eberhardt.

" 'Would you say grace, Sir?'

"And so help me, the Colonel had the effrontery to bow his
head and ask the Lord to bless the food which He had placed
before us, to protect us and our Korean allies, and to bring
peace, brotherhood, and understanding to all mankind."

CHAPTER

5

I MAKE no attempt to convince anyone of the complete sobriety of the Colonel's guests when they entered Baskerville Hall
that ill-fated evening.

"None of us was feeling much pain," Don admitted to me
in my study a day or two after I'd returned from Lisbon, "but
the Colonel poured another one and we sat around the fireplace talking and drinking. We discussed Herb Middleton's
paper, the one he'd delivered at the meeting, and the Colonel
extracted a 1955 London University doctoral thesis, part of

which he said Monsignor Lallou used for his cleric's learned dissertation.

"That reminded Ed Johnson of a monograph on a similar subject, this one tracing the lineage of the Baskerville hound, written in Hindustani by an anonymous author but translated into English by the late Mohandâs Gandhi [a Sherlockian of note]. It was Ed's claim that there were only nine copies in existence, adding, rather proudly, that his was Number Eight, and the only one in the entire Western Hemisphere."

Of course I was familiar with the Gandhi translation, one of the rarest treasures of the Sacred Writings and I could have sworn Ed was correct. I never dreamed the Colonel had a copy since it was *not* on his shelves but, as Don proved, I was wrong.

" 'Not quite so, old boy,' the Colonel said, a smug smile on his face, when Ed stopped talking. He stood up and you know that Penang lawyer that hangs over the fireplace?"

I nodded.

"Well, the Colonel moved it and an original Paget to one side and exposed a small wall safe. Out of this he took a copy of the Gandhi translation and passed it around for our inspection. On the flyleaf was a notation that this was 'Copy Number Two.'

" 'Copy Number One,' Eberhardt told us, 'is in the Victoria and Albert. What did you pay for yours, Ed?'

"Ed admitted he'd paid thirty eight hundred dollars for his at the old Brown Book Store in Chicago. I thought what the Colonel did next was hateful.

"'Mine was eighty cents. Picked it up at a junk shop on South Street.' He gave a funny little chuckle that must have infuriated Ed.

" 'Too bad,' he said. 'Just goes to prove you must keep your eyes open. "Acres of Diamonds" and all that stuff.' And then, damned if the Colonel didn't walk over to his desk, pull out a copy of *Atlanticus*—naturally you know the one I mean—and hand it to Ed.

" 'I've an extra copy,' he said. 'I'd like you to have this one.' "

The gift was a generous one, no question. The April 1913 issue of that long since defunct periodical adds a light touch to the Sacred Writings. On page 53, in the second installment of "The Final Problem" some sloppy printer, aided and abetted by a careless proofreader, allowed the original erratum to remain, changed an "o" to an "i" and Mrs. Hudson's question to Holmes about being "shot" emerges quite differently. Approximately seven hundred copies were either in the mail or hands of subscribers before the mistake was noted and corrected. Don continued.

"Ed was mollified. Then we got talking about current crimes—you know how we usually do—and what methods the Master would have applied to solve them. This was the day our paper had broken the story of Michael Wilson's disappearance and everybody pounded on that one. I didn't cover it myself but I was familiar with the details."

Wilson, as you may recall, was The First National Trust Company's executive vice-president who embezzled a quarter of a million dollars he'd tossed away at the races over a number of years and left for parts unknown. We'd all thought him an outstanding representative of the so-called Establishment. In fact he was a fellow member of several of my clubs, fortunately not the Copper Beeches.

As I recollected—and I have an excellent memory for this sort of thing—Wilson was tending a gas pump in Tacoma, Washington, when the FBI finally apprehended him. He'd not been found for six months and no doubt thought he'd gotten away with his crime. The authorities never revealed the details that led to Wilson's capture, although I have a fair idea of what they were. However, I won't go into this now.

"It was Jack," Don continued, "who said he was surprised it took so long for Wilson's capture.

" 'He was not only a thief but a fool. In this computerized age how can anyone except a complete idiot think he can disappear in the United States? Everybody has a dozen identifying numbers that follow him for the rest of his life. The hospital he was born in probably started this by taking his fingerprints and even footprints. I think most of them do that now, don't they, Marv?'

"Marv nodded. 'All of them, I guess.'

" 'Well, that's his first I.D. Maybe even before he goes to nursery school or anytime during his life he has surgery, which probably leaves a scar. Then there's handwriting. Oh, I can think of a thousand more marks he leaves along the way.'

"Jack paused for breath and Marv added his bit.

" 'What about dental work—that's a permanent record.'

" 'And so are sports,' I said. 'This is the department where they really keep records forever. If the guy played on any of his high school or college team basketball, football, baseball, crew, lacrosse, or what have you. If he was the second string left tackle for Muskingum and they played against Canarsie College in 1912, there'll be a record of that game and what, if anything, every player did. There'll be members of his team who'll remember his particular abilities or weaknesses and most of his peculiarities. And don't think the FBI isn't aware of all this.' "

Don said that soon everybody—that is, except the Colonel who kept silent—was in the act pointing out other sources of identification. These included the "suspect's" driver's license, his signature on bank accounts, and the information he gave department stores for charge accounts, and his insurance forms.

"Charlie said," Don continued, "that unless a man had decided to falsify damned near everything about himself and was clever enough to maintain the deception, he'd still have a hard time of it. And whatever information which couldn't be supplied by the military or anyone else would be supplied by the wife or children who'd known those intimate details."

Then Don told me he brought out the fact that too many people are bearish on the intelligence of policemen.

"That's a mistake many criminals make. I'm not telling you there aren't a lot of stupid cops. What I'm saying is they're a lot smarter than people give them credit for. I'll tell you fellows one case I ran into recently—about a killer who thought he'd disappeared forever after he murdered a friend he got mad at in a card game.

"We've all been speaking about men who have bank accounts, credit cards, went to prep school or college or served in the military and were born in hospitals. The murderer I'm talking about had none of these sources of information in his record. Never was fingerprinted, never had a social security card, never went beyond fourth grade, never had a bank account, and was delivered by a midwife in an Italian slum section of Johnstown, P.A.

"The killer's name was Marchetti and the police had made their routine search, which resulted in exactly nothing despite three years of hard work. Then one day a bright young State Trooper named Jesse Taynton, who'd recently been transferred from traffic to the CID, was going through unsolved murder files when he ran across this particular case."

Don paused long enough for me to refill our coffee cups from the percolator I always keep handy in my study.

"Well, Taynton himself was born and raised in Johnstown only a couple of squares from Marchetti's old neighborhood and he had a lot of friends there. So he asked his captain for permission to work on the case and was told it was OK providing it didn't interfere with current investigations.

"I'm not going to drag this out, Frank, but after a good bit of digging Taynton got a tip Marchetti might be living in Chicago under an alias. That wasn't much to go on and surely not enough to merit the captain's approval for an out-of-town trip.

"But Taynton didn't give up. If he couldn't go to Chicago in person he'd do some armchair sleuthing."

I interrupted with a smile. "Like Mycroft?" I asked.

Don nodded. "Exactly. When Marchetti left for parts unknown he had two kids, a boy, eleven, and a girl, fourteen. That much information was, of course, in the files. So Taynton wrote a letter to both the Superintendents of Chicago's public and parochial schools acquainting them with the known facts and asking for cooperation in a plan he'd worked out.

"Marchetti's son would now be fourteen and the daughter seventeen, which meant the pair should be in high school providing, naturally, they weren't dropouts. Well, Taynton proposed that all the English teachers in Chicago's high schools be instructed to require their students to write, without previous notice, everything they knew about the Johnstown flood.

"Few of us recall much of the flood except in a vague way unless we've just read one of those books in which they keep retelling the story. But *everybody* in Johnstown, man, woman, and child, knows a hell of a lot about that catastrophe even if none of his ancestors was in it—the biggest thing ever to have hit the town. Nobody from the age of five on is ever allowed to forget it.

"The school officials were intrigued. Permission was granted and three weeks later Taynton was advised that a high school freshman named Richard Antonelli and his sister, Maria, a junior, appeared to be the only two out of a good many thousands of pupils who had a comprehensive knowledge of the flood.

"It was duck soup from there on in. Taynton went to Chicago with a warrant for Marchetti's arrest. The murderer was extradited, brought to trial at Ebensburg, the County seat, found guilty of murder in the second degree and is now doing time at Eastern Penn."

Excluding Eberhardt, as I recapitulate, the consensus of the five Sons was that it would be well-nigh impossible for anyone in our highly computerized society to disappear permanently. I believe that at this point had the Colonel no ulterior motive (and since it was by then quite late) his guests would have had another brandy or two, and gone home. However, it's easy to follow Eberhardt's scheming mind. He deliberately baited his hook and the Sons foolishly mouthed it.

This is how Don told me the evening wound up:

"Gentlemen," declared the Colonel, "if a man of superior intelligence were to disappear tomorrow, no one in the world could find him, certainly not those bunglers, Lestrade or Gregson."

Then came the most blasphemous comment a Son could make.

"No, gentlemen, not even the great Mr. Sherlock Holmes himself!"

There were simultaneous gasps of astonishment and before Marv, Charlie, Don, Ed, or Jack recovered their breaths, the Colonel uttered further shocking heresies.

"Let's not fool ourselves about the alleged abilities of the Master. You don't have to look very far to understand why I consider myself an authority on the subject."

He and the other Sons glanced at those vast quantities of the Sacred Writings resting on the Colonel's shelves. Eberhardt went on.

"Holmes' clues were planted by Doyle. In real life they would be nonexistent. Who the hell ever heard of a 'tall, left-handed man, who limps with the right leg, wears thick-soled shooting boots and a gray cloak, smokes Indian cigars, uses a cigar holder and carries a blunt penknife in his pocket?'

"Or 'a man who was more than six feet high, in the prime of life, had small feet, wore coarse, square-toed boots and smoked a Trichinopoly . . . and came . . . with his victim in a four-wheeled cab, drawn by a horse with three old shoes and a new one.' A man who 'had a florid face, and the fingernails of his right hand were remarkably long.'

"Come on, my fellow Sherlockians, this is evidence planted for the benefit of making our so-called Master solve crimes with ease. Doyle makes morons out of the criminals. Who could possibly be as stupid as Jonas Oldacre, the villain who was smoked out of his own attic where he tried to disappear? Any fool could have found poor Jonas in an hour. It took Holmes three days.

"And was there, in real life, a boy quite so stupid as 'the ten-year-old Lord Saltire, only son and heir to the Duke of Holdernesse,' who thought he could walk away from his father and never be found? 'Look for the mother,' our master detective said after wasting precious time. This was a deduction Holmes *should* have made five minutes after he came into possession of the facts.

"Furthermore, gentlemen, I'm getting fed up with that stuff about the Canon's so-called milk-fed morals. Dig deeper as I have and you'll discover not only that Holmes was a faggot but also a despoiler of womanhood, proving he could and did play it both ways. He confesses his 'love' for Doctor Watson and what do you think he meant by *that?* Then, if you'll recall, in 'The Adventure of the Speckled Band,' he admits that 'Mrs. Hudson has been knocked up.' Who but Holmes was the putative father? And if I'm any expert on the subject of deduction, I say an abortion, performed by Doctor Watson, followed. Mrs. Hudson never mentions a son or a daughter and a woman of her loquacity would not have failed to."

By this time I shouldn't have to tell you the Colonel's guests were speechless with anger. Then the Colonel arrogantly played his trump card.

"Gentlemen, I digress on the subject of the Canon's sex life; that is unimportant. What I *am* saying is that without those phony clues Doyle sprinkled so generously in his protagonist's path, the master detective couldn't have found a missing guppy in a fish pond five feet from his very eyes. In real life he would have been just as much a bungler as Lestrade or Mr. J. Edgar Hoover, who publicizes only his successes, not his failures.

"I come back to my original premise. I tell you that despite interlocking communications which provide instant information to police departments all over the United States and the accumulation of data which covers a person's whole life, a man of superior intelligence can disappear for as long as he wishes to."

Wharton was first to recover.

"Colonel," he said as coldly as he could, "are you speaking about just anyone with superior intelligence or have you a specific person in mind?"

Jack, of course, was aware that when the Colonel spoke of a man with "superior intelligence" he referred to himself. Eberhardt smiled and, while I wasn't there, I'm sure it was sardonic.

"I'd be willing to prove my theories," he said, "if you gentlemen have no objections."

From this point on it was child's play for the Colonel to lead his guests anywhere. Even I, who of all Sons had the foresight to question Eberhardt's probity from our very first encounter, might have followed.

Within an hour, stakes were agreed upon and ground rules laid. The prize, as I mentioned before, was the Carl Anderson collection. It was revealed only then that the Colonel was aware he would not have been able to buy it on the open market because Jack had made a previous bid to the Pittsburgher's counsel, a bid which Ben Wolf agreed to honor. If the Colonel won, Jack would surrender his option and the collection was Eberhardt's, to be paid for jointly by the five shorn sheep. If Eberhardt lost he'd buy the prize and turn it over to the five Sons to dispose of as they chose. For the Colonel this would involve no financial hardship; from what Ellen had told Juliet, the Dawson estate was held jointly by husband and wife.

The quintet was permitted to seek advice or direct assistance from any police bureau it wished to consult, including the FBI, or it could hire a private detective. The Colonel agreed, in fact insisted, so vast was his ego, that he would not leave the Commonwealth of Pennsylvania, nor would he travel more than 125 miles from the City of Philadelphia.

Eberhardt was given three days to make his getaway during which time his "opponents" would do nothing to trace his movements nor discuss the Chase even among themselves. To win the bet, Eberhardt had to elude his pursuers for six months.

"That would be," Ed said calmly looking at a wall calendar,

then glancing at his wristwatch, "exactly at 3:22 A.M., Saturday, September 27, 1969."

Eberhardt grinned. "Don't you think it more appropriate for me to make my appearance at the next fall meeting of the Sons? That is, if you gentlemen don't mind lopping off nine or so hours from the time limit."

These, then, were the terms of the most famous (or infamous) wager ever made in the City of Brotherly Love. Jack, Don, Charlie, Ed, and Marv shook hands with their host and were off through the yew trees to Sassafras Alley.

Jack turned around and called out, "Say goodnight to Ellen for me, will you, Colonel?" and almost as an afterthought added, "By the way, what'll she be doing while you're gone?" To which the Colonel answered, "You know what Ruth said to Naomi—'Whither thou goest, I go.'" A fact if not the truth.

CHAPTER

6

IT TOOK about a week before all five Sons became fully aware how deeply they had involved themselves. Each is a busy man, dedicated to the full-time practice of his profession and all are public-spirited citizens who devote many spare hours to civic projects. In addition, with the possible exception of Jack, who leads a quiet life, all have many social commitments. Withdrawing, even partially, from any these activities would be immeasurably difficult and could be embarrassing.

But anger at the Colonel for his perfidy spurred them on and welded their joint determination to "get" him regardless of the cost. We all played the game, as Holmes phrased it, "for the game's own sake." It was distressing to find out that the Colonel, despite his vast collection of the Sacred Writings, was not and never truly had been one of us. He'd taken us in and the revelation was unpleasant. What his basic motivation was for these years of pretense we would discover only later and then never be quite sure.

Those first three days of the "grace" period passed without incident. Very early in the morning of the fourth day, five individual telephone calls were made to Baskerville Hall and each time the response was the same—"I'm sorry but the number you are calling has been disconnected at the customer's request."

The "hunt" was on.

Marv nominated Jack as temporary chairman; the latter accepted and set about arranging a meeting as quickly as possible. Here the first problem was encountered. Don was covering a mine disaster in upstate Pennsylvania and Charlie was attending an architectural conference in Denver. So it was ten days before all were available. By that time I was back from Portugal and in my official position as Historian invited to join them. As a matter of fact, the first plenary session was held in my Jessup Street home.

It occurs to me only now that I never have introduced myself properly to the reader. But because I soon became an active participant and thereby was able to make direct and rather important contributions to group efforts, I feel it necessary to overcome my innate modesty. I will make this "biography" as brief as possible.

I'm fifty-nine, a Philadelphian by birth and a seventh generation resident of the Quaker City so you realize my roots here are deep. You know I am married. My "discipline" is historical research and my particular area is the development of Iberian culture with emphasis on the mid-seventeenth and early eighteenth centuries.

Others may find my vocation dull. To this I say *chacun à son gout,* or in the vernacular of my college days, "that's what the old lady said when she kissed the pig." I have found my life and my work exciting and feel no need to apologize to anyone for the way I've spent the years.

I have one earned doctorate (the University, of course) and "collected" several honoraries. I have written and presented scores of papers, and the University of Minnesota Press published three of my books in hard covers. In 1967 an astonishing event occurred. A New York publisher of paperbacks who previously catered solely to the prurient tastes of the masses, suddenly acquired the rights to an early work.

That one, for a university press, was quite successful. If I recall correctly, almost nine hundred copies were sold to the general public or presented to colleagues at other seats of learning.

I was advised that the first soft cover edition of one hundred thousand was sold out in a fortnight and two editions of like proportions followed. I acquired a New York agent, and a Hollywood-based independent motion picture company purchased the screen rights to what they call my "property." Only two months ago I was informed that a director had been chosen and a star cast for the leading role. My agent tells me there is a chance I may be summoned to the West Coast to become a technical advisor.

What pleases me most, I suppose, is that in the paperback editions not one word of the original manuscript was altered nor a single line deleted. However, at both my agent's and editor's insistence I made one minor concession and that was a change of title.

"Far too long," both gentlemen claimed. What they chose instead I will admit is considerably shorter, but whether or not this is responsible for the astronomical sales, I reserve decision. The University of Minnesota publication was called *The Fructification of Inter-related Sexual Drives within the Confines of Eighteenth Century Spanish Convents*. What they substituted was *The Nuns Liked It Too*.

I once asked my agent, Paul Gitlin, a very decent Jewish gentleman, whatever possessed the Sheiss Press to buy my book. His answer was revealing. "Your editor misinterpreted the meaning of 'fructify.'" I have only one more comment to make about the book and that is concerning the jacket. I find it a bit offensive, although I'm not a Roman Catholic, to see partially undraped Sisters of the Ursuline Convent in strange juxtaposition with equally unclad Missionary Fathers. I assure you I had no control over the artist's imagination.

Within a couple of hours after my Pan Am flight from Lisbon delivered me to the airport and I'd cleared customs, I knew all about the bet. Marv was our first caller and while Juliet unpacked my bags, he filled me in on those events that had occurred since I'd said goodnight to my fellow Sons less than two weeks before.

My anger at the Colonel was no less than theirs although,

as I told Marv, Eberhardt's perfidy was, for me at least, not totally unexpected.

Aside from our personal friendship Marv had a number of purposes in consulting me with such alacrity. First of all, as Copper Beech Historian I have the right to be informed immediately about everything that involves any or all Sons officially. Then, too, Marv and the rest of the quintet must have felt need for my counsel. There was an additional problem that faced the hunters and this, too, Marv brought out.

"With one exception, and you know whom I mean, all of us can afford to lose the seven or eight thousand bucks which our individual share of the prize comes to, plus whatever the hell else it's going to cost to make the search. I'm not even thinking of placing a dollar value on time. We wouldn't like to part with the dough but if we had to it wouldn't be a catastrophe. I'm not the best heeled Son but Helene's got a lot of family loot salted away. She's a good sport and after I told her about the bet she laughed and said the Biddles never gambled money on a more insane cause."

I held up my hands to remonstrate. "Stop talking about losing, Marv. The Colonel *will* be found."

I knew the exception Marv meant was young Donaldson and I gave him a solution to the problem forthwith.

"Suppose I 'bought out' Don's share," I suggested.

Marv breathed a sigh of relief. "Great. But it'll have to be done with all that tact I know you possess, Frank. We certainly don't want to offend him. I know he's worried—he told me yesterday he hasn't even mentioned the bet to Connie [his wife]."

I had no doubts about my ability to provide Don with an "out" he could accept gracefully and thus alleviate his financial worries in the event the bet was lost, a possibility I was forced to admit if only to myself. You may wonder how a man engaged in a discipline as noncommercial as mine can afford to gamble for such high stakes. I assure you that neither my book royalties for *The Nuns Liked It Too* nor the film option, grandiose as they may seem to my university colleagues, place me in the financial category of either Mr. Harold Robbins or Mr. Irving Wallace.

The answer to my freedom from fiscal problems lies in the shrewdness of my maternal grandfather, a one-time pharmacist whose product was a household word at the turn of the century. Some of you may be old enough to recall a large, dark brown, pear-shaped bottle which was a fixture in every late Victorian medicine chest. This was "Kaiser's Kolexian Kurative," positively guaranteed to relieve every one of mortal man's ailments or your money back. Grandpa Kaiser's secret was the inclusion of a high proportion of corn whiskey. I should add that Grandpa never drank the stuff he sold; his preference was Old Overholt, taken neat. He lived to be one hundred and two. I am one of his four surviving heirs.

Don was first to arrive at my home. However, I said nothing to him about changing my status from kibitzer to player until others were present. Then I spoke out declaring that I wanted to buy a share in the wager.

"You know, gentlemen, had I been present at that last infuriating session the Colonel's official opposition would have been six, not five, Sons." (Not for a moment did I believe this; I would have seen through that scoundrel's scheme before he could have foisted it upon those innocents.)

Ed, Jack, and Charlie, briefed by Marv, refused to part with an iota of their "investment," teasing me about my unfortunate absence from Baskerville Hall the night of March 28. But I observed Don's eyes light up with hope. Timidly he offered to "sell" me twenty-five percent of his "stock." I finally pushed him up to three-quarters of his total holdings and that was as far as he'd go. We let it rest there.

This sticky business settled, we chose Jack as our temporary chairman; he called the meeting to order and we proceeded. At the outset what we all felt was most important would be to apportion the amount of time each could contribute to the joint effort. We would then work out a *modus operandi* and assign individual tasks.

The "Chase," which is what I officially recorded the project in my own minor Sacred Writings, began at a time that was fortunate for me and, ergo, fortunate for the rest of the hunters. In my current agenda was the presentation of a paper at the University of Southern California late in August but that would occupy only a few days. Juliet, I truly believe, was delighted I would not be hanging around the house to be fed thrice daily. From this, it is obvious that my hours are pretty much my own.

Jack suggested it might be easier if we worked in pairs, which meant I could accompany a colleague almost any time he was needed for active duty. I'd be able to record all our activities and present them at plenary sessions every Thursday evening at the Architects Club on Seventeenth Street where Charlie was able to arrange for a private room in which we could be served beverages and dinner.

Charlie and Marv were free only rarely during the week (the latter on all legal holidays since he was a city employee) but each pledged every other full weekend. This meant one or the other was available late Friday afternoon to remain on duty until Sunday night or perhaps early Monday morning. As for Ed, unless his presence in court was imperative, he willingly surrendered Wednesday afternoons, normally devoted to railroading, all legal holidays, plus as many Sundays as he could spare.

Don, truly grateful for the fiscal relief I gave him, offered to relinquish his two free days every week plus accumulated overtime which he reported came to 120 hours. Aware that such absences would be unjust to Don's wife Connie and their three small children, we unanimously rejected his generous offer. Instead we accepted a maximum of one day a week and as many evenings as he could spare.

Jack surprised us.

"As of this coming Monday," he said, "I'm in the Chase for the duration, full time. Taking my first real leave of absence after fifty-one years of huckstering."

This drew a round of applause and with good reason. I have no desire to belittle any of the others' intelligence which I rate very high, almost, I would say, at near-genius level. But with the possible exception of myself, and I say this quite objectively, I do believe Jack has, by far, the keenest, most logical and astute mind of all six Sons.

We, therefore, prevailed upon him to become our permanent chairman. He accepted saying he'd call himself "the old Shikari hunter." Shikari was the name Holmes once pinned upon Colonel Sebastian Moran, "the second most dangerous man in London" . . . whose "nerves have not lost their steadiness, nor his eyes their keenness" . . . We fervently hoped Jack was more than a match for our own evil Colonel.

This, I think, was the first time since Eberhardt's cruel attempt to destroy our legends there was mention of the Sacred Writings. The ice was broken. Jack had restored a sense of balance between our two worlds and we could now refer to

Holmes and his deeds without becoming self-conscious. I'm certain Jack did this deliberately, he is very perceptive.

I took upon myself those additional chores normally relegated to a recording secretary. As an initial assignment Jack asked me to draw up a work schedule based upon available free hours. This would make it easier for him to hand out assignments. First of all we would have to determine what these would be and who was best fitted or equipped for the many tasks which lay ahead.

All of us were bursting with ideas but, since it was by then past two o'clock in the morning, Jack suggested we adjourn until the following week. Meanwhile, he thought it might be a good idea if each Son would carefully note, on paper, everything he knew about the Colonel.

"Let's do no more than this for the present," he advised. "I think there's little to be gained if we were to plunge ahead without reviewing all facts in hand."

He grinned. "Remember what the Master said, 'It is a capital mistake to theorize before one has data. Insensibly one begins to twist facts to suit theories, instead of theories to suit facts.' "

Whatever lingering doubts any of us might still have contained concerning the Colonel's true objectives on the night of March 28 were dispelled once and for all before Jack adjourned the meeting. It is hard to believe that despite overwhelming evidence to the contrary Charlie and Jack still were not completely convinced of the Colonel's amorality.

Jack has such a strong sense of fair play and Christian charity that even at this late date he continued to blame himself for seeking flaws in the Colonel's character in order to justify his own defects in judgment.

"After all," Jack said not once but several times, "we must remember he was baiting us and we took him seriously. You can't condemn a man for that.

"And Charlie told me that while Eberhardt had deeply wounded his guests' feelings he might have grinned at us in his charming fashion, declared he'd been pulling our legs and we'd have called off the bet. Another round of drinks, the restoration of good fellowship, and we'd have said goodnight and gone home. The next morning we'd have blamed our gullibility on alcohol, admired the Colonel for putting one over on us, and resumed our normal routines."

But Marv smashed this lingering bit of wishful thinking.

"I kept wondering," Marv said, "just how the Colonel would be able to explain his sudden absence from the Academy. How could a man in his position walk out on his classes in midterm and expect to return? This morning I called the Valley Forge headmaster and discovered the Colonel is on a full year's sabbatical."

I asked when it had begun. Marv smiled grimly.

"Monday, April 1, three days after the spring meeting of the Sons of the Copper Beeches. So, with all apologies due you, Jack, for your forbearance, please don't try to tell me the bet was spontaneous."

The implication was obvious. There was a stunned silence. Jack broke it.

"Gentlemen," he said, "there is no doubt about it now. We have been *had*. Let's get the son-of-a-bitch!"

CHAPTER

7

ALL SIX of us, each radiating self-confidence, were on hand at the Architects Club the following Thursday, convinced by the mass of material we'd brought along that the Chase would soon be ended and the Colonel brought to task.

Because I am an extremely methodical man with a healthy curiosity and a retentive memory, I thought I had compiled more facts about Eberhardt than anyone else. But I do admit I was wrong. In addition to everything young Donaldson recollected within the limits of his association with the Colonel he brought with him a precis of Eberhardt's past. This he read quietly while we listened, totally absorbed.

"Eberhardt was born April 17, 1918, in Lancaster, Pennsylvania, the second oldest of five siblings, three girls and two boys. His father, Kenneth H. Eberhardt, was an Evangelical Lutheran minister. Before H. Wesley had reached the age of puberty the family lived in four different cities. I can't imagine why, unless the good pastor was a victim of wanderlust."

Ed Johnson interrupted.

"Sorry to butt in," he said, "but I think what I have to say bears on the Colonel's character. His father was not a victim of wanderlust; he belonged to the Lutheran Church—Missouri Synod and so did my paternal grandfather. A new parsonage every four years. If the preacher was good or a good politician, which my grandfather was *not,* after six or seven of such moves and right before retirement he'd wind up with a big congregation, a nice house to live in and probably enough salary to feed and clothe his family, providing, of course, he didn't sire more than three children.

"The Evangelical Lutherans were not the most affluent Christian denomination. It was damned rough on kids. No chance to develop lasting friendships or any kind of security, always having to toe the mark. No wonder so many preachers' sons go wrong. That's how my father was raised and he had a rough boyhood. It's a miracle my seven aunts and uncles turned out as well as they did. Go on, Don."

Don glanced at his notes.

"From Lancaster, Pastor Eberhardt accepted a charge in Bay Creek, Maryland. H. Wesley was three when they made the move. The preacher's next 'call' came from Tamaqua, Pennsylvania. That's a town in the hard coal regions. I know it well, pretty dead now but it used to be thriving. This must have been a better deal for the old man.

"After Tamaqua the family moved on to Mahanoy City, another Pennsylvania anthracite coal town. I know that place, too, covered many a story there. That would have been when the Colonel was around thirteen and where he started high school. The last move was to Mauch Chunk; they call the town Jim Thorpe now. It was here that the old man passed on to whatever reward awaits Lutheran ministers."

Don looked up.

"I've got a little more on the Colonel but nothing on the other kids. Shall I pause here for a moment before going on and maybe Ed can give us an educated guess about what happened to them?"

We all nodded; Ed smiled grimly.

"I'll tell you what *probably* took place and I don't think I'll be far off. This was the heart of the Depression and I'll bet you that outside of a small pension all Pastor Eberhardt left his wife and family were debts. So the Colonel's mother had to go out selling pies and cakes she baked herself. Or she did 'genteel' cleaning and sewing for the neighbors. She couldn't possibly raise her family on a Lutheran minister's pension. There'd be no Social Security; it hadn't been started yet.

"They no longer lived in the manse; they'd have left to make room for the new minister. Maybe a kind-hearted parishioner would let them have some unrentable shack he owned on Railroad Alley. That was one way Mother could try to keep the family together.

"Of course the children went to work before school, after school and on Saturday and Sunday, cleaning furnaces, delivering newspapers, shoveling snow, running errands or what have you. Nothing wrong doing that but it would cut into their fun. They might turn out bitter, too."

I slowed Ed down until I caught up with my notes, then motioned for him to continue.

"You can be pretty sure there'd be no stepfather in the picture. A lifetime of drudgery left H. Wesley's mother without much to attract a man. I'll tell you something else. Damned few of the children in any of those split Protestant sects followed their father's calling. Those who decided to do the Lord's work found it more convenient to make the good fight under the aegis of the Anglicans. Better pay, better hours, and better pensions.

"Before he died, one of my uncles who'd gone through all this ended his career as boss of Christ Cathedral up in Poughkeepsie, New York. And his parishioners were Vanderbilts, Rockefellers, and Roosevelts. No life of hardship for *that* priest. I know the whole bit. If the Colonel's mother was lucky enough to be sixty-five or over and the children raised she'd be able to spend the rest of her days in the Lutheran Home at Elizabethtown. This is where my maternal grandmother wound up."

Ed turned to me. "Got most of that, Frank?" I nodded and Don took over.

"I don't have much more but here it is. H. Wesley had just turned seventeen when he went to live with an uncle, Walter H. Eberhardt, his father's oldest brother, in Erie, Pennsylvania. Uncle Walter sent his nephew to Staunton Military Academy in Virginia for one year and then down to The Fortress in

South Carolina. Here he got his bachelor's degree in Military Science. This was 1940 and he was twenty-two years old.

"H. Wesley became a second lieutenant in the R.A. and served six months in the infantry at Fort Benning. He was transferred to Fort Knox where he got his silver bars. From there he came back to Pennsylvania to study at a military intelligence school the army set up in the old Carlisle Indian College. There's nothing—or at least I could get nothing—between this date, December 27, 1941 and January 16, 1960 when Eberhardt was discharged, honorably by the way."

I asked Don if he minded revealing the source of his information.

"Not a bit," he said. "I got in touch with Bob Aucott who's in charge of our Washington News Bureau. What Bob got is simply material any military P.R. man has on hand for distribution to news services or source material for obits. Had the Colonel remained in the infantry there'd be much more available.

"But you have to remember he spent almost his entire career in G2 and their press agents pass out very little information even when pushed hard. Men often get called back into this branch no matter what their ages are."

The last statement of Don's made me raise a point.

"Do any of you believe the Colonel was called back to duty and is hiding out in the FBI, the CIA, or some such agency? I suppose they certainly could provide cover for him, and Ellen as well, if they wanted to and needed the Colonel for some special assignment. And that they'd notified him beforehand so he could develop his own scheme to take us for the Carl Anderson collection?"

This possibility distressed every one of us.

"It's certainly something we'll have to look into right away, before we go ahead and waste time and effort," Jack said. "If he's gone back into the service under the aegis of any one of those agencies I think, gentlemen, we're finished. I'm not going to pit myself against them. The odds are enormous and I'd be ready to put my share of the bet in escrow right away."

Even I would be ready to give up if this were true. I asked Jack whether he knew any way he could have this possibility confirmed or repudiated.

"I'm not sure," he answered, "but maybe Tom [Senator Hart] might help. He's the only person I can think of offhand. He's on the Military Appropriations Committee, or at least he was before he became Whip. We do have to remember that the Colonel promised he wouldn't go beyond his self-imposed one-hundred-twenty-five mile limit and that he'd stay within the borders of Pennsylvania. I feel sure he'll keep his word; his ego won't let him break it. And, it's awful hard for me to conceive of G2 or any of those other secret government agencies having something tailored to measure these specifications exactly at the right time. It would seem to me to almost be impossible."

I sighed.

"Remember the Master's words. 'When you have eliminated the impossible, whatever remains must be the truth.' "

We all chuckled; we could do this once more without being self-conscious. Then Jack continued.

"I *will* tell you something else which puzzles me, something Tom may be able to clear up, too. Why did Eberhardt leave the service, if he really ever left it? There are plenty of precedents, one of our own Sons before he died. Frank knows whom I mean. You others haven't been Sons long enough. This was more than two decades ago. Don't forget the Colonel had the correct rank for his age and he must have been close to being brevetted."

Don shrugged his shoulders.

"I'll buy that possibility, Jack. But *if* he has left the service maybe he just got damned sick of it. Who knows? I had my belly full after twenty-three months, the Colonel was in it for twenty-six years."

"But there was a difference between you two," Ed explained. "He was a career officer and you weren't."

Don chuckled. "I wasn't even an officer."

"Gentlemen, gentlemen," Jack broke in. "Let's not theorize. How about sitting tight until we hear from Tom. I'll call him first thing tomorrow morning. Hopefully we'll know the score by next Thursday."

But the answer came sooner than that. Jack called me early Tuesday evening.

"Be of good cheer, Frank," he said. "The CIA, the FBI, the Secret Service and G2 haven't provided a protective cloak over the Colonel. On the contrary.

"In 1954, shortly before his retirement, Colonel Eberhardt was involved in what the army labeled simply as 'an unpleasant episode.' Only four persons were concerned. One was a Korean woman with whom the Colonel was allegedly living, the second, a native houseboy, the third, the Colonel's driver, a staff sergeant, and the fourth, Eberhardt himself. Tom did not get all the details surrounding the case but what he obtained certainly is sufficient for our purposes.

"There had been systematic stealing from Eberhardt's household. I gather it was the type of petty pilfering which is expected and which usually is ignored. I was in the military during World War One and I knew what Tom meant, although I did not approve of it.

"It was sort of *quid pro quo*. Most of the higher ranking officers who set up housekeeping with native help fully expected this kind of situation to develop. After all, they figured it was taxpayers' money, not their own, so what the heck."

I requested that Jack pause while I caught up with him. One of my accomplishments is shorthand which I do quite well, following a method called Boyd. It's an old system but quite efficient. My ability to take notes in this fashion frequently comes in handy. Jack waited until I was ready.

"One day the Colonel came to the realization that looting in his own household exceeded the norm. I don't know what protocol demanded under these circumstances but what Eberhardt did was not in keeping with the traditions of an officer and gentleman. The Colonel took his riding whip and beat the daylights out of his houseboy, who died shortly after.

"The only witnesses were the sergeant and the Colonel's mistress, who happened to be the boy's sister. Their testimony was in conflict. In any event there was no court-martial. Eberhardt simply resigned his commission and received an honorable discharge. No blemish appears on his record. As a matter of fact he was cited twice for bravery and both times for saving the lives or property of natives."

As Jack requested, I passed this information on to Marv, Don, Ed, and Charlie, asking them, as Jack had advised, that we were all to consider this new information "classified."

So, after this brief but troubled respite during which we might have been forced to surrender all, the Chase was on.

CHAPTER

8

As soon as I completed my round of telephone calls, I conceived and executed a task I thought important, one neither Jack nor anyone else had considered. I laid a large map of Pennsylvania on my worktable and scaled my compass twenty-five miles to the inch. Placing the sharp end in Philadelphia I drew an arc which swept the state for exactly 125 miles in every direction from the borders of New Jersey on the north and east, to Maryland on the south and west. Enclosed, should the Colonel keep his word, was our "hunting ground."

Within these thousands of square miles were a number of fair-sized cities including Harrrisburg, Capital of the Commonwealth; Reading, heart of the Pennsylvania Dutch country; Scranton, Wilkes-Barre, and Hazelton in the dying hard coal regions; and the thriving community of York, center of the "hex" and "bible" belts. There were the populous Quaker City suburban communities of Chester and Norristown and Philadelphia's so-called "Main Line" where once dwelt our better-class citizens.

There was also, I noted, one rather sparsely settled area, the Poconos, where my own family had a summer home before this lovely mountainous territory became a popular vacation and picnic grounds for the masses. Lest you think this is said uncharitably, I hasten to assure you such is not the case. I am quite happy so many members of our middle and working classes have discovered this beautiful territory only a few hours drive from Kensington, Frankford, and South Philadelphia. It is simply that I do not want to enjoy these once delightful hunting and fishing grounds with them.

Contained within this approximately ninety-degree sweep of my compass there were, with the exception of Pastor Eberhardt's one charge "south of the border," those four commu-

nities in which H. Wesley was spawned and grew to puberty—
Lancaster, Tamaqua, Mahanoy City, and Mauch Chunk.

Still keeping to scale I enlarged the map fourfold so that it
almost completely filled one side of my wall. Then I slightly
tinted a different hue each of the twenty-three counties my
original drawing covered. The process took a good many
hours but I felt the effort worthwhile. And when I unrolled
this "work of art" at the next plenary session of our six Sons,
the expressions of admiration with which it was greeted com-
pensated me for my efforts.

Jack opened the meeting with a question, certain he would
receive the correct answer. In which of the Sacred Writings
are there voluntary disappearances? The almost instantaneous
response from every Son present was two: "The Adventure of
the Norwood Builder" and "The Adventure of the Priory
School."

"You didn't want us to include 'Silver Blaze,' did you,
Jack?" Charlie asked with a smile.

"No," Jack laughed. "*Our* hunt is for a man, not a horse."

We all chuckled and Jack went on, this time quite seriously.

"I mention these crimes to see if any of the methods used
to bring about their solution might be helpful to us. I say this
despite the Colonel's sarcastic and ill-spoken comments about
clues he said Doyle planted.

"Over the past few days I've restudied both and I must confess that in neither do I find anything of practical value to us.
What is your opinion, gentlemen?"

At once our minds leaped to a swift but thorough review of
both Dr Watson's monographs in which neither protagonist,
Mr. Jonas Oldacre nor young Lord Saltire, was able to outwit
the Master. Unfortunately we arrived at the same conclusion
as Jack did.

"That is exactly what I was afraid of," our old Shikari
hunter said sadly.

Suddenly another of Dr. Watson's monographs flashed
through my mind. I asked for and was granted the floor. I
should state here that we agreed to observe parliamentary
procedures in order to conduct our meetings with decorum.

"What I have in mind," I said holding my voice down although I felt at this moment I might be making an extremely
important deduction, "does not, strictly speaking, come under

the category of a true voluntary disappearance. The subject returned to his home and family every night."

As though they'd read my mind both Charlie and Ed spoke out simultaneously, " 'The Man with the Twisted Lip.' "

I nodded. This monograph deals with one Neville St. Clair, an impoverished London gentleman-journalist who turned to beggary for his livelihood and by this degrading practice accumulated a small fortune. The point I wished to bring out was that St. Clair remained unrecognized for years although he never ventured more than a few miles from his fireside. Furthermore, he was unquestionably seen upon frequent occasions by close relatives and intimate friends. A clever disguise accounted for St. Clair's success. Holmes, of course, unmasked him.

My colleagues listened with absorption. I continued.

"This is *exactly* the kind of chicanery that would appeal to the Colonel. He wouldn't have to leave Market Street. There are a half-dozen beggars on every block and he could mingle with them. We could all pass him by a hundred times a day and not be the wiser.

Jack looked thoughtful.

"You may have brought out something important, Frank. I remember after we got into World War Two a couple of newspaper reporters strolled up and down Market Street arm in arm wearing U-boat Commanders' uniforms adorned with swastikas and iron crosses and nobody paid any attention to them.

"What troubles me is what the Colonel would do with Ellen. I can't conceive of her as a lady beggar and where would she be hidden out all day or during the evenings if he 'worked' then? There'd be no harm in your looking, Frank. So why don't you accept this as your first assignment. Spend a few hours or a day and see what you come up with. Probably nothing, but this'll eliminate one angle."

I nodded. Then Don spoke.

"What you should be on the lookout for, Frank, is a beggar or peddler not displaying a metal tag about four inches square. That's his legal permit. He pays a fee to the Bureau of Licenses at City Hall; tomorrow I'll check their recent applications."

Jack's next question was again directed to all of us. Was there anything else in the Sacred Writings which might be of help? This was not a new thought. We'd pondered this ever since the Chase began. However, with the exception of Holmes' exploration into the life of Neville St. Clair, nothing seemed to apply. It was a disappointing conclusion to say the least. Faced with the problem of locating the Colonel, we'd all been sure methods the Master used in some previous "caper" could certainly help us in our own Adventure.

"This," commented Jack with a sigh, "is what I was afraid of. Not much appears to fit. But suppose, gentlemen, that the Master were here, how do you think he'd begin?"

There was a long pause, then Charlie spoke.

"I don't want to be facetious but I'll be happy to underwrite Mr. Holmes' round trip transportation, first class on a 747 if one of you can persuade him to join us."

This brought a laugh and a relief in the tension which was building up. I think the seriousness of our situation was just beginning to hit us. None of us was a professional sleuth although both Don and I, in our individual callings, had done considerable investigative work. In a larger sense what we were tackling was quite different. Even though I, for one, was convinced we'd win, I could foresee many difficulties ahead.

There was a great deal of soul searching over the next five or ten minutes. Jack broke our silence.

"I believe, my fellow Sons, that at last we've become conscious of just what we let ourselves in for. If we want to win, and I'm *sure* we will, let's be practical. I advise you and myself as well to surrender a dream that the Master will solve our case for us. He won't. So let's try to solve it ourselves. Frank *might* find the Colonel on Market Street tomorrow but somehow or other I don't think it'll be that easy.

"Gentlemen, the floor is open for suggestions."

Don gave the first.

"I've a few ideas," he said, taking out a pencil and walking over to the map I'd drawn and which Jack had placed on an architect's worktable. We crowded around.

"When you look at it this way, Pennsylvania's one hell of a big state and there's a lot of ground within that one-hundred-twenty-five-mile radius. But I think, temporarily at least, we should be able to eliminate a few million acres. I'd be willing to strike Wayne, Sullivan, Pike, Montour, and Monroe counties. It's April now; the hunting season's over and there'll be nobody around in those thousands of sportmen's lodges which dot that sparsely populated area. If any of the natives saw smoke coming out of one of them, he'd investigate right away.

"A strange man and woman would stick out like sore thumbs there. The Colonel's too intelligent not to realize this. I don't say for *sure* that the Eberhardts aren't holed up in one of those counties but I think it unlikely."

We all gave this some thought.

"I don't know," Marv said. "It seems to me just the kind of place the Colonel would go to. That's vast territory he'd be hiding in and why couldn't he have a good cover story so the natives wouldn't suspect anything?"

Don shook his head.

"Doc, you don't know the problems of setting up house-keeping in one of those lodges. On his own the Colonel could do it but not with his wife along. First of all I can't imagine him taking her to live for a couple of months in one of those primitive cabins without plumbing, electricity, or water. There are lots of them but they couldn't be for Ellen Eberhardt.

"The hunting season's over and this means water and electricity's been turned off and there's probably no propane gas left in tanks for cooking. That means the Colonel, if he were able to rent one of these better equipped places, would have to go to the nearest town, and it'd be a small one like Honesdale or Milford, to get everything turned on again.

"They wouldn't cooperate with Bill Lindeman on our paper. His brother and a couple other guys own a hunting lodge in Pike County and Bill wanted to borrow it for his honeymoon this past March. But the power companies wouldn't cooperate. Said no juice until May 15."

Marv laughed. "Why would a honeymoon couple need light or heat?"

"You've got something there, Marv," Don said. "But I don't think the Colonel and his Lady are still in the same blissful period of wedlock, do you?"

We all agreed Ellen Eberhardt was hardly the type to put up with outside "johns," candlelight, and cooking over the fireplace.

"What I think we have to do," Don said, "is concentrate on areas where the Eberhardts would not be conspicuous. I don't think we should eliminate Philadelphia. They well might be here and if we don't succeed elsewhere we could come back. *My* first choice is not the country but a city of some size where it's possible for people like the Eberhardts to live without attracting much attention. Harrisburg or Reading, cities with around a hundred thousand population. They could fade into the background of communities such as these and live quite well there, too.

"You tell me his lady has no relatives in Pennsylvania. But what if one of the Colonel's brothers or sisters is still alive and he's been in touch with them over the years and maybe even living with them now. We don't know and the only way we're going to find out is to go to the places he used to live in and see if anybody there knows anything. I'm sure that except for Frank's venture tomorrow and my own to back him in City Hall, that's where we must begin."

Don's proposals made sense. Jack glanced at the map, then removed our "work schedule" from his pocket. He turned to me.

"Unless you find the Colonel tomorrow, we'll get started this coming weekend. You and I are the anchor men—always available. So how about Marv pairing with you, I'll team up with Charlie, and Don and Ed can work together.

"We've got four towns to cover. We can't do them all at once so let's try for three. Don, you said you knew Tamaqua well. So how about you and Ed exploring that one. Marv and Frank, if it's OK with you fellows, concentrate on (he looked at the map again to make sure of the town) Mahanoy City. Charlie and I will take Mauch Chunk. I haven't been to that town for fifty years or more. Last time I was there I rode on the old 'switchback' sometime around 1917."

Before the meeting adjourned Don had something else to say. He warned us about chances for publicity.

"This is a good story," he said. "Five (he excluded himself) prominent Philadelphian citizens, devotees of Sherlock Holmes trying to use his methods to track down a seventh Son. I don't see how we can keep it out of the papers much longer. One of my competitors is going to find out and I'm liable to catch hell for not breaking it first."

I saw no reason why we should avoid publicity and I certainly had no objection to a press review. Stories about each of us have appeared many times over the years and when Hollywood optioned my book, all three Philadelphia newspapers ran articles about me. As a matter of fact I suggested to Don that he, himself, break the story. Jack and the others felt differently, saying they preferred to wait until we'd concluded the Chase. Personal publicity means nothing to me, I merely thought this would aid us in our hunt. All we should do, Don advised, was to sit tight. That's the way we left it.

After finalizing plans to meet with our partner in the week-end "team," I decided to walk home via Market Street. This would take me several blocks out of my way but I wanted to see if, perchance, there were beggars still hanging around at that hour. It would be a major triumph if I could spot the Colonel right then and there and inform my colleagues the original deduction I made was correct.

Quite literally speaking I think this was the first time I'd been on the west side of Market for years, even though it is less than a mile from Jessup. With the possible exception of attendance at the two legitimate theaters which have long since ceased to exist, there was no reason for me to be on that tawdry three block "strip" of cheap "B" girl bars frequented by sailors, all-night movies, greasy restaurants, Army and Navy stores, and pawnshops.

To my amazement I discovered that this unsightly section of Philadelphia, a city which has undergone major surgery over the past two decades, was much the same as I remembered from my University days. Benny's pawnshop, in which I once hocked my banjo after a disastrous crap game, was gone and so was the "Gaiety," a burlesque house where we adolescents were given a fleeting glimpse of "something we couldn't see at home." Vanished, too, were those cheap clothing stores with their outside barkers making bold attempts to trap the unwary with "bargains."

But the Nemo, an all-night movie where we Dekes brought dates after the Junior Prom, was extant, its marquee proclaiming a double feature—*Trader Hornee* (I looked twice at *that* title) and *The Swappers,* whatever this meant. The cashier, who but for a thick crop of auburn hair could easily have passed for the Colonel, gave me a wicked leer as I glanced into his glass cage. But Eberhardt, I assured myself, would not be quite so stupid.

Adjacent to the Nemo was a store filled with pinball machines and in front of each of these silly contraptions was a player twisting his body into all manner of contortions. I stood looking at these fools until a group of hippies brushed by me in a hurry to get nowhere. One of them, a tall fellow who appeared to be considerably older than his fellow beat-niks, addressed me in an insulting fashion.

"Go back where you belong, Lord Fauntleroy," he taunted. I'd have liked to have told him I belong anywhere I *chose* to belong in Philadelphia and that *he* probably belonged in Russia or Poland or wherever his parents came from. The impudent fellow kept staring at me until one of his companions shouted impatiently, "Come on, Siggy."

Seconds later I was struck with the significance of "Siggy" and I'm *certain* that was the name used. Sigerson, which might well be shortened into "Siggy" was the Master's *nom de plume* when he visited the Lhassa of Tibet. It is not unreasonable to suppose that Eberhardt availed himself of this alias when consorting with new-found beatnik friends. It was too late to follow this lead, the hippies had scampered around the corner probably heading for Rittenhouse Square, where for the past number of years they'd usurped the benches of decent citizens.

On the east side of the Nemo was "The Odditorium." With fond memories of a doting and long since departed uncle, I recalled my first visit to this "home of nature's pranks" more than a half-century ago. Here, unchanged in a changing world was "Edgar, the Kokomo Giant," "Olga, the Headless Teuton," "Fegar, the Four Legged Fisherman," plus countless "monsters in a bottle," preserved forever in formaldehyde.

I did not see a single "legitimate" beggar displaying his license to prey on the public although there were any number of panhandlers, invariably alcoholics, who sidled up to me, palms outstretched, asking for "two bits, mister, to buy a cup of coffee." A quarter, indeed! Inflation obviously had struck the lowest depths.

As I reached the other side of Sixteenth Street, threading my way through crowds of noisy nondescript men and women bent on cheap thrills, plus soldiers and sailors, thoughtlessly blocking the pavement as they poured in and out of bars, I saw a blind beggar riding upon a little wooden cart towed slowly by a huge, shaggy, long-eared, clumsy mongrel.

My heart pounded madly when I read the crudely lettered cardboard sign hung over the fellow's back—"Your help is all that keeps me and Toby alive."

"Toby," I recalled instantly, was "an ugly, long-haired, lop-eared creature, half-spaniel and half-lurcher, brown and white" which the Master used to track down Jonathan Small in *The Sign of the Four*. This dog was black and white, and part spaniel. There would be no way for me to tell whether or not it was a "lurcher." But no matter, the rest of Toby's description fitted the beast.

I kept watching until I was a dozen paces ahead then came to a dead stop. Without moving my eyes from the fellow's face, I watched the cart approach. Because of the way his legs were twisted to fit into the tiny wagon, I could not gauge his height, but the leonine head, crowned with short cropped gray hair, was not unlike Eberhardt's and his shoulders were as broad and powerful.

The more I looked, the surer I was that I'd come to the end of the trail. I held back my words of triumph until cart, dog, and man were only inches away.

"Colonel," I whispered, bending low so that passersby would not hear me (and to be honest, I was a bit grieved that the Chase was over), "the game is up."

The fellow said nothing for a moment, then looked up over the top of his heavy, dark glasses and snarled, "What the hell do you mean, 'Colonel, the game is up'? Are you fuzz? Scram! I already paid the beat man. See him."

I was confused. It was not what he said that puzzled me. I know what "fuzz" means and I also am aware that there are still a few unscrupulous policemen who accept hush money. So I assumed that the district patrolman knew this beggar could see as well as anyone and was forcing him to pay blood money for the privilege of bilking silly citizens who wear their hearts on their sleeves.

But what did perplex me was the fear that I was beginning to see Eberhardt almost everywhere I looked. The hippie and the "blind" man *could* have been the Colonel and one of them might still be he. The variety of roles to be played and the stages upon which he could play them were limitless. Since I thought I recognized him twice within minutes and in only one small section of Philadelphia, a minuscule portion of the vast acreage we had yet to search, I began to entertain doubts about our eventual success.

As if to prove my point I regarded with particular care a Salvation Army "soldier" cheerfully singing hymns along the curb just west of Fifteenth Street, accompanying himself on a small organ. "All right," I said to myself, "is it possible that this man is the Colonel?" Eberhardt played the piano, I know, and the two instruments are not very different.

"Sure," came the answer. "He's the Colonel's height, he has a military bearing and his rich baritone sounds exactly like Eberhardt's." True, this "soldier" has black hair but it might be dyed. What about those gaunt cheeks, those busy eyebrows and the deep scar on the left side of his face? Makeup? Why not? Holmes and even Lon Chaney did far more than this to enact their parts. The uniform? Rented.

All the while I did not remove my eyes from his face. When he concluded "Jesus, Savior of the *Lost*," I walked close to him and dropped a small coin into his tambourine. "Colonel," I said, honestly not knowing just what was to come next. He smiled disarmingly. "Only a private in the Lord's Army, Brother. You look troubled. Have you a favorite hymn you'd like me to sing?"

I shook my head and walked off. I heard him begin another tune. The melody I recognized but the title would not come. It hit me when I reached City Hall courtyard a few hundred steps away. I hurried back, too late, psalmist and organ had disappeared. This "soldier" could not have completed a single stanza of "You Can Find *Him* If You Try" before he folded his tent and stole away.

I asked a military policeman standing on the corner if he noticed where the Salvation Army man went. He shrugged his shoulders and gave me an odd smile, probably certain I was touched. I was beginning to feel that way myself.

Quite shaken, I retraced my steps, walked through City Hall courtyard to East Market Street. I saw the lights of an H&H and went in for a cup of coffee to steady my nerves. There were only a few stragglers standing in front of those awful tile counters dunking doughnuts and slurping them into toothless mouths. I realized it must have been at least thirty years since I'd set foot in this basement restaurant.

I extracted a few coins from my change purse and looked around for a slot in which to insert them. I wasn't sure what the price of a cup of coffee was. I know it used to be a nickel. A colored bus "boy," my age if not older, regarded me with amusement.

"This ain't no automat no more, Boss," he said, a broad grin sweeping across his black face. "Changed over to cafeteria, long, long while back. Gotta get your java at de counter in back."

I got my "java" for which I paid sixteen cents. "Fifteen for us and a penny for the Governor," the cashier told me. I sat down at a table and tried to think constructively. It was useless, the problem seemed insoluble. I realized my responsibilities and when I talked to Jack or any other Son I'd have to keep up a bold front. I knew they were counting on me, I wouldn't let them down for anything in the world. But I was forced to admit, if only to myself, that the Colonel had a better than even chance to win. What would Holmes have done? Frankly, I didn't know. I was aware this was a different era, unlike the peaceful one in which the Master and Dr. Watson lived at 221B Baker. Grave doubts assailed me. Heresy? I didn't dare answer that question.

I bought an early morning edition of the *Times*, looked for a cab—of course there was none around—and began the half-mile walk to my house. All the while I had a peculiar feeling that someone was following me. I kept turning around but the streets were empty. "This better stop," I said to myself, "or I'll go off the deep end."

I shut off the burglar alarm, entered the house and there, lying in front of the door, was an envelope apparently dropped into the letter slot after my wife went to bed. There was nothing, not even my name, on the outside. Inside was a single sheet of white paper upon which several figures were carefully drawn in ink. They looked like this:

Recognition of their source was instantaneous. I knew they'd been copied from the notes Abe Slaney sent to Elsie Patrick, his old sweetheart: "The Adventure of the Dancing Men." Hurriedly I went into my library to decode the Colonel's message. There could not be the slightest doubt it was from him.

I counted the figures, thirty-one. It was simple to substitute letters for dancing dolls as the Master, himself, had done once he'd broken Slaney's code. What I arrived at was this:

L. ATE. T. ONE ONE FIVE DASH FIVE FIVE NINE

After I once decided that the "ATE" referred not to the act of mastication but rather to the numeral "eight" it was child's play to translate the message.

While there must have been an "F" in Abe Slaney's code, he had no need for it and therefore this letter is not to be found in any of the four messages sent to Elsie. I know this and so does every Sherlockian scholar. What the Colonel did was to improvise and cleverly at that. He made the symbol for "F" by emphasizing the "V" which is used in the second communication. I say this was clever because in English, and other languages where the "F" is found, speaking phonetically it does resemble the twenty-third letter. For example, ask a German to pronounce "five" and see what happens.

Obviously the "T" stood for "top," common usage of the letter among scholars and librarians. So what the Colonel was telling me to do was look at the eighth line from the top of page 115, in book No. 559.

I know my Sacred Writings so well that in the flash of a second I had pulled down my copy of Whitaker's Almanac, that ubiquitous volume the Master used to decode Fred Porlock's message in the "Tragedy of Birlstone." But the eighth line from the top on page 115 of this publication was hardly applicable. "Peel two or three cucumbers," says Whitaker, "cut them in quarters, remove the seeds. . . ."

With a deep sigh I returned the Almanac to its proper place on my shelves and renewed the task of determining which book was meant. I have 4,652 volumes in my general library and I dare say the vast majority of them have at least 115 pages. Had the Colonel suggested page 1115 this would have narrowed the list considerably. But he hadn't. While it was physically impossible for me to look at the eighth line from the top of page 115 in each book containing at least that number of pages, this would have been a most tedious task and surely no challenge to my ingenuity.

No, the choice had to be narrowed. Clearly my best bet was an assumption that the Colonel's reference was to a particular volume of the Sacred Writings. But again I would be wasting endless hours. My collection of Sherlockiana contains more than 1,100 separate works. Again, no challenge.

I sought a clue in one of the Adventures and found none. I looked at publication dates, publishers' and authors' names on frontispieces. Wherever possible I checked addresses and telephone numbers. For a brief moment I thought I had the answer. The firm of Simon & Schuster, Inc. was listed at 559 Fifth Avenue, New York City. In my catalogue I discovered this firm, in all its lengthy history, had published only one volume of the Sacred Writings. With trembling hands I opened their single opus. Alas! The final page number was 114.

I could hear my wife stirring uneasily. I peered into her bedroom. She had awakened, I assured her I was not ill, merely researching. Then I returned to the library. It was almost dawn, and a faint light was coming up in the east. I had gotten nowhere, except perhaps to eliminate a few hundred books. I heard the Westminister chimes in the *Inquirer*'s tower strike the three-quarter hour past five and soon after decided to quit for the night. A big day loomed ahead.

Too tired to sleep, I brewed myself coffee and sat down to read the *Times*. For no reason I can think of I turned to the weather report and the daily tides, items of so little interest to me that I rarely give them more than a glance.

I noted the hours of sunrise and sunset. Then I did a double take. Today, April 18, 1969, I saw that the sun would rise at 5:59. Eureka! Sunrise—the *Rising Sun*. The finest book in my entire collection, in fact one of the rarest of all the Sacred Writings is the so-called Japanese edition of "The Adventure of the Devil's Foot." This Adventure usually runs to thirty-nine pages. This one I possess was handwritten, from memory, by the late Colonel Elic Denbo while he, a fellow Sherlockian, was a prisoner of war in the dungeons of Corregidor. How often had Eberhardt fingered this truly remarkable tribute to the Master from one of his most dedicated and heroic followers!

I was in no hurry now. With calm assurance I returned to my library, reached to the center of the third shelf and removed the loosely bound Japanese edition. At almost the exact second scattered rays of sunshine informed me that the hour was one minute before six, I turned to page 115 for the clue I knew would be there. With steady fingers I counted down to the eighth line from the top.

"I followed you." (Holmes)

"I saw no one." (Dr. Sterndale)

"That is what you may expect to see when I follow you." (Holmes)

Oh, the colossal vanity of that man Eberhardt, a vanity my friend Marv would have called *chutzpah*. How openly he defies us and with what utter disdain this detestable egotist announces his presence in Philadelphia. That *he* had seen *me* there could be little doubt. But just so surely had *I* seen *him*. Let the Colonel beware!

CHAPTER

9

I WAITED until seven o'clock to call Jack; he was already awake making his own preparations for the day's activities. I gave him a full report of my nocturnal actions and suspicions. He was impressed with the speed with which I decoded the Colonel's message and, like me, had not the slightest doubt Eberhardt sent it and that the fellow had not yet left the city. I said nothing about my previous doubts concerning eventual victory; I no longer had any.

"That was a clever job you did with those dancing men, Frank, but I don't believe he followed you last night and I'm not at all sure you *were* followed. It's possible, of course, but you have a robust imagination and it must have been working in high gear when you left Market Street. Eberhardt's clever and he knows us all quite well. I wouldn't be the least bit surprised if he were able to anticipate at least some of our moves.

"Let's assume he knew we'd be sure to look for him on Market Street and try to determine how he came to that conclusion. First of all, he's just as familiar with the Sacred Writings as we are. He's aware, too, that "The Man with the Twisted Lip" is the only Adventure applicable and that we'd attempt to apply it to the Chase. He knows the only Philadelphia street where licensed beggars are permitted to operate is Market. OK so far, Frank?"

I told Jack I could find no fault with his theorizing. But unless Eberhardt had put a tap on all of our telephones (and I definitely doubted that), how could he know I was one of the hunters?

"Let's reason that one out, too, Frank. Under normal circumstances you'd have been present when the bet was made and more than likely a bettor. He also knows you're Marv's best friend and Marv wouldn't want you to miss the 'fun' of putting Sherlockian theories to the test. Correct?"

Again I agreed. Jack continued.

"Whether he's even considered your financial stake in the Chase is irrelevant. You'd be just as eager to win, I'm sure, if you didn't have a cent invested in the outcome. However, knowing Don's money problems and your lack of them, I believe he concluded you would buy out a major portion of our young friend's share, leaving Don enough to save face.

"He knows your time is pretty much your own, Frank, and he may or may not know I'm on a sabbatical, although it would be easy enough for him to find that out. However, he's aware the rest are free, generally speaking, only during the evening and weekends. His rationalization, just as ours, would be to do group planning at a dinner session and our hunting on weekends. Would he know when and where we'd meet? I think so, at least when if not where.

"We've already eliminated Friday, Saturday, and Sunday nights. Every Monday Marv lectures at Temple so that's out. Tuesday's Blue Cross Directors, Ed's general counsel and he never misses. So *that's* out. Let's see who's got what on Wednesday."

I gave him the answer. That's the night Charlie and his mother play duplicate and she counts on it. This left Thursday which was, of course, the night we did meet. Simple enough, at that. Jack went on.

"Since we'd be meeting regularly and to save time at dinner, I think it's logical for the Colonel to conclude we'd have our get-togethers in one of our clubs. The League is out—Marv won't go there. I asked him to lunch with me several times until it finally dawned on me why he kept refusing."

"And he wouldn't go to the Racquet, the Philadelphia, or the Vespers with me," I said. "They don't serve dinners at the

Franklin Inn and the Diogenes, themselves, meet on Thursdays. So what's left? The Architects. Marv would feel welcome there. His neighbor, Herman Beerman, is president. Q.E.D."

Jack chuckled.

"So the Colonel knows you're one of us, that we get together Thursday evenings for dinner, and that we hold our sessions at the Architects Club. Ergo, the Sherlockian deductive processes work in both directions. We may be stretching a point trying to deduce *if* he knew you'd be on Market Street last night where I'm just as sure that I'm talking to you, Frank, as I am that he saw you. But let's give it a whirl anyway.

"The bet was made Friday, March 28. Under its terms we agreed not to begin the Chase for three full days. That would make it April 1 and by that time we'd have come to the conclusion it was no April Fool's joke because we'd have discovered Eberhardt was on a sabbatical. However, it would have been difficult, if not impossible, for each Son to arrange his own schedule for a plenary session by that Thursday nor would we have figured out where. Therefore, we wouldn't all be getting together until April 10.

"What is the first logical order of business? Time scheduling, of course, and a general discussion of the job ahead. Not until last night, April 17, could we have perused the Sacred Writings once more and come to the foregone conclusion that Neville St. Clair was our 'man.' You and I are the only ones who live in town east of Seventeenth Street. I'm no walker but you are, Frank, and you're an impetuous man besides. So it is not unreasonable to assume the Colonel lay in wait. In what role I don't know—beggar, beatnik, or psalmist—or perhaps playing none of these parts."

Like Dr. Watson, I agreed that once Sherlockian processes of deduction were explained they became amazingly simple and the result logical. But unlike the good doctor who invariably piqued Holmes by pointing out this fact, I said nothing. However, I felt that by the end of the long day ahead I would know which, if any, of the three roles Eberhardt had played. We both felt that by now the Colonel, having indulged himself in an *ex post facto* "clue," was no longer in Philadelphia and it was our immediate task to find out where.

"Let's follow through on original plans to seek out Eberhardt's old home sites. And unless you're too tired, Frank, will you check with the Salvation Army? Don might be able to come up with something on the 'blind' beggar—I'll ask him and let you know. However, as far as your hippie is concerned, I doubt if we'll ever discover his identity."

I heard him sigh.

"It would be so much easier all 'round if we could get a lead on Ellen. Where *has* he stashed her while he's on the prowl? I'm certain of one thing, though, he has not left her, that's not the way he'd play the game."

Jack was right. The Colonel, like one of Poe's villains, "had too much ego in his cosmos."

Jack had not finished. "I'll tell you something else, Frank. Before too long we should be getting another 'clue.' You mark my words."

By noon my first lead fizzled. The Salvation Army personnel officer at headquarters informed me that the "soldier" on duty last night at Sixteenth and Market Streets has been a dedicated member of the street corps for the past six and a half years. At the moment he was in the infirmary but if it were important he could be summoned to the telephone.

"He's ill then?" I asked.

"Nothing serious, Brother," was the answer. "Just a touch of dysentery. Hit him like a ton of bricks last night while working."

The P.O. laughed. "Just made it in time, too."

I was waiting for Marv to pick me up for our drive to Mahanoy City when Don called.

"Sorry to give you the bad news," he reported, "but your 'blind' man turned out to be a well-known chiseler—well-known by the cops anyway. And if you'll look on page six of tonight's bulldog edition, I think you'll find a picture of your hippie. Narcotics squad pulled 'em all in on Market Street around midnight. One's a tall, bearded, middle-aged gent who sure reminded me of the Colonel. Looks exactly like the hippie description you gave Jack.

"By the way, my compliments on how you handled the 'dancing men.' "

I'd been in touch with Marv twice that day. He, too, congratulated me. I said good-bye to Juliet, tossed my overnight bag on the rear seat of the car and we were off. I noticed an odd smile on Marv's face as we turned off Lombard Street and onto the Expressway heading north.

"What's up? I asked. "You've got an awfully peculiar expression on your mug."

Marv grinned.

"A strange gentleman left a message for me with Frankie (his oldest son, christened in my honor) about a half-hour before I came home. Wouldn't give his name but you know our number's unlisted so it had to be somebody I know. I've far more than a suspicion who it was."

"Let's see it, Marv," I said and my companion pulled a small piece of note paper from his pocket. There were only four words on it—"I'm out of shag."

I sincerely hope I don't have to explain what "shag" is. Everybody *must* be aware it's the Master's favorite pipe tobacco. There are scores of references to this potent mixture throughout the Sacred Writings. But to which one did this message refer? For three hours we drove through the prettiest part of Pennsylvania seeing precious little of the scenery so intent were we on the problem at hand. "We had left Reading far behind us" (Sacred Writings' "Silver Blaze") and were about to check into the Mansion House, Mahanoy City's only hotel, when we noted the sign above a tobacco shop next door. The name over the door was "Bradley's" and the reference became crystal clear.

"When you pass Bradley's," says Holmes to his medical amanuensis in *The Hound,* "would you ask him to send up a pound of the strongest shag tobacco?"

I was out of the car and into the shop a second or two before Marv, who is fifteen years my junior. A fat old man, his face covered with stubble, was stretched out on an ancient Morris chair, snoring mightily. There was a cowbell on top of a glass counter unquestionably for the specific purpose of arousing Mr. Bradley, whom I assumed the sleeper was. I rang it loudly. He woke with a start, looked at us over a pair of tortoiseshell glasses balanced on the tip of his bulbous nose and wheezed, "What's the hurry, gents?" He made no attempt to change his prone position.

I answered him quietly.

"I'd like a pound of shag, Sir, if it isn't too much trouble." He didn't note my irony. He arose slowly, all five feet of him, shook his head from side to side and leaned both elbows on the counter, a puzzled expression crossing his face.

"Now that's a goddamned funny thing, Mac," he said addressing me. "There ain't been no call for shag in twenty years and you're the second customer wants it the same day. Is it a new fad, or sumpin' like that there pot stuff they're smokin' down in Philly?"

I ignored the fellow's question to ask one of my own.

"What did your first customer look like, Mr. Bradley?"

The tobacconist scratched his head vigorously before answering.

"A tall gent—course pertineer everybody looks tall to me. Well, I don't know what else to say about 'im. Was dressed good, spoke like an educated feller, very polite and din't make no sarcastic remarks like somebody 'round here just done."

That, I suppose, was to put me in my place.

"Did you have any shag in stock to sell him?" I continued.

"Yep. Went down the cellar and dug up one old tin, been there for a hell of a long time, covered with cobwebs. He kinda smiled, picks up the tin and blows off the dust from it. Paper 'round it starts to crumble and you could just about read the label, 'Old Birmingham Shag.'

" 'That's it all right,' he says, his smile gettin' bigger. 'How much is it?'

" 'I'll leave that to you,' I tole 'em. Wouldn't hardly know what to charge. So he plunks down a five-dollar bill and says, 'The shag's worth more than that. But tell ya what I'm gonna do. Wouldn't be a bit surprised if a couple other fellers come 'round later today askin' for shag. Since this is the only can you have I wouldn't want for them to be disappointed. So I'd be most grateful if you'd wrap this up and hand it to 'em when they come in. Just say it's a gift from a friend.' "

Then he reached under the counter, took out a package tied with red and green ribbons and handed it to me. I didn't have to open it, I knew what was inside. Marv, who up to this point had said nothing, turned to the tobacconist.

"Can you recall anything else about the gentleman?" he asked. "Did he say where he was going and did he look the least bit familiar to you?"

"Nope. Can't recall nothin' else and I didn't ask him where he was goin'. Wasn't none of my business. But I gotta admit I had a feelin' I seen him some place before—long, long time ago. When he left he says, 'So long, Mr. Rismiller.' After a bit I got to thinkin' why'd he say 'Mr. Rismiller' unless he know'd me. Rismiller's my name.

"You fellers seen the name on this shop is Bradley's. That's whose place it used to be once and strangers who don't know no better call me that. But I bought out Bradley forty year ago. Just din't get 'round to changin' the sign yet. I been rackin' and rackin' my brain tryin' to figger out who the gent was but it don't seem to come to me."

I'm not sure I would have enlightened Mr. Bradley-Rismiller but Marv did.

"Would the name Eberhardt mean anything to you, Mr. Rismiller?" he asked.

The tobacconist stroked his chin thoughtfully. After a minute or two of silence he nodded his head.

"By God! That's who it was. Young Wes Eberhardt. Old man used to preach up at Evangelical Lutheran. Big, good lookin' fella. Tore into all kinds of sin—booze, dancin', card playin', even tobacco. Boy looks just like 'em. Musta left town 'bout the time I bought out Mr. Bradley. Now what the hell was he doin' back in Mahanoy City? Not comin' here to live, is he? I could use a few more five-dollar customers."

He scratched his head.

"You ain't detectives chasin' him, are you?"

Then he answered his own question.

"Nope, couldn't be. Said you was his friends."

Marv continued the interrogation.

"Does he have any relatives or friends in town that you know of, Mr. Rismiller?"

The latter scratched his head vigorously again. It was an annoying habit.

"Can't think of no relatives offhand. Them Lutheran parsons oncy stayed four years in a town. Not much time for their kids to make friends. So I can't think of no friends neither."

Mr. Rismiller's slaughter of the English language was getting on my nerves. I picked up Colonel Eberhardt's "present" and said good-bye politely enough. But our tobacconist wasn't ready to let us go.

"You fellers checkin' in the Mansion House?"

It really was none of Mr. Bradley-Rismiller's business but Marv humored him.

"We sure are if they have a couple of vacancies."

"Won't have no trouble on that score, Mac. Plenty of 'em vacant every night. Been that way ever since they stopped minin' coal in these parts. Reason I asked if you was stayin' overnight in town was I might think of somebody who know'd the Eberhardts better'n me. And if you'd like I could let you know."

Experience has taught me the most authoritative research is done in libraries. I much prefer this method of inquiry to dependence upon the faulty memory of man, the printed word is more reliable than the spoken one. Nevertheless I have no objection to time-saving methods. I informed Mr. Rismiller that we would be grateful for anything he could give us. However, he had one question he preferred us to answer first.

"If you're friends of Wes Eberhardt and you ain't cops, how come you don't ask him what you want to know yourselves?"

My cover story was ready.

"This is a kind of game we're playing, sort of like hare and hounds."

Mr. Rismiller grinned.

"That's what he tole me you'd say when I ast you."

A young female desk clerk gave us two large, clean rooms with bath and as soon as we'd deposited our luggage—the Mansion House has no bellboys—we hastened to the bar. I had a couple of mediocre martinis, and Marv, a glass of the local draft beer which he said was the best he'd drunk in years. I was about to order my third when Mr. Rismiller walked in. Marv invited him to join us.

"Take a rain check," he said. "On my way home and the little wife don't like to smell no booze on my breath. What I come to tell you is that your best bet is up at Triers' Corner. That's what we call the tailor shop directly across the street from the Evangelical Lutheran oney it's the First German Reformed United Evangelical Lutheran now—couple mergers, one preacher for the lot.

"Well, anyways, Triers' is run by an old, old man, Pop Trier, passed the hundred mark three, four years ago. His helpers is his three 'kids,' Otto, Charlie, and Emma, not one less than eighty and none of 'em ever married. All their noses is pulled out of joint from curiosity."

We thanked the little shopkeeper. He was about to leave when he turned around and scratched his head again.

"What's botherin' me, gents, ever since I talked to you, is how the hell Wes Eberhardt know'd you fellers was comin' to my store today and how'd he know you'd be askin' for shag? Did you tell 'im?"

I said we certainly had not, then waited patiently for Mr. Rismiller to indulge once more in his obnoxious habit. He did and so vigorously this time I could see the dandruff fall on his dirty, blue serge coat.

"All I can say is," Mr. Rismiller continued in wonderment, "that fella must be a regular Sherlock Holmes!"

CHAPTER

10

We had a surprisingly good breakfast in the coffee shop and were at Triers' Corner before 9 A.M. We experienced no difficulty finding the tailor shop. It was, as the hotel clerk said, "four squares up Center Street, right opposite a big, red, brick church." Before entering Triers', I glanced at the parsonage attached to the rear of what used to be the Evangelical Lutheran and was now a conglomerate.

"So this is where the Colonel spent four years," I commented to Marv. "Not too bad, is it?"

Indeed the manse appeared to be quite a pleasant place, brick, three stories in height, with side veranda overlooking a well-kept garden.

"I wonder what the back looks out on," Marv said. A moment later he was answered. There was the high pitched throaty blast of a train whistle so close it nearly frightened me out of my wits. A few seconds later a diesel locomotive rumbled by, pulling a long string of freight cars.

"Can't possibly be more than inches from the back end of the Eberhardt castle," Marv said and I nodded my head and went on.

"And diesels are pretty clean. But can you imagine what it must have been like when H. Wesley lived there? In those days the engines were steam and they must have shaken the house down to the very foundations. And the smoke, that thick black stuff! Old lady Eberhardt must have had one hell of a job trying to keep her place clean.

"It was more than likely that Pastor Eberhardt had to interrupt his sermons each time a locomotive went by. Family conversations broken up in the middle. It's obvious this wasn't the most desirable assignment in the Synod. The preacher had to be on his way down when H. Wesley came to Mahanoy City."

Marv shook his head.

"All this stuff about the Colonel's past is interesting but I don't see what it has to do with our immediate problem. Lets' find out what, if anything, the Trier family has to tell us."

The three steps we took up into the tailor shop led us right into the middle of the late nineteenth century. A tall, gaunt woman was stirring something over a huge, potbellied stove in the center of a long, rectangular room. Seated beside her, his feet on top of a coal bucket, was the oldest human being I ever saw. His porcelain skin reflected the red glare of the coals. He was munching an apple, I could hear its crunch.

Two wooden cutting tables stood side by side opposite the stove. Bent over one was a tall thin man snipping away at a bolt of cloth with a huge pair of shears. Behind this fellow was a scrawny little man wearing a battered black derby, its crown broken to expose a mass of curly red hair. He was pedaling what had to be the original Singer, stitching buckram, nodding his head, the derby bounding up and down and chewing tobacco, all to the rhythm of the machine. I watched him in utter fascination as he directed a stream of brown sputum into a cuspidor at least four feet away.

At our entrance the ancient called out in a strident voice, "Boys! Boys! Stop! We've visitors." All motion gradually ceased. I thought of those children's toys I once had—little figures beating drums, skating or dancing, each coming to a slow halt the moment a spring ran down.

Our appearance was no surprise to "Pop," Emma, Charlie and Otto; they were aware of our mission, just as they knew everything else that went on in the town. But first we had to satisfy their individual curiosities. This I did as best I could without revealing too much. Charlie, the younger son (he was seventy-nine I learned later, Emma's senior by two years and Otto's junior by three) brought in a couple of chairs from somewhere in the back. Pop didn't move from his seat by the fire, Emma by his side, and the "boys" vaulted up the nearer cutting table.

I wear bifocals, my hair is gray and getting grayer and I'm only fifty-nine. The bald spot on Marv's head takes in more territory annually, he wears thick lenses and he's forty-four. But there wasn't one gray hair nor a pair of spectacles among the whole damned Trier family, including Pop, who proudly told me he was born in '66. Had our mission not been so pressing I dearly would have delighted spending that day and others at Triers' Corner. But duty forced me to bring our conversation to a head.

Pop, whose accent was a combination of High German and the lilting, singsong Welsh brogue which typifies so many residents of the coal fields, remembered every one of the Eberhardts well and was eager to tell us all he knew about each. I let him ramble on although, for our purposes, much of what he said was irrelevant. That the family had lived in genteel poverty was beyond doubt.

"Martha, she was Wes' mother," Pop said, "had five other kids to raise. I don't know how she did it. My wife, Gerda, who's passed on, used to send them soup. Pretend she'd made too much for us to eat but Martha understood. Wes was a quiet boy, never said much. He and his brother Joe used to team up together."

We already knew all we wanted to know about how H. Wesley's character was molded. Our quest at the Triers' was to find out how many of the Eberhardts were extant and where they lived. Martha, of course, was dead. Charlie thought there was an older sister, Hilda, in Lancaster.

"Didn't she marry one of the Crawshaw boys, Em?" and Em nodded. "He was an electrician." I made a note.

Charlie continued.

"I know Becky's dead and so's Jennie. Don't know a thing about Joe. Must have passed on by now. Last I heard was more'n forty years ago. He was the wild one. Got in a peck of trouble even while the old man was alive."

Pop admonished Charlie.

"Don't say anything you don't know for sure, lad."

Otto interjected. "But Pop, didn't he get picked up for stealin' a bike and then run off with a carnival?"

"Behave yourself, Otto, and speak when you're spoken to. Otherwise you know what'll happen!"

I was afraid Pop would place his oldest son over his knees and give the "boy" a paddling. We learned only one more relevant fact, that the oldest son, Alvin, had been a successful rancher and for a time had lived in New Mexico.

"He married that pretty Ryan girl from Catawissa Street. Name was Hazel. Went out West to seek his fortune and made it. Might still be out there for all I know," Pop said. "Why don't you talk to Kathy, Hazel's sister, a real beauty, even prettier 'n her."

We got Kathy's address, thanked the Trier family for its cooperation, and said good-bye. We talked to Kathy, *aetat* seventy or thereabouts and no longer a beauty. She had a fairly recent letter from Sister Hazel, apparently still living in New Mexico but planning a visit East shortly.

"Alvin and I will be home for Memorial Day," Hazel wrote. "I'm getting lonesome for the coal regions and for what's left of our friends. I didn't tell you, I wanted it to be a surprise, but we bought the Thatcher farm out in Locust Valley. Al's having Jake Weiss put the house in shape so we can spend this summer there. . . . "

There could be no question as to our next move. The Thatcher "place" was a half-hour's drive from Mahanoy City but the terrain was completely different. The town we left below was surrounded by old culm banks, abandoned collieries, bitter remnants of better days and more recent devastation—treeless wastes laid bare by surface "stripping." Locust Valley, twenty miles away, could have been in another world.

We had to ask directions from a dozen natives before we finally located the Thatcher farm, or what was left of it, in a remote corner of the "Valley." It was dusk when we drove from the secondary highway we'd been traveling on and thence over a narrow road to the farm.

Apparently carpenters and painters had been here some time earlier; a scaffold stretched from ground to third floor of the old wooden farmhouse. In the deepening shadows we could see their tools along the bottom of the Mansard roof's lower slope.

The house had been built at the edge of a small but dense

copse of woods. To the right was a meadow stretching far into the distance and somewhere in the background we could hear swift flowing water. We weren't able to lower a rusty bar holding the broken front gate in place, so we climbed over a low stone wall to get to the front yard.

By then it was getting so dark we could scarcely see more than a few feet ahead, I wasn't quite sure just what we were looking for. Marv whispered he'd go back to the car to fetch his flashlight and left me standing there alone. The wind was rising sharply whistling through the woods. Way off I heard the howling of a dog and while I anxiously awaited Marv's reappearance the sound seemed to get closer and closer. Oh how I longed for the comforting presence of a Penang lawyer in my right hand.

Moments later I heard the car door slam shut, then Marv stumbling along the path. I looked for the beam from his searchlight but saw none. He fell over something, recovered, and then was standing alongside of me.

"Goddammit!" he said. "I told Frankie to keep his big, fat hands off my flashlight. Now the batteries are dead."

I could sense, if not see, that he was looking at me.

"Frank, what in the hell are you and I doing here in the first place? Did we expect to find Ellen and the Colonel camping out in his brother Alvin's farmhouse? We must be crazy." He laughed. "Ain't nobody here but us chickens."

"That so, Marv?" I asked as quietly as I could. "Then how do you account for that?"

The howling, which had ceased for a minute or two, was now so close and so loud that my hair stood on end. I nudged Marv.

"My God! What's that?"

As I turned around to grope my way back to the car my hand brushed against something soft and in motion, man or beast I didn't know which. I must have leaped three feet into the air. Then I heard Marv say, "Come here, Fido, or whatever they call you. Out of the corner of my eye I could see him bend down to pat a huge dog whose tail was wagging furiously.

"Just a lonesome stray," Marv said, "and probably hungry too. Not *the* hound, Frank. Don't be alarmed."

I told him I wasn't the least bit alarmed, simply that the sudden appearance of the animal startled me as it would anyone. To prove my point I patted the beast's head. We fumbled our way to the car, the animal following closely behind. Marv opened the door and our dome light revealed a shaggy, brown, long-haired bitch which fawned all over Marv. This revealing example of canine subservience is the basic reason I prefer cats.

The only food we had was a Hershey bar. Marv removed the wrapper and tossed it to the dog, which moved the candy back and forth with its paws as though it were a toy rather than bolting it greedily as I fully expected.

"Friendly beast, isn't she?" Marv asked. "I wish I could take her home with us. But I'd catch hell from Helene, we've already got two other strays, a cat and cageful of hamsters."

He sighed and tickled the bitch under her neck. "But we can't, old girl, so we'll have to say good-bye and leave you to forage for yourself."

Marv had created a problem for himself, being kind to the dog, then forcing the animal to go away. "Beware of pity," I always say. The bitch thought Marv was playing with her and each time he shoved her, she'd wag her tail, lie flat on her belly, cock an eye, leap up and shove her large head into Marv's stomach. After losing several minutes with this tomfoolery, he was able to slam the door and we were off.

We couldn't have traveled more than a mile or two when I felt something cold and wet against my neck. "Christ!" I yelled. Marv jammed on the brakes so hard I almost flew through the windshield. "Good God!" he shouted. "What happened? Bee sting you?"

"We got company, Frank," he said. "Let's make her welcome."

He turned around and patted the stray, which at once leaped into the front seat and settled down comfortably between us, forcing me to give up half my space.

"Must have hopped in when you opened your door. Nothing I can do now, Frank, except bring her home."

He released the brakes and we began moving again.

"You know we're lucky at that, Frank. This animal obviously was a house pet and not very long ago at that, no chance to have turned wild. Either she ran off on her own or some bastard let her loose. Do it all the time, trick them into getting out of their cars, then tear off and leave the dog stranded in the middle of nowhere. But I don't think this is what happened to our friend here. She wasn't hungry. You could see that. Wouldn't even nibble at the candy bar."

"Perhaps," I said, "Jake Weiss' crew fed her."

"I doubt it," he answered. "This is Saturday night, carpenters and painters don't work Saturdays, so they haven't been around for more than twenty-four hours. She's a good sized hound and I'll bet you she's got a damned good appetite. I'd say she'd been fed within the last couple of hours. All she did was wag her tail and bark when we arrived, almost as though she was waiting for somebody to play with her."

At that Marv and I looked at each other.

"Well, Marv," I said, "go ahead and ask it."

" 'Is there any point to which you would wish to draw my attention?'

" 'To the curious incident of the dog in the night-time,' I answered.

" 'The dog did nothing in the night-time.'

" 'That was the curious incident,' remarked Sherlock Holmes."

At this Marv pulled to the side of the road and stopped the motor.

"Wait a minute. Wait a minute," he said and put his hand under the fur of the animal's neck. "She's got a collar. We just didn't see it."

"Maybe because we weren't looking for it," I answered.

"Good point. We should have realized our lovely bitch is no stray and didn't get where she was on her own."

He felt around for a bit, found a buckle, which he unsnapped. Then he turned on the dome light. In his hand was a brand new collar with a bronze identification tag on it. He examined both, laughed a bit grimly, then turned to me.

"Well, Frank, whom do you think this belongs to?"

I shook my head, afraid to hazard a guess.

"Come on. Come on, try it," he urged.

"All right," I gulped. "Colonel Ross of King's Pyland."

(Colonel Ross was the owner of the aforementioned Wessex Cup winner, Silver Blaze, a thoroughbred stolen and recovered in time because Holmes correctly reasoned that the stable's watchdog did nothing to the thief because she knew him.)

When we'd both recovered from the shock, Marv said with a sigh, "What's the use kidding ourselves, Frank. The Colonel's a hell of a lot smarter than we are and he's able to antici-pate every move. I'll bet you he was somewhere around his brother's farmhouse laughing his head off at us when we drove up, knowing exactly what would happen."

I remonstrated. "How could he know we'd be there at all and furthermore how could he be sure we'd take along the dog with us?"

Marv thought for a moment.

"First of all, Frank, I've a confession to make. You didn't let the dog into the car. I did. I just couldn't bear to leave her out there in the country all by herself. The Colonel knows I'm a softy about animals, stray dogs in particular, so that part of the question he could easily have deduced, once he got us out to the place and turned the dog loose."

"But how did he know we'd be there?"

"I'm not sure I can follow his reasoning completely but I'll try. We've got to remember he's had twenty some years pro-fessional training in the art of deduction, detection, and de-ceit. And to be honest we've had none. Oh, I know we're fa-miliar with the Sacred Writings, but let's admit we've never before tried to put them to practical use.

"So I think the Colonel knew we'd want to explore his background thoroughly and that the trail must lead from Bradley's to Triers', to Kathy Ryan and to Brother Alvin's farmhouse. That's what every investigator would have done and probably in *that* sequence. If the Colonel happened to guess wrong in one of our moves, he'd have little or nothing to lose. For all we know, he may already have anticipated one of our steps incorrectly. But let's go on and assume that in this case we'd be at the right place at the right time.

"How? It's possible, naturally, that we could have gotten to the farmhouse an hour or two earlier or maybe even tomor-row when we'd see it in bright daylight. Could he have known you and me? Would Don and Charlie or Ed and Jack have picked up our affectionate bitch?"

He patted the dog and continued.

"They might have and arrived at the same conclusion. That was the chance he had to take. However, you may remember in advance that the team to come to Mahanoy City would be at one of our sessions, Don once said he'd covered a story in Tamaqua and that he spent a week doing it. So it's logical that he and Charlie would make that town their take-off point. Ed used to talk about how, when he was a child, his parents took him to ride that gravity railroad and he'd love to see what happened to it.

"So who covers Mahanoy City? Whoever's left, meaning us."

I nodded.

"Now we come to a conclusion and a step we must consider taking," Marv said slowly. "I don't know what's doing with our colleagues. I could be wrong but I'm rather inclined to think they won't have done any better than you and I. The old boy may not have teased them the way he's teasing us. I don't know why he's been playing cat and mouse with you and me, Frank, rather than the others."

I knew the answer to that. I, not Marv, was the object of the Colonel's game. I, because H. Wesley Eberhardt was aware *I* was his most formidable antagonist. He wanted to show *me* up so that I would lose confidence. But he should have realized that instead I would become even more relentless. However, I gave no hint of this to Marv and urged him to make his point.

"OK. What do we do next? Sure, you and I will traipse over to Lancaster tomorrow and talk to Hilda Crawshaw, *née* Eberhardt, if we can find her. And providing she'll talk to us if we do. But do you really believe after these last few examples of the Colonel's abilities and intelligence we'll get anything out of Sister Hilda? Of course not!"

I was inclined to agree.

"So where do we go and what do we do next, Frank?"

I shrugged my shoulders. If Marv was ready to quit, *I* certainly was not!

"Look," I remonstrated. "We've been on the Chase for less than two weeks. I don't think we've given ourselves enough time."

Marv shook his head.

"Two weeks. Two months. It makes no difference. We're outclassed. And I'll tell you something else that isn't funny. No one but a louse would take this beautiful dog to the country and let her loose. She belongs to somebody, a kid maybe, you can see she's a real house pet. I'm going to make an honest effort to find her owner and if I do I'll give her up."

Abruptly he stopped talking.

"Wait a minute. Wait a minute, Frank. It just occurred to me, Ellen had a dog, a spaniel, Blondie, didn't she call him?"

I nodded. I hadn't thought of Blondie either, in fact none of us had. Ellen was quite attached to the animal, although when I used to tell her she ought to swap in the beast for a Siamese she only laughed. I never observed the Colonel maltreating Blondie but he certainly didn't tolerate any familiarity either and for this I admired him, albeit grudgingly.

"We should be looking for man, wife, and dog, Frank. That ought to make it a hell of a lot easier."

"Unless they've put Blondie in a kennel."

"For six months, Frank? Come off it! You don't put a house dog in a kennel for a year, the animal would die of loneliness. And Ellen wouldn't have permitted it. No. They must have Blondie with them."

He paused.

"Unless, of course. . . . "

"Unless, of course what, Marv?"

"Unless, of course, he disposed of Blondie. A bastard who'd steal a pet like the lady sitting between us would do anything."

Our trip to Lancaster, where we drove the following morning, was almost totally unproductive except to develop further our insight into the Colonel's character. We located Hilda simply by looking in the telephone directory. She was living in a modest home on Nevin Street, a few blocks from the Franklin and Marshall campus. During a brief conversation held in a dingy "parlor," a gentleman whom I assumed to be Mr. Crawshaw was stretched out on a sofa sound asleep. Hilda simply ignored the gentleman's presence, a task which required a considerable amount of savoir-faire.

Mrs. Crawshaw, a tall, gaunt, weather-beaten woman could have been no more than five years older than the Colonel but she looked as though she were his senior by twenty.

"Wes?" she asked raising her eyebrows. "Haven't seen or heard from my dear brother for a long, long time."

The man on the sofa stirred.

"That was 1942, Hilda. We were living in the big house on Chestnut Street then, remember? [I'm *sure* Hilda remembered.] The son-of-a-bitch was on his way from Carlisle to Washington and he came in for a couple minutes to show off his uniform. He was a young bastard then; guess he's an old one now.

"Done something wrong, maybe?"

This last was uttered hopefully. We answered, "No." Then with an effort he managed to focus his eyes on Marv and me.

"Either of you gents got a cigarette?" Neither of us smoke, we shook our heads. Mr. Crawshaw then promptly fell back on the sofa.

Hilda knew of H. Wesley's marriage to Ellen.

"Saw his picture in the paper with that society girl. Must have been quite a show but Bob and I weren't asked to be among those present."

Did she think Wes might have been in touch with any member of the family more recently than within three decades, her oldest brother perhaps?

Although my next question was totally irrelevant and I knew it, I still asked Mrs. Crawshaw if the Colonel had attended Jennie's funeral.

She shook her head.

"You don't know my brother Wes well if you ask that question. We buried Jennie at Oak View, that's in Philadelphia. My brother Wesley was living in the city then but he did *not* attend his sister's funeral services."

Thus ended our interview with Hilda Crawshaw, and a pair of disappointed hunters plus one shaggy, brown, long-haired mongrel returned to Philadelphia late that Sunday afternoon. I'm telling this out of sequence, and it has little to do with our immediate task, i.e., the search for Colonel H. Wesley Eberhardt, but Marv kept his promise. An advertisement he placed in the "Lost and Found" column of the Mahanoy City *Record-American* the following day brought an immediate response.

"Sandy" either had wandered off or had been stolen (more likely the latter) from a home in Delano, a suburb of Mahanoy City, some twenty-four hours before we came upon the bitch. Her owner told Marv that Delano was a scant three miles from brother Alvin's farmhouse, a superfluous confirmation of an unpleasant thought.

I telephoned each member of our two other "teams," then I prepared my report. While Marv and I had not learned much, the rest of the "hunters" learned even less. For Ed and Jack the trip to Jim Thorpe (*né* Mauch Chunk) proved an almost complete failure. The church in which Pastor Eberhardt once trumpeted from the pulpit had been turned into a garage years back, the manse razed, and the congregation, grown few in numbers, disbanded. The preacher himself was only dimly remembered and Wes not at all. The surviving member of the original Board of Trustees of the Oak Street Evangelical Luthern Church, a Christian gentleman, who sounded the "call" heard by the Reverend Mr. Eberhardt, was senile. I could appreciate Ed and Jack's failure. The Eberhardts had been in Mauch Chunk less than two years when the Pastor died.

Charlie and Don fared somewhat better and emerged from their assignment with a tentative lead. Brother Joe had a friend who, before the influx of television, used to operate a moving picture house on Tamaqua's main thoroughfare. Apparently he and Joe had maintained a desultory correspondence over the years.

The last time this former theatrical entrepreneur had seen Joe was as recently as 1965 at an accidental meeting in New York. What interested Charlie and Don was the fact that during the get-together of the two old friends the retired showman recalled that Joe had mentioned he was in frequent touch with brother Wesley of whom he apparently was proud. Furthermore, while he hadn't seen Joe since, he had heard from him and produced a postal card, written in 1968 bearing an Erie, Pennsylvania, postmark.

"My Lord!" I burst out when Charlie told me this. "I forgot all about that uncle who sent H. Wesley to military school."

"So did we. Somebody ought to go there. The uncle must be dead but perhaps there are nieces and nephews around. Maybe they'll know something."

He suggested we take up the matter on Thursday. I'd been holding back on the peculiar results of our own excursions to Mahanoy City, the incident of the dog in Locust Valley, and our visit with Hilda Crawshaw. Then I dropped my bombshell.

After each had gotten over the shock of learning that the Colonel was not only close at hand but playing games with us, I suggested, and so far it was only a suggestion, that we enlist the aid of professionals. But at our next session, despite Marv's openly expressed opinion that we were hopelessly outclassed, the consensus was we should continue with our own independent efforts.

I believe Jack swayed us by pointing out we'd been on the Chase for less than three weeks and this was too short a time to declare ourselves failures.

"If all of you insist," he said, "I'll yield. However, I do think we should wait a bit longer. Eberhardt's a smart operator—there's no question about that—and he *is* laughing at us from somewhere. But we're not quite so stupid as the Colonel believes. One of these days he'll overplay his hand.

"If this were a matter of life or death I'd agree we need the help of the pros. The stakes *are* high but they're only money and pride. For the present, let's try to work it out strictly by ourselves."

Except for my trip to Erie and Jack's self-designated task of checking kennels in the Philadelphia area to see if Blondie was a registered guest, there were no further assignments. In truth, unless something unforeseen occurred there was little or nothing to be done.

CHAPTER

11

THE ONLY Eberhardt in the Lake City directory was one John C., operator and owner of a good-sized motel at the entrance to Presque Isle Peninsula Park. Fortunately, before I checked into some other hostelry, I discovered this. So it was as a guest, not as a stranger, that I was able to interrogate H. Wesley's first cousin. I found him a gracious, cooperative gentleman in his early fifties. Although I soon discovered his knowledge of the Sacred Writings was nil, he struck me as a rather sophisticated fellow, so I laid my cards on the table and told him about our bet. He roared with laughter.

"Well, you men certainly got yourselves in for something, didn't you? And I hope you win. Even though Wes is my own flesh and blood, I never was too fond of him. Maybe because he was so much cleverer than I and I resented it."

I leaned back in a captain's chair in "The Whitefish Bar" and listened while I sipped a quite superior martini.

"Wes is exactly three years older than me. We were both born September 30, under the sign of Libra, which is supposed to make us highly introverted and intellectual, if you believe all that crap. I don't. You'd have a hard time finding two kids as different as Wes and me. When I was a kid I was great on competitive sports and president of my high school class. At college—I graduated from the Hotel Training School at Cornell—I joined everything in sight.

"But Wes kept to himself. Of course I realize he had a hard life as a kid. Apparently you're aware of his background, so I don't have to go into that with you. And you know, of course, that my dad and Wes' old man were brothers."

I nodded.

"We weren't rich, believe me, but Dad had a good job. He was foreman over at Erie-Bucyrus and during the Depression, even when he got a couple of fat cuts in wages, we weren't nearly as bad off as some of his friends who had no work at all. Well, my father felt sorry for the Pastor, struggling along with a wife and six kids. He sent him dough but he only tried it once, a pretty good-sized chunk for those days, fifty bucks. It came back with a note: 'Thank you, but the Lord will provide.'

"You never knew the Parson. I did, not well, but enough to realize he was a proud man and a stern father. He was the old blood-and-thunder, hell-and-damnation type. Every god-damn thing that was any fun was a sin. You can imagine what my cousins had to endure.

"One summer, when I was around eleven, Dad and Mom packed the old Hup and off we went, my brother Will, too— he's dead now—on our vacation. We didn't have much money to spend and we had only a week but what did we kids care? We spent the first three or four days camping out in one of those state parks where we fished, swam, and had a good time. On Saturday afternoon we landed up in a little town in the hard coal regions where my uncle was preaching. I forget what the place is called."

"Mauch Chunk," I suggested, but my host shook his head and I tried, "Mahanoy City."

"That's it," the innkeeper said and went on. "We didn't say we were coming; we knew they'd be around. Dad was sure his brother would insist we stay that one night in the manse before we shoved off and he was worried sick about eating their food. He knew the Parson'd be more than hard put to feed four extra mouths.

"So in a small town right before we hit Mahanoy City we pulled up in front of an A&P. Dad, Will, and I walked out with a hell of a big ham, a peck of potatoes, a couple fat chickens, and a sackful of canned groceries.

"It must have been around four o'clock in the afternoon when we reached the parsonage. The Preacher was upstairs working on his sermon for the next day but some of my cousins were on the porch. Aunt Martha was in the kitchen preparing whatever they were going to eat for supper. She put on a good front when she saw the four of us walk in but she must have been worried sick."

A waitress refilled our glasses, my host continued.

"Well, to make a long story short, after the Parson greeted us he took a look at the pile of food we'd brought and Aunt Martha hadn't put it away yet. He was wild.

" 'Take it out of here! he screamed. He had one of those German tempers. 'No guest of ours pays for his food in my house.'

" 'For God's sake, Ken,' I can hear my father say. 'This stuff didn't cost me a nickel.'

" 'Where did it come from then, my dear brother?' he says sarcastically. 'Did the Lord leave it at your doorstep?'

" 'Practically,' my father says, 'I won it at a company lottery.'

"At this the Parson almost went off his rocker.

" 'You won it *gambling*? And you say the Lord left it at your doorstep. That's blasphemy. We'll have none of that in *my* household. Take it away before I *throw* it away.'

"So we carried all the food to the car trunk and came back to the house empty-handed. I don't know what Aunt Martha fed us for supper that night or breakfast the next day but I knew we were half-starved and I'll bet our aunt, uncle, and cousins were fully starved. We kids went with our cousins to Sunday School next morning, but Mom and Dad heard Pastor Eberhardt preach. It must have been a beaut. We went after."

There was a brief interlude during which my host left me to

handle some chore. He returned shortly, ordered another drink for me, then resumed his story.

"We were sitting at a restaurant table in the next town when Mom said, 'John! John! What about all that food in the car? It'll spoil. Oughten we buy some ice and pack it?'

"My father only grinned.

" 'No food there,' he said.

"We all looked surprised.

" 'Didn't want that stuff going to waste any more than you. I handled it my own way. I looked around and figured the smartest of that lot was young Wes.

" 'So I got him to one side very early this morning when I knew he was going out to deliver Sunday papers on his wagon. I gave him a proposition. At first I was afraid he'd think I was undermining his father's authority, which of course I was. But I couldn't bear the thought of those kids going hungry and the food going to waste. If he doubled-crossed me and told the Parson that'd be my tough luck. However, I needn't have had such fears.

" 'Here's the trunk key, Wes, I told him. You'll know how to handle the situation better than me, so you're on your own. Just see that I get the key back before we leave. He nodded and didn't bat an eye.

" 'I walked away and when I got into the house I looked out the window. It was just before the Parson came down. There was Wes taking the food out of the trunk, cool as a cucumber and piling it on his wagon. What he did with it I'll never know.' "

My host smiled.

"My father never found out but I did, though it took me almost forty years. I'd forgotten about the incident completely. You know my father paid for Wes' college education. He thought my cousin would choose some small denominational school, not necessarily Lutheran, in fact probably not. Instead he picked a military prep school to overcome any scholastic handicap he might have, then went to The Fortress.

"My rationalization is that Wes was determined to have a career where he'd never go hungry. He chose the right one. That's one place they feed you properly, at least most of the time."

I was waiting for that forty-year-old answer. It came.

"Three, four years ago my office telephone rang and the

desk clerk told me someone insisted on seeing me personally. I walked out and there was a seedy looking guy.

" 'Hello, cousin,' he said. 'Don't you recognize me?'

"I didn't really, although there was something vaguely familiar about him. Turns out it was Joe. I asked him how he happened to locate me and his reply was the same as yours, 'Only Eberhardt in the telephone directory.' 'But how did you know I was in Erie?' 'That's easy,' he says. 'I look up Eberhardts in every city I play in.'

" 'You're an actor?'

" 'You might say that. I'm in show biz. The Lillie DeLisle Company. Assistant Manager. Sometimes when one of the players is indisposed I play his part.' "

My host looked at me, a smile on his face.

"Familiar with Lillie DeLisle and her company?"

I shook my head.

"Low down burlesque. Practically kootch. Ever been to a girlie show?"

Again I was forced to plead ignorance. My education in that area has been almost completely neglected, but my host proceeded to give me a short but interesting lecture on the subject.

"Kootch is where the girls strip completely. No G-strings or pasties. Strictly without talent. Generally speaking they're a pretty scurvy lot and I don't let 'em stay here. I'm not referring to the big name queens—Gypsy Rose or Pagan Jones—they're welcome anytime.

"In the summer and fall the kootchers are on the road, playing small towns under a tent, county fairs and that sort of thing. But their off-season—a pun even if I didn't mean it to come out that way—they travel a burlesque circuit, a third or fourth rate one if they go down that far.

"Joe didn't tell me what his duties were but I knew. When I started in my profession I worked in a little hotel at Salamanca, New York, that catered to this clientele. Joe's job would be to load and unload the props, drive the company truck, post bills, run errands, pimp, and when one of the comedians was too plastered to go on stage, Joe'd take his place.

"I bought Joe a meal, offered to put him up for the night or for as long as he'd be playing Erie. Then I waited for the inevitable touch. It didn't come. 'I'm staying with a friend,' he told me and gave me a wink. From this I assumed he was shacking up with one of the kootchers at the Dodge Hotel, a fleabag which catered to cheap road companies and carnivals.

"Then I asked Joe what had happened to my Mahanoy City cousins. I knew both his parents had died but that was about all. Joe wasn't much better informed although he had attended one sister's funeral—Jennie's. I remembered her as a scared, pretty youngster around my age. But Joe'd lost contact completely with the rest of his family except for Wes.

Now, I told myself, we were getting somewhere.

"When I mentioned his older brother, Joe's eyes lit up. 'That's a real man,' he said. 'Best of a bad lot. Got a mind like a steel trap and knows how to use it.'

"Joe burst out laughing.

" 'Remember the time all of you drove down from Erie on your vacation and brought us a load of grub which we sure could have used? I guess my brother and I were the only ones who ever went to bed with anything resembling a full belly. I don't know how he did it, but he was always able to sneak a couple of sandwiches and a hunk of pie for him and me when the rest of the family was damned near starvin'.'

" 'Can't take care of everybody,' Wes used to tell me. 'It's gotta be survival of the fittest.'

" 'Well, to get back to that load of groceries. When we come in the kitchen and saw it piled up on the table we drooled. That was the most food we'd *ever* had in the house at the same time and we couldn't wait until we tore into it. The old man was a son-of-a-bitch, I hated him and so did Wes. I guess you remember what the noble Preacher told your father to do with all that good grub when he found out it come from gambling.

" 'Wes got me to one side and told me what Uncle John said about salvaging the food. I don't know what your father expected Wes to do with the ham and chickens and all but I suppose he thought that somehow it'd get back into the family larder or budget without the Preacher finding out.

" 'Well, the Preacher didn't find out and nobody else did either except me. Wes always told me everything. He took the stuff down to Wagner's grocery store the next morning and sold it to Mr. Wagner. Even though these were rough times he drove a hard bargain and come out with a wad of cash.

" 'Are you gonna turn it over to Mom?" I asked, and he said, 'How the hell can I do that? She'd tell the old man and he'd whack the daylights out of me. No, kid, you and I are goin' to do something other kids have been doin' all their lives.

" 'What's that, Wes?' I asked, and he says, 'We're gonna have some fun.'

" 'We didn't dare spend the dough in Mahanoy City, somebody'd have ratted on us. We'd never been to a movie in our lives. A sin, that old bastard used to say to us. I don't know what excuse we gave to be away from home pretty near all Saturday, but he hitchhiked a ride over to Shenandoah where nobody knew us.

" 'There was a Tarzan picture playing at the Ferguson with Johnny Weissmuller. I couldn't believe my eyes, it was the most wonderful thing I'd ever seen. We stayed to see it twice. Then, after we came out, Wes took me into a Chinese restaurant and ordered a full meal—Won Ton soup, Chop Suey—the works. First time I ever ate Chink food. I'll never forget that experience.

" 'How'd you like it kid?' Wes asks, and I can hardly answer it's so good. I musta had tears in my eyes. I'da done anything Wes asked me to. Well, I ate it a million times since in Ruby Foo's and some of the best Chink places in the U. S. A. and Mexico, too. But it never tasted as good as it did in that Shenandoah, P.A., joint, probably run by a Polack. I'll always remember that experience and I never eat Chink food without thinkin' of Wes.

"My cousin Joe shook his head, got a faraway look, and I was sure he was thinking of Wes. Then, after a couple seconds, he went on.

" 'I forgot to tell you, John, when we paid our admission to the movies they handed each of us a dish, a bright blue one. That was one of the inducements they used to have to get even kids to spend their money in the Depression. I asked Wes what we'd do with 'em. Give them to Mom, she could use them.

" 'Wes looked at me. "Are you crazy?" he says. "Do you want to get the strap from the Preacher? I'd like to sell them but nobody'll buy. So we're gonna get rid of the evidence." And with that he drops them beautiful, new plates down a sewer.' "

My host asked his cousin the same question I would have asked.

"Do you ever see Wes anymore?"

" 'Nope,' Joe answered, 'but he *always* keeps in touch. I travel around a lot and nobody including me knows my exact schedule. But he writes me every year, three, four times and sends the letters care of *Billboard*. I have 'em forwarded to me so I always know what he's doin' and where he is. Got cards and letters from Wes from all over the world. Know he's married to some rich society dame in Philly. Sent me a wad of press notices. Never asked me to visit him yet but if he does I'll be there with bells on.' "

As an interrogator, I simply could not get over my luck or skill, whatever you wish to call it. Here was an incredible lead. I knew Jack and the other Sons had to be enormously impressed and I myself couldn't wait to say good-bye to my host and, as they say, "get crackin'."

I had one more important question to ask Mr. Eberhardt. Had Joe turned up again in Erie?

"Sorry," was his reply. "That was the last and only time. I had a convention coming in that evening and I didn't even see his show although he handed me 'two on the aisle' before he left. We haven't had burlesque shows here in town ever since although they do get some girlie shows out in the sticks. I'm sure if Joe'd been playing there he'd have stopped in to see me.

"Sometimes we do get the better show people staying with us—Tommy Dorsey always did—and once in a while I ask them if they ever heard of my cousin. They never have. The only thing I ever did find was that Lillie DeLisle was killed in an auto accident last year and the company, or what was left of it, broke up.

"I often meant to go down to the library and look up back numbers of *Billboard* to see if Cousin Wes is still writing to his brother. But I never got around to it. I suppose they have the magazine."

They had excellently preserved bound copies of the publication going back to 1921. I felt there'd be no point checking prior to 1945 when Joe, who was three years younger than Wes, was twenty. Unless I missed one, and I doubt that since I am an experienced, painstaking researcher, the first communication between brothers occurred in the May 7, 1953 issue of *Billboard* as it was labeled then. It later "spun off" to cover only one branch of show biz—the outdoor area—and then it became *Amusement Business*.

Other notices from Wes to Joe followed, not with any great regularity, although one never failed to appear three weeks before Christmas each year. The total was fifty-five, an average of approximately four per year, from the first to the last which ran in the April 12, 1967 issue.

I don't know how significant this was but the issue bearing the last communication from Wes to Joe carried a brief obituary of Lillie DeLisle (*née* Sophie Hammerschlag), killed instantly when a car in which she was a passenger struck a tree on the outskirts of Wenonah, Wisconsin. There was no mention of the driver. If it was Joe, and he suffered the same fate as Miss DeLisle, there went the best lead we were ever likely to have.

CHAPTER

12

MY REPORT at the third plenary session gave all of us the impetus we needed to carry on. There was no question in any Son's mind that the key to the Colonel's whereabouts lay with Brother Joe.

"*If* he's still among the living," Charlie added, "and I doubt it. Otherwise, how do you account for the fact that there were no communications for the past couple of years in *Amusement Business?*"

Ed had more confidence. "Isn't it possible the Colonel knew his brother's address from that time to the present and didn't have to use that 'letter waiting' column?"

This made sense to me, perhaps because I am an optimist by nature. We had two approaches. Marv would handle the first. As coroner's pathologist his motives in seeking information would not be questioned by hospitals in the Wenonah, Wisconsin, area with whom he said he'd correspond on official stationery.

"I should know in a week at the most if Brother Joe had been admitted or only treated at any of these after the De-Lisle accident."

Don, possibly a bit sensitive because he was not a "full" partner in our venture, although heaven knows no one ever referred to this fact, insisted he be permitted to pursue the second approach. This was through *Amusement Business*.

"Let me work this out," Don said. "I don't feel as though I'm carrying my load. I'll find out who the editor is and maybe Bill Hanson, our theater and movie critic, knows him. Whoever he is, he must have had a lot of requests to locate people lost somewhere in show biz. If I tell him what we're up to and he gets interested, I wouldn't be surprised if he gave us a few ideas."

Marv had *his* answer the next afternoon. Instead of writing he telephoned directly to the administrator of the only hospital in the Wenonah area. Joe Eberhardt never was an "in" or "out" patient there. This gave our morale quite a boost.

Don, too, brought us somewhat encouraging words.

"The editor is Irwin Kirby. He used to work on the Minneapolis *Star* with Bill years ago. Seemed like a hell of a nice guy, so I told him the whole story. He laughed at the way we were trapped but said he'd do what he could to help us get out of it. Irwin's got a host of friends in the 'profession' and he told me his magazine has a nonpaid stringer on every fairground in every tent show circus and carnival lot. He knew Miss DeLisle and he was acquainted with some members of her troupe but he'd never heard of Joe.

" 'Don't let that disturb you, Don,' he said. 'There must be fifty thousand guys and girls in outdoor show biz and God knows I don't pretend to be acquainted with all of them. Of course, you must consider the possibility that your boy stuck close to theaters and didn't tie up with tent shows. If that's true, you'll run into problems because there's no one publication that blankets legits in the same way we blanket the outdoor entertainment field.

" 'You got *Backstage* here in New York. They handle Broadway and off-Broadway shows and personnel. There's another in Chicago and one on the West Coast. Of course there's *Variety*. Come to think of it that'd be your best bet. If you don't know Abel Green, who runs it, I'll call him for you and try to set up a date. Knows lots of people and he has a sense of humor. I think he'll get a bang out of your story.

" 'Meanwhile, I'll see what I can do. Give me a ring in a couple of weeks. If I find out anything sooner I'll be in touch.' "

Don said that Abel Green, to whom he'd spoken later that day, was as cooperative as Kirby and laughed as heartily as did his colleague on *Amusement Business*. He was a bit less optimistic about our success, however.

"There's an awful lot of people in show biz," Green said, "and I wouldn't know how you could track down one of them. Every hick town in the country's got a repertory or a college company. Some of 'em are still doin' *Springtime for Henry*.

"Take somebody like your boy, Joe. He could walk into any one of these places with a considerable amount of authority claiming big time experience. Even being assistant stage manager in Lillie's company is a hell of a lot more big time than running the Punxsutawney, P.A., Civic Repertory Theater. If he didn't want too much dough he could land a soft job for himself and have a dozen old biddies chasing him, hanging on to every one of his pearly words.

"If this is what happened, I really don't see how you'll dig him out in six months. But count on me to do whatever I can."

This was a particularly frustrating period. By the following Thursday no word had come either from Green or Kirby. We'd exhausted all leads, temporarily at any rate, and unless one is operating in the realms of fiction, new ones don't come bounding out of the atmosphere. It's all well and good for professional policemen to sit back on their fat haunches at taxpayers' expense and wait for stool pigeons to produce clues. Cops have all the time in the world to solve their cases; they can keep them open forever if they are so inclined.

But for us this was impossible. We'd agreed, or at least five of my fellow Sons had agreed, to solve the Chase within six months or pay the penalty. And already more than one sixth of the allotted time had evanesced. The old Shikari hunter had no assignments, so a rather discouraged group of hunters adjourned the regular Thursday session earlier than usual.

It was a lovely spring evening, a rarity in Philadelphia, I'm sorry to say. While the other Sons went their individual ways,

Jack and I strolled down Locust Street together. We passed Rittenhouse Square, found a vacant bench near the fountain far removed from "hippie heaven" and sat down to talk. Jack seemed troubled. I asked him why. He stared into space for several seconds before answering.

"You know, Frank, I'm treasurer of Half-Way House. For the past twenty years."

I nodded. For an equal length of time I've been a regular contributor to this well-run institution which provides rehabilitation services for patients between their discharge from mental hospitals and their return home.

"Next to your cousin, Archie," Jack went on, "Ellen Eberhardt's been our biggest donor."

I knew that also. Unlike others who show little regard for the way their money is spent I always scrutinize each fiscal report mailed to me from recipients of my charities.

"Since Half-Way House was founded back in 1938, Frank, Ellen's check arrived without fail each April 16, the start of our fiscal year. No solicitation ever was necessary, her check provided a substantial portion of the budget. Perhaps we shouldn't have done so, but automatically we included it in our plans for the oncoming year. As a matter of fact, for the last couple years Ellen's been adding to her contribution, so we've been getting more than we expected.

"The check didn't arrive on the sixteenth but Art Harrison —he's our Administrator—wasn't concerned. You know, anything can happen to mail deliveries these days. Well, it didn't arrive on the seventeenth or eighteenth and on the nineteenth Art called me. I told him to rest easy; Mrs. Eberhardt was away and the check no doubt would be on hand within the next week.

"But I had a hard time convincing myself that this was the case. It wouldn't be in Ellen's character to forget any of her responsibilities. She *knew* we counted heavily on her money and without it we'd have to curtail operations considerably. Actually, we've projected an expanded job-training program and it occurs to me now this was at Ellen's suggestion. Besides being a very generous woman, Ellen's a professional social worker. She's operated on both sides of the fence and she's aware sponsors don't present new ideas unless they're prepared to pay for them out of their own pockets."

I was quite conscious of this. Many a time I've sat through

institutional directors' meetings simply bursting with excellent ideas but forced to remain silent because I'd be expected to assume their financial responsibilities. This may be ridiculous but it is a fact to be faced.

"Frank, I waited until May 1, our directors' meeting, and still no check. As far as the new program at Half-Way House was concerned, we either had to fish or cut bait. It's too late to 'fish' for another sponsor, so we cut bait, an unfortunate situation for clients. I've agreed to make up part of the deficit; a few other board members said they'd go along and maybe you'll help; you must be wallowing in Hollywood money. But it won't be nearly enough."

I have great sympathy for Half-Way House and while I was trying to guess how heavily Jack expected to "touch" me, I asked him if he'd given up on Ellen.

"Not until this afternoon, and what I tell you now is in confidence."

I listened attentively.

"I don't have to explain to you, Frank," he said with a slightly bitter smile, "I couldn't go directly to Ellen and ask her why she'd let us down. So instead I went to see George Hoffman; he's the Trust Officer at Continental where Ellen and the Dawsons have been banking for years. Besides, he's an old friend of Ellen. You know George—he's a member of the League and the Racquet.

"I had to tell him about our bet. He looked at me as though I'd gone out of my mind. Maybe I have, maybe we all have. I asked George point-blank if he knew whether there was any reason for Ellen's failure to send her usual Half-Way House contribution. I was still hoping then that in her absence she'd given George powers of attorney. That's what her mother and father used to do when they were away for long periods of time.

"I waited until George's secretary brought in the Dawson-Eberhardt file. He glanced at the last few pages, then shook his head.

" 'Half-Way House's not the only "victim," Jack,' he told me. 'Nothing went to United Fund, Friends Meeting, Lighthouse for the Blind, Settlement School, Powelton Shelter—all Dawson "pets" for half a century. This is the first year Ellen's not followed through on a single one.'

"I was shocked profoundly.

" 'You mean the Eberhardts made *no* contributions to *anyone?*'

"George gave me a funny look.

" 'I didn't say that, Jack. I told you they'd made no contributions to any of their "pets." '

" 'Don't be so damned enigmatic,' I said. 'Where did the Eberhardts' contributions go?'

" 'I won't tell you how much and I won't tell you which ones. I'll only tell you substantial sums have gone to every Right-wing group in the city, men and women you and I wouldn't be caught dead with.'

"I was horrified. I asked George whether Ellen herself had signed the checks or was the Colonel's signature on them. He said he wouldn't or couldn't tell me that either, but whichever Eberhardt signed, checks would be honored, all accounts are held jointly."

Jack said other ideas occurred to him. What was happening to the Eberhardts' bank statements? Were they being forwarded and, if so, where? What about their mail? Was this going to the Continental to be held for the Colonel and Ellen's return? This would be normal procedure for families without secretaries or direct business connections. Juliet and I have done it scores of times as have our friends.

"George refused to give any more information; he'd spoken more freely than he should have.

"I wouldn't presume upon our friendship to push him further, Frank."

For the first time since the Chase began, I hinted at something which lay deep within me. I turned abruptly to Jack and asked him if he believed Ellen was a victim of foul play, if he thought the Colonel had murdered his wife and disposed of the body. My fellow Son's reaction was not what I expected. He burst out laughing.

"Of course not, Frank. You've been reading too many detective stories. What did the Master say? Somebody's got to benefit from murder and I can't see where the Colonel would gain anything from his wife's death. Absolutely not financially and, outside of political differences, I think they got along reasonably well. You might slay your spouse because she trumps your ace, but you don't kill her because you love the Kennedys and your mate's preference is for Barry Goldwater."

Could there be another woman?

Jack chuckled.

"You know better than that, Frank. Philadelphia's a small town and if H. Wesley played around we'd have known it and *so would Ellen*. If she didn't discover on her own that her husband was a philanderer, you can bet someone would have gotten word to her. That's the one, and perhaps the only, cause for divorce Ellen might accept.

"We have to be objective; it's important. You don't like Eberhardt and you say you never did and I'm not overly fond of him right now. I'm upset that Dawson money no longer supports causes you and I and the Dawsons felt are good. But this again is subjective. Are we so self-righteous and sure of ourselves that we refuse to condone anything else? –

"I'll not try to convince you, not even myself, that Ellen changed her sense of *noblesse oblige* so drastically she readily consented to the use of Dawson funds to support Birchers or Minutemen, groups I suppose George was referring to. I will concede she may have grown tired of endless political theories advanced by her husband and his own set of friends and to keep the peace simply yielded."

I pointed out that this theory didn't hold water when you took into account Ellen's reputation as a quiet fighter for what she felt was right. I asked Jack just what made him think Ellen would have given up the philosophies generations of Quaker heritage instilled in her.

"That's all well and good, Frank. But you must also remember this same heritage gave her a healthy respect for the institution of marriage and a husband's right 'to sit at the head of the table.' This plus a dread of divorce. I never heard of a divorce in the Dawson family and I'll bet—I *must* stop using this word—you didn't either.

"I know I've spoken bitterly about the Colonel and probably made unfair or at least unproven charges against his character—charges I had no right to make. After all, we must remember it takes two to make a bargain. If we Sons hadn't been so anxious to prove our intellect was superior to H. Wesley's and if we hadn't wanted to make him eat crow for his remarks about the Master, there'd have been no wager. We'd be doing whatever it was we were doing before the Chase began and wouldn't be sitting on a park bench worrying."

There are times when Jack's Christian forbearance makes

me want to throw up and this was one of thém. Sitting on a park bench worrying? Indeed I *was* worrying about Ellen's physical and moral well-being. Poor girl, forced to live with a villain like H. Wesley for six months, away from civilized society.

CHAPTER

13

To THE annoyance of my fellow "hunters," the chuckles of the other Copper Beeches, the delight of Baker Street Irregulars all over the world (via the Associated Press), and to the dismay of Don Donaldson, the Philadelphia *Daily News* broke the story of our Chase on Friday, May 9, in a page one, byline story.

SIX SHERLOCKIANS SEEK SEVENTH

SEXTET OF DOYLE'S DEVOTEES
TRY TO OUTWIT COLLEAGUE
PRIZE IS $100,000

Since this past April 1, (sic) wrote Mr. Nels Nelson, a half-dozen members of a local club which exists to perpetuate the legend that Mr. Sherlock Holmes is not a legend, have donned peaked caps, filled their calabash pipes with Trichinopoli and set out to track a Brother.

These stalwarts have six months to accomplish their mission, which is to put the finger on Colonel (ret.) H. Wesley Eberhardt of Baskerville Hall and his wife Ellen (*née* Dawson and you know what *that* name means in these parts).

Should they succeed the hunters will be recipients of the famous Carl Anderson manuscripts, a collection of Sherlockiana valued at up to $100,000 and paid for by the loser. However, should the "fox" elude his hounds until September 29, he, not they, will become proud possessor of this valuable collection.

Under mutually agreed upon terms of the wager, the Colonel and his Lady may not stray more than 125 miles from home base and must not cross state lines. Our travel editor informs us that the point farthest west the intrepid couple is permitted to wander lies somewhere in the wilds of York County's Hex belt. The northern limit is Mahoopany, a village just short of the New York border.

Although we have no official authorization, we believe it reasonable to assume that any of the six will be delighted to hear by telephone, telegraph, or letter from citizens who think they have spotted either the Colonel or Mrs. Eberhardt.

For the record, the name of the club to which the sextet of sleuths belong is known as Sons of the Copper Beeches, the Quaker City branch of a worldwide organization, the Baker Street Irregulars, all members of which are Apostles of Mr. Sherlock Holmes.

There are 86 "Sons" on Copper Beech rolls and we venture to say that more than half of them are listed in the Social Register. Unfortunately, we cannot check this conclusion because our city desk's copy of the Blue Book was mislaid in 1927 and its publishers have not thought to send us a replacement.

We promise our millions of readers we will keep them advised of future developments and consequently urge them to continue to keep in touch. We also take this opportunity to advise the hunters that if they select a one-man delegation (our news room is rather crowded and six extra visitors would be a bit much), upon proper identification, he will be handed what the very highest authority has termed a valuable "clue."

The clue consists of a few dried leaves which at first this reporter, with limited experience in the field of botany, erroneously identified as marijuana. "Not pot," said Sergeant Ralph Earle of the Narcotics Squad, who examined the foliage under a microscope. Ergo, classification of the specimen must remain a task for the Sons should they claim it. We warn them, however, we shall hold on to this mangy bit of dehydrated flora for only a fortnight. It will then be disposed of any way its present owner sees fit.

On the picture page of that same issue were photographs of each of us, together with brief biographies. I must take Mr. Nelson to task for undue liberties when he declared me "a former Ivy Hall recluse who leaped to sudden fame when Hollywood bought his most recent book about sexual deviations in the nunneries of Spain." *Recluse* and *sudden* fame indeed! I venture to say that with the *possible* exception of Dr. Herbert Alexander there is no one in the entire profession better known than I in the field of late seventeenth and early eighteenth century Iberian culture.

I doubt if a single Son subscribes to the *Daily News* or even reads it except upon rare occasions. Yet within ten minutes after the appearance of the story in that scandal sheet, my phone began to ring and didn't cease all day. By noon I had a flood of telegrams and by 5 P.M. there were eight special delivery letters.

Even though all the messages, verbal and written, appeared to come from jokesters and even fellow Copper Beeches who facetiously offered every type of assistance (some of which are unprintable), I insisted on answering each call myself and carefully perused every telegram and letter. Juliet, piqued by the constant commotion, suggested that unless I was enjoying the hubbub, we disconnect the telephone and let the doorbell ring unanswered. I was adamant in my refusal to take this easy way out. "It would be unfair to my fellow hunters. You never can tell in this line of work from what unexpected source an important tip will arrive."

In those extremely brief intervals between phone calls I attempted to reach Jack and the other hunters but always heard the familiar busy signal.

"I'll bet they've taken *their* receivers off the hook," Juliet prophesied and upon this one occasion she was right, as I later learned. At nine o'clock just when I decided to call it a day the doorbell rang. It was Marv and I let him in. He looked exhausted.

"It's been ghastly, hasn't it?" he said and collapsed on a chair. I shrugged my shoulders. "I didn't mind," I told him. "It was my duty."

"Duty, my eye!" Juliet almost screamed. "Marv, that man

enjoyed every minute of it. But it's driving *me* out of my mind."

I had no desire to annoy my wife by telling her she was free to leave the house whenever she wished to but I refrained. Instead, I permitted her to switch the telephone line to our answering service and poured a stiff drink of Fundador for all three of us. As I felt the burning liquid pour down my throat, it was only then I recalled that I'd partaken of no solid food since breakfast. It had been an exciting and strenuous day and I was ravenous. Despite Marv's eagerness to discuss the situation I made him relax while I prepared my specialty, eggs Benedict served with thin sliced Irish rye toasted until it is light brown, then sprinkled delicately with oregano and garlic salt. I made enough for all three of us since I knew that Juliet, after formal but brief protests, would eat as much as Marv and I. It had been a trying day for the pathologist, too.

"You, at least could hole up, Frank, and refuse to answer the telephone or doorbell but I was in the office. Unless I wanted to hide on a slab with the other stiffs I was available for every jokester in Philadelphia. And this, my friend, includes at least half the Copper Beeches. They told me they tried to reach all six of us but settled for me.

"I did some checking. Ed's out of town, Jack's telephone's disconnected, Charlie's secretary's been rebuffing every caller, even me, and I don't know *where* the hell Don is, no answer at his home and all I could get from his city desk was that he was out on an assignment. They wouldn't say where or what."

But soon after we knew where Don had been, we heard it from his lips. My answering service called, apologizing for disturbing me at this late hour but said a Mr. Donaldson was anxious to speak with me.

"There are a dozen other calls waiting," she informed me and I could tell from the excited tone of her voice that she had read the *Daily News* story. I imagine that a large portion of subscribers to the tabloid are telephone operators and their ilk. However, I put her down as firmly as I know how, I had no intention of exchanging social chatter with the young lady. I informed her to advise Mr. Donaldson I would accept his call.

"That, Sir, is not the point," she said. "He's been unable to reach you directly because your line was busy and as long as you're on answering service we intercept your calls. Mr. Donaldson wants to know if he may come to your house now. He'll call me back shortly."

Fifteen minutes later Don was at the door. He had an odd expression on his face and looked as though he needed a drink so, without asking, I poured him a shot of bourbon with branch water, his favorite beverage.

"You'll never guess where I spent the last hour," he said. I had no desire to play twenty questions. I asked Don to tell us.

"At Bartram's" (Philadelphia's Botanical Garden). He took an envelope from his pocket and tossed the contents, a half-dozen dried leaves, on a coffee table.

"Know what it is?"

All three of us shook our heads. But Juliet, who considers herself somewhat of an amateur botanist, picked up one of the leaves which she examined carefully under the lamp. Since Don already knew the answer I saw no particular reason why we should await the results of my wife's analysis. Nevertheless, I sat patiently until she'd concluded her examination. She looked up at Don.

"It wouldn't be gorse?" she asked hesitatingly.

Don nodded and grinned.

"The lady's right. That's exactly what it is. Flowering gorse. And that from no less an authority than Dr. Maurice Katz, Bartram's curator. I see I wasted a lot of time, Juliet, tracking down the good doctor. I should have brought it directly to you."

I may not have recognized the plant since I made no claim to expertise in that discipline. But you can be sure I was aware immediately of its significance in the Chase. And so was Don and so was Marv. We looked at each other.

" 'The heath,' " we quoted in unison, " 'was covered with golden patches of flowering gorse; gleaming magnificently in the light of the bright spring sunshine.' "

We quoted chapter and verse—"Adventure of the Solitary Cyclist," page 91, paragraph three, volume two, *The Return of Sherlock Holmes*, official Morley Edition.

"Another clue from the Colonel? What he'd sent to the *Daily News*, Don?" I asked.

Don grinned. "Right on both counts, Frank. Another clue from H. Wesley Eberhardt and this time he may have overextended himself. Now, if you'll give *me* a refill I'll give *you* the rest of the story."

I poured another bourbon and branch water for our journalistic friend and a couple of brandies for Marv and me. Then to my astonishment Juliet, who usually becomes bored immediately when anything about the Sacred Writings is discussed and rarely drinks a nightcap, poured a stiff one for herself.

"I want to hear it, too," she said. "I've been listening to this private eye all day long and I almost hope the Colonel wins. Go on, Don. Give."

We settled back to listen.

"I started the day with a handicap. The minute I walked into the newsroom, John Raleigh, who was on the city desk, held up a copy of the *News*.

"'Welcome, Sherlock. Do you suppose you'll be able to spare a few hours from your extracurricular activities for an assignment or two?'

"'What's up now, El Jefe?' I asked that sarcastic so and so. Then he showed me Nels' piece. I knew this was going to happen—I told you fellows that—but why did it have to be written by that snide bastard?

"'A rich reporter,' he said, injecting the needle where it hurt. 'I wish *I* could afford to lose twenty thousand dollars on some silly manhunt. Do you suppose your paper might count on an exclusive at one stage in your game? Or are you moonlighting for the *News?*'

"Well, it went on all day; every one of my colleagues pulling some corny gag. I was glad to get the hell out of the office for a bridge dedication.

"I called Nels from a pay station. I knew him well; we used to work together on the *Pottsville Republican*.

"'How does it feel to be a celebrity and have your picture in the paper?' he asked. 'And was the artwork satisfactory? I thought you looked cute in your soldier suit. I vetoed that photograph we took of you when you won the Pulitzer. Too sophisticated.'

"I let him rave. Finally he quit and asked me what I wanted. He knew it wouldn't be an interview. I told him I'd buy him a drink and tell him then."

They met at the Pen and Pencil around five o'clock.

"I got there a few minutes early, there were three or four guys at the bar, including Wilton Krogman, my colleague and the world's chief ribber. It was rough going. 'Here comes

Sherlock' and 'Quick Watson, the needle.' I took it standing, there was nothing else I could do. Finally Nels walked in, we carried our drinks to a back table and in a couple of minutes I found out what I wanted to know.

" 'First of all,' Nels told me, 'the tip came to our city room late yesterday from a caller who identified himself as Colonel H. Wesley Eberhardt. What he had to say was so offbeat that Bergie, who was on the desk, turned it over to me.

" 'This was a funny story and it didn't need verification even though six, well five anyway, prominent Philadelphians were involved. Nobody'd be libeled. I asked the Colonel if this was an exclusive and he said yes, providing I gave him my word I wouldn't tip it off to any of you. He said it would be a lot more fun if it came as a surprise. I agreed.

" 'When he got finished talking he said he'd like to buy me a drink. I said sure but I asked him if he wasn't afraid I'd bring a posse of Sons along. He laughed, said I'd given him my word and that was enough. Pretty damned smart psychology, too, put me on the defensive. I had to trust him then as much as he was trusting me. After all, Don, I *might* have called you and collected quite a few bucks from you rich Sons of Beeches.

" 'Just to make sure it would be the Colonel whom I'd never seen and didn't know, I checked our morgue, got a brief biog and his picture, the one we took when he joined the staff at Valley Forge. He suggested we meet at the Winthrop.' "

I was puzzled. I am a Philadelphian of long standing and I never heard of the Winthrop. Don enlightened us. He said it was a small hotel, very clean, apparently run like a *pension* (Don's word was boardinghouse) for retired, "at liberty," members of the theatrical profession. Not important ones who stay at the Bellevue, he explained, but entertainers in neighborhood restaurants and bars on Saturday nights, members of small traveling dance bands, carnivals or midget circuses which are set up on shopping centers and parking lots.

"There's nothing wrong with the Winthrop," Don continued. "It's quite respectable."

I asked Don where it is and his answer was, "Ninth Street above Locust, right around the corner from the Walnut Street Theatre."

I gasped. Right around the corner from the Walnut Street

Theatre indeed! Almost right around the corner from where the four of us were now sitting.

Marv grinned. *"Chutzpah!* I told you before that's what the Colonel's got. Go on with your story, Don."

" 'The Colonel matched our morgue shot,' Nels told me. 'He seemed like a hell of a nice guy. He could hardly stop laughing when we talked about what would happen to you Sons when my story broke. He says I can picture what several of them will be doing tomorrow night, probably sitting around Frank's house not five minutes from here, tearing their hair out with annoyance. Oh, he says, how I wish I could be around to see their faces.

" 'We had a couple of drinks. Then the Colonel had to go and so did I. He asked me if he could give me a lift but I had my Rambler parked outside. We shook hands and I wished him luck. He was just getting into his car when he turned around and handed me this envelope. I almost forgot, he said. Please turn it over to the hunters. Tell them it's a clue.' "

I informed Don it was too bad his friend, Nels, didn't think of taking the Colonel's license number.

"Don't sell Nels short, Frank. He did."

Well, this was the proper time for refills. I opened another bottle and crushed some ice. Don went on.

"Today's been busy. I finished my desk assignments and knocked off at three. I put through a call to the Bureau of Motor Vehicles in Harrisburg. The 'UD' on the tag made me know it was out of a car rental agency but there was no way of telling which one. I was to call back in an hour. Then I went right to the Winthrop. I once did a feature on Mighty Mame years ago. She remembered me and let me go through her register for the past couple of days. I should have known something was up because she stood over me the whole time, grinning.

"You fellows know what I was looking for, of course, but there was neither an H. Wesley nor a Joe Eberhardt signature. However, two others caught my eye."

Don stopped and looked at Marv and me.

"One name," he said (and I felt he was being over-dramatic), "was Oscar Meunier, the other Jabez Parker. What's their significance, gentlemen?"

It was obvious from Don's glance and chuckle that Marv's and my response was just what was to be expected. Like an old time ministrel end-man I sang out, "Oscar Meunier of Geneva, Switzerland!" and Marv, "Right, Mr. Interlocutor. The other is Jabez Parker, of London, England." Both Meunier and Parker figure in one of the Master's later cases soon after his miraculous return from Reichenbach Fall.

"You guessed right," Don said in what he supposed was a complimentary tone. I should have admonished him, it was *not* a guess.

"When Mame saw me stop at those two names, one below the other on the register for Wednesday, May 1, she asked me if I had found what I was looking for. Then she burst out laughing, all three hundred pounds shaking so hard she could hardly stop to hand me a pair of neatly wrapped packages. She said these were left for me.

" 'For me?' 'Well, not exactly you, Don. The tallest of the two gents said I was to hand them to anybody who was curious about those particular names. He told me he was sure there'd be someone around asking.' "

I was waiting for more of Don's dramatics. They came. From the side of his jacket he extracted the two "gifts," both of which were wrapped although, quite easily, they could have been exposed to Don's view and then retied.

"Just the way I got them," he said and tossed one to me and the other to Marv. A small tag pasted on mine read: "I do think the enclosed is an excellent likeness. O. Meunier."

While the others watched with patience I carefully untied the string and unwrapped the paper. Despite my desire to see what was inside I wanted to preserve all potential clues in their original form. The Master would have done no less.

"Control yourself," I said to my wife who, in her impatience, was practically breathing down my neck. "It might explode." As she withdrew hastily, I removed a thin tissue to expose a small wax bust no bigger than a child's fist. The figure was that of a nasty, effeminate old man with a long, pointy nose, recessed chin, receding hairline and thin, drawn cheeks.

"A likeness, indeed. How ridiculous!" I said, but Juliet, as I anticipated, burst out laughing. "It's marvelous," she shrieked. "Who's Oscar Meunier? He must know you as well as I do."

Don, I could see, was about to make a similar comment but I silenced that young man with a sharp look.

Quite coldly I informed my wife that O. Meunier was a Swiss sculptor who once did a bust of the Master. Marv's present was a cruel joke, a tiny metal lyre from Mighty Mame's second guest, Parker, who, to quote the Master, was "a remarkable performer on the jew's harp."

"I don't know what the Colonel was trying to prove," Marv commented. "But let's hear the rest, Don. What about the car?"

Even before Don told us I informed him in whose name the Colonel would have rented the automobile. "John Clayton of No. 3 Turpey Street, the Borough," I predicted and I was correct. Clayton was the owner of a cab for hire which figured in *The Hound*.

"You are on the button, Frank," Don said. "It was the Colonel's first 'crime.' He gave a false name to the rental agency. I don't know how he got away with it without showing a matching driver's license but he did. It is possible, though, he showed the clerk his own and merely stated the Cadillac was to be used for his boss, John Clayton, or some such covering story."

Marv shook his head in wonderment. "Man oh man! The old boy's really taking us for a ride now, isn't he?"

This was neither the time for levity nor praise of H. Wesley Eberhardt for cleverness.

"Now let me tell you about the gorse," Don continued. "Ever since I read 'The Adventure of the Solitary Cyclist' I always wondered what the hell gorse was but not until an hour ago did I find out."

I might have informed Don that any true Sherlockian would have found out "what the hell gorse was" when he first heard mention of the plant in the Sacred Writings. However, I forgave our journalistic friend and tolerantly attributed this failure to his youth.

"Actually, the Gardens were closed, but I know Dr. Katz well enough to telephone him at his home on the grounds. So I asked his permission to bring the specimens there. 'Gorse,' he said as soon as he saw it, just as quickly as you did, Juliet. He told me the plant is so called furze and that cattle use it for forage. I asked him where it blooms, thinking of the Colonel's one-hundred-twenty-five-mile radius.

"'It's strictly a European shrub, Don. I don't believe it grows anywhere else in the world, at least not wild and certainly not this type.'

"Incidentally, he hadn't read the *News'* story. I gave him

the whole schmeer, the bet and everything else including the extent of the area we hunters had to search."

Don said Dr. Katz was intrigued and, like many others with little aptitude, liked to play detective.

" 'There's got to be something here relevant to your Chase, Don. It *is* a clue, I agree. I told you furze grows only in Europe but I'm only the Garden curator, which means a lot of people working for me know more than I do. Let me see if I can get hold of Joe Spelman. He's our expert on eastern United States flora.' "

Our young journalist paused, then turned to all of us, a satisfied smile on his face.

"We got our answer from Spelman," he said. "In 1959, a Commonwealth botanist experimented with gorse-planting up in the Snyder County State Forest. I'll spare you the details. It grew all right but couldn't be used commercially because it required too much soil care. Well, they kept what they have going hoping that someday they'll be able to find out why it grows wild every place in Europe but not in Pennsylvania or other parts of the country."

The map I'd drawn so painstakingly was in Jack's possession but I do have an atlas which we consulted. The eastern end of Snyder County was well within our 125-mile limit.

"What in God's name would the Eberhardts be doing up in Snyder County?" Marv asked. "I don't know the section well but every couple of hunting seasons I get a call from their coroner asking me to help figure out whether some sportsman's been murdered or shot accidentally. This is one of the areas where the Colonel and his Lady would stick out like sore thumbs. Not much in that neck of the woods except farms, villages, and hunting lodges."

Don interrupted.

"Wait a minute! Wait a minute! See if McClure's within the boundaries. It's only a little bit of a town."

McClure wasn't on my map. None of us were in the mood to wait until the next day.

"I'll call Jack," I said. "It's only eleven o'clock. He doesn't usually retire until midnight."

Jack was exhausted from the day's trials but he could not sleep. When I briefed him about the development of our new set of clues he perked up. He checked McClure on my map; his answer was disappointing.

"One-hundred-and-twenty-nine-and-a-half statute miles from City Hall," he told me. Official distances from Philadelphia to all other points are measured from a marker in the center of City Hall courtyard.

Don shook his head. "Something's wrong. Ask him to check again, will you, Frank?" I did and Jack's answer was the same.

"Look fellows," Don said, "I've a hunch, I'm sure I'm right."

We pressed Don to tell us what his hunch was but he refused, albeit with a smile.

"Who'll gamble and drive to McClure with me tomorrow? I'll be free about three P.M. and we should be back before midnight."

I acquiesced at once but Marv claimed he had an obligation he simply could not slough off to anyone else.

"Let me ask Jack right away," I went on, "before he does go to sleep," and Don wanted to check with his "partner," Ed Johnson. As it worked out, all four of us, Jack, Ed, Don, and I met in front of the *Inquirer* office at three. We'd asked Charlie to come along but he, like Marv, had other unbreakable commitments. We used Ed's car, a roomy Mercedes, rather than Don's light uncomfortable Volks.

Before we pulled away Don carefully noted the speedometer reading. "I'll add exactly five-tenths of a mile," he said, "the distance from here to City Hall. We'll check again when we get to where we're going."

He had a funny smile when he looked at Jack, who was sitting in the rear seat with me. "I'm sure you were accurate," he said, "but I'll still bet we won't go one-hundred-twenty-five miles."

Even though three of us, far more mature in our judgments than Don, had blindly agreed to accompany him on what might well prove to be a wild goose chase, he refused to tell us where we were going until we'd turned off the main highway at Selinsgrove and headed northwest.

"Any of you fellows ever hear of The Bean Soup?" he asked.

A silly question. Of course we'd all heard of bean soup.

"I don't mean *bean soup*. I mean *The* Bean Soup."

This sounded like double talk but apparently it made sense to Ed.

"My God, Don," he said. "I haven't heard of the McClure Bean Soup since I was a kid. Isn't that where they cook bean soup the way they did during the Civil War and serve it to a hell of a big crowd of maybe thirty, forty thousand people?"

"Right, Ed," Don answered. "That's the main part of the show. There's more to it than that. Let me tell Frank and Jack what it's all about and why I think we might end our hunt tonight."

Now Don had our complete attention.

"I won't go into the whole history but The McClure Bean Soup—and that's just what it's called—is about the biggest annual celebration in Central Pennsylvania. Why it isn't better known I don't understand. It began this way. In 1891 the local GAR post held its first reunion and their old cook prepared bean soup the way he'd prepared it during the war. That's all they served except for hardtack and it went over big. Next year they did it again only this time the vets brought their families along.

"The gathering kept getting bigger and bigger. Everybody from the surrounding farms and villages, as far as fifty miles off, started pouring into McClure. The celebration stretched out first to two days, then three days, and now it's a full week. Well, the politicos couldn't pass up the chance to talk to captive audiences that size. So, for the last half century The Bean Soup is where statewide campaigns for Governor, U. S. Senator, and all the lesser lights of both parties unofficially launch their campaign. It's a sort of trial balloon."

I couldn't see where this had the slightest connection with our mission. I advised Don that unless he had something far more specific in mind, something applicable to the Chase, I felt we were wasting valuable time. I, for one, had no desire to hear what *any* candidate of *either* party had to say; I'd heard it all before.

"Relax, Frank," Don said, "I'm coming to that."

I'm the most relaxed person in the world and I detest anyone suggesting that I'm not always at ease. But I merely shrugged my shoulders and waited.

"This won't be the first time I'll be at The Bean Soup. When Ray Hendrickson ran for Governor, I covered his campaign trail which started right here. By that time The Bean Soup had developed into an enormous 'homecoming celebration.' They'd built a huge grandstand where they put on free acts, bands from six or seven central Pennsylvania counties played and in addition they brought in a circus or a carnival."

The trend of Don's reasoning was becoming apparent. We all felt the Colonel might be hiding out with Brother Joe, if the latter were still alive. The younger Eberhardt had been in show biz. Why couldn't he be connected with a carnival or circus? What an ingenious place for H. Wesley to hide out. And Ellen, too, if she was a good sport.

I expressed this opinion aloud.

"That," said Don, "is what our trip is all about. This morning I checked with a friend. He used to work on the *Inquirer* but retired about six years ago and bought out the Snyder County *Plain Dealer,* a good weekly. I wanted to make sure they had some grandstand acts and a carnival. They had a circus earlier in the week but it left. The carnival's still there and it's a pretty good-sized one. He did tell me the name but I've forgotten it.

"We'll be arriving at the peak hour. The grandstand and midway'll be jammed. I think we ought to separate and spread out. Let's meet every hour at the *Plain Dealer* tent. Jon Mungie who runs the paper said it's just to the right of the grandstand. He'll either be there himself or his wife'll know where he is. We're to see him later."

Don appeared to be taking over the arrangements but I had no particular objection so we let him go ahead.

"Suppose you, Frank, and Jack start your 'tour of duty' on the midway, one of you on each side. Meanwhile Ed and I will cover the grandstand. Don't pass up anybody or anything suspicious [as if I would]. Ed and I will cover the grandstand performers, I'll get one of the Mungies to introduce us to whoever's running the show and also the carnival owner. See if we can get anything from them, although they're a pretty clannish lot and protect their own."

He paused, looked at each of us and sighed deeply.

"I think we've better than an even chance of making it tonight. I sure hope so. Everything points that way."

I could see why Don would want to wind up the Chase for fiscal reasons alone. Even though his financial interest in the result was far less than any of ours, I did feel sorry for the position in which he allowed himself to be maneuvered. However, I did *not* see why "everything pointed" to a successful conclusion. I almost felt we'd been unduly swayed by this young man's enthusiasm.

All of a sudden we found ourselves in a minor traffic jam as cars seemed to pour out from nowhere. It was hardly what you'd expect to find on a narrow country lane in one of the few remaining rural areas of our highly industrialized state.

"We're almost there now," Don said. He didn't have to point that out to us. Not far ahead we could see the lights of a ferris wheel turning rapidly and hear the sounds of people, a hum at first then, as we approached the entrance gate, an undulating roar.

"Look at your speedometer," Don then advised Ed who made a swift mental calculation. Including the distance from the *Inquirer* to City Hall, he told us we'd traveled exactly 123-4/10 miles. Don smiled. "McClure's two miles west. At the most, The Bean Soup grounds couldn't be more than a mile from the entrance gate. So even if the Colonel were at the far end he'd still be within his 'territorial' limits."

As a State Trooper directed Ed to a parking lot a few hundred yards from the gate, our nostrils suddenly were assailed by a marvelous fragrance. We'd eaten nothing but a tasteless sandwich on the Turnpike in one of those wretched, expensive, clinical Howard Johnson's. We sniffed the new bouquet hungrily.

Don grinned. "That's it! The bean soup. Two bits a plate. The first round's on me."

Beneath a large shed just inside the entrance gate huge iron vats of liquid were simmering over banked wooden fires. Don tossed down a dollar on the counter and a man, dressed in Union blue, filled four plates and handed one to each of us. I've eaten the famed onion brew they served after three A.M. in Les Halles, the bouillabaisse and vichyssoise in a dozen three-star Michelins. But never in my life did a soup so tantalizingly delicious as that served in this hick village pass my lips.

We had three more "rounds." With deep regret I refused Don's offer to buy the fifth. But I did ask the gentleman behind the counter if he had a container large enough to hold a few quarts of this incredible soup to take home with me. He smiled, produced a large glass jar which, for the modest sum of $1.50, he filled to the brim. I persuaded the Union "soldier" to hold it for me until our departure time. One of the great regrets of my life is that by the time that evening ended so much occurred that I actually forgot to pick up my prize jar until we were more than half-way home. Had I been alone I certainly would have been tempted to return to McClure. But the hour was so late I thought this would be unfair to my companions, all of whom, including myself, were harboring feelings of frustration, bewilderment, and chagrin. Yet, in this otherwise unpleasant potpourri was a smidgeon of well-founded hope.

, CHAPTER

14

A BANNER fully thirty feet wide and ten feet high announced that the carnival playing on McClure's "Homecoming" lot was "Gibson and Fowler's Giant, Uncomparable [sic] American Shows." Don pointed out the newspaper tent and we synchronized our watches. Then he and Ed took off for the grandstand, Jack turned left on the midway and I turned to the right. This was the first time I'd been to a carnival in perhaps a half-century and I'd all but forgotten the sounds, sights, and smells that assailed my senses.

There were countless attractions. In addition to the tallest ferris wheel I'd ever seen, there was an enormous merry-go-round adorned with thousands of spinning lights and from its center a calliope was emitting nostalgic tunes. There were other amusements not all reminiscent of my childhood—rocket ships, trips to the moon, and space gliders.

These were stretched along the center of the midway. On my right, and I presumed the same was true of Jack's left, were endless numbers of stands containing gambling wheels, bingo tables, and other games of chance; in front of each hard-looking, gravel-voiced men were barking, "Tellya what I'm gonna do." I noted that a good many of the yokels were heeding their calls, foolishly tossing away hard earned money they certainly could have used to better advantage.

One beady-eyed carnival worker—"pitchmen," I believe they're called—viewed me speculatively. I supposed to his trained eye I appeared quite different from the badly attired array of men parading along the midway. This furtive fellow, with a large Semitic nose, said softly as I approached, "I need a winner. Tellya what I'm gonna do. Everybody's supposed to score a hundred to win one of these prizes."

He turned around and pointed to shelves filled with wrist-watches, radios, and portable television sets. I know something about merchandise and unless my eyes have grown dim the prizes on display were as acceptable as anything seen, for example, in Wanamaker's.

He continued in a conspiratorial fashion, putting down a wet, malodorous cigar, and pushing his thick lips so close to my ear I felt contaminated.

"But for you, Sir, I'll lower the score to seventy-five and I'll give you a 'red one' to start out with. That counts for twenty so you only need fifty-five more points to be a big winner. All I wanna make sure of is that you'll let these hillbillies see the radio, television set, wristwatch, or movie camera a *real* gentleman won."

He winked again.

"The first roll's free, Sir. Here," he urged, "take these eight little balls and throw them on this board. See how high a score you can make."

I have a reputation for the care in which I examine any project I undertake, large or small, weighing all contingencies. So I meticulously noted that the board had six rows of deep indentations, each bearing a number from one to eight. Providing that only four of the balls fell into these holes, my average, by every law of mathematics, had to be a minimum of sixteen points per throw. Ergo, if the winning total was seventy-five, it should take me a maximum of five throws to reach eighty, five more than the required amount.

I accepted the offer; what could I possibly lose? I took the balls in my right hand, bent low, and tossed them directly to the center of the board where I noted the largest collection of high numbers was bunched. The carnival man gasped in amazement when he began the count.

"My God, Sir! You've hit forty-eight your first roll. Sure as my name's Gypsy Joe I never seen nothing like that and I been in this business twenty-five years."

I *was* pleased. Of course I didn't let the fellow know I play a rather fast hand at backgammon. Actually my count was only twenty-one points but I could have been in error. The fellow admittedly was in the "business" for a quarter of a century so his addition surely was more accurate than mine. He had already removed the balls from the board so there could have been no recount even had I insisted.

I smiled pleasantly enough at the fellow and began to walk away. After all, I had more important tasks that evening than to demonstrate certain of my innate skills. But the carnival man crooked his finger and called me back to the counter.

"Just a second, Sir," he said, turned around to raise a canvas wall in the back of his stand, then looked furtively to the right and left. Once more he whispered in my ear.

"Sir. My boss is a thief. I'm quittin' him after we tear down tomorrow night but I'd like to see that he gets took good before I walk out on the son-of-a-bitch."

I was totally disinterested in discussing the morals of Gypsy Joe's employer. But never have I been consciously rude to anyone regardless of his social or economic standing. So I listened to what he had to say.

"You got forty-eight your first roll. Like I said, Sir, I never seen nothin' like it before. You need only twenty-seven points more to win anything on the shelf. Gimme a buck. Maybe you'll have the same luck next time but even if you don't let *me* do the addin'."

He winked once more. This was fair enough so I opened my change purse from which I extracted the required bill, handed it to him, and rolled again. I let Gypsy Joe make the count. Possibly because I was overconfident this second time my total was only eighteen. But the carnival fellow appeared quite pleased; he must have detested his employer.

"Now, Sir, you need ony eight points more." Surely forty-eight and eighteen make sixty-six leaving nine, not eight, to be earned. But perhaps the Gypsy was giving me a bonus of some sort. My third roll would cost two dollars, Joe said, but should I make those few needed points he would permit me to select any two items on the shelf.

"That'll fix my goddamned boss right," he told me out of the corner of his mouth. By this time a rather large crowd had gathered around the stand to witness my manual dexterity. Naturally they were unaware of the enmity between the

Gypsy and his employer and as far as they were concerned, the winning number was one hundred points. Neither Joe nor I enlightened them. My third roll, which I thought was extremely poor, almost sent Joe into ecstasies.

"Six and a half points," he practically shouted. "This gentleman needs only one and a quarter points to win." I hadn't noticed before that some of the holes bore fractions of numbers. However, at this stage of the game, when I needed so few more points to win, I thought that to complain would be caviling.

"It's four dollars this throw, Sir."

I had no singles left so I took a ten-dollar bill from my wallet, making damn sure I received the proper change. This time, there would be little chance of failure to reach seventy-five. I could then walk off with *three* prizes. Or, if I so chose, Joe advised me, I could have $150 cash in their stead.

I was about to roll when I felt a tap on my shoulder. I turned around; it was Don accompanied by a tall, handsome gentleman whom he introduced me to as Sheriff Dave Roberts. I was a little annoyed at the unwarranted interruption when I was so close to winning. I assumed the law officer was looking for Joe's employer to take him into custody. Instead he spoke sternly to the pitchman.

"How much you into the gentleman, Joe?"

The Gypsy grinned cheerfully.

"Six bucks, Dave. We oney just got started."

The sheriff looked at me.

"Is the amount correct, Sir?"

I nodded. That was the sum involved, it was true. However, this was not the appropriate moment to talk about the proposal Joe had given me *sub rosa*. So I graciously accepted the six dollars he peeled from a thick roll of bills. This time it was I who winked. "See you later," I whispered. But the Gypsy shook his head dolefully, frustrated at the last moment in his try to seek revenge against a dishonest employer.

Don told me why he had to stick his two cents in.

"You didn't show up at the newspaper office a half hour ago. We thought maybe you'd tracked down the Colonel and needed our help."

At Jack's suggestion, Don informed both Jon Mungie, the newspaper publisher, and the latter's friend, Sheriff Roberts, about the bet. Both of these men agreed to assist us in combing the carnival midway. I wondered whether my fellow Sons realized that by bringing Sheriff Roberts into the picture we had, for the first time, sought the help of a professional. However, he did us little good except, perhaps, save some of our time.

Before we left the midway I was convinced Colonel H. Wesley Eberhardt either was on the lot that very night or had been with the carnival quite recently. I am sure of my ground because no reasonable person could attribute solely to coincidence the quantity and quality of evidence I uncovered.

At the first of our hourly meetings in the newspaper office, Don and Ed admitted that their initial investigation into the background of personnel performing for the huge grandstand audience revealed nothing. Including the Snyder County veterans' band, consisting of eighty-six players plus their leader, a total of 127 men and women had appeared on stage. The agent who billed all acts was able to vouch for each of his entertainers. As for the band, every member was a local resident and either Sheriff Roberts or Mr. Mungie could testify to that fact.

Don and Ed had been introduced to the carnival owners who, at the moment, were elsewhere but there was present a Mr. Sillman, a rather slick-looking fellow wearing a hound's-tooth vest. Mr. Mungie told us this was the carnival "patch" who acted as the liaison between management, labor, and local law enforcement authorities. Mr. Sillman certainly got off on the wrong foot. It was obvious, from the fellow's initial remark, that either Don or the sheriff, both possibly, without any knowledge of my understanding with the Gypsy, had pointed the finger of scorn at me.

"I hear *you* were trying to take *Joe*," Sillman said, a wise smirk on his oleaginous face. I didn't bother to answer and barely touched the fellow's fingertips when we were introduced. However, I do admit being resentful of Don, who had the effrontery to place me in the same category as those yokels streaming past me on the midway.

The patch promised his cooperation, whatever that might be worth, and I had a feeling it wouldn't be worth much. He'd been told whom we were seeking without revealing details of the bet. The sheriff furthermore assured Sillman that the missing Colonel was not wanted by the law.

"You *have* to say that, gentlemen," he informed us after

Sillman had left, presumably to question certain recent employees. "Carnies are a very clannish lot. They'll tell you nothing about any of their co-workers no matter how hard they're pressed, so you need the cooperation of the patch. Even on a carnival like Gibson and Fowler's which is about as legitimate as they come, a man could hide forever. Well, if not forever, at least until the season's over."

He shook his head.

"There are fifteen hundred employees on this lot—bums, con men, freaks, alcoholics, dope addicts, gamblers, wife beaters, fugitives and quite a few good guys including, to my knowledge, at least two college professors who travel with carnivals as soon as their school terms end. But all these diverse men, women, and children who come from damned near every walk of life and all fifty states have one thing in common. They protect their own—always!"

I did not agree with the sheriff on this point. Perhaps his personality was such that *he* was unable to draw these people out. Admittedly carnies were a close-mouthed group who did not betray confidences to strangers. Yet, in the course of only a few minutes hadn't I made a friend of one who squealed on a fellow carny, his boss at that? But I did not want to hurt the sheriff's feelings so I remained silent. He went on.

"This is my fifth, four-year term of office. I'll bet you I've tramped fifty carnival midways from end to end looking for somebody who's wanted. Or maybe just showing my face to let 'em know we're on deck. Otherwise they'd separate our gullible citizens from their last buck.

"G&F's not the only carnival we get in Snyder County which covers a lot of square miles. Four or five others come 'round every summer. Most of them are considerably smaller than G&F's and several have broken down equipment and all manner of crooked wheels and games. We must keep after them every minute they're open. Otherwise you can't imagine how they'd take our local citizenry."

I could imagine it quite easily, with all those thieves mingling among these unsophisticated farmers and hillbillies.

"Once in a while," the sheriff went on, "we get a really hot fugitive, wanted for a serious crime. The FBI or our state police are sure he's on a Snyder County midway. Between my men and theirs we turn the lot upside down and inside out.

This way we mostly get our man. It's a hell of a lot of hard work. We've used as many as twenty officers and agents to flush out a small carnival with perhaps no more than seventy-five employees. Even under the best circumstances we've often found our bird flown."

He shook his head.

"You can imagine how tough it would be to finecomb a carnival as big as G&F's. Look at that midway!"

We turned around. Men, women, and children were packed so tightly they had to inch along. We thought we'd grown inured to the noise but suddenly it became overpowering. We understood what the sheriff meant.

"Take at least fifty cops plus the cooperation of the owners and we still couldn't be sure we had him," Sheriff Roberts went on. "Besides, I have no legal right to interfere. As far as your knowledge goes the Colonel's committed no crime."

Ed answered. "That's correct. We couldn't swear out a legal warrant nor do we have the right to ask you to make an arrest. And that wouldn't be our game, even if we could."

The sheriff nodded.

"You bit off a pretty good-sized mouthful, gentlemen, and I wish you luck. I repeat, I wouldn't be at all surprised if your fox was on this lot right now, so look well before you go home. I'll even be more surprised if you find him. He sounds like a smart cookie. I wouldn't want to be up against a pro like the Colonel if he *was* wanted. To pick a carnival lot and be accepted on one shows an astute brain and characteristics of a chameleon."

He grew thoughtful.

"I don't have the same peace of mind you do about Mrs. Eberhardt. But then I don't know either her or her husband except what you tell me. If I were you I'd concentrate on the lady. You tell me he promised to take her wherever he goes. You believe him. I'm not sure you're right. If you are then she's here, too.

"But can you picture a real lady running the dice game or duck pond or working at the cookhouse in blackface? Maybe she could hide out in the Dark Ride or the Mirror Maze but it would get awfully boring after ten or twelve hours. Unless the Colonel has her stashed away in his own trailer or camper I'd say she'd be in a nearby motel. There are quite a few in the vicinity. However, you've no legal right to look at their registers. And I doubt if they'd show 'em to you voluntarily."

He smiled.

"Might embarrass quite a few of our young folks and possibly some of the older ones also. But this shouldn't stop you from making the effort."

I'm not sure our meeting with the sheriff did anything for us except perhaps stress the difficulties of our Chase. As a parting shot he added another element—that of fear.

"What troubles me most," he said, "is the gorse."

We looked puzzled, considering it merely another one of those clues the Colonel insisted on taunting us with.

"Are you troubled about 'our' gorse or gorse in general?" Ed asked.

" 'Your' gorse. Anybody's gorse."

"But why?" Ed persisted.

"Before I went into politics I was going to be a ranger," Sheriff Roberts went on. "I got my degree in forestry at Penn State. My major was botany."

He smiled.

"I'm not trying to demonstrate my erudition, gentlemen. After all, I'm only a hick sheriff. But the word 'gorse' comes from a Latin root, *hordeum,* the verb *horrere,* to bristle with fear. This I think is why the Master used it in 'The Adventure of the Solitary Cyclist.' "

Don was first to ask the question.

"You're a BSI, Sheriff?"

Roberts shook his head.

"A mere devotee, unfortunately the only Sherlockian within fifty miles. Which may be the reason I've spent so much time talking with you gentlemen instead of being where I should be, in our field office on the midway. If you'll excuse me I'll say so long and wish you the best. Call me if I can be of further help. Meanwhile, if you don't have any serious objections I'll do a bit of checking myself."

Don said we'd be grateful and invited the sheriff to be his guest at the next Copper Beech meeting when we'd either have won or lost our bet. We shook hands, then Roberts departed. It was past nine o'clock but I was by no means ready to abandon our search of the midway no matter how my fellow Sons felt. I suggested we make our rounds in earnest. While I knew my first call would be on my new-found friend,

Gypsy Joe, whom I intended to pump, I said nothing of this to the others.

I wanted to end the Chase quickly. I, too, began to feel concern for Ellen's safety.

CHAPTER

15

MUNGIE, THE newspaper publisher who'd said little or nothing during our talk with the sheriff, took Don and Ed to the carnival office. There they had permission to go through personnel records, a task we all agreed was essential although not one of us believed this would turn up information about the Colonel or Brother Joe.

With Sillman their reluctant escort, our two Sons would then speak to several selected old-time carnival laborers—roughies is what they were called—in an attempt to ferret out information.

"You're not gonna get much from these fellows," the patch said. "They just won't talk. I'm only doin' it because the sheriff asked me to."

It turned out Sillman was right. Meanwhile Jack and I resumed our respective walks around the midway. I pushed my way through the crowd directly to the Gypsy's stand which had quite a few people in front of it. I wasn't sure I wished to re-involve myself in that scheme to punish Joe's dishonest employer. However, I had already committed myself, and my own sense of integrity would not permit me to withdraw without explaining why to this humble fellow with obviously decent instincts and a sense of justice.

Joe, however, was bent down over his counter talking confidentially to some denim-jacketed hillbilly and I had difficulty attracting his attention. When he finally saw me he rolled his eyes heavenward and shook his head violently. I managed to get close enough to hear him say, *"Please* go 'way, Professor. I been told to lay off." By this I took it to mean his boss had returned and made threats. So I assured the Gypsy I'd return later. "Don't hurry," he answered, and I thought this was kind of him.

I passed several more gambling stands each of which was not unlike Joe's although some of them had wheels. It may have been the quality of my attire (although the truth is I was wearing one of the few ready-made suits I own) that attracted the attention of every "agent," which is what the sheriff called them. Each of these fellows appeared to single me out of the crowd to offer me special attention. I had a duty to perform and politely, yet firmly, refused to listen to what they were "gonna do."

Very shortly thereafter I found myself in a section of the midway where games of chance apparently were outlawed. In this area were the Dark Ride and the Mirror Maze, both mentioned by Roberts as potential hideouts for Ellen. I pondered these for a couple of moments, trying to make up my mind whether to engage their cashiers in conversation. However, both were so busy selling tickets I was afraid they'd have no time to talk, so I abandoned the idea and moved on.

A loud-mouthed barker (the man who stands on a platform and urges the marks to pay an admission fee) was proclaiming that inside a large trailer behind him was "The Royal Rolls Royce." He kept speaking directly to me so I walked up and asked the fellow what was meant. He informed me that inside was the limousine once owned by Edward, Prince of Wales, and in it he and his Baltimore-born wife, Wally Simpson, took many a ride. With the utmost care I informed the barker I wouldn't walk across the street to speak to Mrs. Simpson let alone pay out a half-dollar to gaze at the spot where she had placed her Commoner behind. I might also have let him know that in Philadelphia we do not accept the Princess Grace who, after all, is nothing more than a bricklayer's daughter.

"Little Irvy," the "thirty-eight-foot, twenty-ton Frozen Whale," was in an adjoining trailer; I refused to pay the admission fee for that either. The Colonel, in my opinion, was not likely to play the role of Jonah, and I doubted if there'd be space for Ellen inside "Little Irvy."

No sooner had I passed this "attraction" when I heard a raucous voice call, "Sir! You with the coat *and* the tie *and* the vest."

I turned to see where the sound was emanating from and at whom it was directed. Some twenty feet to the rear of a counter filled with baseballs I saw a clown in back of a mesh screen swinging on a perch above a tub of water. A sign over the top of the game read: DUMP BOZO!

To my annoyance I discovered this crude buffoon was addressing me. His words, steeped in scorn, followed as I moved away.

"Hey, Mister. Think you're out slummin'? Why don't you get with it, man? Shed those fairy clothes and be like the rest of the people."

Everyone in the tip stared at me and quite a few of these yokels began to laugh. I would have hurried along if Bozo's next words did not slow me down.

"Society's passin' us by, folks. Watch that Philadelphia gent beat a quick retreat."

"How do you know he's a Philadelphia gent, Bozo?" someone called out and the clown's reply brought me to a dead halt.

" 'Cause I'm Mr. Sherlock Holmes," was the buffoon's answer.

That did it. The effrontery of this uncouth fellow daring to play the role of the Master was a bit much. Believe me, at no time was I completely convinced this was H. Wesley Eberhardt, swinging like an ape over a tank of black water. However, that possibility did remain and I could not pass it by. As I pointed out before, I am a tireless investigator and never omit a single opportunity of searching for the truth, no matter how veiled it may be. While Bozo did label me a "Philadelphia gent," I credit this guesswork plus the fact that unquestionably I stood out from the crowd of local hillbillies who gaped while I turned around and moved up to the counter.

There was nothing subtle about the purpose of the "game" nor the manner in which it was played. The object was to strike dead center of a small target some two feet in diameter, over Bozo's head and outside the screened area. A direct hit released a catch, the bench tilted, and sent the fellow plunging into the tank.

I removed twenty-five cents from my change purse and gave it to the young lady in charge. This action caused Bozo to make another crude comment.

"Where'd you get that one, Sir? Thought they stopped using

them pocketbooks before the Civil War. Look out for flyin'
moths everybody!"

This brought loud laughs from the buffoon's appreciative
audience. I said nothing, doffed my jacket which I folded
neatly and laid on the counter, then took careful aim. My first
toss missed but not by more than an inch. This did not daunt
Bozo whose harsh voice never ceased hurling imprecations at
me to the delight of the stupid louts who crowded around. I
smiled, if only inwardly; not for nothing had I spent those
years pitching for the Academy's champion Nine. Again I
twirled my arm, took aim, then let go. Moments later a loud
splash brought gasps of surprise from the tip and deep satisfaction from me.

"Lucky pitch!" the clown, dripping wet, shouted as he re-
mounted his perch.

"Lucky, was it?" I asked and threw the last ball. Another
bull's-eye and this time the crowd cheered. I donned my coat,
grinned at the tip, gave them a prizefighter's salute, both
hands clenched together over my head, said, "So long, Sherlock," and walked off, blending into a large crowd assembled
at an adjacent attraction.

This one was labeled "The Girls from Paris." I've been to
the Folies Bergère often enough to recognize real class when I
see it and I did not see it here. Mounted on a platform were a
half-dozen scantily clad, large-breasted women, twisting their
hips in what they must have felt was a provocative fashion. A
fellow, wearing a straw hat, stood in the center of his "young"
ladies urging "all red-blooded Americans from sixteen to sixty
to come in and see what you can't see at home."

I pondered for several minutes. The admission price was
two dollars, a great deal to lay out on the off-chance that H.
Wesley Eberhardt might in some way be connected with "The
Girls from Paris." I wished then I had asked the sheriff for
passes which I'm sure he had in ample supply. However, I
was not going to restrict my research because of a paltry sum,
so I bought a ticket and fortunately was able to get a seat on
the first row where I would have an unrestricted view should
the Colonel come on stage.

The performance lasted for three-quarters of an hour and
at no time, though my eyes never left the stage, did I see the
object of our Chase. I even paid another dollar for a special
men's show that followed. This also turned out to be a disap-

pointment. As I got outside I glanced at my watch, it showed ten minutes past the hour. In my desire to do a thorough job of research on my side of the midway, I missed our ten o'clock rendezvous and was a bit late for the next. However, I assumed my colleagues would understand, a return to our meeting place would have taken at least a half-hour, the crowds were so dense.

I paid another admission fee, this one only fifty cents, to enter the freak show. It was certainly possible that among those "Ten of Nature's Pranks," graphically portrayed on the outside banner, the Colonel might well be masquerading. Upon entering I discounted the "Polish Giant," all eight feet six inches of him; Mary King, "Fattest Woman in the World"; "Hugo, the Human Skeleton"; and "Alvin," the half-naked "Anatomical Miracle," who contorted his body into all manners of hideous shapes.

These four obviously were real people and despite the Colonel's training in deception no amount of occupational skill could have enabled him to take any of their places on the podium. In similar fashion I dismissed the near-naked "Gerald-Geraldine," obviously a hermaphrodite unabashedly displaying both male and female genital organs. No matter how anxious Eberhardt may have been to win the Carl Anderson manuscripts, I was sure he would never degrade himself to this extent.

Even with my limited knowledge of anthropology I needed but a single glance to eliminate "Eng, the Wild Man of Borneo" howling savagely at everyone from inside a snake-filled pit. I am afraid "Mr. Eng" was only a kinky-haired African albino. "Olga, the Headless Teuton" was an obvious fake. Even a child knows a truncated body cannot maintain life. Yet these yokels could not take their eyes from the lower half of a woman whose "head" consisted of an inverted bell jar. Through this apparatus were tubes of red and white fluids; the "doctor" in attendance averred it was blood flowing in and out of his "patient's" heart.

I wanted the "physician" to realize that I, unlike the other members of his audience, knew Olga was a fake. I whispered "mirrors" and winked as I passed by. A rather sophisticated gentleman dressed in a clean white jacket and sporting a neatly trimmed Vandyke, the "doctor" responded by nodding his head and winking broadly. I do not think either of us were observed, so intent on the optical illusion were the silly yokels.

"Prince Eric," the sword swallower, had a huge, bright red handlebar mustache and a full crop of hair the same hue. He seemed to be the Colonel's height and bore himself well when his head wasn't bent back in readiness to swallow some metallic object. But I could not conceive of H. Wesley inserting a long lighted neon tube down his gullet. The tube was no fake; it lit up "Prince Eric's" insides revealing all manner of human obstacles which, if I may pun, are better kept dark.

I wasted little time gazing on the tattooed body of Mrs. Astoria Gibbons, nor had I trouble resisting the Master of Ceremony's offer to prove the truth or falsity of Mrs. Stella MacGregor's full-blown beard by giving it a yank. Neither possibly could be Ellen or her spouse. There remained then, in this freak show, only one act, that of sawing a woman in half, something I had not witnessed for a good many years. I needed no one to tell me that this, too, was an optical illusion. Nevertheless I did watch carefully as a top-hatted fellow removed, one by one, a dozen long, pointed daggers and swords from a rack behind him, crossed these weapons through holes in a box and allegedly cut small segments out of an attractive blonde woman who lay inside it.

I believe I researched the freak show as thoroughly as anyone could have done so under the circumstances. I felt there was little to gain by witnessing another performance although the MC assured his audience it was welcome to remain as long as it chose with no additional cost. I noticed quite a few yokels remained, no doubt feeling that was the only way to get their money's worth.

The midway was still seething with humanity. Another large crowd, a "tip" Sillman called it, stood before "Harem Delights," a vulgar display of near-naked, busty women, gyrating to the sounds of a weird-sounding musical instrument. You can be sure I was the only person present able to identify this almost forgotten woodwind as the flageolet. I paused, hesitating momentarily to consider whether it would be worth my while to spend another two dollars on research. I decided in the negative. The hour was growing late and unless I hurried I would not be on time for our midnight rendezvous. I had missed the previous one.

However, I did want to spend a moment or two with my

friend the Gypsy so I retraced my steps in order to pass his
stand. Alas! The place was closed and Joe nowhere in sight.
Obviously the boss had fired him and, unable to get a replacement on such short notice and too lazy to operate the game
himself, he preferred to shut up shop. I regarded the Gypsy's
departure as a blow to our Chase. In view of the confidences
he revealed so soon after a casual meeting, I felt sure he
would have checked Gibson and Fowler's personnel and sur-
reptitiously reported the results to me.

Within sight of the newspaper tent my eye was caught by a
very tall, heavily bearded fellow wearing dark, horn-rimmed
glasses who averred that for fifty cents he would guess within
three pounds or three years anybody's weight or age. If he
failed he'd pay a penalty. What threw me off balance was the
man's first remark, one addressed directly to me.

"Come right over, Doc. Let's see if they feed you properly
on the Main Line."

Now the so-called "Main Line" is where better bred Philadelphians once lived. Even though most of these Quaker City
leaders have long since moved elsewhere to make room for
nouveau riche, the appellation still has significance as a term
denoting a man's social standing. Could this be the Colonel? I
asked myself looking directly at his face. His eyes were concealed by those dark glasses and I was unable to pass judgment.

Inside of a small, dimly lit tent directly behind the "agent's"
huge "butcher's scale" I could see the outline of a woman
silhouetted against the canvas. She was moving her hands rapidly in a manner which let me know at once she was knit-
ting. Ellen used to knit furiously claiming it relieved tensions.
Had I come to the end of the trail? Could this be Ellen and
her husband? I looked directly at the "weight guesser." His
physical appearance was much like the Colonel's. I wanted to
stare into his eyes but those thick black lenses concealed them
from my view.

I stood facing him for a moment, then walked up, extracted
a half-dollar from my change purse and said, "OK. Go ahead.
Guess my weight." The fellow stood me on a little wooden
platform and without uttering a word began to pat my arms,
legs and shoulders. By this time a number of yokels were
watching the proceedings. Finally, after several moments, he

turned to me and in a loud voice said, "I calls this gentleman to be one hundred and seventy-two pounds."

This was within the three-pound margin of error which surprised but did not overwhelm me. But what startled me was that the "weight guesser's" accent was German, the kind of thick German stage accent used by Weber and Fields at Keith's Vaudeville house on Chestnut Street. He had *no* accent whatsoever when he first addressed me. Of this I am *positive*.

I had no sooner stepped down from the scale when three or four "roughies" brushed by, blocking the weight guesser from me and from the crowd which surged inward. I had no idea what was happening but a few moments later a pair of state troopers forced their way through. However, by that time the scale was no longer there, the tent was down and both the Colonel, if that's who it was, and the lady had vanished.

I heard one of the police officers turn to the other and say, "Boy! Word gets around fast. Quicker than the grapevine." The other trooper looked in my direction. "Check your wallet, Sir, and see if it's still there." I patted my coat and reassured the officer that the wallet was still in my possession. I have too much sense to leave it in its usual place. It was in my inside coat pocket, a safety pin fastened over the edges.

A few moments later I saw Mr. Sillman hurry by and engage in a tense conversation with the troopers. Not wanting to interfere, I waited until the officers left and then walked up to the patch and told him whom I thought the missing weight guesser was.

He raised his eyebrows.

"Could be. Oney usin' a different name. Happens all the time, that's why we got to watch out pretty careful if we want to keep the lot clean. We always check their records. Didn't finish checkin' his yet. Takes about two weeks. Meanwhile we give him his privilege and let him go to woik. That was last Saturday. Short of good A&S men this season. Very popular. But if I'd have known how it was gonna turn out I'da never let him on the midway. He was no JCL though. Knew his way around."

I asked for an explanation of the patch's terms and was told that a "privilege" was a temporary weekly lease, that "A&S" stood for "Age & Scale," and "JCL" was an abbreviation for a "Johnny Come Lately," a newcomer in other words. There were still several unanswered questions and I insisted on having them.

"OK," Sillman said. "I got no objections tellin' you what happened. You'll get it from the sheriff anyway. This is the way it went. The fuzz got a complaint so they come over to investigate. It looked like this A&S man couldn't care less how much he took in on his guessin'. He had a front man peekin' pokes and then lead good prospects off to a G tent."

All this was too much for me. I have more than an adequate understanding of the English language and I was a minor in philology, but I admit I am no expert on slang or carnival terms. The patch comprehended my bewilderment and smiled.

" 'Fuzz' stands for cops. [This I knew.] A front man is a shill, a shill is a guy workin' the outside inside the tip, and the tip is the crowd. Peekin' a poke is oney tryin' to find out how much dough a mark's carryin' on him. You're a mark, Sir, if you'll excuse me the expression. Comes from easy mark. [I could have refuted this derogation by telling Sillman about my experience with Joe but I refrained, not wishing to get the Gypsy in trouble.] A G tent's a gamblin' tent.

"How they work is like this. A mark'll open his pocketbook to pay the A&S man. The shill's close enough to see if it's stuffed with bills. He oney needs a quick glance. If it is then he and maybe another shill kinda separate the mark from his family by handin' out passes for rides to his kids and his wife. When they get the mark alone one of the shills'll tell him they know how he can win a lot of money for him and for them.

"They usually say they had a fight with their boss who's a crook. And they need a local man he don't know to act as a front so they can take the boss good. They tell him how he can grab onto a lot of dough. All the mark has to have is a little larceny in his own heart. They never loin."

I wanted to point out that I, personally, would have little or no sympathy for any "mark" who enters into such a conspiracy. The truth is, he deserves to be taken. However, there was little to gain by entering into a discussion of ethics with one of Sillman's breed.

What was most important to me was the alias used by the Colonel if that were he. Sillman pulled a three-by-five card from his pocket.

"Voiner," he answered. "That's what he tole me his name was. Said to call him Doc."

At first the name meant nothing to me and I almost dismissed it from my mind. It was only later, when we were on our way back to Philadelphia, it occurred to me that a man who says "woik" when he means "work" and "oin" when he means "learn," might well say "Voiner" when he means "Verner." Dr. Verner was "a distant relative of Sherlock Holmes," who bought out Watson's practice.

CHAPTER

16

DESPITE THE potentially encouraging information I was able to turn in re Dr. Verner, a sense of frustration swept over us on the return trip home, a feeling that somewhere we had missed a golden opportunity on the carnival lot we were putting behind us at seventy miles per hour. My fellow hunters had far less to report than I although, upon at least one occasion, Don was sure he had seen the Colonel. Furthermore Don claimed a female ticket taker on the "Dip of Death" was a dead ringer for Ellen.

"I went back a few minutes later to check but by the time I reached the cashier's cage she'd gone," Don reported. "I asked one of the workers where she went but he claimed he didn't know who the hell I was talking about."

Jack said that for more than a half-hour, until he could find Mr. Sillman, he was certain a tent photographer was the Colonel's brother.

"I hate to admit it," Jack went on, "but I'm still not sure. The 'artist' looked enough like H. Wesley to be a close relative. I watched him work for a bit and probably stared at him too hard. I was even thinking of letting him 'do' me; instead I went looking for Mr. Sillman. By the time we both returned to what Sillman called a 'mug joint' someone else was in charge. Whoever that was denied the very existence of another person, swearing he was alone and hadn't left the place all evening.

"'That's one of the things we got to contend with,' Sillman told me. 'I don't doubt in the least you spotted another operator. But you kept lookin' at him, he got suspicious and took off. Happens all the time. Too many of our personnel got guilty consciences and with good reason. So if anybody gives 'em the eye, they fade away.'

"Sillman promised to check for me although he held little hope for a solution, adding that the man might well be a hundred miles away by then."

Charlie Starr is a realist, seemingly swayed not by emotions but measured facts, so when he told us he believed the Colonel was still on the Gibson and Fowler midway we were a bit surprised.

"I don't know what it is makes me say this but I have a hunch that somewhere on that lot we're leaving behind, we saw Colonel H. Wesley Eberhardt and that he, in turn, saw us."

However, Jack, usually an optimist, shook his head. We'd stopped for coffee at a Howard Johnson's on the Turnpike.

"What's happening to all of us," Jack warned, "is that we're beginning to 'see' our fox or his brethren almost every place we *want* or *expect* to see them. Wishful thinking carried to a high degree. Look how many times Frank 'observed' the Colonel during his first stroll down Market Street, weeks ago. And look what happened to each of us tonight. Half of our six months is over and in my opinion, at least, we've not accomplished much.

"Sure your 'mug' man, Ed, might be the Colonel's brother Joe and your 'Doctor Verner,' Frank, could be the old boy himself dishing out still one more clue. But I don't see how we're going to find out for certain. I don't want to follow that carnival or any other all around Pennsylvania for the next ten weeks, or whenever it is their season ends. And if H. Wesley is with G&F's show and they go beyond the one-hundred-twenty-five-mile radius do you suppose he'd quit to join another carnival? I wish I knew."

The next two Thursday night plenary sessions were depressing; our operations had come to a dead halt. There was little to discuss, no leads to follow and no new clues, *ex post facto* or otherwise. That work schedule we'd drawn up so optimistically only three months before looked ridiculous. Jack had no assignments to hand out.

Charlie asked for and was granted permission to take a brief trip to Paris. "On business," he said, but I knew otherwise. Marv drove his wife and offspring to their rented summer cottage near Harvey's Lake south of Wilkes-Barre and remained there for ten days. Ed was off to Denver by train at that for a conference, taking his wife along. I was sure he wouldn't be back in a hurry. Don, too, was furloughed. His two-week leave was spent as counselor at the Treasure Island Girl Scout enclave on the Delaware where his two oldest daughters were campers. This left Jack and me to hold the fort. We had a leisurely dinner together at the Penn A.C. where he, not I, is a member.

I was irked and showed it. That very morning the postman delivered a package quite clearly addressed to me and even though marked "personal" Juliet took the liberty of opening it. Inside was the photograph of an almost nude burlesque dancer at the bottom of which she had inscribed: "To my darling Frankie from his Pagan."

"From *his* Pagan, indeed!" I said to Jack. "I never even met the woman!"

"But did you ever actually *see* her?"

"I did. She was one of the featured performers on the midway."

I looked Jack squarely in the face.

"How can I, how can anyone, do a thorough research job without entering every single place the Colonel might be hiding?"

I hadn't mentioned that I'd been inside the "Girls from Paris" tent. Nor had I asked any of the other Sons or Jack to share the out-of-pocket expense. I noticed his eyes lit up when he slowly scanned the photograph I'd brought with me.

"I understand," Jack said with a slight smile.

However, I'm sure he *didn't* and from his amused expression I gathered he considered me, at this moment at any rate, "a dirty old man."

"Well, it *is* another clue, of course, Frank. Charlie knew what he was talking about. The Colonel was on the midway, probably laughing his head off. What a stupid fix we got ourselves into!"

He shook his head.

"What to do? What to do?"

I could not furnish a satisfactory answer, there was nothing more we could do. All six of us were present at the August 18 dinner session. Never before had I seen Jack quite so upset. We'd scarcely sipped our second martini when he took the floor.

"I have some disturbing news, disturbing to me in any event and I'd like to get your opinions. It has to do with Ellen. You may recall some time ago, not too long after the Chase began, I told you I was concerned about the Colonel's Lady.

"I had good reasons which I mentioned only to Frank, not that I haven't just as much trust in each of you but because one of his close relatives is involved Frank would have heard it anyway, I'm sure."

Then Jack proceeded to inform the other Sons about Ellen's surprising failure to make any of her usual anticipated charitable contributions. They were just as shocked as I'd been. Jack continued.

"This morning I went over to Morgan's to get one of Veda's prescriptions filled. John Morgan is a very old friend of mine."

John is an old friend of mine also. My family's been dealing with the Morgan Apothecary—*not* drugstore, please!—for a hundred years or more and so have many of us. All of John's sons, and John's father before him, are alumni of the Academy and have the same social standings as those not engaged in trade.

"The first thing John mentioned," Jack continued, "had to do with Ellen. Had I seen her recently? When I said 'no' he shook his head.

" 'That's strange, Jack. I haven't either, nor has my son John.'

"I asked him what was strange about this since I was sure the Morgans and the Eberhardts were not personal friends. Couldn't it be that Ellen was either trading elsewhere or had no prescriptions to be filled? He shook his head again.

" 'I'm not basing this on the fact that the Dawsons have always dealt with us from 'way back. Certainly she and the Colonel are entitled to trade anywhere they wish. Heaven knows we've lost many patrons who prefer to have their prescriptions filled where they can also buy groceries, have their film developed, or eat lunch.

" 'No, my worry about Ellen goes deeper than loyalties.'

"He excused himself, walked to the rear of the shop and returned a couple of minutes later with a small glass jar in his hand. I could see it was filled with liquid.

" 'Jack,' he said 'I never discuss patrons' ailments with anyone except their physicians. In this case I'm taking certain liberties because I know about your wager and because you and Veda have been friends of the Dawsons for a long, long time. But were you aware that Ellen is highly allergic to wasp and bee stings?' "

I couldn't keep quiet at this revelation.

"My God, gentlemen! That bottle contained some sort of serum. The Colonel's prevented Ellen from picking it up, then exposed her to a bee or wasp, she was bitten and died. This is murder! Where do you suppose he's hidden the body?"

Jack smiled.

"That's the conclusion I jumped to. I didn't voice it to the Doc but he had to know what I was thinking and reassured me. Five years ago, or even four, this could have happened but not now. He claimed Ellen had built up considerable immunity and had been getting the shots once a week for the past seven years.

" 'That is, until about three months ago,' he said."

Marv interrupted.

"Something's wrong with that story, Jack. Why would Ellen pick up the prescription herself? The patient never has that responsibility. Morgan would have mailed it directly to whomever's giving her the shots. I'll bet I can tell you who that would be. Ed Holling at Hahnemann. He's a member of the team that developed the serum.

"Jesus! The possibilities for murder sure are there. If the victim is highly allergic to insect stings and probably penicillin as well—they usually go together—she could have a horrible death."

I shuddered.

"You and I get stung by a bee and what happens?" Marv asked rhetorically. "The injured part swells, gets red, and if it's a real bad bite there's considerable discomfort for a short while. When you were a kid and that happened Mom spread calamine lotion over the bite. Now you do it yourself. In a couple of hours, or at the most a day, what remains is nothing more than a conversation piece. I'm talking about one or two bites, not a swarm.

"But for Ellen, it's different. There's little redness and no swelling. The diaphragm is almost completely paralyzed, the victim has enormous difficulty breathing, goes into a deep coma and is dead soon after. That is if no serum's available. Nothing else could save her."

Jack nodded.

"That's just about what Doc Morgan told me."

Marv had not yet finished.

"We had a case like that a little while back, maybe two, three years. It was no problem to determine the cause of death. Young guy about twenty tried to get rid of his kid sister with whom he'd been having an incestuous relationship. The girl wanted to quit, got herself a boyfriend and threatened she'd squeal to the old man if her brother tried anything funny.

"Between the D.A. and our department we reconstructed the murder which the brother later confessed to. The girl was highly allergic to the same things. There are perhaps a hundred, no more, in the entire United States with as severe allergies as these. The murdered girl wore one of those Medical Alert Tag necklaces they issue out in California. Never supposed to remove it, even when they go to sleep in their own home. Stamped in it is a list of the allergies, the name, address and telephone number of the attending physician and an identification number.

"In addition she carried a kit with antihistamine serum and three hypodermic needles. The extra ones were in case she got nervous and broke two of them while she was giving herself an inoculation. She was taught how."

I asked Marv if he thought the Colonel had subjected Ellen to a fatal insect sting, pointing out how easily this could be done. Marv thought for a moment before answering.

"Obviously it wouldn't be much trouble for the Colonel to capture a bee or wasp and then place his wife in a position where she'd be attacked while she was sleeping. Then if he hid her emergency kit so she wouldn't be able to give herself an inoculation she'd go into a coma and die.

"But the Colonel would be putting himself in one hell of a fix. How to get rid of the body? Bury it himself in a secluded spot where some kid or picnicker invariably discovers it within a week? Sounds like fiction but happens all the time. Burn it? No. There's always something left. It's really difficult to dispose of a human body as many a murderer's found out."

Ed raised his hand.

"Hold it, Marv. Let's consider the Sacred Writings."

We all knew at once what Ed meant. He was referring to "The Disappearance of Lady Frances Carfax" whom the would-be murderer placed in the bottom of a double coffin.

The upper half was occupied by the body of an aged woman whose death was certified by a registered physician. Fortunately for Lady Frances, Holmes deduced the criminal's *modus operandi* in time to rescue the victim from death by suffocation and furnished Scotland Yard with sufficient information to arrest Henry Peters, alias the Reverend Dr. Shlessinger.

Marv, who had vast experience in the field, was quick to reply.

"Of course he could make a deal with a crooked undertaker but H. Wesley would be putting himself in a very vulnerable position and he's too damned smart for that. He wouldn't be able to have Ellen buried legitimately. First of all Pennsylvania and all the other states with the exception of Mississippi require a coroner's inquest unless a registered physician has been in attendance within twenty-four hours preceding death. Even a third year medic should be able to determine the cause of death if it's an insect sting. Can you imagine the publicity?"

He turned to young Donaldson.

"That would make a great story, wouldn't it, Don?"

Don nodded.

"It would indeed, no question about that. But again we're taking the easy way out, making the Colonel a murderer to balance our own ineptitude. Forgive me for this seeming blasphemy, we all might be coming to the realization that the Sacred Writings are not applicable *every* time. Let's let Jack finish his conversation with Doc Morgan. Maybe we'll get somewhere with that."

Jack continued.

"You're right on several counts, Marv. Doc Morgan said Ellen's allergist *is* Ed Holling and the prescriptions *are* sent directly to him."

"And I'll bet, Jack," Marv interrupted, a smug smile on his

face, "Ellen stopped into the store just to have them fill her emergency kit with fresh serum before it went out to Ed Holling. Did Morgan tell you how much of an immunity Ellen had built up? That is important to know."

"Yes, Marv. He said Ellen would have at least an hour's grace. But let me tell you what it is that troubles both John Morgan and me as well."

Marv was nodding his head vigorously and I could see he was about to butt in again. I motioned for him to be quiet. I'm fond of the man but there *must* be something in his racial heritage which compels him to demonstrate an admittedly superior intellect on every possible occasion.

Jack went on.

"John said he always kept the fresh serum in his store until Ellen came in, then sent it on to Holling's office. But when Ellen didn't show for several weeks he called the allergist's secretary only to discover Ellen hadn't kept any of her appointments. As a matter of fact, she hasn't been to Holling's office for at least three months.

"Next day Ed Holling himself called John. He, too, was upset. The gist of their conversation was this. That the longer the interval between Ellen's shots, the greater her chances for lessened immunity. Both doctor and patient had put in years of time and effort to develop that single hour's safety factor, something Ellen wouldn't toss away lightly.

Holling completely discounted the possibility that Ellen changed either pharmacist or physician. Ellen's prescription was not refillable and could be delivered only to a registered M.D., although not necessarily an allergist. The only drug company in the world making the Serum is Smith, Kline, up on Spring Garden Street. Ed was so disturbed when it suddenly dawned on him that Ellen hadn't been around that he called Smith, Kline. Apparently they know him well enough to give him the information he requested—that Morgan's was one of only thirty-five pharmacies in the United States who'd received shipments of this particular serum within the past one hundred and ten days. Beyond this period of time the efficacy of the drug would not be guaranteed and no reputable drugstore would dispense it. I have the names and addresses of these stores. John gave them to me."

He turned to Marv.

"Here's where you come in."

Marv nodded his head violently.

"I know what you want me to do even before you ask. The answer is 'yes' I'll write to every one of them on our official stationery and request them to advise me if within the past three months they filled a prescription for Ellen Eberhardt."

He paused.

"Or anyone else since she and the Colonel might be living under an assumed name, that is providing the druggist hadn't known the person for more than three months. Better still I'll send telegrams and if they reply in the affirmative they can wire me the answer collect. We ought to know in a couple of days at the most, I've done this many times in the past. I'm assuming Jack can get the original prescription from Doc Morgan so I can include it in the telegram."

Jack said he'd already done this and handed a Xeroxed copy to Marv. Then he addressed all of us.

"Gentlemen, I think you'll agree we have some cause for alarm about Ellen's safety although I am not yet convinced she has been harmed. There is still the possibility that when we find the Colonel or he seeks us out to collect the bet in a little more than a month, Ellen will be by his side."

He smiled.

"Or at home since we don't allow the distaff side to attend Copper Beech meetings. Perhaps our fellow Sons will permit us to make an exception in Ellen's case."

"I'll make that motion at our picnic next week," Charlie said. "I'd be that glad to see her. I don't know the Lady as well as any of you do but I must confess to twinges of worry. What do you think we should do, Jack? Wait for replies from Marv's telegrams? Or have you something else in mind? You said at the beginning you were interested in our opinions."

We were quiet until the dinner was cleared and the B&B served, but the moment our waiter closed the door Jack continued.

"Gentlemen, I don't like to say this since, in a sense, it's a concession of failure if only in degree but I think it's time we called the pros in for an assist."

Ed pretended to be shocked.

"You mean, Jack,' he said with a grin, "you're conceding the Sacred Writings aren't enough to go by?"

Jack smiled.

"Maybe even that. Perhaps they don't cover every contingency. Now if we could persuade the Master to come out of retirement that would be different. Don't forget he is an expert apiarist. I am suggesting we ask Tom Hart if he'll set up a date to talk to the FBI in Washington."

Don shook his head.

"We don't need Tom for that. The local office over in the Widener Building is cooperative and I know Francis Gowen, Agent-in-Charge. If you'd like I'll see him tomorrow and if anyone wants to come along with me I'd be happy to take him.

"Actually, my own opinion is that they will *not* be interested. I don't think they'd have any legal right to help. We've no proof anything's happened to Ellen and as far as the outside world's concerned, all we're doing is trying to win a bet. Since it's within those terms the Colonel accepted, I for one, have no objections calling for aid from the professionals. We've already established that precedent."

All but I looked puzzled. I knew what Don meant.

"We laid our cards out for that Sheriff Roberts up in Snyder County, don't forget. We asked his assistance. I've a lot of confidence in the guy—he strikes me as a very smart operator—and I don't think he's dropped the Chase. I wouldn't be at all surprised if we heard from him sometime.

"In line with Jack's thinking, I've another suggestion to make. There's an extremely bright woman I know down at police headquarters. She has only patrolman's rank and technically she's merely in charge of the files in the Missing Persons Bureau. But she really runs the department and has for the last fifteen years at least. You ought to know whom I mean, Marv. You must have worked with her one time or other."

Marv nodded violently as was his increasingly annoying habit.

"Millie Tomassio, of course! I should have thought of her. Not only worked with her but I used to date her when she first came out of school before either of us were married. She'll be marvelous and cooperative, I know. Maybe she won't be allowed to help us officially but she'll listen and give an opinion and some advice. Want me to go with you, Don?"

"Why don't you go there instead of me, Marv, since you know Millie better? Take Frank along if you want company."

I certainly did not like the way Don passed my services

around to all takers and I'd already suggested I'd accompany him when he saw the FBI. But if Marv needed me I would, of course, go. Apparently he did because he looked at me for acquiescence. I told him I'd telephone him as soon as our conference at the FBI was ended. Don felt this could be arranged the first thing in the morning.

Despite our concern for Ellen, we all felt considerably better after these decisions were made. Even the realization that we had only a bit more than five weeks to wind up the Chase didn't dampen our renewed enthusiasm.

CHAPTER

17

OUR MEETING with Gowen, the FBI Agent-in-Charge, was not encouraging. Gowen, or the S.A.C. as he was called, was attentive and gave us as much time as we needed to tell our story. Don did most of the talking (some of which I thought unnecessary and spared none of the details. Despite its length, Gowen listened without interruption. Don cited reasons for our concern over Ellen's safety, her failure to make contributions to her favorite causes, the missing house pet, the gorse, and finally the most serious of all, the matter of those serum inoculations. When he concluded Don turned and asked me politely if he'd omitted any important point. However, his presentation on the whole, I must say, was fairly accurate and I could add nothing.

"You have a problem, admittedly," Mr. Gowen said. "But I'm afraid that much as we'd enjoy the fun, we can't enter your Chase and can't be of assistance. First of all you are not able to furnish proof the Colonel has committed any crime."

He smiled.

"Except, of course, as a participant in an illegal wager. But then, you Don, and your friend here, and the other four Sons, are just as guilty as Eberhardt. However, I don't think your 'crime' is serious enough to warrant a Federal investigation."

While I realized Mr. Gowen was only joking—at least I hoped he was—I had given no thought to the fact that our wager *was* illegal. Ergo, if we wanted to adhere to the strictest letter of the law, we six law-abiding citizens would call the whole thing off. I held this face saving thought in reserve and allowed the S.A.C. to continue.

"Perhaps you don't know, Don, since we're not on your regular beat, that the FBI may not enter a case unless certain basic conditions are met. We may enter a case on our own—by that I mean we have original jurisdiction where a bank with membership in the FDIC has been robbed. Or we have the right to go after military deserters. In either case we must first secure a warrant for the arrest of the wanted person or persons.

"Otherwise we have to be called in by the local District Attorney and this usually follows informal discussions, conducted in a friendly manner. In the event our services are requested by a local agency certain conditions must be met. There has to be the commission of a felony involving the crossing, or assumption of the crossing, of state lines. And we *still* have to get a warrant just as we did under original jurisdiction.

"These are the basic points which must be met before you can call on the FBI for help."

He smiled again.

"I think you'll concede, Don, and you too, Sir, that you haven't met them."

To this we agreed.

"Now," Mr. Gowen went on, "I'll talk to you both off the record. You suspect murder and/or kidnapping. You may be right on both counts but believe me you've far from sufficient evidence to merit a warrant. All you have is suspicion, not too badly founded, I will say.

"Don, you know Arlen Specter [our District Attorney] as well as I do. Can you imagine what he'd say if you asked him to have a warrant issued for the arrest of H. Wesley Eberhardt! And if you swore out a warrant yourselves and hired an agency to execute it they'd have to find the old boy themselves. I can't think of any private agency with those facilities. Then if you do catch him and he is innocent you'd be on the wrong end of a whale of a big damage suit.

"I don't blame you for being concerned about Mrs. Eberhardt's safety. Personally I would be, too, but officially I can't.

I gather that your feelings are—and correct me if I'm wrong —that the Colonel has used a bet with six. . . . "

He grinned at Don.

"Well, five anyway, highly respectable citizens of Philadel-phia as a cover for the murder of his wife and given himself time to collect the fortune they hold, or held jointly, then fade from the scene forever."

"That's just about it, Mr. Gowen," I said.

The S.A.C. sat back, filled his pipe, lit it, then continued.

"Unquestionably you've come to the conclusion you've pit-ted your wits against a very smart operator with probably as much professional training as any of us in the field. Without wanting to disparage your intelligence, you're *not* profes-sionals and you are *not* a match for the Colonel. As I see it, the only way he'll be trapped, if at all, is by his own ego.

"Again, not to denigrate your individual abilities, the Colo-nel had to be aware of a fact that I don't think most people realize. Despite credit cards, social security numbers, bank ac-counts, insurance policies, and so forth and so on, it's very easy for anyone who has not committed a felony to disappear in the United States and stay away just as long as he or she cares to. That's true even if they've been fingerprinted.

"Thousands of men, women, and teenagers and some even younger than that vanish every year. Most of them are never heard from again until they, themselves, want to be. These are people who suddenly get fed up with their jobs, their wives or husbands, they're harassed by creditors, they have love affairs they want to end. They reach a point where they say, 'to hell with it all' and they take off.

"The Bureau gets letters and telegrams every hour from desperate parents and the spouse who's left behind. We feel very sorry for these people but unless those conditions are met there's nothing we can do except offer sympathy."

He paused, leaned back in the chair, both hands clasped be-hind his neck, then puffed hard on his pipe. We waited pa-tiently for a few moments. He continued.

"Let me try to assay your chances of 'getting' the Colonel. First of all you cannot eliminate the possibility that she is with her husband because she wants to be with him enough to toss aside ingrained social responsibilities. It's happened, the hus-band comes first. Meanwhile the Colonel's having a ball, needling you with those clues he sends. If this is all in the spirit of fun then you deserve just what you let yourselves in for.

"It's quite conceivable he'll show up at the next meeting of the Copper Beeches with his wife in tow, or if you won't let her in she'll be waiting outside. You'll be the subject of a great many jokes and the Colonel will have a conversation piece which should last him for the rest of his life. You, Don, will have a good story for the *Inquirer*, an even more complete one than our friend Nels told."

I hadn't realized that the S.A.C., too, had read that annoying item in the *Daily News*.

"However," Gowen said in a far more serious vein, "I can't convince myself that is the way it will be, a happy ending for all except you six Sons. The Colonel quoted the Book of Ruth when you asked him whether his wife would be with him. That's a Delphic response and you accept any meaning you wish to. There's no way of telling what he meant. He may have phrased his answer the way he did to protect his ego—to prove he stuck to the truth and you were too stupid to accept it other than literally.

"I'm inclined to think Mrs. Eberhardt is not with her husband voluntarily. From what you say this would be completely out of character. So, if she's not with him of her own volition, where and how has he concealed her or what means has he used to force the lady out of sight?

"I'm also certain his ego will not permit him to go beyond the one-hundred-twenty-five-mile limit he, himself, set. He is, or has been, where he can observe your movements or at least where he can make an educated guess as to your whereabouts. To watch you floundering would be great satisfaction for his ego.

"Furthermore, I believe he was on the carnival lot; that you saw him and that he saw you. You may have even seen his wife. This, too, would help satisfy his sense of superiority."

He paused again and smiled slightly.

"I hate mentioning this to such aficionados of Mr. Sherlock Holmes, so please forgive me if I suggest you consider Poe's 'Purloined Letter.' I'm sure you will recall how M. Dupin successfully concluded that the 'hidden' envelope was not really out of sight."

Both Don and I nodded. Naturally we were familiar with the efforts of the French detective. I myself had even less confidence in Dupin than I had in Gaboriau's Lecoq, whom the Master labeled a "miserable bungler," but who somehow managed to achieve small successes. I could not refrain from quoting aloud a far more aptly put phase from the Sacred Writings.

"The world is full of obvious things which nobody by any chance ever observed," a comment Holmes once made to Dr. Watson.

Mr. Gowen grinned.

"Well spoken, Sir. You know exactly what I mean. Now, permit me to give you another thought and then I must ask you to excuse me."

We listened carefully.

"If I'm not greatly mistaken the Colonel will present you with one more 'hot' clue before the deadline. His ego will compel him to. This, or these, should be good ones so follow them through. Remember what Dupin said, or if you prefer, reflect upon the words of Mr. Sherlock Holmes. This is the one way you have to win your bet. A superiority complex has beaten better men than Colonel H. Wesley Eberhardt, believe me."

Even before I met Marv to keep our afternoon appointment with Miss Tomassio of the Police Department, the S.A.C. prediction came true. Upon Don's return to his office he found a note from Irwin Kirby of *Amusement Business*. In the envelope was a clipping from the "Personal Notices" in the current issue of that periodical. Don read it to me over the telephone.

"If this should meet the eye of any of my fellow Sons, I advise them to review page 163 of the Sacred Writings, C.M.M. [Christopher Morley Memorial] edition of the Sacred Writings."

This time we were one jump ahead of the Colonel. The passage to which he referred I knew without doubt was the one I had quoted to Mr. Gowen. Kirby's note, which he was most kind to have sent, explained that the advertisement was placed via a prepaid telegram sent from Chester, Pennsylvania, and signed simply, "Little Ivy." There would be no point tracing the sender in some Western Union office even if it were possible; beyond question the message had been dispatched by H. Wesley.

Another clue which led to another problem. What was the

Colonel doing in the grubby little city of Chester which I
have often heard described in the coarse but accurate phrase
as "the asshole of Pennsylvania"?

CHAPTER

18

YEARS OF experience plus the ability to apply my familiarity
with the Sacred Writings have taught me that certain profes-
sions or trades attract certain types of individuals and leave
their marks upon them. For example, I've rarely seen a fat ac-
countant or an overly intelligent one for that matter. "Grinds"
they were in college and "grinds" they are today. Physicians
have pink skins and an acquisitive look about their sharp
eyes, holders of Doctorates in Philosophy carry themselves
with a sickening aura of superiority. A plumber, with his pig-
gish nose and bathroom scent, looks like a plumber.

All the foregoing is preface to an admission of a serious
mistake I made in prejudging Millie Tomassio. The fact that
Marv had dated the woman once and found her attractive
then, meant little to me. After all, I know Helene, whom
Abrams refers to as his "beautiful roommate," and I would
not consider his wife nearly as attractive as that nickname
would imply.

Somehow I pictured Millie as an ungainly, square-toed,
flat-chested female with straight gray hair pulled back to expose a low forehead, and wearing some kind of drab uniform
upon the shoulders of which I would observe sprinklings of
dandruff. Little can be farther from the truth. When Marv
took me into the Missing Persons Bureau of the Philadelphia
Police Department and introduced me to the dark-eyed exotic
beauty wearing a low cut black dress which exposed an ample
view of creamy white skin, I could hardly believe my eyes.

This, I freely concede, is one of the few times I would gladly have traded my age and the wisdom acquired in fifty-nine
years for the advantage of being as young as Don Donaldson.

I have no intention of belaboring the point I make of Millie's physical charms. This is not the story of *that* kind of Chase. I shall say now, and for the last time, she was, or rather is, a beautiful woman who exudes sexual charms and let it go at that. Nor shall I hint that anything beyond platonic friendship developed between any of our Sons and the lady policeman who heads Philadelphia's Bureau of Missing Persons. Such, alas! would not be the truth.

When my loquacious friend concluded, Millie turned to us.

"I'm utterly intrigued with the whole situation. I share your concern over Mrs. Eberhardt, and I want to become involved within the limits of my duties here. First, however, I'll have to clear it with my boss, Inspector Fox. So, if you'll excuse me for a short while, gentlemen, I'll handle that chore right away."

Millie returned to her office in less than ten minutes, a broad smile lighting her face.

"It's OK. As you can see, we're less restricted here than the FBI and the fact that you're a city employee, Marv, Don a newspaper reporter, and you other gentlemen prominent citizens didn't hurt. I've no reason to believe I can solve the case but at least I can open certain channels for you and smooth your paths a bit."

She picked up her telephone and asked the operator to get the Chester Chief of Police.

"Hello, Dan," she said. "This is Millie."

We could hear with what evident delight the Chief took in asking Millie what he could do for her.

"First tell me what carnivals are playing in Chester and the rest of the country."

Millie turned to us while we waited for the answer.

"The cops always know beforehand. That's the way they keep ahead of the drifters, con men, and pickpockets. I won't go into the details—they've no bearing on your case—but the authorities work through a liaison, a sort of fixer. Every carnival has one."

I interjected.

"You mean a 'patch,' Millie."

Quite surprised, she smiled, showing a set of pearly white teeth and seemed amazed at my inside knowledge of carnival-ese. But before Millie had a chance to compliment me, as I'm sure she intended to do, the Chief of Chester fuzz came back on the line.

Despite the fact that from where I sat the clearly written notes Millie made rapidly on a sketch pad were upside down and backward I was able to read them just as easily as I had once read type when I was makeup editor on the University's Daily. According to the Chief a fair-sized carnival was currently playing within Chester's city limits and another, a small one, was scheduled to open the following week in Avondale, a village I knew well, near the Delaware State border. Two more would be in the county before the season ended but both of these were scheduled to open beyond our six-month deadline so that our interest in these was not even academic.

With our permission Millie informed the Chief about the bet and gave him a description of Colonel Eberhardt plus what she knew about Brother Joe. We could hear the Chester County officer's loud guffaws, but apparently he agreed to do a bit of checking both in his own bailiwick and in that of a fellow chief's at Avondale.

I was quite pleased that Millie politely but firmly brushed aside what appeared to be the Chester fuzz's persistent efforts to buy her a drink with dinner to follow. "Some other time," she kept saying, then thanked the officer and hung up.

"I saw no point in either of you wasting time at Chester," Millie told us. "Dan'll do a thorough job and if anything develops he'll advise me."

I would have been more confident of the results had I been permitted to handle the Chester County investigation myself, with Millie, perhaps, accompanying me to make the necessary introductions. Naturally I would have paid all expenses from my own pocket no matter what they were. However, there was no graceful way to change the plan now, I did make up my mind that should further research be required outside of Philadelphia, I would not yield so readily. After all, this was our Chase, not an official one, yet. With Millie's knowledge of police procedure and my ability to ferret out deeply concealed evidence, I saw no reason to ask any fellow Son to accompany us. Even though it might be necessary to spend several days in the field, all financial costs would still be mine.

Millie, naturally, was unaware of my thoughts but if she had been, I'm not sure she would have rejected the opportunity to get away from her humdrum existence. She smiled again, showing those pearly teeth from bright red lips.

"Dan knew all about your wager. They've been laying a few odds themselves. I think you six Sons may have provided some 'off-track' wagers in more than one station house. The Chief's betting against you. Offered to buy me a meal with the winnings. 'No dinner,' you heard me say. 'The faculties become refined when you starve them.' "

Marv and I almost leaped out of our chairs.

" 'The Adventure of the Mazarin Stone!,' Millie," I sang out, "I had no idea you knew the Sacred Writings, and so well."

"A hobby. The Master's been my hero for years. But I've no one to discuss him with. All my colleagues here read is Mickey Spillane. No females in the Copper Beeches? Apparently you Sons never heard of the Women's Liberation Movement."

Her eyes were twinkling when she said this but I'm not sure she wasn't hurt by our antifeminism and I decided at once to do something about this bigotry.

"Millie, Millie," I answered reassuringly. "This is a situation I, for one, intend to rectify. I've been a Copper Beech for as many years as you are old. [Slight flattery but under the circumstances I felt it more than justifiable.] I'll raise the point at our next meeting."

"It's a deal. If it can't be permanent I would like to be in at the killing."

An odd choice of words, I thought to myself, in view of what transpired later. Then Millie grew serious.

"I'm going to do some further checking with a couple of Pentagon friends. I'd like to get more details of the Colonel's career and his subsequent discharge. I don't believe you've been told the whole truth. If I get it, I'll call you, Marv."

I suggested that Millie get in touch with me instead since Marv had a full-time occupation and I, on the other hand, was devoting my energies exclusively to the Chase. He shrugged his shoulders noncommittally and agreed reluctantly, I'm sure.

"OK," she answered.

I gave her my telephone number. I think Marv was quite annoyed. This had been a day of surprises and they hadn't ended yet. Millie opened a desk drawer and removed a long,

thin cigar from which she deliberately bit off the tip. I was not
alert enough to offer the young lady a light but Marv was.
This was the first time I'd ever witnessed a member of the opposite sex engaged in smoking what I had heretofore regarded
as a male's prerogative. After I recovered from my initial
shock I must confess that on Millie it looked good. She took a
few deep puffs then settled back in her chair.

"If you'll forgive me for saying so, gentlemen, it really is
unfair of me to have passed judgment on the Colonel's character solely upon your assessment. But that's exactly what I
did, something contrary to all I've been taught. You cannot
exclude the possibility that your missing Son [I winced] has
done nothing which merits police interference."

I waited impatiently for Millie's telephone call. Meanwhile
we held our picnic on the Doylestown, Perkasie, and North
Wales Short Line Railroad. All six of us were subjected to
some good-natured teasing but certainly less than we expected. The afternoon and evening were stimulating. Normally
there are neither speeches nor presentations of papers at these
annual alfresco affairs which are devoted solely to conviviality. However, a goodly number of Copper Beeches prevailed
upon me to brief them about the Chase. I responded and
when I finished a great many toasts were drunk to our success. This in a broader sense would be a success not only for
our fellow Sons and BSI sodalities all over the world but also
proof that the Sacred Writings had never lost their timeless-
ness.

The evening ended on a high note and my neighbor, Arthur
Redstone, the brain surgeon, drove me home. He was cold
sober. I do believe he'd experienced some difficulties during a
recent operation which I gathered was not as successful as the
patient and his widow were led to expect. Since then Redstone
has been "on the wagon," to use the vernacular. I had some
few problems with my latchkey but suddenly the door was
flung open by my spouse. I could tell she was quite out of
sorts. She never did give her full approval to my membership
in the Copper Beeches and was openly hostile to my involvement and, I guess you could say, leadership in the Chase.

"Some woman's been calling you all evening," she said
coldly. (Actually there were only two calls but then my wife

is inclined to exaggerate.) "You're to get in touch with a Miss Billie something or other who claims she's a policeman."

My wife regarded me with disdain.

"What have you been up to now, Frank? Drunken driving again?"

I have never been arrested for driving under the influence of alcohol and Juliet is well aware of this. She was referring to an incident that occurred more than twenty years before on the Pennsylvania Turnpike when a Trooper, making a routine inspection of *all* drivers, offered a friendly suggestion that I permit my wife to drive the rest of the way home.

When Juliet dredged up that silly old incident for perhaps the thousandth time, I remained silent. This was no time to get into one of those endless marital arguments. So, with dignity, I retired to my study, shut the door and made sure my spouse had not picked up the extension telephone in her bedroom. As I dialed Millie's home number (for that's what I was sure it was), my heart leaped at the thought of news this intelligent policewoman may have received about H. Wesley. Her voice was so soft I thought at first I had awakened her but she assured me she had not yet retired.

"I have some queer news about the Colonel, Frank."

I listened eagerly, torn between a desire to learn anything new about our antagonist at once and the thought that what Millie had to say should be discussed privately and not on my telephone which might well be tapped. I had in mind a small, unfashionable but excellent restaurant in the Frankford section of Philadelphia where we would not be interrupted. The martinis there are quite potent but infinitely superior to those served at the so-called better in-town places. Then I heard a familiar click on the line and realized my wife had picked up the extension receiver. So, aware that Juliet would completely misunderstand my motives, I forbore to mention this better arrangement and resignedly sat back and listened to Millie in the limited privacy of my study.

"My friend at the Pentagon, the one I told you about, pulled the Colonel's file for me, something we've done for him on many an occasion. The information is not 'top' secret, it isn't even classified. It may all be public knowledge someday but meanwhile I would appreciate it if you and the others kept it to yourselves."

Without question, I would regard in the strictest of confidence whatever Millie told me. I didn't doubt that my colleagues would be just as worthy of her trust. At least I hoped they would, it was a chance I had to take.

"Your 'fox,' " Millie said, "has an incredible military record, one which should have put him at the head of the class. Let me say this, Frank [I could almost hear my wife gasp at the familiarity], my friend at the Pentagon volunteered none of the details nor did I request any. All I asked for was the broad picture and I got it, plus a bit more.

"During World War Two his assignments were to seek out and *destroy* person or persons plotting against the security of the United States Armed Forces. His objectives were not merely to gather information from collaborators, plotters and such, and this he did expertly, but to be the Avenging Angel as well. He succeeded, beyond reasonable expectations, to put the fear of God into those of the enemy who believed we were a bunch of silly sentimentalists and the worst that would happen to these civilian men, women, and children was a slap on the wrist. H. Wesley Eberhardt, then a Major, taught them that was far from the truth.

"You should know that all these missions were behind enemy lines. Obviously they required skilled advance planning, coolness under great danger, ability to outsmart the enemy at close hand and . . . "

Here Millie paused.

" . . . utter contempt for human life."

I shuddered. According to this H. Wesley was a trained executioner. And yet, at this moment my feelings about him were blurred and tended to become somewhat ambivalent for perhaps the first time. I had to admit that when we were at war men with such qualities as his could be a military necessity and their actions probably saved American and Allied lives. I may even have been a trifle envious since my own efforts then, surely through no fault of my own (age and myopia), were restricted to the promotion of Savings Bonds. However, I did rather well at that, as a wall plaque I glanced at while Millie talked so testified. I permit the decoration to remain where it is although it was signed by that *awful* man in the White House.

Millie had not yet concluded.

"The more I learn about the Colonel, the more astonished I am and the more I realize the difficulties of your problem.

Were you aware that he speaks four foreign languages fluently?"

I was not aware of this. She went on.

"He does. French, Italian, Russian, and German. Not bad for a poor parson's son, is it?"

Agreed but I hoped Millie wasn't becoming overenthusiastic about H. Wesley's charms and that she was not being swayed in his favor. I asked her if she agreed that murder, even legalized, was "not bad for a minister's son" either.

Millie laughed.

"Oh I'm not switching sides, Frank. I'm still with you, the Colonel's a dangerous man."

She continued.

"All the perils the Colonel braved and the successes he achieved during the two years he spent living as a civilian in France, Belgium, and Germany were taken into consideration when he came up on that charge after the Korean episode. The original complaint was murder, not excessive brutality.

"Any of those times while he was behind enemy lines he could have been hanged as a spy. He was a railway clerk in Linz, an undertaker in Bordeaux, and a baker in Antwerp. And he was so good at every job he tackled the enemy believed it had been his life's work. He was considered a master of disguise and deception and blended into the lives of every community in which he lived. Hiding from the Sons must be child's play for H. Wesley Eberhardt. You can see now, Frank, what we're up against."

I saw it only too well. One consolation was the fact that Millie had said "we" and not "you." Her next words were even more heartening.

"There are other developments which might very well let me join the Chase officially, that is if you'd like me to."

You know what my answer was to that.

"I'm going to work on that angle first thing in the morning. Do you think we could get together tomorrow sometime, Frank?"

My heart leaped. I wished only that Millie had not addressed me quite so familiarly. I could almost hear Juliet's outraged gasps.

"Certainly!" I answered, regardless of the cost. I thought once more of that little restaurant in Frankford. It was not to be.

"Good, Sir," Millie answered and the change in her tone of voice and salutation made me know that she, too, must have realized a third party was listening.

"If it's all right with you let's make it at headquarters around three o'clock. I'm sure you'll try to have the other Sons on hand and I think I can promise Inspector Fox will be present."

As you may well imagine I had little sleep that night even after Juliet wound up a long diatribe which began the moment Millie said goodnight. I tossed and turned for hours, finally dozing off lightly just as the sun rose. However, by ten o'clock I had already briefed the others, reaching Charlie Starr last. His mother said she hated to awaken her son; he'd just returned from a "convention" in Paris only hours before. But I finally prevailed on her, stressing the importance of what I had to tell him.

I arrived at police headquarters a few minutes early. Millie looked particularly attractive in a simple, tight-fitting blue blouse with a matching mini-skirt which revealed more of her shapely anatomy than I thought regulations would have permitted. I told her she looked stunning adding I was sure her outfit was a Hattie Carnegie original.

"So sweet of you to notice, my dear," she answered, patting my hand lightly. "You look beautiful, too, and besides I'll bet you're the only male in this joint who even heard of Hattie. Sorry to disappoint you, though [as if she ever could!] it comes from Sear's basement."

I know she was teasing, Sear's basement indeed! However, there was no time for the exchange of further amenities; within moments the others arrived and shortly after that we were all summoned to Inspector Fox's office.

The officer was a tall, slender fellow with salt and pepper hair, cropped short, sharp blue eyes and a most pleasant, almost deferential manner, as though he was aware we were not the usual run of guests. He addressed both Marv and Don by their first names. Both had informed me the inspector was a graduate of Northwestern University's Police Training School and the FBI Academy and was Commissioner Rizzo's right-hand man.

"Be seated, gentlemen," he said, "and you, too, young lady."

He shook his head from side to side, smiling as those bright blue eyes swept over the policewoman from head to toe.

"Thank God for Millie!" he commented. "What a dull place this would be without her."

Then he grew serious.

"First of all so that I don't waste any of your valuable time, let me say I'm completely familiar with the details of the Chase. Don, who's an old and trustworthy friend, and Marv, who is my colleague, filled me in."

I was slightly put out at this revelation, assuming that as the duly elected Copper Beech Historian this was my prerogative. But no matter, I sat back and listened.

"I know the terms of the bet and I know about those clues the Colonel's been taunting you with. With the exception of certain classified information, which my informants assure me is irrelevant, I've a reasonably complete dossier of his military background. And with an assist from a few of her old friends who are becoming as concerned over the lady's whereabouts, a fair knowledge of Mrs. Eberhardt's character."

There was a twinkle in his eyes.

"I've even pored through the Sacred Writings, something I'm forced to admit to you dedicated Sherlockians I haven't done since high school days. While I don't pretend to be an aficionado of the Master, at least I have a working knowledge of his methods.

"As it stands I have no justification for involving the Philadelphia Police Department on an official basis. . . . "

He paused and looked all of us in the eyes.

" . . . despite some well-founded suspicions that a crime may have been committed. Our operation's not unlike the FBI's and you've been given the reasons why they can't participate. In the past we've stretched a point just as we're willing to do now. Millie can tell you that every day in the week we get requests to help locate a missing person. If it's a minor, a wife deserter, or we're dealing with a felony, we muster as much force and know-how as we can.

"Unlike the Mounties, we don't always get our man. This is particularly true when we're dealing with someone like the Colonel who's disappeared of his own free will and is not a fugitive from the law. Lots of silly teenagers take off and we can't find them either. We could do better if we had more men but every time we ask Council to increase the budget we can hear you taxpayers scream from way up here."

He sighed.

"Things are not the way they used to be when I was a beat cop. I won't go into that now but you gentlemen know what's going on in our streets and schools so I don't have to tell you how the Force is deployed a large percentage of the time.

"What I'm trying to say is that we've long since passed the good old days when we had the time to investigate something on 'spec.' It meant the prevention of a crime or at least getting the jump on a potential criminal. Call this 'preventive medicine' if you like because that's what it is."

He smiled again.

"I'll get off my soapbox now. Millie has a hunch and from past experience I'd be a fool to disregard it. She realizes she's got a full-time job here from eight-thirty to four-thirty and no substitute available, which means she'll have to keep up with routine assignments. How she spends the rest of her hours and spare time is up to her. And I promise you, gentlemen, that whatever facilities we have are at your disposal. If this is agreeable to you six 'hunters,' Millie has my OK to join you under the conditions I outlined."

Jack, as chosen leader and self-proclaimed Shikari hunter, nodded his assent. He added, quite unnecessarily, I felt, that since we had failed to turn up the Colonel ourselves, outside help was more than welcome. This was almost an admission that the Sacred Writings were limited in value. As Historian, I added that all the notes I'd made so laboriously and my analysis of them I would turn over. The inspector seemed pleased.

"Gentlemen, I've one more point to make and I hope you'll regard what I say as confidential. For the past two years we've been aware of a slowly expanding group of men whose views are of the extreme and illegally violent Right. We've a complete dossier on most of them and you might be surprised at some of their names and prominence in city, state, and even national affairs. So far they've done nothing to merit more than continuous surveillance and that, of course, we're doing.

"They meet weekly, we know when and where and we have reasonably accurate knowledge of what they say. Your Colonel began an association with these fellows eighteen months ago and quit them abruptly. He met with them for the last time March 25."

The inspector paused and swept his eyes over us.

"As you gentlemen know this was three days before the bet was placed. There was no overt reason for his sudden withdrawal from the group and we've been unable to come up with a hidden motive either. The only conclusion we drew is that he just got fed up, decided there was no future in this association and determined to find another or perhaps decided it was all talk and no action. I, myself, think the last reason is the true one. But let me tell you, some of the suggestions he made to his erstwhile colleagues and his methods of executing them were brilliant, even though they'd displayed complete contempt for human life. What an ego! When anyone had the nerve to disagree, he gave them a tongue-lashing that must have made the culprit feel like a village idiot."

That bit about the Colonel's ego was hardly anything new to me.

"Gentlemen," the inspector went on, "the man's a genius but I think he's cracked and getting worse. He *must* show his superiority constantly and that is why, as I'm sure you realize, he issued the challenge and keeps taunting you with clues. I've told you about the Rightist group not because the Colonel's membership has a remote connection with your bet but simply to demonstrate just what his potential is."

He smiled and quoted the Master.

" 'I said it in London, Watson, and I say it again now, that never yet have we helped to hunt down a more dangerous man than he. . . . ' "

What the inspector left unsaid, I'm sure, was the possibility that H. Wesley eventually would tie up and perhaps take over the leadership of another extremist group willing to do more than spout philosophy. I should explain that while I may have strong dislikes for certain socialistically motivated organizations—the Civil Liberties Union to name one—I have equally strong distaste for Rightist oriented associations. Hence, it should be obvious why I was willing to cooperate with the Philadelphia Police Department and the FBI as well in the apprehension of H. Wesley Eberhardt.

CHAPTER

19

I SAW Millie socially for the first time the day after her official entry into the Chase. I felt it important to establish an informal relationship since we'd be working together so closely, I, the Historian, and she, our link to officialdom. As far as I was concerned, I'd gladly have sacrificed a dinner engagement Juliet and I had that evening but Millie, unfortunately, was not free.

Instead of dining at that quiet Frankford restaurant as I planned, we lunched in the noisy police department cafeteria where the food was better than passable although we were forced to serve ourselves, a barbaric custom, in my opinion. This, coupled with the annoying discovery that alcoholic beverages, even *vin ordinaire*, were not available, caused our meal to be something less than a gourmet's delight.

The time we spent together was not a total loss, however, despite the good-natured, albeit constant, raillery to which she was subjected by her associates. One of the more literate officers insisted upon calling her "Kitty Foyle." I understood the allusion since Kitty's creator was a Founding Member of the BSI. I'm not certain Millie did.

During those few moments we were left to ourselves, I learned that Millie's maiden name was a good old Anglo-Saxon one—Weston. She'd been a widow since 1960 when her husband, a police lieutenant, was killed in an encounter with a deranged sniper. There were no offspring; she was presently living with her mother. Millie's spouse had been considerably older than she.

"But then I always did like older men," she confessed. "They're much more comfortable to be with."

She shook her head.

"I get so tired of these married wolves around here."

I should have liked to assure her that while I was married I

163

am *not* a wolf and am prone to respect a woman's virtue as long as the woman, herself, holds it sacred. However, there was no chance for this disclosure. I wasn't even given the opportunity to light Millie's cigar; the moment she bit off the tip there was a sudden flurry of flicked cigarette lighters and matches around her mouth. All, including myself, who'd been waiting for that moment, were "beaten to the draw" by a brash young officer. I yielded gracefully, the others did not. They turned on the "winner," raucously denouncing him with all sorts of epithets.

It was solely business when we returned to Millie's office. No sooner had she closed the door when a call came in from the Chester Chief. Millie motioned that I was to pick up the extension line but put her forefinger over her lips, meaning, of course, that I was to keep silent. The information Dan gave Millie was encouraging and probably our first break. Joe Eberhardt *had* been in Chester the day the telegram was sent to *Amusement Business*, in fact he was there the entire week of August 18.

"He and some broad were running a 'mitt camp' [a fortune teller] on the Wallace Wondershow's midway," the Chief reported. "I got this dope from their patch who owed me a couple favors. He had nothing on the Colonel but told me it was quite possible the old boy was on the lot. I *know* that and so do you, Millie.

"Best place in the world to hide out, a carnival. Wallace runs a pretty good size outfit—over eight hundred employees —and the labor turnover's heavy, particularly in midseason, which is now. Ain't no way possible to keep track of who's on hand and who's not. They're so desperate for help they'll hire anybody they can get even if they stay for only a day, drunks, thieves, you name 'em. They don't bother to check 'em out.

"I went over to Western Union myself. Girl clerk who took the message don't remember a thing about who sent it. It was a crazy signature, the one you tole me, 'Little Ivy,' but it didn't faze her a bit. Doesn't even recall lookin' up at whoever it was paid for it. Could have been Joe, could have been the Colonel, or could have been the three-eyed man for all she knows."

Millie asked the Chief if he'd checked the "broad" in Joe Eberhardt's mitt camp.

"Give me some credit, Millie," he answered sounding a bit aggrieved. "It wasn't the Colonel's wife."

We knew now, almost beyond question, that H. Wesley was on a carnival midway within the 125-mile limit. I said "almost beyond question" because, as Millie pointed out, it was possible the Colonel had set Joe up as a Judas goat and was elsewhere himself. So far we could make no assumptions about Ellen except take H. Wesley's word that she would be with him until the Chase ended one way or the other. This we had to do despite the fact that all of Marv's telegrams about Ellen's serum brought negative responses from druggists and not one of the kennels I reached was boarding a dog answering Blondie's description.

Millie stared into space for several moments, then turned to me.

"The Colonel's really got us where the hairs are short, Frank, hasn't he?"

I wasn't quite sure what she meant by that expression but I nodded my head in agreement.

"I'm going to take it for granted he's on a carnival midway with Joe and that's where he sent the clues from. So it's reasonable to believe he was with Gibson and Fowler up in Snyder County and with the Wallace shows in Chester. What we'd like to know is which carnies went from G&F to Wallace."

She shook her head.

"And that's going to be very, very tough, if not impossible —heavy turnover, aliases, you know the whole bit, Frank. But we'll make a stab at it anyway. I'll find out where each of those carnivals is playing now then I'll ask the sheriff there to get the payroll list and send it to me pronto."

I pointed out the possibility that either or both carnivals might be well past the limit or, as a matter of fact, in another state.

"True," Millie answered, "but even so, if we had that information think how much easier it would be for us when we checked a new midway, knowing beforehand the names or aliases of employees who'd been on the other lots. There can't be too many. If the same ones appeared on the payrolls of a third carnival I'd say we'd be fairly safe assuming we had our man. That is if we get him before he slips away."

She paused to remove a cigar from the desk drawer. This

time I had no competition and leaned over to light the cheroot. Millie met me half-way, rising from her chair and bending over to expose her lovely breasts.

"Don't burn your fingers, Frank," she warned, then sat back, inhaled deeply, shaped her lips into an oval and blew a series of beautifully formed tiny smoked rings into the air. This was something I'd been trying to do all my life from the time of my first Sweet Caporal at the age of eleven.

My face must have been flushed. Millie asked me if the room was too warm and when I replied that it was just right for me, she continued.

"I've another thought which might be easier. I don't know for sure whether any of the rides, gambling joints, or exhibits move from one lot to another during the season but I rather suspect a few of them may. Let's say the same Dark House you saw in McClure was also in Chester with the other carnival and then we caught up with it on another midway, I'd say we've got it made. There can't be nearly as many equipment changes as there are personnel. So let's give that a try.

"First, we'll have to find out where Gibson and Fowler and Wallace's midway are playing this week. Can you handle this end, Frank?"

I couldn't help smiling with pride as I opened my briefcase and extracted the latest issue of *Amusement Business*. While she watched I turned the page to the "route list." Millie whispered an appreciative, "Well, what do you know?" walked around to my side of the desk and with her hand resting lightly upon my shoulder we combed the columns together. My knowledge of perfume is sketchy at best (Juliet uses only Ivory soap and water on her epidermis, plus some foul smelling antiseptic after-bath deodorant) so I had no idea what fragrance Millie applied. However, the effect was overpowering and it became increasingly difficult to concentrate on the task at hand. I finally managed after she asked me whether I suffered from emphysema. Somewhat piqued I assured her with asperity that at my last annual physical examination, one of the city's most respected internists found my body functions those of a man twenty years my junior.

Gibson and Fowler was playing at Troy, New York, which put it out of range. Wallace's Wondershow's midway had a scheduled opening at Punxsutawney which was in the Commonwealth, all right, but at least 250 miles northwest of Philadelphia. Millie then proceeded to demonstrate the advantages an official law enforcement agency has over others including talented, resourceful amateurs with background knowledge of the Sacred Writings. It would have taken the Sons weeks to accomplish what Millie, as a representative of the Philadelphia Police Department, did in a few minutes.

Her first telephone call was to the sheriff of Rensselaer County in which Troy apparently is located. While she waited on the line I mentioned that I was acquainted with one of the Van Rensselaers who holds a nonresident membership in the Racquet. I suggested he might be of assistance should I be able to reach him. But Millie, while appreciative, shook her head and smiled. "I think the sheriff will cooperate."

After identifying herself, Millie told the officer what our problem was. She received his assurance that a man would be assigned at once and promised that a teletyped list of all carnies who had left for parts unknown after the Bean Soup would be dispatched through proper channels before the day ended.

"What happens now," Millie explained, "is that a deputy will put the heat on G&F's patch."

I interrupted with a smile.

"Mr. Sillman," I said, calling upon my prodigious memory and Millie looked amazed.

"You should have been fuzz, Frank, you've the talent. At any rate the list will arrive simultaneously at State Police Headquarters in Harrisburg, the barracks nearest Punxsutawney and right here, too. Since it'll be on the record that this is an official request from us the Officer of the Day in Harrisburg will instruct the Punxi sergeant or lieutenant to turn the list over to the local chief of police. And that guy I know well, so I'll alert him on what to expect."

This incredible exhibition of police interplay was not lost on me. Nor did it fail to make me ponder once again upon the colossal nerve of Colonel H. Wesley Eberhardt who, by now, must be aware we Sons had become party to a mutual pact with law enforcement agencies all over the country.

Millie needed no introduction to Punxsutawney's chief with whom she was on a first name basis. In addition to checking the personnel list with the Wallace patch, Millie requested that "Chuck" find out whether any equipment—rides, games or exhibits—had gone from G&F to Wallace. Apparently the second half of the assignment was easy. As the chief told Millie the Wallace outfit owned practically all of its own materiel and therefore would be unlikely to permit more than a few independents to operate on its midway.

Then Millie turned to me.

"Now, Frank, let's take a look at that list again and find out what's playing in 'our' territory, big, medium, and little and see where that takes us."

This was Saturday, August 30, with Labor Day, the biggest summer weekend coming up. The number of carnivals scheduled to open then within the 125-mile limit reached the staggering total of seventy-three. Millie was even more surprised than I.

"We can't possibly check them all," she said, "no matter how fast we move our asses."

For a moment I was aghast at Millie's use of such a Rabelaisian expression. However, on second thought, I found it quite descriptive, admittedly conjuring a not unpleasant image of the actions involved were I to accept the phrase literally. I experienced some difficulty concentrating on her next words but I got myself together and listened with as much attention as I could muster.

"We're too short of manpower, Frank, to do any kind of thorough job on that many. Let's not fool ourselves. I can't ask the inspector for anybody else. Maybe later but right now I'm *it*."

My chagrin must have been apparent. Millie smiled, reached over the desk and patted my hand.

"Of course, Frank, I have you and the other Sons. My reference was to official fuzz."

I was mollified; Millie went on.

"I've hunted for enough missing children to know that most of that list of seventy-three are little, locally run street fairs set up for 'homecoming' week or church bazaars or volunteer fire department benefits. There'll be a merry-go-round, a few other kiddie rides, Bingo and a couple different games of chance. If there's a mug joint this'll be run by the hometown photographer and if they have a mitt camp you can bet the fortune teller inside the tent will be a housewife, dressed up in costume.

"They won't have a Bozo, a Dark Ride, a Mirror Maze, a girlie show, or a ten-in-one, all of which are good potential hideouts. There's no real midway, only Main Street roped off for two blocks and you can go through the whole bit in ten minutes and check off everybody. I've done it; I know. We won't find the Eberhardts this way."

She shook her head.

"No, 'lover,' " she said, and at this unexpected term of endearment even if uttered casually I could feel myself growing red, "if the Colonel and Company are to be found on a carnival lot, and I'm sure they will, they'll be with a damned sight bigger operation than these."

Millie leaned back in thought, blew some more contemplative smoke rings, then continued.

"I don't see what else we can do except sit tight till we get the word from Chuck out in Punxi and take it from there."

I reported the results of my conference to Jack who, in turn, notified the others, asking each Son to hold himself in readiness for a hurried trip should the necessity arise. I got the word from Millie the following afternoon, just as Juliet, our neighbors, the Redstones, and I were having cocktails on our terrace. We'd all planned to spend Sunday and Labor Day following with their son, Horace, whose spacious houseboat was docked off Kent Island on the Chesapeake. This has been our custom for some time. However, with my usual foresight, I had already warned my own spouse of the possibility that duty might call me elsewhere. I shall not elaborate upon Juliet's comments except to say I wished for an absence of guests when she made them.

There were, Millie informed me, a total of five men, three women, and two sixteen-year-old Bozos who had transferred their allegiance from Gibson and Fowler to the Wallace Wondershows. The Chief interviewed all and results were negative. Three of the adult males were the wrong color, the fourth was a con man, known over the years by Chuck, and the fifth was presently in the county jail charged with indecent exposure. No matter how evil the Colonel, I could not possibly imagine him committing this degrading crime. None of the ladies was Ellen—one was black, one was pregnant, and one's body was covered with tattoos.

The only equipment making the journey from Troy to Punxsutawney was a "duck pond," a "cork gallery," and a "sit down grab joint." The brief but thorough education I received at the Bean Soup came in handy. Consequently I was able to share my erudition with Millie. The first, I explained, was a stand where marks, upon payment of twenty-five cents, were permitted to lift any one of many plastic ducks from a stream of fast flowing water. Each fowl had a number on its underside which, to win, must match a corresponding number on a prize displayed behind the counter. I told Millie—and she realized I was speaking with quiet authority—that the prizes, for the most part, were penny novelties, "slum" I had heard them called.

The second was a cork board filled with inflated balloons, which marks tried to puncture by hurling darts at them. A sit down grab joint (a most descriptive nomenclature, by the way) is a minuscule restaurant where patrons put their weary bones on uncomfortable stools in front of a counter while munching that unpalatable greasy American phenomenon, a bolus lebeled the hot dog, then wash down the indigestible mess with a warm, sweet, carbonated swill.

While Millie was amused at my descriptive powers she felt the news from Punxsutawney was disappointing and agreed with me it was unlikely that our "fugitives" would attempt to hide in any of these joints which had gone the route from New York to Western Pennsylvania. Chuck confirmed the fact that the operators of these stands and their assistants were not the Eberhardts. Besides, even at this late hour with less than four weeks to go we still clung to the belief that our fox was staying within his self-set geographic boundaries.

Millie scanned the list again.

"Let's see what big ones we've got for Labor Day openings. World of Mirth's scheduled for Allentown. That's one of the largest fairs in the state and World's is one hell of a good-sized carnival. There'll be at least a half-million people on their midway before the week is over. I'll find out who handles their security. Probably the Pinkertons but I'll make sure."

It was the Pinkertons. Millie talked to their regional chief and received assurances that should anyone answering the Colonel's, Ellen's, or Brother Joe's description be found the Philadelphia Police Department would be notified.

"I can't ask the Allentown cops or the state police for an assist. It wouldn't be right, we've no real emergency and they'll have plenty of trouble themselves searching for fifty or more runaway kids and keeping the drifters out of customers' pockets and clearing the way for ambulances. But the Pinkies *have* to cooperate. They're nothing more than armed civilians and they need us more than we need them. So what does that leave us?"

Millie answered her own question.

"Witkin and Egan's up in Carbon County Fair at Lehighton; Dell and Travers Giant Amusements open Labor Day in York. I don't know much—in fact I don't know anything—about Witkin and Egan, the Carbon County Fair and who'll be on security, so I'll have to inquire. But the York Fair's a huge one, just about the size of Allentown's, with another mile-long midway and a daily attendance of a hundred thousand. God knows it would be like trying to find the proverbial needle there."

Again I became acutely conscious of the Colonel's brilliance in choosing this form of hideout. For that's where he was, I *knew*. I was *not* discouraged. We, Millie and I, and perhaps the other hunters, would find him and Ellen as well in one of the hundreds of "attractions"—the Mirror Maze, the Dark, the Fun or the Glass House, the Side or the Girl Shows, or the Snake Pit. Could he be working one of the rides—the Sky Dive, the Ferris Wheel, the Merry-go-round, the Double Dip, the Matterhorn, the Trabant, the Scrambler, the Tilt-a-Whirl? I knew them all. Those few hours I spent at the Bean Soup had long since proved their worth. Was the Colonel operating a crooked joint (I wouldn't put it past him), the Big Cat, Crazy Ball, the Penny Pitch, the Razzle? I wished I could have another confidential chat with my friend, the Gypsy. I'd find out, believe me I would.

A few telephone calls later we knew that the Lehighton Fair and the carnival there were both medium-sized operations. Protection of the public was in the hands of the local fuzz—four patrolmen, a sergeant, and a chief—augmented by scores of local citizens sworn in for active duty *pro tem*. Security at the York Fair was provided by the William J. Burns Detective Agency. Like their rivals, the Pinkertons, this outfit readily agreed to cooperate. There would be no need to supplement these organizations with any Son at either York or Allentown, Millie felt. I was in complete accord. She hadn't yet made up her mind what to do about Lehighton.

"I don't know the chief there but I can easily get a contact. I probably wouldn't even need one, although in small towns

like that it's better. They don't have much use for lady cops.
I'm just wondering if we shouldn't handle this one ourselves."

She eyed me speculatively.

"What are your plans for tomorrow and Monday, Frank?"

I gulped, not knowing what to expect next but hoping
against hope she meant what I thought. I assured her I was
completely free.

"So am I, lover. I'm off until Tuesday morning. Shall we
make the trek to Lehighton together?"

You know my response to that. I arranged to pick Millie up
at her home about noon the following day, leaving unanswered the delicate matter of motel accommodations—two singles or one double? I would let circumstances dictate the solution. Then I hastened home to break the news to Juliet, a
most difficult task, believe me. I don't want to go into the
acrimonious harangue to which I was subjected. After the
gush of verbiage subsided sufficiently for me to speak I pa-
tiently tried to explain where my duty lay.

"Duty, hell! Playing cops and robbers again. Grow up, Bus-
ter, Sherlock's dead," she said scornfully and slammed her
bedroom door. She emerged a half-hour later and strode into
my study.

"You want to louse up a beautiful weekend with the Redstones, something we've been looking forward to all this stinking hot summer. OK, I'll louse it up with you. *I'm* coming
along."

"Good," I answered, calling upon strategy which has served
me so well in the past. "You'll love Lehighton. We'll make a
real weekend of it."

She looked at me.

"Lehighton? Where's that?"

I opened the atlas on my desk, turned the pages to a map of
Pennsylvania and located the town for her.

"What's there?"

I shrugged my shoulders.

"Not much except the fair. It's a little Dutch farming
town."

I must give the devil her due. My wife is a most tolerant
woman. Only rarely have I heard her speak disparagingly of
any ethnic or racial group with the exception of what she calls
the "Dumb Dutch." Her strange antipathy for these solid, unsophisticated souls was brought about by one of them, a child-

hood nurse who kept her charge under control by threatening to "put a hex" on her should she misbehave. Juliet was thoughtful.

"What are you going to do there?"

I told her that in the company of a member of the Philadelphia Police Department and probably the local sheriff I would spend my time combing the midway in search of Colonel H. Wesley Eberhardt. Her eyes narrowed into slits.

"And what will *I* be doing then? Sitting around in the hot sun twiddling my thumbs or riding the ferris wheel with all the Dumb Dutch. No thanks. You do what you like. *I'm* going with the Redstones."

I suppressed a "winner's" smile of victory, snickering to myself at the memory of that long since departed nurse who controlled her charges by witchcraft. This, alas, was a mistake. Moments after Juliet left the next morning and I had my suitcase half-packed debating whether or not to include pajamas, I began to sneeze violently. Within seconds my eyes teared, my nose grew red and my sinuses clogged.

"Jesus Christ!" I shouted in fury. "Hay fever. I'll be one stinking, sniffling, repulsive mess for the entire weekend."

I hadn't had an attack like this for more than ten years. "One of the compensations of getting old," my allergist said. "You outgrow it."

I clenched my fist, beat the air savagely and looked up at the ceiling.

"You son-of-a-bitch of a Pennsylvania Dutch nurse, wherever the hell you are. You put a hex on me. May you rot forever in purgatory!"

In every possible respect the weekend was a ghastly failure. I rummaged through our medicine chest and found a half-empty bottle of an antihistamine I used to take. Hastily I swallowed six tablets, triple the normal dosage. But the drug had lost its efficiency and all they did was make me so groggy I surrendered the wheel to Millie. In fact, it was only by summoning up great willpower that I managed to get from Jessup Street to Frankford.

Disappointed as she must have been I couldn't blame Millie for laughing when she saw my red eyes and dripping nose. There was no opportunity for explanation or apology, I fell asleep almost at once and remained in that condition, more or less, until our return to Philadelphia early Monday afternoon.

There were a few times during the night when paroxysms of sneezing, at least a fifteen force on the Beaufort scale, awakened me and unquestionably awakened Millie in the adjacent cabin. Then I redosed myself with antihistamine and promptly fell asleep again.

A young deputy sheriff whom I dimly remember meeting and who was most solicitous of my welfare although I saw no reason for him to call me "Pop," was Millie's escort on the midway and her dinner companion as well. We had made no formal pledge to keep our liaison a secret, yet I know the young lady mentioned it to no one; you can be sure I didn't. A thorough search of the small Witkin and Egan midway Millie made in conjunction with the local fuzz and state troopers uncovered no member of the Eberhardt family. It's possible I could have done better; I never had the chance.

Millie insisted on driving me to my doorstep; she herself went home by taxi. I'm a son-of-a-bitch if my hay fever didn't vanish the very instant I stepped inside the house. Weary with frustration and too debilitated to curse the Fates in the form of that miserable Dumb Dutch nursemaid, I simply crawled into bed, there to remain until loud, persistent bangs on the door knocker aroused me about six A.M.

Of all the times for our failing postal system to remind me of its once vaunted efficiency, this was it. I signed for a special delivery, tore open the envelope and with eyes still red and swollen I noted the contents—a pair of tickets for a Labor Day dance sponsored by Reading, Pennsylvania, Local No. 161, of the Amalgamated Association of Gasfitters of America, AFL-CIO.

"Oh, Eberhardt, you misbegotten monster! Where are you now?" I uttered aloud with near despair at this further demonstration of the Colonel's cleverness. Lips trembling with suppressed rage I quoted the source of H. Wesley's "inspiration" purloined from the Sacred Writings in "A Case of Identity."

"A flush stole over Miss Sutherland's face, and she picked nervously at the fringe of her jacket. 'I met him [Mr. Hosmer Angel] first at the gasfitters' ball.' "

CHAPTER

20

EVEN THOUGH Millie was present our plenary session of September 4 was most depressing. We Sons had nothing to report, Millie's answer from the York County Sheriff was negative, and Jack had no assignments to hand out. In retrospect I think it was at our meeting the following week that we descended to the nadir of our despair. This, despite Millie's continued insistence that the Colonel's ego would compel him to furnish us with one "live" lead before the Chase was over.

"He *must*," she claimed, "and we must be ready to take advantage of it when it comes. I know his type. They have to flaunt their superiority even at the risk of capture. And that's what traps them finally. I could show you a hundred cases in our files to prove my point."

Whether Millie was merely talking in an attempt to raise our low spirits or whether she meant what she said I don't know. We had no intention of asking her to submit those hundred cases for inspection. What troubled us more than anything else was our growing concern for Ellen. Should anything evil happen to her we were, at least in one sense responsible. By subscribing to the wager we became party to her disappearance.

All well and good for us to say aloud to each other (regardless of what we said to ourselves), "Just wait and see. Five Sons heard him declare, 'Whither thou goest, I go.' We never had any reason to doubt the Colonel's word before so why doubt it now?"

And yet we had to take into account that damned enigmatic reply to a simple question. Was there anything in the deal we entered into which called for Ellen's presence at the payoff or at any other time for that matter? The answer to that was "no." We had neither the legal nor moral right to demand proof of his wife's existence or good health.

There was the matter of motive. If we sought bizarre reasons for murder between spouses I could cite that fatal bridge game many years ago, out in Denver I think it was, where a husband shot his wife to death because she trumped her partner's ace. The jury heeded defense counsel's plea of justifiable homicide and acquitted the accused. But H. Wesley did not have those mitigating circumstances to offer; neither he nor Ellen played bridge.

True, they were poles apart politically and may have had violent arguments on that score although I doubt this because of Ellen's genuinely equable disposition and her old-fashioned belief in a husband's position of authority. In our circle, at any rate, men don't go 'round killing wives because one is registered Democrat and the other Republican.

What could Eberhardt possibly gain by Ellen's death? Still another "nothing," at least as far as we knew, certainly not any financial benefits. We were aware that Ellen's great wealth was held jointly. Another woman? Possible but not probable, he wasn't the type. And, as I pointed out before, you can't get away with an illicit romance in Philadelphia without someone of your own social level finding out. It's been tried. I have an ear for this kind of thing and I'm sure I would have known.

What's left? We think H. Wesley's an amoral man, a trained, ruthless, efficient murderer, perhaps even a psychotic who, if these terms are not contradictory, needs no logical purpose to kill. Webster says, "Where these facts are admitted . . . the *rationale* usually appended is that their source is a diabolical one." We suspect that the Colonel has "done away with" poor Ellen but can we prove it? Of course not! We don't even possess the usual *corpus delicti* always available in the Sacred Writings.

Suppose the Colonel shows up at the duly appointed time, collects the Carl Anderson manuscripts, closes Baskerville Hall or sells it and takes off for any place in the world he wants to go. Who can stop him? Not us. There's not a damned thing we can do except pay up. He's under no obligation to produce Ellen for the six Sons or anyone else.

And if he wants to stick around Philadelphia to finance a new political party of the Right, that's his business. This is a free country, or so we've been told since nursery school. I must admit that during those early weeks of September all of

us drifted into a state of lethargy. We abandoned our erstwhile positive approach and in its place substituted the fatal-
ist's philosophy—"What will be, will be." Even Millie had no
further suggestions. "Wait and see," she kept saying. "There'll
be that give-away clue. Don't worry."

But we did worry about Ellen, at any rate, and on September 15, with the deadline a mere two weeks off, we had
further cause for concern, even alarm. This is what happened.
While neither Ed nor his associates ever represented the Dawsons he was brought into the picture by Bill Moody whose
firm does, or rather did, for three generations.

Ed called me that Monday morning. He said he had disturbing news and asked whether I, myself, was free for lunch
and also would I get the other Sons to join him at the Benedict (a lawyers' club) of which he is a member. I said I could
make it and would contact the others. I suggested bringing
Millie along and he thought this a good idea and changed our
meeting place to the Carlisle. The Benedict is for gentlemen
only, no exceptions are ever made.

We might just as well have met at the Benedict; Millie was
unable to get away on such short notice. She did ask me,
though, to call her immediately after we adjourned. Of the
other Sons only Jack was available so there were just four of
us including Bill Moody whom I knew slightly. How Bill managed to become a partner in this distinguished law firm is evidence of our changing times. Bill is a Roman Catholic, a
graduate of Villanova and, if memory serves me correctly, an
unsuccessful Democratic candidate for Legislature in 1962.
However, this information has little bearing on the Chase, I
mention it only in passing.

I was surprised at the excellence of the Carlisle's martinis
and meant to ask their bartender which brand of vermouth he
used—the gin was Beefeater, unquestionably—but after Bill
presented this new problem, or if rather an extenstion of an
old one, I forgot, and have not been to the Carlisle since.

From his briefcase Moody extracted a letter which Ed already had seen. It was dated September 8, had been sent air
mail, special delivery and came from one of those two dismal
cousins of Ellen, the ones we'd met at the Dawson-Eberhardt
nuptials. The return address was Sioux City, Iowa; apparently
I'd been in error "locating" them at Indianapolis (or was it
Peoria?). The communication follows:

William R. Moody, Esquire
Bailey, Banks, Linton, and Stauffer
Land Title Building
Philadelphia, Pennsylvania 19107

Dear Mr. Moody:

I do not want to cause you any trouble but my sister, Ada, and I were wondering if you have been in touch with our Cousin Ellen Dawson Eberhardt recently. We have not heard from her since March 24, which was my birthday. My sister Ada's was August 4 and this is the first time in more than thirty years that Ellen has forgotten it. We usually receive at least four letters, about once a month, from Ellen between those natal dates.

Please believe me, Sir, our concern is not for her gifts, generous as they were, which she always included in her greetings. My sister and I are quite able to support ourselves on adequate pensions and own our home on the banks of the Mississippi. As a child Ellen spent more than one summer holiday with us when her dear parents, and our as well, were still alive.

Despite the great disparity in ages and although we saw her so seldom—in fact not since the wedding—I know she feels close to us. Perhaps that is because we are her only surviving relatives, when we pass on she will have no one else.

I wrote to Ellen on March 25, thanking her for the gift. Since the envelope bore our address and it was not returned I believe delivery was made. I wrote again in April and this was not returned either. Ellen never answered it and that is highly unusual. This past June the National Association of Librarians held its annual convention in Pittsburgh, Pennsylvania. My sister Ada, who used to be head of the Carnegie Library here in Sioux City before her retirement in 1966 was invited to attend. She accepted and I accompanied her.

We sent a note to Ellen beforehand thinking it would be nice to visit her since we would be only an eight-hour bus drive from Philadelphia. We said we did not want to impose on her and her husband's hospitality and would stay only two nights if that was convenient and if not, we

would stay at the YWCA. At least we would be able to
see her. We never received an answer.

My mother passed away twenty-nine years ago and
on the anniversary of her death, which is September 5,
Ellen always saw to it through a Sioux City florist shop
run by young Mr. Vincent and his father before him
that fresh cut flowers were placed on "Aunt Willa's"
grave. This year, when we went to the cemetery as is our
custom, to place our own wreath, there was no bouquet
from Ellen. Mr. Vincent said he had not received an
order.

Ada and I fretted so much over this we decided to
make a long distance call to Ellen but the operator told
us the line was disconnected. That was last Sunday,
September 7. This is why we are taking the liberty of
writing to you. We got your name from a letter you sent
us April 16, 1951 when Ellen endowed a bed in the
Harkins General Hospital in our parents' memory.

Both my sister and I would be deeply grateful if you
will let us know whether Ellen was in touch with you
recently. I have enclosed a self-addressed stamped envelope for your reply.

Respectfully yours,
(Miss) Bertha O. Franklin

Moody was silent until we finished reading the communication. Then he turned to us.

"Ed knows we haven't represented Ellen for quite a while,
we never did represent her husband. I always liked Ellen—she
was a lovely, gracious woman and taken on face value this letter is disturbing. However, it didn't give me the right to investigate her absence. After all, I don't know the Franklin 'girls';
they might well be crackpots and Ellen could have a perfectly
valid reason for severing the connection.

"George Phillips represents the Colonel and it would hardly be ethical to inquire about a former client. Maybe if I knew
him better I could do it informally but he's a stiff old man, as
Ed knows, and I was sure he'd resent me. After all, the
whereabouts of a client is none of my goddamned business
and he has every right to tell me to go to hell.

"We all know about your bet, so I called Ed, here, thinking
he might enlighten me. Instead he only added to my concern.

You fellows more than anyone else can understand why. So I asked Ed if he'd mind getting in touch with George."

Moody looked at Ed.

"Did you reach him?"

"Yeah. About an hour ago. He was formal with me, too, even though we've been acquainted for a long time. He didn't tell me to go to hell but I didn't get much out of him either. George had no idea where Ellen is, on the other hand he had no reason to see her. He did not know the Eberhardts socially and I couldn't ask him directly when he'd last seen the Colonel. But I gathered it hadn't been for a good many months. There wouldn't necessarily be any occasion for a conference between the Colonel and his lawyer. You've probably handled some estates, Bill, where you don't see your clients for ten years. So do we.

"Well, at any rate, this is the way George and I left it."

We—Ed rather more than I—felt Bill Moody had a right to be informed about details of the Chase. So we briefed him on our progress, or lack of it, and his concern became as deep seated as ours. He asked a few sharp questions and I was glad I could supply the answers.

Yes, as I'd reported to the other Sons, I checked the Colonel's car and Ellen's as well. This became one of my first chores and after peering into the Eberhardts' garage and observing neither vehicle there I did some probing and learned that H. Wesley's Imperial and Ellen's Porsche were leased on an annual basis. Both contracts expired simultaneously March 31, 1969. This, naturally, did not preclude the probability that some other rental agency was involved or that the Colonel bought a car. However, the task of gathering this information was impossible without official aid. I made a mental note to discuss this with Millie.

What had been done with the Colonel's mail? I had a partial answer to this. I knew he had a P.O. Box—he'd once told me so himself—but who was storing accumulated mail or where it was being forwarded were questions government employees refused to answer. In fact, a postal inspector to whom I was referred at the main branch became quite nasty when I persisted. I finally had to tell him I was a close friend of Senator Hart to whom I would report this incivility. Even that didn't calm him down.

As you must know by now I do not easily abandon a project once I begin. When I was unable to develop clues at the post office I took several additional steps. Late one afternoon, and with considerable trepidation, I raised the bronze panel over the mail slot and with the use of a flashlight I'd thoughtfully brought along, peered inside. I can state positively the opening was not jammed nor was there a pile of mail on the floor.

Still not satisfied I waited one morning for the approach of the postman who delivers on the 1900 block of Spruce Street. I used, as a pretext, the story that I wanted to know when an invitation I'd mailed the previous day would be delivered. He shook his head.

"There's a stopper on all Carriage House mail," he informed me. "You'll have to check with the inspector."

We adjourned our session at the Carlisle with nothing accomplished except an intensification of our anxieties.

CHAPTER

21

EVENTS MOVED so swiftly those last ten days of the Chase that I have succumbed to the temptation of listing actions and counteractions in chronological order. On Wednesday, September 17, Millie telephoned me. I'd been up early poring over my notes on the case so that her call at eight A.M. neither awakened nor disturbed me. She sounded amused, puzzled, and even slightly embarrassed, a strange admixture indeed.

"I don't quite know how to ask this, Frank, but did you by any chance send me a gift last evening?"

I was as puzzled as she.

"No. Why do you ask?"

"Well, yesterday was my birthday and when I came home from work there was a present for me."

"Millie, Millie, had I known I would have sent you flowers."

There was a click on the line by which I knew Juliet had lifted the receiver.

"It wasn't flowers," she went on, "it was a canary."

"A canary? Are you fond of the birds?"

(I, myself, loathe the greedy creatures who, contrary to popular belief, do not lift their heads in pious gratitude at every swallow but, in reality, are merely clearing their gullets for faster intake. However, thinking it was possible Millie had a predilection for canaries, I did not speak ill of them.)

"No," was her answer. "I'm completely neutral. Never had one before in my life and never felt the urge to buy one. Mother has no particular fondness for them either."

I felt better.

"Who delivered it?"

"I don't know. Mother said some boy rang the doorbell but by the time she got down from the third floor there wasn't anybody on the stoop, only a cage with the canary in it."

"Wasn't there any kind of gift card?"

"Nope, nothing. All I had to go by was the name of the pet shop. The bird was bought outside of Philadelphia, there's no pet shop by that name here or in the suburban directories. I checked that right away."

I thought for a moment, an idea dawning.

"What was the name of the shop?"

"Wilson's, it said on a printed label tied to the cage."

"Millie, Millie, he's done it again!"

"The Colonel, you mean?"

"Yes, the Colonel. I *know*. I quote from the Sacred Writings, 'The Adventure of Black Peter': . . . 'an inquiry which was carried out by him [Mr. Sherlock Holmes] at the express desire of His Holiness the Pope—down to his arrest of Wilson, the notorious canary trainer.' "

There was a bitter taste in my mouth.

"He's seen us together; he knows who you are; he knows where you live and he knows you're on the Chase. How *did* he find out?"

"That," said Millie, less distressed than I thought she'd be, "is our problem."

We held our regular plenary session of September 18 at the Press Club. I'd heard of it but never had been there before; it is not one of our better clubs. It was Don who suggested the change, he was on a rough work schedule and this was the only club to which he belonged. It was easier for him to receive messages there than at the Architects. I went along with the suggestion although I was sorry I hadn't been firmer. I almost regurgitated after a sip of my martini which had to be made with bathtub gin. Despite nostalgic feelings it gave me about those old Prohibition days, it also gave me a severe case of heartburn.

The dinner which followed worsened my dyspepsia and deepened my melancholy. There were no menus, we took Don's recommendations which might or might not have been an error. I have no intention of returning to the Press Club to explore other unmentioned possibilities. I expected a truck driver's delight and I was not disappointed. The tomato juice was slightly fermented ("turned," my mother used to say) and the salad was brown-hued lettuce covered with a bitter mixture of peanut oil and acetic acid.

The rolls were edible providing none of the rancid butter was spread upon them but no amount of catsup could disguise the taste of oft-used lard in which our french fried potatoes were scorched. I prefer not to become involved in any discussion of the entree. Suffice it to state that the maximum elapsed time between the hour when the steak last grazed peacefully on some pasture and its appearance on our table could not possibly have exceeded a week.

The so-called working press, of which there were some dozen nondescript shirt-sleeved members present apparently enjoying the "chef's special," after a jocose word to Don, ignored us completely.

Millie told us she'd officially realerted all sixteen county sheriffs within the "hunting grounds," stressing the probability that the Eberhardts were most likely to be found somewhere on a carnival midway. There were thirty-one then in progress under these specified jurisdictions.

Jack suggested we get together nightly until the Chase ended—a matter of eight days—and I suggested we dine at the Architects, as usual. Don shrugged his shoulders resignedly and Charlie promised him there would be a night line plugged into our meeting room to make communication with Don's office easier.

I had a sleepless night, not aided a whit by my wife's violent reaction to the new work schedule. In the morning our mailman delivered a small package with no return address.

After a malicious warning to be careful since bombs fragmented upward, Juliet stomped downstairs and noisily slammed the kitchen door. I did hesitate for a second, then boldly alashed the string with my pocketknife, tore off the paper and opened my "gift" box. Inside, wrapped around with Kleenex were a bronze toy block, a top, the kind we used to whittle when we were children, and three very old, warped, and unlabeled phonograph records. Concealed somewhere in Sherlockiana there had to be a direct reference to these oddly assorted items. Yet, though I know the Sacred Writings as well as any man alive, I could not discover what it was even after long hours of intense concentration.

I tried the records, ancient 78's, probably pressed more than a half-century ago. When I played them on our stereo they emitted a waxy, low, undulating hum even when I turned the volume as high as it would go and cut down the bass. It was impossible to hear any musical sound.

I crawled to the back of our cellar storage bin from which I took (despite my wife's anguished cries) a dusty portable, hand wound Victrola, circa 1910, hoping that a combination of ancient records and ancient machine would blend more happily. I turned the handle, fully expecting the spring it controlled would have long since lost its elasticity. To my surprise the turntable moved just as efficiently as it had when my father proudly presented it to my mother on their first wedding anniversary, a year before my birth. Unfortunately this time I could not even hear the low murmur; all I got was needle noise. Nevertheless I determined to bring the Victrola to our evening session recalling that Charlie, who is a hi-fi buff, might think of something.

I re-examined the package. The postmark was blurred but by using my magnifying glass I determined it had been sent from Allentown, Pennsylvania, September 13. I consulted the previous week's issue of *Amusement Business* and there it was on the "route list." Gibson & Fowler's played the Great Allentown Fair the week of September 8 closing Saturday, September 13. So much for those hick sheriffs! They had missed the Colonel again.

As I felt certain he would, Charlie, by a clever device, extracted sufficient sound from all three records for us to identify the tune. In place of the needle he used one of Millie's long fingernails, holding it steady in the groove as the turntable revolved, something I wish I had thought of. Very quietly we put our heads close to the speaker horn. Then came faint sounds as though a military band were playing softly in the distance.

Chills ran up and down our spines. There *was* significance here, we all felt. Someone was dead or was going to die. We now had the Colonel's word for this. From each record came the same, sad strains of Chopin's Funeral March. But even this gruesome warning, if that's what it was, did not help solve the immediate problem. Which chapter and verse in the Sacred Writings had H. Wesley applied for his selection of a child's block, a top, and three phonograph records? It was Millie who helped us find the answer.

We must have been sipping our fourth B&B, each calling upon his own vast Sherlockian knowledge when Millie picked up the block for perhaps the dozenth time.

"It could be part of an arch," she said thoughtfully. "You can see the way the sides slope inward when you hold the wider end on top."

Charlie asked if he might take another look and Millie dutifully handed the block to him. He examined it for only a second.

"Of course!" he said. "That's exactly what it is, the keystone of an arch. I've seen thousands of them on blueprints. I should have recognized it at once. My apologies. So what have we?"

He answered his own question.

"A kid's top and twine to make it spin, three phonograph records and a bronze keystone."

"Not bronze and not a stone," Ed almost shouted. "Brass. A brass key."

And at almost the same moment Charlie sang out, "Not three *records,* three *discs.*"

"Wrapped in wrinkled Kleenex."

Then I quoted chapter and verse.

" 'From within he [Sherlock] produced a crumpled piece of paper, an old fashioned brass key, a peg of wood with a ball of string attached to it, and three . . . old discs.' "

"The Musgrave Ritual." The Colonel had struck a blow close to home for it is from this classic Adventure that we Sons have chosen our Sacred Vow. Yet despite the grim connotation in those morbid discs plus the implied warning to be found in the strange murder of Sir Reginald Musgrave's faithless butler, we still regarded this latest "clue" as only another expression of H. Wesley Eberhardt's colossal vanity. Oh what foolish innocents we were!

I can recall Jack saying, as our waiter served the last round, "Well, gentlemen, the joke's sure going to be on us if the Colonel shows up next Friday night with Ellen on one arm and Joe on the other. What will you do, Frank, if H. Wesley asks you to cosponsor his brother's application for Copper Beech membership?"

That was a decision I was never called upon to make. On Monday, September 22, Juliet, who usually wins the race for the morning mail, handed me a letter with a Lancaster, Pennsylvania, address, written in a feminine hand on the back flap.

"Who's *that* from?" my wife asked even before I'd slit the envelope. I paused before replying although I knew the answer at once.

"Mrs. Hilda Crawshaw."

"Who's she?"

"The Colonel's sister."

I recalled giving my card to Mrs. Crawshaw with a request that she advise me if she heard anything about her brothers, the Colonel and Joe. She had complied; Joe was dead, victim of a heart attack. The note was brief, almost curt, as though the writer since regretted a promise made to a stranger with only a selfish interest in the Eberhardt family's vital statistics.

Joe was a passenger in someone else's car when he complained of heart pains and, as Mrs. Crawshaw phrased it, "He passed on in the Myerstown Community Hospital two hours later. We buried him on Saturday at Glen Hill. My brother Wesley was not at the funeral. I guess that's all you wanted to know."

It certainly was not all *I* wanted to know. I called Jack first, then Millie. We arranged to leave for Lancaster early the next morning, those two, the old Shikari hunter and I. I'd wanted to take off at once, but Marv was in the midst of an autopsy and Millie had to get Inspector Fox's permission for out-of-city travel.

What all of us had in mind, of course, although only I had the courage to express it aloud was the possibility that Joe's coffin contained not one but two bodies. This was why I insisted that Marv and Millie come with us. We planned no *modus operandi*. "Let's play it by ear," Millie said.

Her first call was to Dave Braveman, the chief of the Lancaster Police Department. She took Marv with her. I reconciled myself to this exclusion despite the fact that as Historian I should not be excluded from *any* discussion in which Sons are involved. But, after all Marv was an official of Philadelphia while I was not.

Jack and I waited for at least a half-hour.

"Mostly protocol," Millie explained when she and Marv rejoined us. "Their men would do the same thing if they came into somebody else's jurisdiction. Now, if we need help, we can call on the chief and get it. Incidentally, he had no knowledge of Joe Eberhardt's death, which means the Lancaster newspapers didn't run an obit. Otherwise it would have been in the files.

"He knew the Crawshaws ran a rooming house, their name was on the list of acceptable student homes. He was not aware that Hilda's husband was a heavy drinker; there'd never been a complaint filed about his conduct. That's where we stand."

We didn't want to descend upon the Crawshaws en masse so this time it was Jack and Marv who waited outside while Millie and I continued the investigation. Hilda was more friendly than I expected which may have been due to Millie's experience in such matters or my sympathetic approach. Inadvertently I glanced at the empty couch. Mrs. Crawshaw caught my eye. "He's upstairs sleeping one off, he won't bother us."

Millie conducted the gentle interrogation, explaining that the purpose was not to cause her hostess any more sorrow than she was presently suffering but an attempt to locate the Colonel's wife who Millie said (not altogether untruthfully) was needed to sign some papers. Whether Mrs. Crawshaw believed this, which is irrelevant, she answered all questions to the best of her ability.

When Joe died he'd been using an alias. "Otto Schiele, or his stage name, 'Otto the Great,'" Hilda explained. "Otto Schiele was a kid we used to play with in one of those towns we lived in. I forget which, there were so many. But Joe's social security was in his right name and the card was in his wallet. They also found an old letter in his pocket with my name and address on the envelope. That's why the coroner got in touch with me to identify the body and claim it.

"Myerstown's up in Lebanon County you know. I didn't see much point tryin' to reach my brother Alvin but I did anyway. He wouldn't come with me or even promise to go to the funeral but said if we needed money to bury Joe I was to tell him and he'd pay the tab. I told you before we weren't a close family and you better believe me. I went to Myerstown by myself, couple hours' ride each way. You gotta change buses in Harrisburg.

"I had to get back the same day—can't stay away overnight. [Fearful, I suppose that her drunken sot of a husband would burn down the house.] So I didn't have much time to find out much about what Joe's been up to these last eight, ten years."

She almost broke down but after a few sniffles, managed to gain control of her emotions.

"There wasn't any question about the cause of death. They told me it was a massive coronary and he didn't feel any pain after it struck him. That was one good thing, anyway. That's the way the Pastor went to his reward."

This last was said bitterly and I assumed she was speaking of her father's demise.

"They let me see the police report. Gave the name of the man who Joe was riding with and who took him to the hospital. Want to know what it is?"

Both Millie and I nodded. Mrs. Crawshaw stood up, opened a desk drawer and after fumbling around for a moment, pulled out a small piece of paper.

"Jerry Kaufman," she said. "But it won't do you any good. All this guy said was that he'd met Joe a few days before at a carnival. He offered to drive Joe to some other place they were going to play the next week but he didn't say where. That Mr. Kaufman didn't even know Joe's right name. Sorry, but that's all. Not much help, I guess. Nothing mentioned about Wesley."

Mrs. Crawshaw was right, she hadn't offered us much information. I had a question to ask. Why was Joe Eberhardt buried in Glen Hill and not in the family plot his sister told me was in suburban Philadelphia?

"A good reason," the lady answered. "We're filled up except for space for Alvin and me. Glen Hill's where *his* family's from."

She raised her head and looked up at the ceiling, referring to her husband, whose snores we could hear.

"It's only a farm cemetery but they got room for an awful lot of people. Been burying Crawshaws and their kin there since before the Revolution. Don't seem to mind if a stranger 'moves in' long as he pays the landowners what they ask and takes care of the State burial license. 'Course the undertaker's bill is separate."

Mrs. Crawshaw looked at us.

"Drive along the rural roads in this or York County which is where Glen Hill is and you'll see that pretty nearly every old farm has its own burial grounds. Used to be the custom. Some folks still do it. It's much cheaper, all right, I can tell you that. Glad we were able to make arrangements to bury poor Joe that way. We don't have much money ourselves and I didn't want to accept Alvin's."

She sighed and began to cry again.

"It was a very small funeral. *He* [Hilda pointed upward] again wasn't in any condition and the least Alvin coulda done was to be there with that slick wife of his. But neither of 'em showed up. I was the only family representative and no matter what Joe did, he deserved better than what he got.

"Services were held in a tiny church just outside Glen Hill. Except for a couple old ladies who I guess go to every funeral around, there wasn't anybody else. Minister was an elderly Lutheran who rides circuit. Never knew Joe, and so he couldn't say much except what I told him. Wouldn't make any difference, the Pastor spoke in Pennsylvania Dutch.

"Undertaker had to furnish all the pallbearers. Must have charged plenty for them, too, but since somebody else was paying, it didn't matter to me as long as it wasn't Alvin."

This raised a point.

"Then who did pay the undertaker?" I asked.

Hilda shook her head.

"Never did find out for sure but I think I know. There was a card in Joe's wallet showing he belonged to some carnival association. On the back it said they were to be notified in the event of a member's death. I sent them a telegram and told them where Joe'd be buried. When I talked to Mr. Beebelheimer, the undertaker, to ask how much the funeral would be before he went ahead, figuring I'd have to borrow some cash, he told me all his expenses were taken care of. Naturally I figured the association paid the bill. God knows there wasn't enough money in Joe's wallet to pay. All he had was eight dollars and forty cents, no watch, no ring, no other kind of jewelry. And as far as we could find out he didn't carry any insurance, not even burial."

"Did you send them the undertaker's name?" Millie asked.

Mrs. Crawshaw shook her head.

"Guess not. Didn't know who he'd be. I suppose they found out somehow. There's only one funeral director in Glen Hill, this fellow Beebelheimer, and I'm sure he takes care of every-one in the whole area."

The membership card was in Mrs. Crawshaw's possession.

"This is to certify," it read, "that Joe 'Otto the Great' Schiele is a member in good standing of the International Independent Showmen's Association of Gibsonton, Florida." It was signed, "Barney (Slim) Kelley, President." On the back was the information Mrs. Crawshaw mentioned, together with the association's telephone number.

Millie pressed on.

"When you looked around the church or at the grave, did you see any stranger, some man, I mean?"

Our hostess shook her head.

"Nope. No one. I'm sure of that. If you're thinking Wes was there in disguise, forget it. I'd have known him no matter how he was made up and I can tell you he was *not* among those present."

I admit I was thinking of H. Wesley and so were the rest of us. If, as we fully believed, he and Joe had been traveling to-gether since the Chase began, it was hard to reconcile his ab-sence from the funeral even granting that the Colonel was not given to sentiment. But Joe was the only member of a large family with whom the Colonel had any rapport and probably the one person he trusted. I could not see H. Wesley executing his plans without outside assistance and if it weren't Joe, who gave it? If the pair hadn't been traveling together, then the framework of the entire structure we'd built would collapse.

There was little or nothing to be gained by further interro-gation of Mrs. Crawshaw. We thanked her and left. Our question was whether to head for the Myerstown coroner or go to Glen Hill first. Marv made the decision.

"I probably know the coroner, or he knows me. We work with them all over the state. So let's see if he can give us any more dope than he gave Mrs. Crawshaw."

It was lunchtime; we stopped at a much advertised roadside Pennsylvania Dutch restaurant with its "seven sweets, seven meats, and seven sours." Washed down with two seidels of cold draft beer, an excellent local brew I must say, this was not the type of noonday meal to induce thought. I fell asleep on the way to Lebanon, the county seat. With Jack, who also was a bit drowsy, I waited in the courthouse parking lot while Millie and Marv went inside to pay their respects to the coroner.

They emerged with a little additional information but its value was moot. Kaufman, who'd been questioned briefly by both the coroner and Lebanon's Chief of Police, had been operating a "penny pitch" at the Happy Day Shows, which played Central Pennsylvania and Eastern Maryland. Again, my familiarity with midway terms came in handy. I explained to my colleagues that a "penny pitch" was a game where marks tossed coppers into a shallow cut glass plate. If the coin remained inside the dish they won this useless piece of merchandise.

As Mrs. Crawshaw told us, Kaufman's acquaintance with Joe Eberhardt was indeed tenuous. They were on the same midway for less than a week and had never met before. Joe was still operating a mitt camp but the woman with whom he'd been working this fortune-telling racket took off with someone else. Apparently it was Joe's intention to seek a substitute elsewhere, hence his departure from Happy Day.

The cause of Joe's death was determined quickly and Kaufman was released as soon as the medical report reached the coroner. Kaufman, or so he told the chief, was headed for Frawley's Frolicks, another small carnival where he and his very temporary passenger had hoped to set up. Unless we were able to find Kaufman and interrogate him, there was no way of knowing whether Joe had mentioned Brother Wes.

This new data was confusing. All our previous thinking indicated that the Colonel and Joe were together and would, of necessity, be on a large midway where concealment was far easier than in "forty-milers" such as Happy Day and Frawley's Frolicks. Why had the brothers separated and was this fraternal split permanent? Or was it part of a plan wrecked by

Joe's unexpected death? We could count on one factor, however, that the Colonel would not be left without an alternative. During his military career as a legitimate killer he must have faced many a similar situation. That he survived is sufficient proof of his skill at improvisation.

We had another decision to make. Should we try to locate Kaufman and interrogate him or proceed directly to Glen Hill, where we wanted to speak to the undertaker who buried Joe? It was 4:30 P.M. by then and the York County village was a good two hours away. We weren't even sure the funeral director would be at home or in his mortuary. If he were I felt he would talk to us; Millie and Marv's presence assured us of Beebelheimer's cooperation.

I solved the dilemma. With my usual foresight I brought with me the current issue of *Amusement Business*. Frawley's Frolicks was playing at Hummelstown, Pennsylvania, which, fortunately, was almost on the direct route from Lebanon to Glen Hill. By taking a slight detour over a secondary route we would lose at the very most thirty or forty minutes. Should our luck still hold, we ought to be talking to the penny pitchman within the hour.

I was getting a bit hungry and the thought of a thick chunk of that famous Lebanon bologna (processed not a hundred feet from where we sat) and a Bermuda onion between two slices of rye bread and washed down with a seidel of that excellent draft beer we'd drunk for lunch, was mouth watering. But my normal conciliatory attitude forced me to pass up a snack now and settle for a full dinner later in the evening.

Our luck held. Kaufman, a beady-eyed little Semite with a hooked nose, was just setting up his stand when we approached him. The fair, really only a four-day street carnival —what carnies term a "still date"—had not yet opened.

"Fuzz," he said with surprise and looked Millie up and down when she produced her I.D. card. "I thought the patch took care of you."

Almost simultaneously he took out his wallet and was about to extract a bill when Millie stopped him with a shake of her head.

"Philly fuzz," she said. "Just want to ask you a couple questions about Joe Eberhardt. You're under no obligation to answer if you don't want to."

He shrugged his shoulders.

"I tole 'em everything over in Lebanon. But if I don't do it over again for you I guess you'll call in the locals. So what do you want to know?"

Millie told him.

As far as this pitchman was concerned, Joe had no other confederate or associate except for the woman who helped him run the mitt camp.

"Y'unnerstan', I din't know Joe too good. Jest got acquainted that week, our joints was next to each other. I can oney say this. The first day I seen him he seemed like a quiet, easy goin' guy but when we took off together he was awful upset. Maybe that was too much for his heart. I figured it was the broad that left him got him all bothered, but from what he tole me he couldn' a cared less. Something else was buggin' him. He never said what it wuz.

"All we talked about was the different lots we wuz on and mentioned a few mutual friends. He was still 'with it' but I think he'd been out of show biz for a long time and jest come back in a season or two before. This year he'd been workin' on some of the big midways and I couldn't figure why he switched to gillies like Happy Day or this one here, Frawley's.

"As for me, them small ones is all I ever wanted to be on. Don't like too many people 'round. But if that's what Joe wanted, that was his business. In our racket you don't ask for no more than a guy wants to give and this guy din't want to give nothin'. He wuz awful poor company."

That was the extent of information Millie was able to extract. Before we left I thought it a good idea to impress the pitchman that I, too, was "with it" and knew my way around.

"Did you ever run across a carny named Gypsy Joe?"

Kaufman raised his eyebrows and regarded me with curiosity.

"That gonif! Sure I know him; he'd steal his mother's gold teeth if he got the chance."

I didn't wish to get into an argument with the fellow so I refrained from pointing out that my own association with the Gypsy, tenuous though it was, led me to form a contrary opinion. And I consider myself a far better judge of character than Mr. Jerry Kaufman.

I assure you that despite severe personal discomfort I have often abstained from both food and drink for long periods of time rather than interrupt intense research. But in this case I believed it would be beneficial to group morale if we were to take our dinner break before proceeding to Glen Hill. I say this because even the cookhouse grease on the Frawley lot began to develop an appetizing aroma. While it is hard to believe that a nation which claims to be as advanced as ours is without a Michelin Guide, such is the sad truth. Consequently the hungry traveler must depend upon the hearsay evidence of self-proclaimed gourmets who wouldn't know the difference between a 1902 Chateau de St. Emilion and a bottle of Manischewitz's Sweet Grape.

Fortunately for my fellow travelers I have an almost unerring sixth sense about the quality of restaurants, so it was without fear that I suggested we pull into the parking lot of the Stockyard Inn, just outside of Lancaster. Although our dinner certainly merits detailing, I will postpone its deserved delineation until a more appropriate occasion and mention only those thick, beautiful sirloins, tender, rare and aged, and the dessert, lush ripe red strawberries, swimming in deep bowls of rich, country cream.

Yielding to the impatience of my colleagues whom I felt were overly anxious to be on their way, I rejected a second Courvoisier and climbed into the rear seat of the car, where I rested my eyes. It was well past nine o'clock when we reached Glen Hill and Mr. Beebelheimer's establishment. Marv and Millie entered first, thought better of it, and in a moment came out and asked us to join them before they talked to the undertaker.

I roused myself and followed Jack into the funeral parlor which was dimly lit and reeked of cheap incense. From somewhere in the dark background came the muffled strains of "Ah Sweet Mystery of Life" pumped into the air by some unearthly organist. In a moment the dark shadow of a man emerged. Noting that we did not look like customers, he snapped off the mood music and snapped on bright overhead lights. He eyed us in a friendly enough fashion, introduced himself as Mr. George ("Call me Chorch") Beebelheimer, sole owner of the establishment.

"Chorch" is a short, fat Pennsylvania Dutchman, bald except for tufts of pinkish hair which stuck out like miniature coxcombs on both sides of his large, otherwise bald, head. His accent is incredible, at times so thick we had trouble translating it into English. At first, in writing this history, I attempted to phoneticize Mr. Beebelheimer's speech but since my linguistic expertise lies with Iberian dialects, I soon gave up. With the exception of a few of the mortician's particularly choice words and phrases, I am permitting him to speak the English language after his peculiar fashion.

He was quite cooperative in his answers, however, perhaps because he, himself, had been puzzled by certain aspects surrounding burial of the late Joe Eberhardt. Soon after Marv (professionally closer to the undertaker than any of us) outlined the background of the Chase to his fascinated listener, the latter confirmed the accuracy of our deductions beyond the shadow of a doubt and in so doing, re-established our faith in the Sacred Writings. Shortly after "signing for the body," Mr. B. had a visitor, "a tall, fine looking 'chentelman' who looked like a 'Brussian Cheneral.' "

Millie wanted to know if the gentleman gave his name.

"Give me his calling card. I got it back some place but I don't know where. Want I should look for it now?"

I shook my head.

"Was it Ezekiah Hopkins?"

I don't know which of the two looked more startled, Millie or the undertaker. The latter nodded.

"That's it, zir. Are you aguainted with the chentelman?"

I nodded. At another time I would explain to Millie that the name of the late Ezekiah Hopkins figured in the Master's "The Red-Headed League." His home was supposedly Lebanon, Pennsylvania.

Mr. B. continued.

"I asked him if he was kin to the deceased and he says 'no, chust a friend who wants to make sure everything is done brober and in the best of daste.' I thought I knowed what he meant but I wasn't sure. I should exblain to you, young lady, and to you chentelmen, that in certain circumstances we are sometimes forced to use blain, bine coffins. They're bainted good outside and they look OK but they ain't in the same league with mahogany, cherry, or black walnut and naturally they don't hold up so good."

Mr. B. eyed us as a teacher might regard his class of fourth grade pupils.

"The damp and the insects, if you know what I mean."

I knew *exactly* what he meant and hoped Mr. B. would refrain from further detailed confidences. I was beginning to feel a bit queasy; those mushrooms pickled in vinegar and marinated in garlic sauce which our Stockyard Inn waiter had served with martinis were, in second gustation, not so "divine" as Millie originally pronounced them.

"Who was going to lift the tab I still didn't know yet. I run a quick credit check on that Mrs. 'What's her name,' the deceased's sister up Lancaster way and I knowed damned soon she ain't got nothing, not even a savings account and every bill bast due. Lived in the same house nigh on twenty years and the mortgage chust as big as it was the day she and that drunken Mister of her'n moved into Nevin Street.

"Beeble come in here—they're full of grief—weepin' widows—them's the worst. Keep bendin' my ear about what a good man they lost. Talk, talk, talk, and more talk, you can't hardly shut 'em up. But when you ask did that good man of their'n carry funeral insurance and if he din't who was gonna be responsible for the bill, that shuts 'em up all right. Some of 'em get mad and tell me I gotta nerve bringin' up such a filthy thing as money when they got all these other troubles."

I was growing more and more annoyed; we were drifting far from our objectives. Deliberately I took out my pocket watch and noted the hour. It was then past ten o'clock and I would have interrupted the mortician's verbiage except for a wink from Millie as though to say, "Let the man rave on. He'll get to the point eventually." I realized we'd need Mr. Beebelheimer's cooperation, so resignedly I sat back and let his drivel flow in and out of my ears.

"Expenses! Man, they eat you up alive no matter how much you economize. Cost blenty to decently put a body six feet under the sod these days. You can bet your sweet ass on that!"

He suddenly became aware of Millie's presence and, with acute embarrassment, apologized.

"Exguse me, lady. I always get upset when I think about what's going on in the profession. Ain't like it used to be when my vodder started the business.

"Cut a corner here, cut a corner there. Zom of my competitors use green wood. Say it don't really make no difference in the long run and maybe it don't. Could tell you stories but I won't. And some of 'em shoot in brinters ing 'stead of embalmin' fluid. That's sumpin' I'll *never* do; that's not for good Christians.

"All right. I give you this. Brice of supplies gone sky high. It's those damned chobbers gouchin' us. All a bunch of . . ."

He looked at Marv and substituted another label for the one I'm sure he intended to use.

". . . Voreigners, every damned one of 'em. Ought to ship 'em back where they come from. Takin' advantage of us Americans. Raisin' the brice of supplies pretty near two hundred percent last five years. And the cost of labor! You beeble don't have no idea what we gotta pay bearers these days. Used to be when my vodder was alive you could get six good men chust for the fun—egsguse me—the privilege of helpin' out a neighbor plus all they could eat at the home of the bereaved."

He raised his hands in despair.

"They god social security for themselves. They god Blue Cross for the hospitals and this here Blue Shield for the doctors. They god Medicare for the old folks and I hear the dentists is tryin' to dip their greedy hands in the till. But *nobody* thinks about us. Vell, we got a man down in Vashington now, tryin' to verk on Congress. Ve'll see. An election's comin' up and there's a zolid organization behind."

My patience was at an end. Unless Mr. B. had something to offer I intended to shut him up regardless of Millie. But our host stopped, this diatribe completed, temporarily at any rate.

"Now let me see, folks, where was I? Oh, yes. I was tellin' you about the military lookin' chentleman who come 'round to inquire about arrangements for the deceased. Like I said, he vanted everyting in the best daste.

"And *then* he says he vants him buried in a 'bridal suite.' I tell you Miss and you chentlemen, ven he says *that* instead of 'casket' or 'coffin' I know he knowed the game. 'Bridal suite's' somethin' ve say only among ourselves. *Never* in front of a client. Beeble like you volks vouldn't know vhat that meant, vould they?"

I, for one, would not. My thoughts ran to a ghoulish honeymoon; I could not repress a shudder at the imagery this conjured.

"Vell, folks, a bridal suite ain't vhat you think it is. It's the fanciest, richest coffin they make. It's like everybody's dream come true."

Mr. B's eyes rolled heavenward.

"Made outa imported ebony," he whispered almost orgiastically. "Veighs half a ton, need eight strong bearers. Handles is solid brass and box edges is trimmed in fourteen-carat gold. Inside's lined with satin and all the cushions bordered with handmade lace and stuffed with real down, none of your jeep kapok.

"This vas oney the second one I ever sold in my whole career and that goes back forty year. First was a young couple died together and buried together. Had chenerous funeral policies made out to each other."

At the recollection Mr. Beebelheimer drooled and with the back of his hand wiped his wet lips.

"Din't have no other survivors. It was beautiful! Chust beautiful!"

He went on.

"Another advantach of the bridal suite is that it's so big a body's god plenty of space to move 'round in."

"Jesus Christ!" I said to myself. "What the hell does this idiot mean by 'space to move around in'? Don't they always make sure the deceased *is* deceased?"

Then Mr. B. really gave me a bad turn. Through narrowed slits, he looked me over from head to toe and shook his head violently.

"You'd be lost in a bridal suite, zir, if you don't mind my zayin' zo. Too skinny. Ve could bury two like you in one of 'em."

I shuddered. Was this Ellen's fate? Marv's usually florid face turned white; I could feel the blood rush into mine, Jack fanned his brow and I didn't dare even glance at Millie. Yet it was she who first recovered from the shock.

"Mr. Beebelheimer," she said very quietly, "what you've just told us could be of vital importance. It might even mean that a felony of the gravest nature was committed. Now I would like to ask you a few questions."

The undertaker appeared shaken. He nodded.

"You still haven't told us who lifted the tab, Mr. Beebelheimer. We've been informed it was a carnival association the deceased belonged to."

Mr. B. looked puzzled.

"Don't know nothin' about no carnival association. Thought you unnerstood it was the chentelman who paid. While he waited I called up the casket company out in Altoona and asked them if they could deliver a bridal suite right away—naturally I don't keep none in stock—and how much would it be. Told me and said if I give them the order they'd put it on their truck right away. I give 'em the order to ship at wunst.

"Then, while the chentelman waited, I made up his bill. Since he seemed so unnerstandin' I figured he prolly wanted to pay the whole works hisself. So I included, with the bridal suite, my own charges for professional services and a fee for my assistant, a new coat, tie, tie pin, shirt, and cuff links for the deceased."

Mr. B. paused in the midst of the inventory.

"I alvays try to persuade a patron to use French cuffs, they look better than the button kind even if they cost a bit more and you need links for 'em. But I point out you save on the pants, shoes, sox and suspenders 'cause oney the upper half shows. The lower's covered vith a sleep blanket."

Again I wanted to interrupt and again Millie motioned me to refrain.

"Well," the mortician continued. "I listed vages for all eight bearers, four sprays of flowers for inside the church, and a special wreath for the grave, a limousine for the bereaved and a chauffeur, a tombstone to be erected later vhen the ground settled. They vas a couple other charges like for the organizt and choir, a mourners' book for friends to list their names, cards and envelopes vith black borders for the bereaved to answer, a chanitor to glean up the church aftervard, two gravediggers' vages, shovels, and a pick in case the earth's hard. Last item's an honorarium for the preacher. It come to quite a bit but not as much as somebody else might charch 'cause I got a sort of deal goin' with the local merchants and the preacher's my brother-in-law.

"I dotalled the bill up and handed it to the chentelman, after I first exblain that seein's I doan know him I couldn't take no checks and we ain't on Diners or none of them credit cards yet. He looks at me. 'T on T,' he says with a smile. I smiles back and say, 'T on T' it is."

I noticed Marv was chuckling. I was going to ask him for an explanation but Mr. B. gave it to us.

"'T on T's' another somethin' we say but oney in the trade. Means cash on the line."

Marv appeared satisfied with the interpretation and Mr. B. continued.

"The chentelman skims through the bill real fast like he doan give a damn. But then he comes to the last item and vhen he sees that he gets red in the face, sucks in his breath hard and stares at me like a crazy man.

" 'Honorarium for the breacher!' he perty near shouts. 'Not one goddamned cent for no barson. Take that outa the bill or I'll call the whole thing off and have my friend cremated. If you want a breacher, then pay him yourself. I won't!' "

Could there be any doubt that the "chentelman" was Colonel H. Wesley Eberhardt?

"There was nodding I could do bud sgratch the barson's honorarium. If the chentelman vanted to save a buck or two by refusin' to pay for a Christian eulochee, that wuz his business. Somethin' I vouldn't stand for but I didn't say nothin'. After, I chust tole my brother-in-law he must do it for nothin'. Owes me a few bast favors anyvay.

"The chentelman calms down, looks at the bill vunst more to see if I got the breacher's bill took off and vhen he seen that he takes out a thick roll of bills. All of 'em was C-notes as far as I could tell. He slips off the money clip and doan make no vhimper vhile he peels off enough to pay. Never seen nothin' like it in my whole life. That's the vay a real chentelman does business.

"There's about sixty dollars in chanche left over from the last C-note comin' to him, so I dig into my own pocket for chanche.

" 'Never mind,' he says. 'Keep it for the kiddies. There's one thing I'd like you to do for me.'

"Anything, zir, I says, anything you say. Churst ask.

" 'How soon will you and that assistant of yours finish the job? Don't tell me embalmin' takes all day. I know better.'

"Couple hours, I says, if we get to work right avay.

" 'When will the bridal suite get to your place?'

"Tonight, I answered. No later than ten o'clock. That's vhat they bromised.

" 'OK. I'll be 'round then to see. I won't be able to stay for the funeral, so could I be alone with my poor dead friend for a short while?'

"OK, I answers. Then he gives me another hard look, starin' down at me and I almost got scared. He seemed like the avenging anchel.

" 'And I mean *all* alone.' "

Even now, a week after the event, the fat little undertaker could not repress a shudder.

"At quarter past eight, more'n an hour ahead of schedule, the bridal suite's delivered. Company musta been glad to get *that* order. Delivery men uncrate her, put her on a dolly and wheel her in.

"She's so beautiful you can't imachine. I look her over from every side very careful. Not a scratch or a mark, everything perfect. And she's so big, berty near fills up the room. I sign for her and the truck leaves. Then I hurry back to the chabel vith a soft chamois and I vipe her off all over, very, very slow."

Mr. B's eyes grew dreamy and he stared into the distance, his high-pitched singsong voice dropped at least a full octave, soft and caressing. If you can imagine a Dutch accented Charles Boyer making love, you will understand what I mean. His absorption was so complete I hesitated to break in, but after a few moments of complete silence in which we all participated, our host, with a deep sigh, continued.

"The little girl who's been keebin' house for me since my vife passed on a year ago I sent home, so I vuz all by myself vhen the chentelman showed up at exactly ten like he said he vould."

"What about your assistant?" I asked, thinking Mr. B. might cunningly have posted him in some spot where he could have had a keyhole view of the Colonel's actions.

Mr. B. frowned.

"Assistant! Who's got an assistant? Never had none, do every chob myself."

I repressed a cynical comment but since I knew it would not alter Mr. B.'s ethics I held my tongue. Millie then asked our host what kind of a car the undertaker's visitor drove. So contagious was Mr. B.'s accent that Millie actually said "chentelman" and for hours after, I found myself calling my fellow Son "Chack."

"A long black Cadillac," Mr. B. answered. "Vhen it first come into sight I vuz out vaterin' the lawn. This here's a special kind of autymobile they make oney for us. Seats nine inside comfortable. Nobody's able to gape at 'em. They got silk shades you can pull down over every window 'cept, of course, the ones up front with the chauffeur. In our profession we call it a 'Black Diamond Empress.'"

"Vell, that night it's plenty dark outside but I got the borch light on. Before he turns off the Caddy's lights, I can see the shades in the car is all down. The chentelman valks out and before he comes over to me, he locks all the car doors careful vhich is crazy. We doan lock nothin' in this part of the country. Everybody 'round here's honest.

"Chentelman ain't zo friendly. Says good evenin' all right, then doan vaste no more time. Asks is everybody oud and I says, 'yes zir, everybody.' 'You're sure?' and I nods my head. He looks at me like daggers and I tell you chentelmen and you, too, Miss, I'm scared. I'm thinkin' of a moo'm bixture we seen on the late, late show vunst vhere they got that tall bloodsucking wampire feller drivin' stakes in beeble's hearts.

"The chentelman's wearin' a dark suit and he's got long black gloves on that goes past his wrists and vay up under his goat sleeves. He doan offer to shake my hand and you can bet your life I ain't sorry."

Although tempted to do otherwise, Mr. B. said he followed instructions, after showing his visitor the bridal suite, the undertaker walked out of the house, got into his car and drove off.

"I din't know chust vhat the chentelman vuz up to and I ain't sure I vanted to. But right before I rounded the curve down our street I looked in my mirror and I seen the car backin' up against the side of the house vhere I got a double door for unloadin'. Then the borch light vent off. I din't come back for two hours like I promised and by then the chentelman vuz gone and so vuz his Black Diamond Empress."

Jack asked the question all of us had on our minds—did Mr. B. examine both corpse and coffin.

"That's the first thing I done. I had brought back the little girl keeps house for me to stay out front, see if maybe the chentelman is comin' back and I valk in the chapel to make the eggsamination. My heart's poundin' avay and I ain't gonna take no chance on nothin'. Maybe the chentelman decides to come back anyvay and he's hidin' some blace in the voods back of the house vatin' to see vhat I do. Zo I doan put on the top light even though the chapel vindows is made outa stain glass and the oney thing you can see from outside is shadows.

"I light a candle and move it up and down along the body tryin' to see if it vuz touched. I don't see nothin,' corpse is

chust vhere I left him in the middle of the bridal suite, lookin'
calm and peaceful. Even smilin' a bit if you look glose. I done
a beautiful chob, I tell you, but this vuz not the time to be
chuching my verk. I chust vanted to get the hell oud fast as I
could.

"Then I hear that little girl who comes in to keep house for
me vunst in a vhile give a vhistle like she vuz apposed to do if
she heard somebody. My heart chumps and I start to run oud
of the chapel. Then, chust as I'm turnin' 'round I notice the
sleep blanket's a bit mussed and maybe the body's layin'
slightly on the bias. But vhether I done it or the chentelman
done it I don't know and I ain't never gonna find out."

Mr. B. concluded by saying he and the little girl scurried
upstairs, moved a heavy chest against the bedroom door and
retired for what was left of the night. The funeral apparently
proceeded on schedule the following day, but we did not ask
whether the mortician was able to persuade his brother-in-law
to give the eulogy "on the house." There were more important
questions to be answered.

CHAPTER

22

BEYOND ANY shadow of doubt the body of Joe Eberhardt must
be disinterred and the lower portion of the bridal suite checked
for an extra corpse (a "freeloader" Marv phrased it rather
crudely), one we were all convinced was Ellen Eberhardt. I was
beginning to feel gas pains and suggested we retire somewhere
for the night and hold off action until dawn, by then only four
or five hours away. But the others, particularly the old Shikari
hunter, backed by Millie, were adamant, insisting there was
no time to waste and that decisions must be made at once.
Reluctantly but with grace I yielded.

We gathered around a large, circular table in Mr. B.'s dining room, which he told us he rented, catering services included, to clients whose homes were unequipped for the entertain-

ment of more than a few mourners. Moments later the young lady brought in a most appetizing platter of liverwurst and Bermuda onion sandwiches on rye bread and a tall, frosted pitcher of ice cold draught birch beer.

The basic issue was how to dig up the coffin without delay and without interference. Marv assayed our chances for legal disinterment. He was pessimistic.

"If we had a week I think I could persuade Arlen [Arlen Specter, the Philadelphia District Attorney] to ask this County Court for papers. We don't have a week. Including today, we've less than seventy-two hours."

While we debated the issue, Mr. B. said nothing. Finally he interrupted.

"Chentelmen, chentelmen, there's no broblem. I'm Chustice of the Beace for this Downship. If you want, write out the order and I'll sign it. But you don't have to do that. Chust go right ahead. Ain't nobody 'round here got more par than me."

I'm not sure I was relieved or troubled by Mr. B.'s display of "par." A gruesome task lay ahead, one requiring steel nerves and strong physiques. I was able and willing to supply the former which I possess in abundance, but a future hernia operation bars me, upon my surgeon's advice, from any form of physical labor. Our store of manpower was indeed limited, Millie could not be asked to help and Jack was past seventy. This left Marv, who pants at the slightest exertion, and Mr. B., who didn't appear as though he would enjoy anything more exhausting than raising food from plate to mouth.

There were six feet of earth to be removed and the heavy bridal cover unfastened and lifted out of the way. Who could be summoned for the arduous task at this hour? I could not even guess; I wouldn't know where to begin. However, Mr. B. did. He smiled.

"Chosie," the undertaker called out and in a moment the young lady appeared.

"Show 'em your muscles, girl," he ordered.

Grinning from ear to ear Chosie rolled up her sleeves to reveal the most powerful set of biceps I have ever seen. Then, like a professional strong man displaying his wares, she flexed them. Rippling like waves they rose at least four inches. Mr. B. sat back with pride.

"Now you, zir," he said looking at me. "Feel how hard they be. Chust like iron bands."

I obeyed. Mr. B. had not exaggerated one whit.

"Vunst," the mortician informed us, "vhen the gravediggers vent on strike, Chosie done their chob for them and done it faster and better, believe me."

I believed him. There was another brief exhibit—this time Chosie's calf and thigh muscles—and then we were on our way. All of us rode in Mr. Beebelheimer's slightly smaller version of a Black Diamond Express.

This was a night I do not care to remember. My colleagues had the rear of the car to themselves, but I was forced to sit up front between Mr. B. and Chosie. The latter had an extremely earthy odor from which I could not escape, and insisted on raising her left arm and putting it around my shoulder. The only comparable olfactory experience I recall was on the Metro during rush hour when I was packed between crowds of unbathed, undeodorized French women of the lower classes. In mitigation for such seeming snobbery I should state that Parisian ladies of the upper classes would be equally malodorous but for their profligate use of perfume.

It began to drizzle almost the moment we left Glen Hill's main street and turned onto a muddy country lane so narrow I could hear the constant swish of bordering brush against the undertaker's oversized Cadillac. There was no other sound except that of the wipers' steady beat and the occasional howl of a dog from somewhere in the distance. We saw no other car and every farmhouse we passed was as dark as the night surrounding it.

Mr. B. promised that the ride to Crawshaw's private cemetery would take no more than a half-hour, and a few minutes before that time elapsed he eased the car onto a still narrower road, actually, a rutty, weed-filled lane. He came to a halt.

"This is it, ladies and chentelmen," he said. "Get oud blease."

We obeyed, grouped together on one side of the automobile, and awaited further instructions. Mr. B. turned to his housekeeper.

"Here's the drunk key, Chosie. Get the bick and shovel."

Mr. B. removed an electric torch from the glove compartment, switched it on and snapped off the car's headlights. Then he motioned for us to follow him. We walked single file down a winding path for perhaps a hundred tortuous feet, past neglected graves and crumbling tombstones either toppled to the ground or standing at some crazy angle. Far to the rear I could hear the clank of Chosie's shoulder-borne tools and twice I almost fell as my foot struck an unexpected pot-hole.

The mortician, slightly ahead of Millie, turned the beam in our direction. We caught up with them and formed a circle around a fresh mound of soil.

"This is it, chentelmen," Mr. B. informed us, then bent down to pick up a piece of earth which he expertly rolled between his forefinger and thumb.

"You won't need no bick, oney the shovel, Chosie. Get goin'."

Chosie marched ahead, spit on her hands, grasped the shovel and began the task of removing the earth from Joe Eberhardt's resting place. I caught a glimpse of the little un-dertaker's face glowing with satisfaction as he watched his housekeeper piling earth on both sides of the grave while she sank deeper and deeper into the hole. It could not have been more than an hour before we all heard a clank as Chosie's tool struck the top of the bridal suite.

The mortician then waved his torch over the grave while he inspected the housekeeper's work.

"Gut. Gut. Now clean up enough schtuff from 'round the casket so's to give the lady and the chentelmen a blace to vatch."

Then, as an afterthought he added considerately, "One side's enough for 'em to stand on, Chosie."

Swiftly more dirt came flying up from the pit while Mr. B. peered below.

"OK, Choise, you done chust fine. Come up now and let me go down."

I heard Jack muttering to himself; I moved closer.

"Good Lord!" he said in awed tones. "Do you realize we have just witnessed a miracle in logistics. That young lady, within one hour, dug up seven tons of wet earth and tossed it an average distance of five feet. It staggers the imagination; if I didn't see it with my own eyes I would not have believed it possible."

In retrospect this may sound humorous but as we stood huddled together, Millie, Jack, Marv, and I, wet, miserable and absolutely desperately fearful of what might lie ahead, it was not the least bit funny. For the first time I understood what some of my students call black humor.

Marv and the undertaker extended their right hands, Chosie grasped them and was pulled out, her face positively beaming with joy. Mr. B. gave Marv the lamp and with a spry leap landed in the pit on top of the coffin. From the light of the torch I could see he was grinning broadly. It looked as though now that Chosie had concluded her performance her partner was eager to begin his own turn on the stage.

He brushed aside a thin layer of earth remaining on the casket, then took a wrench from his belt and began to loosen the bolts which held the coffin lid in place. Still smiling contentedly and as though he were enjoying every minute, he looked up.

"They turn easy, folks. Schpring action. Guaranteed for life."

I wondered if Mr. B. was jesting; if he was, the pun was uncalled for. But I decided this was beyond him. In less than three minutes the last bolt was removed.

"OK, folks," Mr. B. sang out cheerfully. "I'm ready for you. Chosie, help down the lady."

The moment I most dreaded had arrived. Softly, I kept muttering over and over again those portentous lines from the Sacred Writings, " 'It's an ugly business, Watson, an ugly, dangerous business and the more I see of it the less I like it.' "

My heart never pounded more wildly than it did as I followed Millie, Jack, and Marv down into the grave and stood there silently waiting for the curtain to go up on the next dreadful act. My eyes were closed; my hand wet with cold perspiration, clutched Millie's. I sensed Josie's presence and heard her grunt as she and the little Dutchman tried to raise the heavy lid. Twice they failed and twice the top fell back with a clunk. Then Marv volunteered his aid. Suddenly the lid was off and the body of the late Joe Eberhardt exposed to view.

At first, through barely opened lids, I merely peeked, then gaining courage I opened my eyes wide to look squarely at the remains, stretched out full length in his elegant, though final, resting place. The dampness and the sweet, sickening smell of death overwhelmed me and I felt my face grow pale and my limbs tremble. Oh how I wished I had not yielded to the temptation of eating that last liverwurst and onion sandwich on the platter.

I closed my eyes trying to gain a modicum of composure. Then I squinted as the undertaker swept his torch up and down the grave casting shadows on the moldering body and the glistening satin upon which it lay. Despite some evidences of decay I noted at least a familial resemblance between the faces of the corpse and Colonel H. Wesley Eberhardt. Against my will I found myself fascinated by the scene.

An owl hooting once far off in the distance was the only sound save for our labored breathing. Otherwise the silence was absolute. Marv broke the silence.

"Well, Mr. Beebelheimer," he said, "let's see if Joe's got company." With Marv's help Mr. B. lifted the body.

"I see you cut a corner here and a corner there, didn't you?" Marv commented. "I don't see any sleep blanket and this doesn't feel like real satin to me."

He rolled a piece of the material knowingly between thumb and forefinger.

"More like muslin, seconds at that. Fifty cents a yard on South Street. What did you charge the 'chentelman' for it, Long John?"

The irony was lost on "Long John," who did not deign to answer. I wanted to get on with the horrid task ahead and was afraid Marv might comment on the absence of links on the deceased's cuffs, but all he did was lift the sleeve and raise his eyebrows cynically. Then, while Chosie held the torch, Marv and Mr. B. removed Joe's remains from the bridal suite and tried to stand them upright in one corner of the hole. But they sagged, one arm dangled over the edge of the casket and the other hung limply against the body while the head wobbled from side to side. Marv attempted to wedge the body between coffin and wall but the last remains of the late Joe Eberhardt slumped to the wet ground where it lay, one bare foot protruding.

Then as the horror mounted, Marv plunged his hand down into the depths of the bridal suite and felt around for what we were certain would be the body of Ellen Eberhardt. He groped furiously, joined by Chosie and Mr. B., but all their fingers encountered were yards upon yards of soft cotton wadding which they tossed aside. Millie, Jack and I leaned over the edge of the casket and looked down; we saw nothing either.

"There *has* to be something here besides this goddamned cheap packing," Marv said as he wiped the sweat which was pouring from his face. "The Colonel wouldn't let us down."

I objected to the phraseology but in my heart I knew Marv was correct. And then, at the very bottom of the bridal suite, he found it—a replica of the Master's famed Persian slipper. Marv passed this up to me and while Millie, Josie and the others looked on, I put my hand into the toe and extracted a small, white, sealed envelope. I quickly ripped it open, and out came a single sheet of paper upon which was hand-inscribed the Secret Ritual of the Sons of the Copper Beeches. In hushed tones I read it aloud:

> Whose was it?
> His who is gone.
> Who shall have it?
> He who will come.
> Where was the sun?
> Over the oak.
> Where was the shadow?
> Under the elm.
> How was it stepped?
> North by ten and by ten, east by five and by
> five, south by two and by two, west by one and
> by one, and so under. . . .

It was dawn by the time we returned to Glen Hill to pick up Jack's car and go home. Mr. B. refused our rather lukewarm offer of help to return Joe to the bridal suite and refill his grave.

"Chosie and me'll do it after breakfast," he said. "Chust sometime exblain what this is all aboud, blease," and this we promised faithfully.

"Gentlemen," Millie said as we pulled away from the village, "I don't know how you feel about it but until I get a shower and put on some clean clothes I can't talk about a single thing."

We stopped in front of a small wayside motel, explained our needs to the clerk and rented two rooms, one for Millie and one for Jack, Marv, and me. We'd all brought changes of linen but Millie was the only one who had clean outergarments with her. We bathed and waited; she emerged from her room looking fresh as the proverbial daisy.

The night had taken much of our energies and I felt faint with hunger. I took it upon myself to ask the motel proprietor if he could fix breakfast for us. We were still in Pennsylvania Dutch territory and I suggested, if it were any way possible, summer sausage, fried potatoes, scrapple, and shoofly pie. I think our host was surprised at my knowledge of area culinary arts and seemed delighted to oblige. Within a half-hour we were seated in the family's dining room with each delicious dish I requested before us. In addition there were thick slices of country cured ham. I am sorry to say that my colleagues' recuperative powers are not as great as mine; they merely nibbled politely at the tempting viands served to us on a clean, checkerboard tablecloth. Millie, able to imbibe only apple juice and a cup of coffee, regarded me with admiration as I downed every bit of food on my plate and much of hers as well. The coffee did not come up to my high standards, but since I am not one to cavil I drank it without comment.

The ride back to Philadelphia took less than three hours, but before Jack dropped each of us at our individual homes we arrived at some definite conclusions, one of which was particularly encouraging. Before we began the discussion Millie wanted an explanation of the Ritual itself and how it applied. Without going into the details which she, herself, could read later, I told her the Ritual was the key by means of which the Master uncovered the body of Sir Reginald Musgrave's butler and located the actual crown worn by Charles I.

"OK as far as it goes," she said, "but I'll have to know much more about the Musgrave Ritual than the outline you drew for me, Frank. I'll study it as soon as I get home."

She smiled.

"I bought my own copy of the Complete Works. It's only a paperback but it's all there."

We all shuddered at the thought of anyone perusing Holmes in soft covers. I determined I would rectify this deplorable situation by presenting Millie with the Folcroft Edition, two beautiful, hand bound volumes printed by Winich of Manchester, England, in 1927. While by no means a collector's item, they are nevertheless worthy of a place on any Sherlockian's shelves.

It was Millie's firm opinion that the Ritual, stuffed into Holmes' Persian slipper, was H. Wesley's "giveaway."

"Remember I've been telling you all along that the Colonel's ego will compel him to furnish you with one last clue and if you solve this, you've got him. It's his final gesture; he's giving you a 'sporting chance' which in his opinion isn't sporting at all because he's convinced his intellect far outweighs ours. And, gentlemen, let's admit it, at this point he's right.

"I think we should concentrate on the Ritual and nothing else, we have so little time left. If we're able to figure out how it applies to the Chase before your meeting tomorrow night, you may still win the bet.

But *application* of the Ritual was a different story, like belling the cat, far easier said than done. What stumped us was our need for an oak close enough to an elm so that the first tree was in a position to cast a shadow upon the second. Without this set of conditions, there was no possible way we could begin to unravel the problem.

Old Musgrave himself had a specific pair of trees in mind when he concealed the Stuart family's royal jewels where their future recovery depended upon the ability of a descendant or someone else (the Master and Brunton, the butler, in this case) to decipher his clever code. But even Holmes had to have a starting point from which he could begin to step off that "north by ten and by ten. . . ."

There is an abundance of old oaks on Philadelphia's tree line streets. I know of one at the corner of Jessup and Lombard Streets, only yards away from my home and while I never checked, I would not be surprised to learn there are at least three oaks casting shadows over Baskerville Hall. Elms, however, are a rarity. I'm not an arboreal expert but I *am* an observant man and I venture to say there could be a mere few of this species within city limits or, as a matter of fact, in the suburbs. I know the reason; a blight which swept the entire East Coast two decades ago destroyed most, if not all, of the genus. I pointed this out to my colleagues.

Jack recalled a large tree in front of the Diogenes Club where, as you know, we Sons hold our meetings. He thought this was an elm.

"It's not," Marv said. "It's a horse chestnut. I know. I'm always picking up brown nuts from the ground to bring home for my kids in September.

He grinned.

"Good for rheumatism, too."

We made several other equally futile attempts at a solution to the problem and decided to postpone further efforts until the final plenary session we'd be holding as usual that evening in the Architects Club.

"Meanwhile," Jack said, "I think we should be prepared to pay off. I hate to break it to Don but if he needs time, one of us can advance the cash for him."

I said I would since I already owned seventy-five percent of his "stock." It was nearly ten o'clock in the morning by the time Jack dropped me off. Juliet was less irate than I expected and even made a sympathetic comment which I thought at first was spoken in irony. But to my amazement I found she was sincerely sorry our Adventure had turned out so badly.

I shut my studio door and slept fitfully for a few hours, awaking both exhausted and depressed. Most thoughtfully Juliet brought me a tray of sandwiches about one o'clock. Then when I thanked her politely but said I was unable to eat, she spoiled her gesture by saying, "You must be damned upset, Frank, to turn down food."

So, rather than subject myself to a bitter tirade, I managed to swallow three or four bacon, lettuce, and tomato on toasted Danish rye (my favorite, obtained only in the Reading Terminal Market) and wash them down with a quart of milk. I should state that I have no respect for those ridiculous theories about cholesterol; for milk to be potable, it must be Grade A or better.

The balance of the afternoon I spent re-reading the Musgrave Ritual and pondering its potentials. It was obvious the Colonel referred to some spot where he had been or still was in hiding. I looked for symbolism in that "strange catechism to which each Musgrave had to submit when he came to man's estate." I found nothing. Where was that elm and where did it cast its shadow? From which point should we begin to count?

We dined that evening seemingly without hope. The entree, Chateaubriand, was tasteless and the wine, a moderately good Nuits St. Georges, 1962, which I normally find quite palatable was bitter while the predinner martinis might have been concocted from fusil oil and horse piss.

No one said much, it was hard to penetrate the thick aura of defeatism which cast a pall upon us. Don told us he had invited Sheriff Roberts to be his guest at the regular Copper Beech session the following evening and that the Snyder County lawman had accepted with alacrity.

I had still another guest in mind but I did not mention this, holding off until I completed arrangements. I was determined we Sons must keep up with the times, break precedent and set a place for a woman—Millie—even if it meant some pawky neophyte had to eat alone on the Diogenes' first floor lounge. I intended to take action on this the moment I arrived home by calling Bill Starr, our Headmastiff and Millie, in that order. Although no woman ever had attended a Copper Beech meeting (nor has any since), I felt that my forensic powers were sufficient to persuade Bill to yield in this one, highly unusual case. As for Millie, I was confident that the young lady would accept and I would escort her myself.

It was then that Marv displayed traits which made me regret being his chief sponsor at the Copper Beeches.

"I've a surprise for you, gentlemen," he said, a silly smile covering his fat, oily face. "You'll be delighted to know I'm bringing Millie to the 'payoff' tomorrow night. I cleared it with Bill while you were showering this morning."

(Later I learned that Bill was extremely reluctant to yield —"Against my principles," he protested—and, as a matter of fact never officially granted Marv permission to bring Millie to our meeting. I think the Headmastiff was completely justified in his attitude. However, Bill is a Philadelphia gentleman of the old school, and under no circumstances do I believe he would have created a scene once Millie was present. "I smacked Marv down pretty hard afterward," he told me confidentially.)

Outraged, I sucked in my breath preparing to bring Mr. Abrams to task for such highly unethical conduct, conduct not befitting a gentleman. But Millie smoothed things over. She kissed me lightly on the cheek.

"I knew this would please you, Frank," she said. "Remember it was you who suggested it a long time ago. You're *such* a dear."

Jack reported that he'd picked up the Carl Anderson manuscripts from Jason Fox a few hours ago.

"I'm having it giftwrapped at Wanamaker's," he said wryly. "Costs a buck but this'll be my extra contribution." He turned to me.

"Will you make the 'presentation,' Frank?" he asked and my answer was, "Like hell I will!"

Furthermore, I added that I'd like to see Ellen in the flesh before we made the payoff but Jack demurred.

"That's not part of the deal, Frank. She could be in Timbuktu or the fat lady on a carnival midway. Makes no difference where she is. The Colonel's under no obligation to produce her."

I was forced to accept Jack's decision and, to prove that to a gentleman a "gentleman's agreement" is far more binding than a legal contract, I handed Jack a check for my share of the wager. What I expected to do *after* the payoff was my business. I determined then and there I would let no stone go unturned until I found Ellen Eberhardt, dead or alive. Even at this bitter moment of defeat I planned eventual victory. I would begin work at once, perhaps this very Saturday evening if Millie were free to join me for dinner in that little Frankford restaurant. There we could quietly lay our plans together.

The Friday of our meeting I told Juliet I'd paid off my obligation. Her answer was that as long as it came out of my personal account, she had nothing to say, then proceeded to say it in three or four thousand well chosen words. I listened without rebuttal and spent the balance of the afternoon poring over the Ritual and again seeking some light.

The elm, unquestionably, was our key. I didn't give a damn how unethical I was being but three times that day I circled Baskerville Hall—east on Spruce, south on Nineteenth, west again on Sassafras Alley and east on Locust. I persuaded Juliet to accompany me partly as a gesture of goodwill and partly because she knows botany. She pointed out several chestnut trees, maples, a ginkgo, a gorgeous copper beech in front of the home of Frank Eustace (a Master Son and our Recorder of Pedigrees), plus a dozen oaks. Two of these last were huge old trees on the east side of Baskerville Hall and had it been morning instead of afternoon, they would have cast shadows not only on the house itself but also over that terrifying forty-foot walkway leading from Sassafras Alley to the Colonel's side door.

There was no sign of life in the Hall; shutters were tightly closed as they had been for the past half-year and what little grass there was on the small front lawn was in desperate need of cutting. If the Colonel and his Lady were inside, they concealed themselves well. It was my wife's belief they spent the night in some suburban motel and would make a joint appearance only after the Copper Beech meeting was officially opened. I had grave doubts about any "joint" appearance.

It was five minutes before six o'clock when I left my home. As I turned on to Camac Street I noted a cluster of newspaper reporters, photographers, TV interviewers, and cameramen swarming around the clubhouse entrance, apparently awaiting the arrival of the Colonel or perhaps that of our six involved Sons.

By using the Diogenes' side entrance it would have been an easy matter for me to evade these eager representatives of the working press but such pusillanimity is not in my character, I never take the easy way out and quite boldly walked into their "lair." Apparently I was recognized, for I had no sooner adjusted my tie when bulbs flashed, cameras began to grind, and a half-dozen microphones were thrust into my face. I have been "on camera" so many times and subjected to so many interviews that when such a confrontation occurs I never become ruffled. With complete aplomb and a confident smile on my face I answered every question hurled at me. "Did I pay up my share of the wager?" "Did I expect the Colonel to show?" "Would the Colonel receive the Conan Doyle award?" "Had we consulted Philadelphia's Police Commissioner Rizzo?" "Had my wife filed suit for divorce?" "Was the Chase only a publicity stunt to lure new members into the Copper Beeches?"

I waited a few moments to make sure the last question had been asked and then, as the motley crew scurried off to impale someone else, I walked ahead to the club entrance. There a half-dozen male and female pickets bearing crudely painted signs marched up and down on the sidewalk in front of the door.

"SHERLOCK WAS A FINK. Friends of Nero Wolfe."

"HOLMES IS UNFAIR TO FEMALES. Women's Liberation Movement."

"HOLMES AND AGNEW FOREVER. Schuylkill River Pilots Association."

"BLACK IS BEAUTIFUL. HOLMES WAS BLACK. The Black Panthers."

I had a feeling the whole operation was promoted by the Union League still smarting over the kidnapping of their chef and under the misapprehension that the Diogenes somehow was affiliated with the Copper Beeches.

It was quarter past six when I cleared the vestibule so jammed with laughing, noisy Sons that I could hardly plow my way through to the bar. Don, with his guest, Sheriff Roberts, Charlie, and Ed were already there, elbows bent. Jack walked in shortly, carrying a beautifully wrapped package inside of which I knew were the Carl Anderson manuscripts.

It was six-thirty before Marv, smiling smugly, and Millie, looking absolutely magnificent in a low cut silk knit dress which clung to her body and a mini-skirt which displayed to best advantage her shapely legs, arrived. The whistles, cheers, and catcalls were deafening.

Except for Colonel H. Wesley Eberhardt, every living Son, anticipating the most exciting meeting in BSI's international history, was present waiting for the first Canonical toast. Three nonambulatory members—Dick Nalle, operated on only recently for double hernia; Bill Miller, head bandaged from ear to ear, the result of being thrown from his mount at the Devon Horse Show; and Ralph Earle II, both legs in casts—were wheeled in by fellow Copper Beeches. I have no idea how many neophytes dined by themselves downstairs and listened to the ceremonies via a loudspeaker.

I noted the presence of John Koelle, the famed Irish Sherlockian and was amazed to see Joe Gillies who told me he flew in from Canberra for the sole purpose of attending the meeting and had reservations to return to Australia the following morning. He wouldn't even see his first grandson, born two days before in Wilmington, Delaware.

There were at least a half-dozen more out-of-towners, in fact out-of-state and out-of-country guests, some of whom I knew and some of whom were complete strangers to me. But all shared intense anticipatory excitement.

Precedent was smashed at the first Canonical toast.

"Gentlemen," said Charlie, "I give you the loveliest lady in all Sherlockiana, Millie Tomassio, a worthy successor to Irene Adler!"

"Hear! Hear!" we responded in unison and raised our glasses on high.

Now, in as calm, coherent and dispassionate a fashion as I am capable of let me attempt to reconstruct the rest of the dreadful evening that followed. At seven o'clock the final of our seven symbolic toasts were drunk, and slowly we ascended the stairs to the dining room above. Colonel H. Wesley Eberhardt had not yet made his appearance.

I took my usual place between Tupper Lewis III, who holds the George W. Kreuzberger Chair of German History at the University, and Thomas Stix, Sr., Board Chairman of the Second National Bank. I had not seen nor spoken to Tups since the last meeting. He sat enthralled as I recounted the details of our own Adventure. Even in failure, I told him we brought no disgrace to the Sons. Then quite ruefully I added, "If we could have found one goddamned elm near Baskerville Hall, I'm sure we'd have laid bare Eberhardt's secret and proved the eternal value of Dr. Watson's Sacred Writings."

At 7:15 when all Sons were back in their seats after a brief comfort stop, our Headmastiff called the meeting to order, beginning as usual with another one or two unofficial non-Canonical toasts. At 7:45 the first course, a delicious lobster bisque, was served. I have no intention of detailing the menu. Suffice it to say François, the chef, on this occasion outdid himself and Tom, who belongs to the League but not the Diogenes, openly expressed his bitterness about the "kidnapping."

At 9:30 the last B&B was served. Our Headmastiff pounded his gavel trying to get order so that homage could be paid to Sons departed from this earth since the spring meeting. A hush swept from table to table until the only sound heard was the ticking of a grandfather clock in the hallway.

At 9:33 in strode Colonel H. Eberhardt. He was alone.

There was no applause, not even polite handclapping. I saw to it that every Son had been alerted to H. Wesley's perfidy. They also were aware of my petition to strike him from the roles, a procedure used only once before in our long and honorable history. That, of course, is another story.

As I looked squarely at Eberhardt when he turned around from the Headmastiff to face us, I could have sworn the man was already 'round the bend. His eyes had a strange look

which could not be attributed solely to the overpowering glee
he undoubtedly felt at his moment of triumph.

Jack, a true Philadelphia gentleman, arose prize in hand
and slowly moved toward the dais.

"Colonel," he said quietly and looked at his watch, "with
six hours, twenty-five minutes, and forty-one seconds to spare,
you have fulfilled, successfully, all terms of the wager. We
now fulfill ours."

With that, he laid the giftwrapped package in front of the
Headmastiff and walked to his seat. An uneasy quiet followed.
I think we all felt the contradictions in this odd situation. It
was almost as though George Washington, honor-bound to
fulfill a previously made commitment, was awarding a medal
to Benedict Arnold.

I must give the devil his due. With complete self-possession
the Colonel removed the ribbon tied around the prize and
held the manuscript aloft for all to see and for all to envy. He
glanced questioningly at H. W. Starr and when the latter nodded approval, Eberhardt made an about-face and, for the last
time, addressed his fellow Sons of the Copper Beeches.

"Gentlemen," he said in tones as cold as ice, "what I have
to say will be said in as few words as possible. For the past six
months, as all of you know, I completed an experiment, the
results of which were for me, at least, a foregone conclusion.
At the same time I demonstrated the ineptitude of the profes-
sionals whom my 'hunters' felt compelled to summon when
they realized their efforts at detection were failing."

He paused, then looked directly at Millie, seated at the
head table.

"I bow to the obvious physical endowments of one such
representative of law and order. I pay no homage to her occupational prowess."

Bitter cries of "Hear! Hear!" resounded throughout the dining hall but our Headmastiff pounded his gavel and restored
silence. The Colonel went on, his voice dripping with sar-
casm.

"Chivalry, I note, is not dead. So, in mitigation, I hasten to
add that a large portion of the lady's time and much of her ingenuity was spent eluding an aging, gluttonous Lothario with
yearning, if not success, in extracurricular romance."

For a moment I was certain H. Wesley referred to Marv,
Millie's dinner escort. Then a wave of unrestrained tittering

broke out, shouts of "Challenge him, Frank!" and "Let me be your second, Frank!" came from everywhere and I realized the Colonel meant me. I literally trembled with rage at this unjust inference and, had it not been for Tups and Tom, I would have risen to the floor and issued a challenge. The Colonel went on.

"To the other official aide of our six intrepid hounds, I have only this to say. You, sir, with knowledge of my physical characteristics passed me by a dozen times and twice lit my cigarette. Were I a Snyder County taxpayer, I would demand more for my money. Holmes, at least, never sucked the public trough."

At this blatant discourtesy to a guest came even louder outbursts of "Hear! Hear!" silenced once more by H. W. Starr.

"I beg you to indulge me a bit longer, gentlemen," the Colonel said. "I have almost concluded. I wish merely to emphasize certain unassailable facts I elicited from the Book of Holmes, something I pointed out months ago to my would-be captors, something I don't doubt they have repeated to the Brethren.

"The truth is that the Sacred Writings are as practical to modern detection as a witch's incantations to a patient with terminal cancer, that Mr. Sherlock Holmes was an admitted deviate whose one venture into a heterosexual relationship resulted in the impregnation of his 'virtuous' housekeeper, and that John Watson, M.D., was nothing more than a greedy abortionist forced to abandon his flagitious practice every time Scotland Yard caught up with him."

At this infamy, a gasp swept through the Diogenes' Banquet Room. However, in accordance with time honored custom, no Son arose from his seat or interrupted the speaker.

"Now gentlemen, go on with your play acting, live in your world of dreams, indulge yourselves in romantic fantasy. I shall sit back and laugh."

He raised his glass.

"I propose a toast."

We raised our glasses; custom demanded it.

"Maligned by those who should honor him most, I give you, my colleagues for the last time, the only *real* man in *all* Sherlockiana—Sir Arthur Conan Doyle."

The shock was overwhelming. To propose a toast to that villainous literary thief was like asking the Holy Father and his College of Cardinals to wish Martin Luther a long life. But drink the toast we did, every single Son of a Copper Beech, choking down the B&B in one huge gulp. The Colonel nodded, a sardonic smile on his lips, then seated himself on the chair reserved for him on the right side of the Gasogene. His eyes swept the room, his lips uttered nothing. Nevertheless we knew the bastard was thinking—"Carry on now, *if— you—can!*"

It was not easy but we made the effort, doing our best to concentrate on the first monograph, Ken Souser's "Preliminary Report of London's Railroad Stations." Ken always does a beautiful job of research and under normal circumstances we could have listened to him with complete attention. But now the balloon was punctured. H. Wesley, looking down upon us, a cynical smile never leaving his face, had cruelly demolished our private escape route from a troubled world. Whether we could ever rebuild it was, at this moment, highly questionable. I think Tom Stix sounded our mood as well as anyone. "I feel like Alice," he whispered. I knew what he meant.

" 'Who cares for you?" said Alice,' I quoted [she had grown to her full size by this time]. 'You're nothing but a pack of cards.' "

I no longer paid attention to Ken nor to Bill MacMurtrie who followed with a "History of the Fifth Northumberland Fusiliers, Dr. Watson's Regiment." I was concentrating on those questions Colonel Eberhardt had failed to answer. He practically admitted he'd been a carny but on which midways had he played? How was he disguised when Sheriff Roberts lit his cigarettes? Why didn't he mention Brother Joe? Was it application of the Sacred Writings which enabled him to follow our movements? Where had Ellen been all the while? Where was she now? Why hadn't he produced her?

If he held us in such contempt, why, then, was he an avid collector of the Master's works? I could comprehend his use of the wager to provide a six months' cover for some nefarious scheme. But this did not explain his long-time quest for Sherlockiana, the accumulation of a treasure second only to that of Lord Philip MacKlein of Aberdeen, Scotland. Furthermore, did H. Wesley intend to sell his acquisitions on the open market? Or would he take them with him wherever he went?

I knew only too well he had no moral or legal obligation to reveal more. He was a free man, he could walk out of the Diogenes, leave Philadelphia, go any place in the world he chose and stay forever. God knows he had the wherewithal. If, after the Headmastiff pounded his gavel for adjournment and Colonel H. Wesley Eberhardt disappeared from our lives, the mystery of Ellen Eberhardt might never be solved. That it was, and on this very night, is because of my ability to take advantage of a coincidence, even though in so doing I almost suffered an untimely death.

Tup, my partner on the right, is more than a moderately heavy drinker but after the first highball he becomes befuddled and for the rest of the evening sits in a stupor, seeing nothing and hearing nothing. "I'm a cheap drunk," he used to say, another fact if not a truth since it never stops him from indulging himself. But that night he drank nothing at all. I have no desire to make a mystery of Tup's sudden sobriety; he'd been warned only that day by his internist that while one drink of Scotch might not kill him, two probably would.

In the midst of Joe Gillies' monograph on "The Curious Experiences of the Patterson Family in the Island of Uffa," Tup nudged me.

"What's the name of that judge who lives in back of Baskerville Hall?"

I thought for a moment before answering this seemingly irrelevant question.

"Ulmebaum. Phineas T. Ulmebaum. As I recall his mother was a Bowen."

But Tup rudely interrupted.

"Oh, crap on his pedigree, Frank. I'm trying to tell you something important. Do you speak German?"

My knowledge of Spanish, Portuguese and even the Basque patois is superb and if it were not for my strikingly Nordic appearance I could easily pass for a native anywhere on the Iberian peninsula. But I say, and without regret until this moment, that my knowledge of German has been restricted to Teutonic drinking songs. I shook my head.

Tup grinned.

"Too bad," he said in his patronizing fashion. "Otherwise you could have prevented the shellacking that bastard Eberhardt gave us tonight."

"What do you mean, Tup?" I asked, barely controlling my anger at this unfair criticism.

"What I mean, Frank, is that the German word for 'elm tree' is *ulmebaum*. Comes from the Latin root . . ."

But I no longer listened.

"*Ulmebaum! Ulmebaum!*" My mouth opened wide. I gasped.

Where was the shadow!

Under the elm.

"Thanks, Tup," I whispered fervently.

Marv sat directly in back of me. I turned around, motioned for him to follow and the pair of us, wishing neither to be rude to the speaker nor to be observed by Colonel Eberhardt, slunk out of the banquet room. There, in the second floor hallway, I told Marv. He was as excited as I.

"My God! Frank," he said. "You've got the answer. Let's get going."

I thought we should ask our fellow hunters to join us but Marv felt otherwise.

"Huh, uh! That'll be a sure tipoff if he sees Jack and the rest leave. The two of us may get away with it but if we all pile out he'll be damned sure something's up."

Marv looked at his watch.

"Ten after ten. We've two hours at the most."

There was no point driving; the Diogenes is less than three blocks from Baskerville Hall. As we scurried along Philadelphia's deserted streets and neared the darkened carriage house I tugged Marv's sleeve.

"Don't you think we ought to notify the police? After all this really is their job, not ours and we should have told Millie."

"For Christ's sake, what's with you, Frank? The cops'd think we were crazy. You and I know what we're looking for but we've nothing to go by except our suspicions. Can you imagine explaining the Musgrave Ritual to Commissioner Rizzo. We can't swear out a warrant, no court would give anybody the right to make a search under these circumstances.

"And we can't involve Millie. We might have to break into the house. She'd *never* let us."

I hadn't thought we'd go that far but additional argument was pointless. Marv had made up his mind. My heart pounding wildly, I followed him to the rear gate of the silent house and stood listening.

"If a red car spots us or a beat cop comes around," he said softly, "just let me handle it. If they yell 'Stop' once we get inside the gate, do exactly what they say. Much as I'd like to solve the mystery, I still don't want a bullet up my ass."

I didn't either. The very thought of an involuntary rectal injection of lead made me wince. We stood, quiet as mice, beneath the penumbra of a street lamp on the opposite side of narrow Sassafras Alley and surveyed the scene. Directly in back of us was the somber Ulmebaum house, a five-story Georgian monstrosity. Our first obstacle was an iron fence about eight feet high, topped with six spears arranged in organ-like fashion, the highest in mid-center. On the other side of the barrier was that dreadful forty-foot path leading to the side entrance of Baskerville Hall. How *many* times, I recalled, had I scurried along this dark yew lined passage, heart pounding wildly, certain I would never reach the door alive. How clearly I pictured the Colonel's sneer, his inward laughter, his sarcastic greeting—"The hound's dead, Frank. Relax."

And this upon nights when I knew that close by were five or six convivial Sons, seated in front of a cheerful fire, and Ellen, warm and gracious, hovering in the background. Now it was just Marv and me. Only God knew what horrors might be waiting for us in that huge dark old house which loomed ahead.

CHAPTER

23

"THE FIRST thing we got to do," Marv whispered, "is get over or though that lousy fence. Too bad my sport was wrestling, not pole-vaulting."

He told me to remain beneath the extension of the Ulmebaums' garage roof, almost completely concealed from view.

He took a small flashlight from the medical kit he always carries with him.

"Hold this," Marv said and passed the black bag to me. Then he crossed the alley and examined the lock with care. He came back and was about to say something when out of the night came the widening scream of a siren, a flash of red lights and the roar of a car traveling south on Eighteenth Street.

"Somebody saw us and phoned the fuzz," I said. "What'll we tell them?"

But the vehicle, an ambulance, sped on toward Graduate Hospital, and once more all was silent.

"Come along and hold the torch for me," Marv ordered and I obeyed. He unzipped the kit and extracted a sharp instrument.

"I use this for cutting out cadaver hearts. Has a nice hook on it," he grinned.

My body was covered with goose pimples.

"This is no time for levity," I hissed.

He inserted the tool into the keyhole, gave it a few twists and the rusty lock sprang open.

"Wouldn't be surprised if the Colonel knew we'd be around and wanted to make things easy for us," he said, still grinning.

"You're kidding, Marv."

"I'm kidding."

He drew in his breath then added, "I hope."

He put his shoulders to the gate.

"Hang on to your hat, Frank, I'm going to swing it open. Get ready to scram if an alarm blasts off."

He paused again. "Unless, of course, it's a silent one and only rings in police headquarters."

No sound greeted us. Marv shut the gate while we quietly waited inside the grounds for at least five minutes.

"I guess we're safe now. Let's see what the hell we do next."

My suggestion was that we apply the Sacred Writings, specifically the Musgrave Ritual.

"OK, Frank. You apply."

I nodded. We had our elm; now to find the oak which would cast a shadow over the alley. This was easy; on the Nineteenth Street side of Baskerville Hall, towering above the thick border of yews was a giant oak.

"That must be the one," I said confidently. "So we do just

what the Master did. We take ten paces north, then five paces east."

"Beginning where?"

I hadn't thought of that.

"Let's try from the gate," I suggested, "and see where it lands us."

Marv by my side, we paced off ten steps north. This led us in the direction of the side door but still some ten feet away.

"Going to try five paces east now?" Marv asked and I realized at once that five paces, or roughly fifteen feet in an easterly direction would bring us to Nineteenth Street. Even though it was almost pitch black—Marv had extinguished the flashlight—I could sense his dissatisfaction.

"No matter where we start from Frank," he whispered, "if we follow the Master's directions and turn east, we're bound to land outside."

I was compelled to agree. But how had we miscalculated? The error had to be ours; the Sacred Writings are quite explicit. I was extremely upset.

"Truth is, Marv, we've fouled up somewhere along the line."

He gave a bitter laugh.

" 'The seeming truth, which cunning times put on,' " he quoted, " 'to entrap the wisest.' "

"The Talmud, I think. But it's been a long time since I was a Bar Mitzvah boy."

I corrected him.

"Shakespeare. *The Merchant of Venice.*"

"No wonder I misquoted it. I used to rip the goddamned pages out of that play in everybody's books at Central High."

This was hardly the time or place for a discussion of the Bard's alleged anti-Semitism. My thoughts were upon the Colonel and I kept praying he had not noticed our absence and was still seated on the dais. I did not remember what other monographs were on the agenda. I could only wish they were lengthy.

We took three more strides north. This brought us just short of the side entrance where we stood for a few minutes contemplating the next move. Despite the density of the yews the darkness was not quite total. Faint rays from a sliver of moon directly overhead reached us and I could see Marv scratch his head. He took a deep breath as though he'd come to a decision.

"Scalpel, nurse," he whispered, an anomalous grin on his face. I was still holding onto the black medical kit which I couldn't seem to unzip. He took the bag from me, opened it and removed a pocket flask and a shiny instrument.

"You need a shot, Frank," he said, unscrewing the cap and passing the bottle to me. I took a long, long pull and could feel the burning liquid, whatever it was, all the way down my gullet and into my stomach. I shuddered and was prepared to risk another.

"Enough! Enough! That's no way to enjoy 120-proof mescal. Besides, I need one myself. Here's to you, Colonel H. Wesley Eberhardt, you son-of-a-bitch," and he took a hearty swig.

A few twists of the scalpel and the lock snapped. Marv shook his head.

"Got your trusty .38 with you, Frank?"

The question was ridiculous; I never carry a dangerous weapon; it is illegal in Philadelphia without a permit and I have never applied for one.

Marv sighed.

"I wish I had H. Wesley's Penang lawyer or that scimitar he has. I'd feel better."

He took another deep breath.

"Well, Frank, let's go before I lose my nerve and let you carry on alone.

The door opened easily, we stood stock still for a couple of seconds waiting for an alarm to sound and when it didn't, stepped into the darkness of Baskerville Hall.

The heavy wooden shutters were closed tight, but because we both were fairly familiar with furniture arrangements in the foyer, living room, and library we managed to grope our way through these rooms encountering only a few obstacles we'd either forgotten about or which had been moved. A glimmer of moonbeams struck the glazed upper half of the first floor powder room.

"Power of suggestion," Marv said. "I gotta go."

I waited close by. He whistled.

"Well, what d'yu know? Seat's up, Pop's home."

I turned around in mortal terror, convinced the Colonel

was directly behind me. And then a minute later Marv automatically flushed the toilet. The roar of rushing water was deafening. "Niagara Falls," I hissed, sure the sound carried to Spruce Street. I cursed my companion for his thoughtlessness as we both dashed toward the front door. This time my arm struck something and I heard an object crash to the floor. Marv banged his shin on a low hunt table which he should have known was there. He leaped up and down swearing furiously, hugging the injured limb.

We waited, poised for rapid flight, then turned back. He closed the bathroom door, shutting out what little light there was and, of course, plunging the house into darkness again. He turned on his pocket torch, one of those tiny rechargeable things which never give much light.

"Wonder if the electricity's turned off," he said. "We could stand more than we're getting from this."

He flashed the beam onto a switch and before I could stop him, pulled it. Thank God we were not flooded with light which most certainly would have revealed our presence despite the closed shutters.

"No electricity, Frank. We'll have to settle for this, such as it is. Now what do we do and what *are* we looking for? You move, mein Fuehrer."

I repeated passionately that we were seeking anything that would reveal Ellen's present or past whereabouts. Furthermore, I was certain we would find a clue once we discovered how to apply the Ritual. We needed a starting point.

"Want to take a look upstairs, Frank? See if her clothes are missing?"

I shook my head.

"No! There's nothing in the Ritual about that."

We sat down to think in front of the cold, dead fireplace, Marv haphazardly swinging the beam around the room. The light suddenly played on that object I'd inadvertently knocked to the carpet. He picked up what appeared to be a glass bowling ball.

"Now where the hell do you suppose this comes from, Frank?" he asked and handed the round object to me.

It was a pure plastic globe about ten inches in diameter. On the surface I discovered a small hole into which I could insert my thumb as far as the first knuckle. The moment I felt threads I knew something belonging to the ball was missing. I bent down and ran my hands over the carpet in the same general area where Marv picked up the globe. A few feet away I encountered a long metal cylinder with threads on one end and a series of flutelike holes along a side. Each of these was threaded. As I anticipated, the tube fitted perfectly into the plastic ball.

"Get your fat *tochis* off the chair, Marv, and help me."

"What am I supposed to be looking for?"

"Seven stems, wood or metal, which will screw into the holes of the tube."

Marv found the second, a free-form aluminum cylinder with one end shaped like the arrow of a weathervane.

"A jackstraw," he said, and that was close enough. The lower end of the straw was threaded. It took us another few minutes of floor crawling but we finally picked up the other six. When screwed into the tube as tightly as they would go every one pointed in the same direction. Even in the faint light which Marv's torch threw off I could see the workmanship was that of a craftsman whom I recognized at once.

"Hold it upside down, Marv," I said, "and you find an *A* and a *C* etched into the bottom of the glass."

He followed my suggestion. He was surprised but I wasn't.

"How'd you know?"

I couldn't resist.

"Elementary, my dear Doctor. It's an Alexander Calder. Remember the big one on the first floor of the Art Museum?"

He made a noncommittal grunt.

"Well, this is one of the four signed miniatures Calder made. Each one cost a fortune. Why in the hell did the Colonel want one of these moderns for Baskerville Hall? Everything here is conventional, Victorian monstrosities the Dawsons must have had for a hundred years."

"I think I can tell you, Frank. There ought to be a slight irregular indentation on the base of the globe."

He was right, I asked him how he knew. Before he replied I sensed, even if I couldn't see, his silly grin.

"Elementary, my dear Holmes."

The hour was late and getting later. This was no time for jokes. I told him to get on with it.

"The globe's got to fit into its convex counterpart somewhere in this room."

"But why?"

"Because, Frank," he answered softly, "*this,* not the gate is our starting point. Let's get going, man, and find it. I've a feeling we're not too many jumps ahead of H. Wesley Eberhardt."

We were in the library. I didn't believe we'd find what we were looking for there because I'd knocked down the piece after I'd gone through it in our hurry to reach the front door.

"Must be in the living room," I said. "I was running tiptoe and my right shoulder barely brushed against it, now that I recall. Happened just before we reached the foyer."

"If you hit it with your shoulder while you were running, that means it's got to be on a ledge about five and a half feet above the floor."

This narrowed the search. I was afraid to look at the luminous dial on my wristwatch and I had the horrid feeling that our sole source of light was losing its efficacy. Marv had the same idea. He snapped off the switch and asked me if I could feel my way in the dark along the wall into the living room without stumbling. I said "OK" and swung my left hand in front of me to prevent bumping into anything and my right pressed against the wall, moving it up and down from neck to eye level.

With Marv close behind I'd almost reached the foyer when we heard the pounding of footsteps moving along Spruce Street toward Baskerville Hall. Whoever it was had the type of wooden heels which the Colonel always wore. We stopped dead in our tracks. I thought I was going to faint.

"Goddamn," Marv said. "We haven't a thing to protect ourselves with. Wish I had that scalpel but I left my kit on the floor back there when I picked up this hunk of junk."

What a way to speak of the great Alexander Calder's work! Even in my agony of fear I wanted to admonish this uncultured friend of mine. As we listened the footfalls continued on past Baskerville Hall and faded into the night. A moment later my fingers touched the shelf and I breath a sigh of relief. Marv relit the torch, handed it to me, then placed the bottom of the globe over a slight rise on the shelf. The fit was perfect, the ball would not move in any direction unless it were lifted and every arrow pointed the same way.

"South, southeast, about twenty-three degrees," Marv explained. "See how being a Boy Scout pays off. Were you one?"

I didn't deign to answer. As a matter of fact I never was a member of the Boy Scouts. At that period in my life my father always sent me to a good Maine camp. But this was beside the point; I let Marv enjoy his petty triumph.

"OK, Frank, let's see where this takes us," he added cheerfully. *"Que sera, sera.* If the Colonel returns before our treasure hunt's over, we'll have to face him. Do you think he'll believe I got lost on my way to a professional house call? Besides I started to get the feeling we're the victims of a huge practical joke."

"Joke!" I said. "This is no joke. We've a chance of being murdered by a madman with every legal right to shoot us as housebreakers."

With Marv in the lead we paced off the ten prescribed steps which brought us to the far drape covered wall of the Eberhardts' living room.

"Well," my fellow conspirator said, "unless there's a secret door behind these drapes, we're off the track again."

But we were not off the track; there *was* a door behind the heavy damask which I moved aside and a dank, musty smell assailed our nostrils. Luckily we did not move; when Marv flashed his light ahead we could see the door was at the head of a steep set of stairs leading down. We stood there motionless peering into the depths below.

"Wait here a second, Frank, don't budge." Marv said, turned around abruptly and left me alone in the darkness. I followed the beam and the shadows it cast before it as Marv's broad shoulders disappeared into the darkness weaving around the furniture. I thought of the watchtower atop the original Baskerville Hall where Stapleton, the killer, could often be sensed slithering through the Great Grimpen Mire, his torch darting hither and yon until it was lost somewhere in the bogs.

Marv finally returned with the medical kit. He opened it and removed the flask.

"That ought to stop your teeth from chattering, Frank. Take a swig of this Dutch courage, but save some for me."

I tried to swallow the potent beverage; the liquid simply would not go down. My companion polished it off with no trouble, drew a deep breath, then flashed the beam downward.

"OK Chief. Let's see where the next ten paces takes us. How many steps to a pace?"

I suggested three since the wooden riser was about a foot high.

"All right," he said. "You go first. I'll hold the beam so you can see ahead."

There was no banister or rail to cling to and the stairs were almost as steep as a ladder's. I counted twenty-one steps before my foot hit bottom, Marv right behind me. We stopped for a moment. There was an extremely musty smell and the air was dank and chilly. Marv sniffed.

"I think we're under Spruce Street out behind the house."

I listened intently for some sound to come from above, but there was none. Then I pressed my ear against the wall and from far off came a very faint rumble.

"You're right, Marv. We *are* under Spruce Street. That was a train I just heard go by on the Locust Street subway extension.

The left side of my face was damp from contact with the wall, flakes of whitewash clung to my jacket. Marv wondered what the room was used for and I suggested a wine cave, the temperature and moisture content seemed perfect. "But not in the Colonel's time," I added.

We couldn't see far, certainly no more than a half-dozen feet but I sensed that the room was huge. It occurred to me then this probably was the hostler's repair and storage room, when Baskerville really was a functioning carriage house and the Fosters owned it. If that were so, somewhere there should be a wide trapdoor for lowering equipment into the basement.

I pictured the layout as it might have been in Doctor Foster's day, borrowed the flashlight and threw the beam up at a likely place for the trap; it was where I thought it would be. While only traces of the opening remained, an old pulley, with tackle attached, still hung. With a shock I recalled the tragic fate of young Master Foster, trampled to death seventy years before by his Shetland pony within a few feet of where we now stood.

I told Marv the story; he listened impatiently but before I concluded he grasped my shoulder.

"Wait a minute. Wait a minute. Then that runaway slave station's got to be here. Isn't this the dungeon where those Negro men and women died of starvation?"

My hair stood on end. I'd forgotten about that.

"Yes," I whispered. "It must be close by but not in this

room. Too exposed here; there has to be a better hiding place."

"We've *got* to get to it, Frank, and damned soon, too. We're going directly where that old bastard Eberhardt expects us to go and I want to find out what he's got in mind. Then out fast before he gets back. This torch isn't going to last much longer."

I suggested we retrace our steps, return to the Diogenes for Jack, Ed, Charlie, Don, and perhaps Sheriff Roberts as well.

"After all," I said, "we have no right to exclude any of them from witnessing the last chapter. They'd be furious."

"No," Marv hissed. "God damn it, no! How many paces left?"

I sighed. Marv is a stubborn, reckless fellow. I tried to remember the Ritual.

"Three," I answered. "Then . . . east by five and by five . . ."

He interrupted a bit irritably.

"I know the Ritual. Come on."

Marv decided to save the power remaining in his torch so in the pitch darkness we groped our way along the wall. We stopped at the requisite number of steps but all we felt was more wall.

"Our strides are too short, let's take a couple more."

Within a few feet I felt a break in what I thought was a solid wall. Marv turned the light on again and we could see a deeper, smaller, chamber ahead. Five paces brought us to still another door. We paused. I could hear Marv's heavy breathing and I'm sure he could hear mine. He tapped the wall, there was a slightly hollow sound.

"This *is* it. How the hell do we get in? Let's look for an entrance."

We found one, a gate no more than three feet high in back of a long abandoned coal bin. Marv touched the gate and it swung open. Either the chamber we now entered was blacker than the others or Marv's torch had grown dimmer so that for several seconds we could see absolutely nothing. Yet I knew instinctively this was the place where those poor benighted darkies had died their wretched deaths a century before. I kept telling myself I would find no traces of their existence, sure that Jasper Patterson's survivors cleaned up the mess those slaves had made.

At this crucial moment the flashlight ceased to function, we were plunged into total darkness. Never before in my whole fifty-nine years had I experienced anything quite so fearful. I know my teeth were chattering and I hoped my upper denture would hold. Then I heard Marv softly humming:

> Where was Moses when the lights went out?
> Down in the cellar eating sauerkraut.

I could have strangled him in cold blood.

"You haven't a match on you, Frank? I know I haven't."

I felt in my pockets but the conclusion was foregone. I don't smoke and the package of matches I carry to light others' cigarettes and Millie's cigars I'd left on the Diogenes' banquet table.

Sometimes this works," Marv said and banged the torch on the ground. The response, thank God, was instantaneous, the beam appeared even brighter than it had been.

"Won't last more than a minute or two," Marv added pessimistically. "Then it'll stay out until it's recharged."

But the light lasted long enough for us to accomplish our purpose. Stretched across the rafters from wall to wall we could see a huge canvas banner—OLGA THE HEADLESS TEUTON. There, in one corner, sat Olga, just as I'd looked at her on Market Street in the Museum of Oddities and on those two carnival midways. The bell jar with the glass tubes had been removed and rested on the floor by her side.

The joke was on us! With Brother Joe's help, and even without it, it was easy to see how the Colonel kept reasonably close check on our movements. I was ashamed to admit it but I, myself, had jested with him in a casual fashion at the McClure Bean Soup. As I recalled, the "physician" in charge of the exhibit was in the most simple of disguises: a white jacket, a pair of dark, horn-rimmed spectacles, a well trimmed goatee. I couldn't think of anything else. He must have left all the talking to the MC because I could not recall anything he'd said.

The diabolical cleverness of H. Wesley's choice of a place to "hide" came from the fact that everyone, including his pursuers, concentrated on the freaks or illusions and not on their exhibitors. It's what the prestidigitator does with his left hand while you watch his right. Or you might consider this a classic use of the "Purloined Letter" technique.

"Want to pinch Olga," I asked Marv sarcastically. "I understand a great many marks do."

"No, thanks. I've seen her before. But I was always under the impression they used a live one and concealed her head in back of a mirror. Otherwise what's the point having a headless Teuton if she's not human?"

"What's the difference? So the Colonel used a papier-mâché model."

He sighed.

"OK. Maybe you're right. Now let's get the hell out of Baskerville Hall before the boss gets here."

We were halfway up the stairs when Marv stopped.

"Frank, there's something screwy about what we saw down there in that chamber of horrors. Why was the mirror removed? We could see right through where Olga's head should have been. The Colonel *wanted* us to."

"For God's sake, Marv. We'll debate the question some other time. Please!"

But Marv is stubborn as a mulc.

"I'm going back for another look. We missed something. You can leave if you want."

There was no use arguing, Marv had the flashlight and I couldn't face walking through those empty rooms to Yew Alley alone.

"I'm with you. I just hope your flashlight holds out."

But the light was beginning to fade even before we reached the bottom of the stairs. Marv banged it against the wall and the beam miraculously brightened. With the most incredible willpower I ever mustered I followed him into the storage room through the gate into what he rightfully called a "chamber of horrors."

Marv walked over to Olga. He scratched his head; stood in front of her, in back of her and viewed her from either side. He couldn't see much, the light was dimming again. She was wearing the dress I recalled seeing her in on the various midways, a light blue, knee-length frock with a rather modest neckline exposing the breasts only slightly, just enough to give marks a perverted thrill.

Suddenly, with one hard yank Marv ripped off the dress. I could see flecks of dust rising. Then he bent down on his knees, held the torch close to a small section of the torso, his eyes only an inch or two away.

He jumped up.

"That's not papier-mâché!"

"Then what in God's name is it?" I whispered although I was afraid even then that I knew the answer. "Are you sure?"

"I'm sure. Come over here and I'll prove it to you if the goddamned light doesn't go out."

Almost in a hypnotic trance I obeyed and bent my head close to Marv's

"Look at these fine hair patterns, those skin creases and the pits. Nobody can duplicate them by hand, not even Madame Toussaud. This was once a living breathing woman, with a pretty good sized pair of tits. A thirty-six C would be my guess."

I began to feel faint and moved back to lean against the wall. The Colonel's Lady was, in the vernacular, "well stacked."

"Ellen, do you suppose?" I could barely ask the question.

"I wouldn't be surprised but we won't be able to tell without an autopsy. I'll order one tomorrow. Eberhardt *is* crazy. No question about that."

I gasped for breath. This, I thought, was the climax to a night of horror, but for me it was not yet over.

"Listen, Frank. We can't leave the body alone. One of us has to remain with it until the cops come."

"Why? Why can't we both go together right away?"

"Because if the Colonel gets here first there's no telling what he'll do. I want the corpse just like it is."

He turned around and flashed the beam on Olga, or perhaps I should say what was left of poor Ellen.

"A beautiful embalming job; Mr. Beebelheimer might learn a thing or two. Didn't that report Millie got on the old boy's military background say undertaking was one of the Colonel's undercover activities?"

Marv, to my disgust, felt the space between Ellen's shoulders.

"Clean a decapitation as I've ever seen and I've seen plenty in my day."

There was a hint of admiration in his voice.

"Must have used that scimitar. Wonder what he did with the head?"

This callousness shocked me. Had my fellow Son no feelings? I was aware of his profession but he was not discussing a nameless cadaver, he was talking about a friend, a lovely woman we both knew.

"Marv! We're *not* going to look for the head now, I protest. Come on. I don't see why both of us shouldn't leave together so we can protect each other if he shows up."

"Nope. One of us has to stay here."

"Why can't we wait upstairs near the door?"

"Because, Frank, there might be another entrance to this room, one they took the slaves out of. The Colonel could come in, snatch the body and disappear with it. We might never find him or Ellen. We can't take that chance. Make up your mind but do it soon, the Copper Beech meeting must almost be over.

What an awful choice to make! Should I remain in the dark with the body and perhaps be murdered by that madman creeping through a subterranean passage only he knew about? Or should I feel my way through the silent house with the possibility of H. Wesley lurking behind a door waiting for me, his sharp scimitar poised, ready to swing at my head? And then even if I got through Baskerville Hall that long, horrid stretch of yews lay ahead.

"I counsel you," Holmes had said, "to forbear from venturing upon Yew Alley in those dark hours when the powers of evil are exalted." Then a childhood riddle came to mind. "If you were up to your neck in shit and someone threw a brick, would you duck?"

My decision was just as difficult to make but after as much thought as Marv permitted I decided not to stay with the body, providing he would surrender his torch.

"Take it. I've an extra scalpel you're welcome to. If you're forced to use it get close, aim for the heart and flick your wrist like so. Don't try to swing, the Colonel's probably a karate expert."

The offer of a scalpel did not tempt me. I would have to rely upon other skills. With the flashlight in hand I said farewell to my companion, turned around and began my fearful trek. No sooner had I reached the top of the stairs when the light went out. I banged it against the floor as Marv had done but nothing happened. So in total darkness I moved on, once falling over a misplaced ottoman, landing with such force that my glasses flew off my nose. I moved my hands over the rug trying to feel for them but failed. I suffer from myopia and while with spectacles my vision is twenty-twenty, without them I cannot identify, even in broad daylight, any object smaller than a pony.

Then I really had to grope my way. I stumbled, this time over a coffee table, then bumped my head against the library door Marv in his haste had forgotten to close. For a moment I lost consciousness, the pain was excruciating and I could feel blood pouring down the side of my face over my right eye. I was only yards to the front of the house thinking I would make my escape to Spruce Street. When I finally reached it I leaned against the door to catch my breath. Then, with trembling fingers I unfastened the security chain, pulled hard but the door would not budge. I realized it was a double lock and no key in the hole.

Hoping it would be hidden where we sometimes conceal ours, I jerked up the mat and as I did I heard something metalic fly off into the dark. It had to be the key, and on hands and knees I groped for it frantically. My head was bleeding so profusely I could no longer see with my right eye.

Suddenly, out of the night came the measured beat of wooden heels on the sidewalk, at first only a faint tap, tap, tap, then louder and louder they came until I thought I would scream. This time I *knew* it was the Colonel. I abandoned my search, stood erect and, misjudging distance, cracked the left side of my skull against an antique umbrella stand, an old Dawson relic I wished they'd given to the Volunteers of America, as I'd often suggested.

I was as close to a complete blackout as I have ever been; only my indomitable courage made me stay conscious. For a fleeting second I thought of returning to Marv, alone with Ellen in the chamber of horrors so that together we could face H. Wesley. But I knew I could never make it before that murderous villain caught up with me in one of those silent rooms I had to pass through.

The only remaining choice was the side exit even though it led into that long, gloomy stretch of yews. I turned around and this time ran through the corridor, bumping shins, arms, and once more my head against unidentified objects. All the while, like offstage sounds, came the steady, ominous tread of those wooden heels moving closer and closer.

With one final plunge through the dark I reached the door, twisted the knob and peered out. I could see no more than inches ahead, a heavy fog, typical of Philadelphia in early autumn, had descended since Marv and I entered the Hall. I listened, all was still save for the barking of a dog somewhere in the distance, I could no longer hear the Colonel's footfalls. Then, almost directly behind me came other sounds, but what they were or who was making them I had no way of telling.

I took a deep breath, leaped forward and dashed between the yews for the safety of Sassafras Alley. I had almost reached the gate when I heard Marv shout, "Duck, Frank!" I obeyed instantly and dropped to the flagstones. There was a swish where my head had been and the tall figure of Colonel Eberhardt stood over me, holding something. I never knew a man as fat as Marv could run so quickly but before H. Wesley could swing again, Marv hurled my would-be assassin to the ground.

It must have been loss of blood which caused me to faint although before I lapsed into a complete coma I recollect seeing light spring up from all around, hearing a revolver shot and the sounds of voices.

CHAPTER

24

JULIET WAS on a chair by my side when I awoke in Graduate Hospital, sunlight pouring over the bed. She stood up and looked at me with an expression combining concern, annoyance, and affection.

"Well, for a man your age, Frank, you really got yourself into a peck of trouble. How do you feel?"

"I'm not sure yet. What's the matter with me?"

"Not much. Harold [our physician] says you'll be home tomorrow. Couple bumps on your head and a cut over your eye. Had to put in a stitch to close it up.

I looked around. An untouched breakfast tray stood in a corner.

"I'm starved," I said. "What's to eat?"

She raised the bed, moved the tray over, and removed the aluminum lids.

"You won't like it," she said. "The orange juice is canned, the eggs aren't basted, the toast is burned, and the coffee's lukewarm."

But I was ravenous and so weak from hunger that anything was a banquet.

"If I served you that mess at home," Juliet said in tones of utter disgust, "I shudder to think how you'd have screamed."

This was totally unfair. "Hunger," someone said, "is the best sauce."

"What day is this?" I asked.

"What day? It's Saturday."

I reflected.

"You mean I've been in a coma for over a week? No wonder I'm famished."

"A week! You're crazy. You've been here less than seven hours. They brought you in around one A.M. and it's not quite eight o'clock. If I'd known you'd feel so chipper I wouldn't have sent those photographers, TV interviewers, and reporters away. I told them they could get the story from Marv."

I jumped up in fury.

"Photographers, TV interviewers, and cameramen here? You had the nerve to send them to Marv? Where are they now? Get them right back."

"They'll be back later. Don't you want to get yourself prettied up meantime? Harold says you can remove all the bandages except the one over your eye. The rest, he said an intern put on to get practice."

I ignored the irony. I wanted the working press to see me just as I was. It would be sheer hypocrisy for me to remove a single bandage.

"Besides," Juliet continued, "haven't you even an academic interest in learning what happened to the Colonel and poor Ellen? Don and that policewoman, whatever her name is, have been outside in the lobby the last hour waiting for you to awaken. I hope your allergies don't act up. That female positively reeks of cheap perfume."

It was *not* cheap perfume. I happen to know because I'd bought it for her. However, this was hardly the time to prove my wife's olfactory sense was faulty.

Juliet flounced out and returned with Don and Millie, who looked positively radiant despite the fact that she'd not been to bed at all that night. She greeted me a bit less warmly than I'm sure she would have under other circumstances. She was about to light one of those delicate cigars, then, after a glance at my wife, thought better of it and returned the cheroot to her pocketbook.

Eager though I was to learn about poor Ellen—it was she, indeed, who'd become an unwilling Olga—and what transpired after Marv and I left the meeting, I graciously yielded to Don's request that I pose for pictures. He'd brought a staff photographer who was standing in the corridor waiting for my OK.

"It won't take long," Don promised. "I don't want to tire you but I'd like to get at least a small jump ahead of my colleagues. After all, I was part of the Chase."

I told Don and his man to take as much time as necessary, this was the very least I could do for a fellow Son. Quite a few nurses and several interns peeked into my room during the procedure. It seems as though I was somewhat of a hospital celebrity, although I paid no attention to these intruders and assumed all of the many poses the *Inquirer* photographer requested. When he had enough he thanked me, said I was most cooperative and left. Don remained for only a few minutes more.

"It's quite a story," he said, "and I want to get back to write it. So I'll wish you luck and take off. Millie'll fill you in on the details. If you're up to it by next Thursday, we're going to get together for one final session at the Architects."

I settled back to listen.

"You know I was sitting between the Sheriff and Don," Millie said. "When we saw you and Marv leave we knew something was up. Don had an idea you were headed for Baskerville Hall. But as long as the Colonel stayed where he was up on that platform, we figured you two would be safe.

"We decided we'd leave the moment the Colonel did *if* he did. But he didn't seem to budge, just sat there looking down at everybody with contempt. Then came that last 'intermission.'

There was no place for me to go even if I had to, so I didn't move. I was talking to Dave Roberts when all of a sudden we looked up and Eberhardt was gone."

Had I been in their position I know *I* would not have taken my eyes off the man but I suppose Dave was so intrigued with Millie he neglected his duties. However, I said nothing.

"Don was just coming back when Dave grabbed him and the three of us scrammed. You should have seen us tearing down those stairs. I didn't spot a red car until we got to Eighteenth and Walnut. I blew my whistle, flashed my badge and the officer, Don La Van, who was riding solo stopped. I told him what was up, he radioed his district for an assist, we piled in the car and took off for Baskerville Hall. Believe me, Frank, we got there just in time; another minute and you'd have been a goner."

At this, my wife let out a gasp and I could see she was upset. I merely shrugged my shoulders; danger and I are old comrades. Millie continued.

"La Van was out first, he had a police positive in his hand, I followed with my .38 cocked. Dave wasn't armed. We heard sounds coming from the back of the house and La Van flashed his light through the gate. There was Marv with the Colonel on top of him and you, Frank, out cold.

"The gate was locked, La Van yelled out and the Colonel turned around, we could see him stare even if he couldn't see us in that bright beam. But he didn't lose his cool.

" 'I caught a couple of housebreakers,' he said. 'Go 'round to the front door and I'll let you in.'

" 'Then what are you doing with that garrote in your right hand?' Dave yelled. 'Drop it.'

"But the Colonel didn't. He must hate you, Frank. Quick as a flash he moved away from Marv who was groggy and was getting ready to slip the thin wire around your neck. La Van fired a warning shot but that didn't stop the Colonel. Then I fired and winged his right arm just below the shoulder.

"He dropped the garrote. La Van smashed the gate lock with another shot and we dashed through. Eberhardt was game, I must say that for him, even if he is crazy. He stood his ground; broke Dave's shoulder with a karate chop but La Van managed to clobber him hard on the head with the butt of the gun and the Colonel fell down. By that time we had reinforcements—three red cars, and the lieutenant's command car."

How desperately I wished that fall in Yew Alley hadn't rendered me unconscious. This is the sort of action I crave. It was too late for it now, a fact I will regret forever. Millie went on.

"Somebody put the cuffs on Eberhardt and brought him here."

I nearly leaped out of my bed.

"Here? In *this* hospital?"

"Yes," Millie answered. "In this hospital."

She smiled.

"We're keeping our eyes on him."

Then my wife had her say.

"They pointed out the guards to me, a couple of husky young cops. You don't have to worry."

I assured my wife I was not the least bit worried. My concern was for the safety of the public. A prison cell most certainly offered better protection from that maniac's sudden attacks than a hospital.

"Eberhardt'll be charged with first degree murder," Millie explained. "That *was* his wife, all right. Marv did the autopsy himself last night, or rather early this morning. We haven't been able to question the Colonel yet but the D.A.'s coming over to talk to him today and you, too, if your doctor says he can."

It was only because my constitution is rugged and my recuperative powers great that I was able to survive the excitement of that day without a relapse. Shortly after Millie left I sent Juliet to a neighborhood delicatessen which, as I recalled, made excellent corned beef sandwiches on rye and supplied kosher pickles with them. I knew only too well that without further sustenance I would not be able to carry on.

It was while I was washing these down with a chocolate malted milk, a beverage most authorities claim provides quick energy, that a pretty nurse brought me early editions of the *Evening Bulletin* and the *Daily News*. The young lady refused to accept payment asking only for my autograph which I graciously gave her.

Both periodicals, I noted at a glance, carried our story on page one under what is known in the profession as a "banner headline." My picture in the *Bulletin* was the excellent likeness I'd provided them with when my book was sold to Hollywood. But I was furious at that other so-called newspaper which showed me laying on the ground, Marv bent over me rendering first aid. I suspect the police of furnishing that miserable example of yellow journalism and I intend to take up this invasion of privacy at a later date with my good friend, Inspector Fox. There was no time to peruse either article, however. Scarcely had I glanced through the *Bulletin's* story once when Marv arrived. I really was glad to see him although his opening comments were annoying. He sniffed the air.

"Nice going, Frank. An invigorating mixture of Chanel Number Five and garlic. Smells like a combination of Millie and Day's Delicatessen."

I laughed politely and asked Marv if he'd please give me what information he had. He said Ellen had been dead for approximately six months.

"She was pickled in embalming fluid so it's impossible to say when the Colonel did her in. Our guess is it happened right after we left Baskerville Hall the night the bet was made. Apparently the Colonel had all the necessary preservatives on hand and knew how to use them. Homicide found Ellen's head about an hour ago."

At this point Juliet gagged and asked to be excused. Marv continued.

"Remember that bust of von Clausewitz which used to rest on the mantel? Well, Ellen's bronze-plated head was there in its place and detectives found the poor old general relegated to a corner of the basement."

Marv had little additional information. He said he'd return for a longer visit that afternoon and promised to bring me a flask of martinis. I felt that by then I would need a stimulant of sorts. The press came, interviewed me individually and en masse; I did a live telecast, a "remote" I think they call them, for Marciarose's noon program and then I taped at least a dozen more for assorted TV and radio stations.

About three o'clock, just as I finished a light midafternoon snack, the First Assistant District Attorney, a young fellow named Richard Sprague, dropped by.

"I'm sorry to bother you now," he said apologetically, "but since you'll probably be the Commonwealth's chief witness I would like to get a few facts straight."

I was perfectly willing to go back to my first meeting with H. Wesley, but Dick said this would be unnecessary and at the moment was concerned with the last week of the Chase and, of course, the final encounter. When I'd concluded I asked

Sprague if he'd spoken to H. Wesley. He nodded and said he'd talked with him for several hours before coming to see me.

"Until his lawyer arrived, the Colonel spoke quite freely although I warned him about Constitutional rights. Somehow I had a feeling his frankness was part of a buildup for an insanity plea. I don't know; we don't have a complete psychiatric report yet. Our own headshrinker, Nick Frignito, examined the Colonel briefly and made a tentative diagnosis of psychopathy. We'll see. Meanwhile I'm preparing my case for murder in the first degree.

"He admitted killing his wife a few minutes after your friends left on the morning of March 28. Said she was taking a shower.

" 'I picked up the scimitar which I always keep honed and went upstairs to her bathroom. I didn't feel like wasting any words, so I pulled the curtain aside, didn't bother to turn off the water and gave her a fast slice. Off rolled her head. I picked it up; her lips were open and I could tell she was going to ask 'why?' had I given her the chance. I would have told her it was because she bored the hell out of me and I was setting an example for husbands all over the world.

" 'Her tongue was sticking out and I shoved it back. I wouldn't have to hear any more about how peaceful and humble the Quakers are and I ought to be more like them. I'd answered her a thousand times before that with all their goddamned humility and brotherhood, the bastards meanwhile accumulated more money than anybody else in their City of Brotherly Love by buying properties they rent out for gin mills, whorehouses, and tenements.' "

After this, I knew there would be no sympathy for Colonel H. Wesley Eberhardt, at least among Philadelphia's better class citizens. Sprague said the Colonel either could not or would not give a logical explanation for his other actions.

Some weeks later I learned the rest of the Colonel's story. Brother Joe, whose sudden death did not appear to disturb H. Wesley, was an old time carny and made all the arrangements, even to "framing" their joint. Apparently they'd parted company when Joe discovered Olga was not living up to her billing as a "true" illusion, if this is not a contradiction in terms.

It was as easy for the Colonel to keep track of his hunters

as it was for him to furnish us with those *ex post facto* clues; any student of the Sacred Writings could have done as well. I think he realized the challenge of that last one was a dead give-away; he issued it regardless. Perhaps he actually wanted to be caught and Dr. Frignito, with whom I've conferred concerning the trial, expressed the same opinion.

No doubt he married Ellen for money and planned her conquest with as much care as he planned the wager. As for his accumulation of Sherlockiana and love for Holmes, I think it was genuine enough until he thought himself superior to the Master. Well, as you know, I proved otherwise.

That day I spent at Graduate Hospital came to a brilliant end. Late in the evening, after visiting hours were over and all had gone, my agent, that pleasant Jewish gentleman named Gitlin, called from New York. He'd just read about me in an early edition of the *Times* and wanted to know if I were willing to write a book about the Chase.

"We have a chance for a movie sale, too, if you can add a romance somewhere along the line."

I promised I'd do my best. It occurred to me that if I were to cast Millie in a more important role, I might get her a Hollywood bid. I called her at home, told her the interesting news and said I should like to discuss it further at that little Frankford restaurant.

Millie said she'd let me know but I'm sure she'll acquiesce. She must realize that for someone of her inferior social status, I have much to offer.

For the Sunday cyclist... for the cross-country tourist... whether you ride for better health, for sport, or for the sheer fun of it,

GET
THE COMPLETE BOOK OF BICYCLING

The First Comprehensive Guide To All Aspects of Bicycles and Bicycling

JUST A FEW OF THE HUNDREDS OF EXCITING TIPS YOU'LL FIND:

- A simple way to increase your cycling efficiency by 30 to 40%—breeze over hilltops while others are struggling behind.
- 13 special safety tips for youngsters.
- How to read a bicycle's specifications to know if you're getting a superior one or a dud.
- How to know whether to buy a 3-speed to start with, or a 10-speed.
- How to select the right kind of equipment for touring or camping.
- How to minimize danger when cycling in the city.

▼ **AT YOUR BOOKSTORE OR MAIL THIS COUPON NOW FOR FREE 30-DAY TRIAL** ▼